DOWN HERE

BY SHERRY ROBERTS

Down Here
Up There
Crow Calling
Warrior's Revenge
Down Dog Diary
Book of Mercy
Maud's House

DOWN HERE

A NOVEL BY
SHERRY ROBERTS

Osmyrrah Publishing | Apple Valley, Minnesota

Osmyrrah Publishing
Apple Valley, Minnesota 55124
www.osmyrrahpublishing.com
info@osmyrrahpublishing.com

ISBN: 978-1-7340113-5-7 (print)
ISBN: 978-1-7340113-6-4 (eBook)

Library of Congress Control Number: 2025918140

Printed in the United States of America

First Edition

TO SABRINA, IVY, AND OWEN
WHO MAKE MY HEART SOAR WITH EVERY SMILE

There are two worlds: Up There and Down Here.
Up There is the name for the wind and sky.
Down Here is everything that is *not* Up There:
the ordinary grind, the arguments and the resolutions,
the meanness, the kindness.
And the secrets.

CHAPTER 1

WALKING IN THE AIR

THE MEADOW ROSE LIKE an earthen wave. It swamped Ruddy Turnstone with vivid memories and mixed emotions. His first shattering kiss with his wife Ariel Lee Turnstone—a moment when the earth moved as if hundreds of giant bison were pounding it—had occurred here. But this was also the spot where he saw her die—or thought he had.

The meadow climbed up, up, up like no other place on the Stevens farm then leveled off for several feet before curling over the edge of the cliff and crashing into the valley below. Ages ago, native hunters drove giant bison over the meadow's cliff to their extinction. That history alone should have warned Ruddy that this place was not an easy one to love.

And yet, Ariel adored this wind-possessed piece of geography. Standing with Ruddy on the edge of the meadow, she buzzed with excitement, energized by the swirling air. Here she felt the ultimate connection with Up There—her name for the wind and sky that swept her out of this world and into another. In Up There, Ariel could be strong and fearless, the complete opposite of how she felt on land.

Ruddy, a meteorologist by training and nature who looked for the predictable but had grown to accept the unpredictable, thought he was prepared for a life with Ariel. But, like the weather, his wife continued to surprise him. He was married to a woman born with a special gift—a wife who could step off a cliff with no parachute, no bungee cord, no chance that he could save her.

And now she was taking their daughter with her.

Ruddy, the acrophobic man who kept firmly to the ground, hated this. His greatest desire, his job, was to keep his wife and child safe—and he couldn't do that Up There.

Once again, he tried to dissuade his wife from today's exercise. "She's too young," he argued.

"We only have a few months before school starts," Ariel reminded him.

"I know, but this seems so soon, so drastic. She's only four."

"About to be five," Meriweather Turnstone piped up.

"I can't keep her safe if she doesn't know how to handle herself Up There," Ariel insisted. "And the only way I can do that is to teach her how to be who she is."

Who she is.

Like her mother, their daughter was born with the gift of flight.

A worried Ruddy studied Ariel, his daughter Meri, and Gus the family dog sitting at Meri's feet. "I don't like this. Please don't take her Up There," he begged his wife.

Ariel was more composed on the outside than she was on the inside. All her life, she'd had to balance the natural lightness of her physical being with the inner heaviness of worry and fear. She gazed past the horizon. Was this a mistake? The first time she had left the meadow and chosen the cliff she had been eleven years old, alone, and petrified. It had been her first experience *descending* instead of *ascending* with the wind. Lifting into the air had seemed safer and easier than stepping into nothingness. But then her young mind had heard the wind's irresistible beckoning . . .

Now, the wind whispered, *Trust us. Trust you.*

Ariel lifted her chin. "Don't worry," she said to both Ruddy and the wind. "I've got her."

Then squeezing Ruddy's hand, a silent plea to have faith in her, she turned to the child standing beside her. "Ready?"

Meri's chin imitated the lift of her mother's. Their eyes met, and she nodded.

Tension choked Ruddy. *No, no, no,* his inner being shouted.

Then, without warning, Ariel dropped his hand, clasped Meri's tightly, and launched a race through the meadow's tall grass. Gus dashed beside them, his frantic barking mixing with their happy laughter in the welcoming air and the bright May sunshine.

"Wait!" Ruddy shouted and chased after them.

He followed them as far as he could go.

Then he watched as the two loves of his life flung themselves past the daunting edge.

Ruddy skidded to a stop, unable to look into the valley below.

"Come back," he whispered.

As Ariel's and Meri's legs left the earth, they kept running in the air, just as those long-ago bison must have done when the hunters stampeded them over the cliff's edge and into the valley kill site. But Ariel and Meri weren't running *away* from something. They were running *to* something—the unimaginable feeling of being Up There.

When Ariel stepped into the world of Up There, she followed the path of her Hamilton ancestors, the women on her mother's side of the family who had passed down to her the extraordinary gift of flight. And now, Ruddy thought, she was showing their entirely too breakable daughter the gift that she too had inherited.

Suddenly, strength left Ruddy's legs, and he collapsed to the ground. Gus sat beside him with a whine and nudged his shoulder.

"I know," Ruddy said, with a shuddering breath, "being left behind is the worst."

Gus woofed.

"They'll be okay," Ruddy assured himself as much as the dog.

Neither the dog nor the man could take their eyes off the airborne woman and child. Ruddy's hand flew to his heart as Ariel and Meri dipped for a moment below the edge of the cliff and out of sight. When he heard Meri shriek with laughter, Ruddy scrambled to the edge and searched the area below, even though the motion of looking down made his head swim. After a moment, mother and daughter rose back into view, turned in his direction, and floated, bodies dangling from the clouds in a space where humans were not meant to be. As he shuffled back from the precipice, his mind played the same thought: *I can't get to you if something goes wrong.*

Eventually, Ruddy tamped down his nerves. He was able to sit quietly and, finally, absorb the beauty of the moment. Ariel's and Meri's wind-tossed tresses fanned around them as if they were drifting on their backs in the family lake. Their bodies floated with grace. Ariel had dressed casually for this momentous walk: T-shirt and ripped jeans. Meri, on the other hand, had chosen for the occasion one of her quintessential ensembles: it was ruffly, fluttery, and pink. Ruddy thought his daughter looked like a pixie flitting in a sequined princess dress.

Ariel kept a firm grasp of Meri's hand, and as they gently wafted on the currents, Ariel engaged the child in conversation. Meri nodded in understanding to her mother's discourse. Ruddy knew Ariel was explaining the fine points of how this whole riding-the-wind thing worked. For weeks, she had been preparing Meri for this moment.

Occasionally, Meri waved to Ruddy. "Hi, Daddy," she shouted with a giggle.

That laughing voice, those words. Each time she called his name, each time her small hand patted his arm to get his attention, each time she posed one of her infinite questions, his heart swelled. He swallowed the lump in his throat and waved back.

His eyes met Ariel's. She smiled at him, the same luminous smile that lit their daughter's face; the same smile, he was told, that had glowed like a lighthouse on the face of Ariel's grandmother when she came home from being Up There. Some days, like this one, he hated the gift that wind-walking Anne Hamilton Stevens had passed on to his family.

The cry of an eagle startled Ruddy from his thoughts of Anne. The bird circling high above, the sun catching the glint of its distinctive white tail feathers, soared the same currents that held his wife and daughter aloft. The eagle and his family shared the same world. It was a scary thought.

This was his life now. They were part of Up There, and he would always be Down Here.

Waiting.

CHAPTER 2

WHEN LOVE STRIKES

RUDDY HAD BEGUN WAITING for Ariel when they were in sixth grade. That was when he fell in love with her on a tall slide at the annual autumn festival. Frozen by his fear of heights, he had clung to a support pole, trying to fight off the pack of boys who'd pushed him to the top of the slide. As the wind grew and shook the platform on which he was standing, he looked down with terror and saw Ariel's hand beckoning him. She reached for him, and suddenly everything calmed. He knew instinctively that she would get him to the ground safely. And she had.

It took Ariel longer—years, in fact—and a crazy dance with a tornado for her to realize that she loved Ruddy as much as he loved her. Ariel was stubborn; she held onto beliefs longer than was often good for her. But being dropped from the sky by a tornado and waking up days later in a hospital changed her perspective.

The tornado came for Ariel on the day of her mother's wedding in the meadow, just days after her first unexpected kiss with Ruddy. The small group of friends and family had just begun to congratulate the happy couple when a raging wind rose unexpectedly. As everyone ran for cover, Ariel hadn't moved. Instead, she gave Ruddy a sad smile then stepped into the swirling arms of the tornado. Ruddy hadn't known then that women like Ariel existed, that they were born to calm what others could not, that they were destined to soothe the anger and confusion of storms and rescue the people they loved.

And so, just as her grandmother had often steered storms away from the small town of Cosette with her gift of flight, Ariel had ridden a tornado to save their home. She had done the unthinkable—risked her life—at a time when Ruddy thought their relationship was on a path to forever. It had scared him and angered him. But then, in a quiet hospital room, she opened her eyes and said to him in a soft voice, "There's something I must tell you . . ."

That phrase never boded well for the person to whom it was directed, Ruddy thought. A sinking feeling came over him, and he hid his face in his hands.

The blinds, which should have been silent that day in the closed hospital room, began to clack. They mixed with the usual sounds of the hospital: squeaky wheels on gurneys, gossiping staff ambling down the corridor, the beeping machines attached to Ariel.

Ruddy listened to them and wondered: *How could everything carry on as normal when his life was about to fall apart?*

But then Ariel took a deep calming breath, and the blinds stopped flapping. Ruddy lifted his head. She gave him a crooked smile, the kind people wore when they were about to deliver devastating news, and immediately Ruddy leaped from the side of her bed where he had been sitting. "I'll get Doctor Echo and your mom."

With the hand shackled by an IV, Ariel grabbed at his arm to stop him. "No! Wait. Let's talk first."

But Ruddy had not wanted to talk. He'd wanted to stall. He'd wanted to go back to the days before a tornado spun through their lives, before he'd had to excavate Ariel's body from a pile of storm debris at the foot of the Harriet Bunyan statue in the city park.

With desperation in his voice, he whispered, "Don't say it. Please, Ariel, don't say it."

Unable to meet her eyes, he studied the tiles on the floor, his shoulders slumping, his long wavy hair covering his face in a coppery curtain. They had spent the past weeks in Cosette together, reviving their twenty-year friendship and taking it closer. They'd kissed, held hands, and he had begun to dream. Maybe he wouldn't go back to his job as a meteorologist at a Vermont television station, and maybe she wouldn't return to the Twin Cities where she had built a reputation as an environmental reporter. Maybe they could finally be together.

But, in that hospital room, he felt it all ending, and his heart was breaking.

Then Ariel threw him a curve that set him on his heels.

She said, "Ruddy, I want to marry you."

His head snapped up.

"What?"

Ariel said tentatively, "You did say I should stay in Cosette . . . with you."

He rushed back to her, gently cupped her bandaged face in his hands, and kissed her. "I thought . . . I thought you were going to tell me that these past days had been a mistake. That we were a mistake."

They stared into each other's eyes. When she slowly grinned at him, he cautiously lowered himself to the edge of her bed.

He didn't want to jiggle or hurt her. She had a broken arm, a dislocated knee, two broken ribs, a concussion, and more stitches than he wanted to think about. The tornado hadn't been messing around.

"We're not a mistake, Ruddy Turnstone," she said, and suddenly, everything was all right.

He bent close to kiss her banged-up knuckles and began to chatter. "I'm tired of being apart," he said, "tired of waiting for your emails and texts, tired of only seeing you on brief trips home to Minnesota. The long phone calls are nice . . . but, Ariel, I need you."

Ariel laughed then suddenly sobered. "I need you too, but there really is something I need to talk about . . ."

"I don't care what it is, as long as we're together."

Ariel pressed her fingers to his lips to quiet him. "Listen. You have to hear this."

Ruddy heard fear in her voice, and it frightened him.

Ariel began, "I am a Hamilton woman, and we Hamilton women are not easy to love. My grandmother, Anne Hamilton Stevens, believed the men who fell in love with us had the right to know what loving us meant—all the good and all the bad."

"Ariel, I've loved you for so long . . . I do know you."

She held up a hand and interrupted him, "You don't know everything, Ruddy. Sometimes the women in my family are born with an unusual gift. It doesn't always happen. It can skip generations. It missed my mama. But it did come to me."

Ruddy gave her a baffled look.

"Ariel?" he said. "What gift?"

He watched her gather her courage.

"I was born with the gift of flight, Ruddy."

Silence.

Then he began to laugh. "Do you have X-ray vision too?"

When he realized she wasn't laughing with him, he considered her earnest face. "You're serious."

Ariel continued, "Growing up, there were things I could never reveal, never talk about, never show. My mother insisted: I must always keep who I am a secret—for my protection. But I can't, not with you. This is who I am, Ruddy."

"Who you are . . . you mean, this flying thing is real?"

"What do think happened during the tornado, Ruddy?"

His memory wouldn't allow him to accept what he really had seen: that the woman he loved had actually stepped off a cliff and into the arms of a tornado.

"I had hoped there was a reasonable explanation, like the tornado had just reached up over the cliff and kidnapped you, Ariel. But you intentionally walked into the tornado, didn't you?"

Ariel rubbed her forehead. "That's what some of the women in my family do. Sometimes, we ride the wind for fun, but other times, it calls to us and asks for our help. We ride the winds and try to calm them. The tornado was my first time trying to settle a storm. It was just my luck that it was a twister."

Ruddy was stunned. He thought of the wind rattling the blinds on the closed windows of the hospital room and of dozens of other small moments over the years when the weather seemed to perfectly match Ariel's state of mind. Slowly, it dawned on him—he loved a woman of the sky, and he was a man who hated heights. For a student of science, this gift of Ariel's was almost impossible to believe, and terrifying.

A tear dripped down Ariel's cheek. She reached up to wipe it away, forgetting her arm was in a cast, and banged her head. She winced at the pain. Ruddy immediately was at her side, lifting the tear from her face with a gentle finger.

"If this is too much, tell me now, Ruddy," blubbered Ariel. "If you see the real me and turn away . . ."

For a moment, Ruddy saw himself doing exactly that: getting on a plane and flying back to his old life in Vermont, facing the cameras in front of a weather map of the Green Mountain State, and waking up each morning in his lonely apartment. He could forget he had ever heard her words, ever seen her step off that cliff.

Or he could stay and do what he could to help her. Hadn't that always been his role, since they were kids? Sometimes she called him her zephyr, a gentle wind that soothed her fears. He was the one in her life who always could bring her back to an even keel when she was upset and lost. She would need him.

"I'm not leaving, Ariel."

* * *

Now, as Ruddy sat in the meadow, nervously watching his wife and daughter in the sky, he recalled that decision made so long ago in the hospital. He remembered how she'd cried with relief and had flung her arm around his neck, nearly strangling him with the IV line. She had whispered, "Thank goodness. I couldn't choose between you and Up There."

That was the first time he had heard of Up There, Ariel's name for the wind that called her and the sky that welcomed her. With sparkling eyes, she had told him, "I am alive Up There, Ruddy, so much that sometimes it hurts to come back down here and feel the ground beneath me again. I begin missing Up There almost from my first step back on land."

There was no doubt in his mind that he had made the right decision on that long-ago day, when he had tied his fate to a woman who could fly. But that didn't stop him, especially during times like these, from feeling jealous. He wanted her to love him more than Up There. And now, Up There was staking a claim on both Ariel and his daughter.

With relief, he watched Ariel and Meri step from the clouds. As soon as their feet touched the ground, Ariel released Meri's hand, and the child barreled toward her father. Laughing, Meri flung herself at him, knocking him onto his back. His arms enclosed the tiny body atop him in a tight embrace. *She's back,* a voice inside him cried. *You can breathe now.*

He looked up at his wife, who gave him a hapless grin. She knew trusting Up There with the ones he loved was difficult for him.

"Was that so bad?" she asked.

Every bone in Ruddy's protective and acrophobic body revolted.

"No," he lied.

CHAPTER 3

WHEN THE UNIVERSE FALLS

RUDDY CARRIED AN EXUBERANT Meri on the walk back to the house.

She chattered, "Did you see me? Did you see me?"

"Yes, I saw." Ruddy clasped Meri to him with one hand and with the other rubbed the still-tight muscles in the back of his neck.

Meri dipped and weaved her hand through the air imitating her adventure. "We went right off the cliff. We went up and down. We ran in the air." Her small hand paused to pat his cheek to make sure he was listening. "Did you see?"

"You were magnificent," he told her, although what he really wanted to say was *You must never do that again.*

Meri smiled at the trees they passed, at the birds sweeping over their heads, at the clouds she already missed.

With barely a pause, she switched gears and asked, "Where does air come from?"

The twisting labyrinth of almost-five-year-old Meri's questions made her parents look at each other and grin. Like her father, Meri greeted every being and every experience with kindness and an open heart. Her insatiable, and sometimes troublesome, curiosity, however, came from her journalist mother.

"You take this one, Mr. Meteorologist," said Ariel.

Ruddy thought for a moment. "Do you want the technical definition or the unicorn one?"

Without hesitation, Meri replied, "Unicorn."

The family stepped out of the thick woods of their farm and into the backyard, which was governed by a spreading oak tree and patrolled by a windbreak of spruce trees. The spruces did a terrible job; the wind always seemed to be able to penetrate the barrier of tall conifers to reach Ariel and Meri.

Ariel and Ruddy crossed the grass toward their home, the farmhouse where Ariel's ancestors had once lived. Gus dashed ahead of them to chase a rabbit from the garden.

"Air is the breath of unicorns," Ruddy explained. "If you squint your eyes and look into the air, you will see that it sparkles. Those flashing, buzzing specks are unicorn energy, and they are always moving."

Meri squinted her eyes and gasped. "I see them!"

"Some people call it prana," said Ariel. "It means life breath."

"It's magical." Meri smiled at her mother. "I am full of unicorn prana."

As they entered the house, Ruddy announced it was time for "short nap," which was different from the "long nap" of bedtime. While Meri had outgrown naps, she *still* needed rest time—and so did her parents.

"Are you sure?" Meri questioned this statement. "Is it two, zero, zero?"

Ariel said, "Look for yourself." Meri, who was obsessed with numbers and counting, consulted the digital clock on the microwave and frowned. She didn't know how she would rest for a whole hour—the length of short naps. The wind was still inside her filling her with excitement, still seeking her.

Ruddy mounted the stairs with Meri in his arms. He could feel the energy zinging through her, like unicorn breath gone wild. This nap time would require more than one book to settle her into sleep. He opened the door to her room and, as usual, paused. He could never enter this room without remembering the day infant Meri first revealed that she was truly her mother's daughter.

Meri had been about six months old. He'd heard excited gurgles coming from the nursery and had gone to investigate. It was a cold Minnesota day with snow softly swirling outside the house. The windows were shut tight. He was always concerned about keeping the nursery warm enough for Meri. Everything should have been quiet and still. But it wasn't.

His infant daughter was conducting a symphony with the stars and moons that dangled on strings from the ceiling. The nursery had been Ariel's childhood room. They'd replaced her old double bed with a crib, a rocker, and a thick, soft rug. They'd left the construction paper stars and moons young Ariel had hung from the ceiling long ago.

On the day the universe danced to the tune of his infant daughter's raised fist, her eyes sparkled with delight as stars spun, moons collided, and strings tangled.

Ruddy stood in the doorway, in shock and awe. When Ariel joined him, he asked, "Is she—is she doing this?"

Ariel gave him a sheepish grin and leaned against him. "I'm afraid so. I was levitating rattles at her age."

"Levitating rattles?"

Ariel watched the performance with pride; Ruddy, with astonishment. Eventually, infant Meri threw her whole being into it: arms waved wildly, chubby legs kicked, body wiggled. That was when disaster struck.

The universe exploded. Stars streaked across the room, and moons fell. Some celestial bodies barely held on by their strings. Meri stopped and began to cry. The Milky Way wasn't waltzing for her anymore.

While Ariel had picked up the baby to comfort her, Ruddy had fetched the stepladder and painstakingly reattached the fallen stars. He bandaged the torn moons. He put Meri's sky right again.

Now, the room held a white kid-size bed instead of a crib, and his daughter was more interested in counting her many stuffed animals than dancing the stars. Meri had to make sure no animals had escaped while she'd been Up There.

"I'm not sleepy," she said with a yawn, snuggling into the nest of soft creatures.

Sitting on the floor, with his back against the bed and Meri looking over his shoulder at the pictures, he read two books by Dr. Seuss: *The Lorax* and *I Had Trouble in Getting to Solla Sollew*. Ruddy personally found *Solla Sollew* too intrigued with violence, but it was an old favorite of Ariel's.

When he finished, Meri whispered, "I wish you could go Up There with us, Daddy."

He shifted so that he was facing the bed and rested his chin on the mattress. "I don't think I would be very good at being Up There," he said. "I'd probably drop to the ground a lot."

"That's what Mama says." After a pause, Meri said, "Don't be sad, Daddy, about being stuck Down Here. I love Down Here too."

This was the first time Ruddy realized that his daughter

saw the world in all its duality. She even had a name for it: Up There and Down Here.

He leaned forward and began rubbing her back. "What did it feel like Up There?"

Meri wiggled closer to the edge of the bed until father and daughter were nearly nose to nose. She lowered her voice and placed a hand on his cheek. "Daddy, the clouds kissed me," she said with awe in her voice. "And the wind *whispered* to me."

The thought of his young daughter already communicating with Up There sent Ruddy's universe spinning. "What did it say?" he asked.

Meri's eyes fought to stay awake. "It said 'Welcome.'"

Ruddy handed Meri her sleep mask, a fuzzy white cat face with big eyes and long lashes, and shut the door to her room. He stood for a moment listening to his daughter sing to herself. A song always meant sleep was not far away. Ariel said her musician father used to sing her to sleep when she was a baby, but adult Ariel seldom sang, or even hummed. It was up to Ruddy to join Meri in counting songs and "Baby Beluga."

Ruddy raked a hand through his long hair. He leaned wearily against the door jamb and wondered, *How could he compete with Up There?*

He straightened and started downstairs.

Up There had welcomed his daughter.

He supposed it was better than the alternative.

CHAPTER 4

THE RETURN OF THE SHOES

WHILE MERI NAPPED, ARIEL and Gus searched the barn.

"Where did I put it?" Ariel glanced at the dog stretched on the barn floor. "Do you know where it is?"

Gus just looked at her.

Years ago, Gus had followed Ariel home to her apartment in the Twin Cities and cleverly inserted himself into her life. He was an alley dog abandoned on the streets of Minneapolis. If Ariel had been looking for a half-eaten hotdog in a trash bin, he probably could have helped her.

The concrete of the barn floor was cool on Gus's belly, just the way he liked it. When he first came to the farm with Ariel, he was younger and afraid of the barn. It was the kingdom of cats, spitting, hissing creatures that did not like him. Their attitude puzzled him. He was a reasonably good-looking mutt, part German shepherd and part who knows. His coloring blended inviting shades of black, striking tan, and exceptional browns. Okay, so his one eyebrow looked a bit wonky. The coloration of that one brow, a tan swipe, gave that eye a supercilious appearance. It made him seem to be either mystified by everything or someone who knew it all. Gus preferred the latter perception.

Back to the cats, so many cats. They appeared every time Ariel and Meri were outside. Eventually, he and the cats came to a truce regarding the barn. They decided that despite his overwhelming size he lacked aggression, and he decided they were smaller than their hisses claimed. He could live with that unspoken agreement. After all, he was permitted into the house, and they were not.

Ariel continued to paw through storage boxes, unearthing a calico kitten on one shelf. She lifted it down and placed it on the floor. When it padded over to Gus and curled up beside him, the dog heaved a sigh of resignation.

Ariel's uncle Kal had built the cubicle shelves in the barn long ago. Kalahari Stevens, now a conservation officer with the Minnesota Department of Natural Resources, had always spoken to animals. No one knew if they answered, but at least both the wild and the tame tolerated him and didn't bite him, much. When he was a boy, Kal had rescued injured animals and nursed them to health in cages slotted into the barn cubicles. The cages were long gone, replaced by more than a dozen plastic storage boxes that contained mismatched dinnerware, books that couldn't fit on the house's many bookshelves, winter clothes, sports gear of all seasons, family knickknacks, and memories. Of course, nothing was labeled. Neither Ariel nor her mother were organizers.

After plowing through several boxes, Ariel pulled down one large but suspiciously light box. Prying off the top, she smiled. This was it—all the memories she'd packed away when they turned her old bedroom into a nursery for Meri. She fingered the pinecones and rocks that had once adorned the windowsill of her room. She lifted the bison bone her grandfather, Will Stevens, had unearthed while plowing one day at the bottom of the meadow. This hard piece of rib or leg (no one can remember) had started a quest that took her grandfather to the natural history department of the University of Minnesota. There he had learned that it was not a regular old cow bone but the remains of a now extinct species of giant bison. The bone became a talisman to Will, a reminder that he was simply a caretaker borrowing this land. At the urging of his wife, Anne, he never plowed that field again. Ariel and Meri had flown over that protected bison cemetery this morning.

Digging deeper, Ariel unearthed more precious childhood belongings: a ceramic butterfly, a hawk's feather, a penny flattened and imprinted with the head of an eagle, a scrap of her favorite Christmas-themed paper. Finally, she reached the really good stuff: the platoon of stuffed animals and one doll. She put the animals aside to give to Meri later and examined the doll—the object of her hunt.

Harriet the rag doll.

Ariel's aunt Giselle, the wife of Ariel's other uncle, Gobi, had sewn the doll. Giselle was the family's best and only seamstress. Harriet was Ariel's hero, and the doll had kept Ariel company every night during her childhood and into college. The doll was modeled after the statue of Harriet Bunyan in the Cosette city park. According to the legend developed by the Cosette Chamber of Commerce, Harriet was the sister of lumberjack Paul Bunyan. While Paul loved chopping things down, Harriet loved building them. A pamphlet in the visitor center claimed Harriet was a heroic environmentalist who defied her big brother and his land-clearing ways to save the natural beauty of Cosette. The statue of Harriet, carved by local artist Lars Diego, stood taller than one man standing on the shoulders of another and was an irresistible photo destination for Cosette's tourists.

Keeping the stuffed animals and the Harriet doll aside, Ariel returned the plastic memory box to its cubicle. As she turned away, her attention was caught by a weathered cardboard box shoved back into a dark, cobwebby corner atop the shelves. Ariel unfolded a stepladder, climbed up, and tugged the box into the light.

On the side of the box printed in black marker were the words: *NEVER OPEN AGAIN*.

"That's an invitation if I ever saw one," Ariel told Gus. She lowered the bulky box down, placed it on the floor, and crouched beside it. As she was about to unfold the top flaps, a sudden wind tunneled through the open barn door. It said, *Don't open it.*

Don't be silly, Ariel told herself and the wind.

Gus's head snapped up as the wind brushed past his ear. He gave Ariel a hard look.

With shaking fingers, Ariel untucked one cardboard flap after another. She peered inside the box and what she saw sapped the strength from her legs. Suddenly, she found herself sitting on the cold floor.

Gus made a sound and crept toward her.

Shoes. The box was filled with shoes. Her shoes.

Still trembling, she reached inside the box and retrieved one of the shoes. It was small, about a child-size six, and well-worn. The toe and heel were scuffed. The leather was deep brown. The shoe was heavy, so heavy that it pulled her down into a sea of memories that took her breath away. She heard the clatter of the shoes as she stumbled through the school hallways; she felt the stares of the children; she saw the dodgeball flying toward her and knew she wouldn't be able to move fast enough to avoid it or to stop everyone from laughing at her.

She didn't realize until Gus bumped her foot with his nose that she was crying.

* * *

That was how Ruddy found her: falling apart on the dusty barn floor surrounded by shoes.

"Ariel?" he asked, taking a tentative step into the barn. Afternoon sunlight flooded through the windows, spotlighting the sobbing woman sitting among a scattering of footwear. A cat rubbed against his leg as he passed, but he didn't stop and give it the usual pat. He went to his wife, kicked some shoes aside, and sat down beside her. He pulled her into his arms.

And still she sobbed.

They stayed like that for a long time. Finally, when Ariel seemed to be settling, he whispered, "Can you talk about it?"

Silence.

"Okay, why don't we start with why you came out here in the first place? Were you looking for something?"

Ariel sniffed and held up the Harriet doll. "I wanted to give Harriet to Meri."

She smoothed the doll's jean pants and flannel shirt with the lace cuffs. "Harriet was my favorite growing up," she explained. "I wanted Meri to have something special to remember this day. Her first true trip Up There."

Suddenly, she motioned toward the shoes and cried in frustration, "But then I found these."

Ruddy went to lift one of the shoes, but she stopped him. "Don't touch them. They're evil."

He pulled his hand back.

"These were mine," she said in a sad voice. "You probably remember them."

Ariel thought everyone in the entire town had to remember the little girl who clomped around in specially made shoes, who refused to say why she needed them, and who miraculously one day was able to stop wearing them. The shoes were a stigma—as if someone had imprinted on her chest: D for Different, O for Other.

Ruddy vaguely remembered the shoes she wore as a kid, but didn't recall them being a big deal.

Ariel hugged the Harriet doll. She told Ruddy, "When I was a kid, I wore these so I wouldn't get hurt."

Ruddy stiffened. "Hurt?"

"The heavy shoes were Mama's idea. When I was wearing the heavy shoes, the wind couldn't lift me into the air so easily, couldn't toss me around or knock me into a tree or the house."

Her words shocked Ruddy. "Those things really happened?" He pointed to the sky. "Up There?"

"I don't blame Mama because she really didn't know what else to do. And I don't blame the air either; it just wanted to be with me. In fact, I loved being Up There, until I got hurt." She tried to make light of her strange childhood. "You know how it is, it's all fun and games until you're thrown against a house and break your arm."

A thoughtful Ruddy wasn't buying the act. His mind had already leaped ahead to what this could mean for his family. "These things could happen to Meri, couldn't they? If the wind took her?"

"Yeah," she said. "That's why I didn't put up a fuss when you attached a harness and leash to her."

The first time his baby daughter drifted out of his arms and wiggled in the air, Ruddy nearly passed out. His shout brought

Ariel running to the backyard, and she immediately stepped into the air and snagged the laughing baby by the back of her onesie. When mother and child were safely on the ground, Ruddy wrapped them in a tight bear hug. Then, without uttering a word, he marched to the car. He came home later from the hardware store with harnesses in three sizes and leashes of varying strengths and lengths. As Meri aged and grew, this crude solution was replaced with child safety backpacks—plush and playful unicorns and monkeys—that Meri could wear and still be attached to safety harnesses and tethers.

On walks, Ruddy had learned quickly how much lead to give baby Meri—enough so her chubby legs were running in the air just above the grass but not so much that he couldn't yank her back to the safety of his arms.

Meri lived up to her name, always happy, never walking when she could run. She danced to music only she could hear. She chose to wear bright dresses every day and loved to make them billow and swirl. She often became tangled in the leash as she pirouetted in the air.

It wasn't until Meri was three that the tough questions began: Why didn't her father walk in the air too? Why did she have to wear a harness and Gus didn't?

Ruddy studied the shoes strewn around him. They ranged from pink contrivances with a flighty nature to serious-looking inventions resembling torture props out of a boarding school wardrobe.

"You were worried about Meri, too, and yet you never suggested we try these shoes. Why?" he asked.

After a long moment of silence, Ariel answered, "Because of what they would do to her."

Ruddy didn't understand. "What do you mean?"

"They made me feel even more different than I already was.

I hated them, how they made me see myself and how others saw me. They were another secret I could never explain. I don't want that for our daughter."

"Me neither. But, Ariel, I don't know how we're going to keep her safe in this world. I stay awake at night worrying about her."

Ariel threaded her fingers between his. "I spent much of life pretending, keeping secrets, desperate to be ordinary, to be something other than the Clodhopper in the hideous shoes." Ruddy winced at the name. That was the ugly moniker classmates had stamped Ariel with in grade school. Even after she learned how to navigate Up There when she was ten and no longer needed the clunky shoes, "Clodhopper" followed her into high school.

Ruddy thought of all the years he'd known her, and not really known her. Sometimes, he felt clueless around his wife; how she saw the world and how she lived in it amazed him. So many forbidden secrets. So many guilty deceptions. The Turnstone household where he grew up had not been haunted by secrets. Compared to Ariel's life, the Turnstones were ordinary. They were an open book. His father watched birds and built websites, and his mother gardened and baked.

He sighed, "Why can't we all just be who we truly are?"

In a wistful voice, Ariel said, "No secrets, no hiding behind masks. That would be nice. But it's not possible—for me or Meri." Her voice turned more urgent. "Ruddy, I don't want our daughter to become a Clodhopper."

He raised her hand to his lips and kissed it. "She's not a Clodhopper. I would never let that happen. It's the world that's confused, not you. Your secrets will always be safe with me. You are not alone."

That brought a smile to Ariel's face. "From the very

beginning, from the moment I felt her stirring inside me, I knew our baby would be special, and I swore she would never wear the ugly shoes. Now, here they are." Distressed, she kicked at the mess of footwear. "I don't know why Mama kept them. Maybe they're a sign. Maybe I found them now for a reason. Maybe I did it all wrong. Maybe I should have . . ."

"Stop it," said Ruddy. "Every parent thinks they've screwed up their kids. We're doing all right. We haven't been to the emergency room . . . much." In fact, the one mishap had been when the leash became tangled in Ruddy's hand while toddler Meri was twirling and broke his finger.

With sad eyes, Ariel considered the box and the words penned in wobbly letters: *NEVER OPEN AGAIN*. "I don't re-member writing those words, but that's my handwriting."

Ruddy immediately began tossing the shoes back into the box. "We're getting rid of these. Right now."

"But—"

"I'll take care of it. You never have to see them again, and Meri will never know about them."

"What will you do with them? They're hardly Goodwill material."

Ruddy said, "I'll bury them in the deepest hole I can dig, and I will never tell you where it is."

And that was what he did.

CHAPTER 5

THE VOLCANO ERUPTS

WHEN ARIEL WAS PREGNANT with Meri, she suffered terrible backaches. At night she was unable to sleep, until Ruddy swept his hands in soothing motions down her back, swirling, pressing, relieving. She wanted the back rubs to go on forever, but they always ended as Ruddy drifted to sleep. She would feel his hands slow, grow still, drop to his side. And then all the rocks in the bed would come alive again, the pointy mattress peaks would gouge, and everything that touched her became too hard to bear.

Some nights, anxious not to wake Ruddy with her tossing and turning, she slipped from their bed and padded barefoot into the backyard. There she closed her eyes, took a deep breath, and leaned back into the arms of Up There. In moments, she was horizontal on a cushion of air. She floated a couple of feet from the ground, staring up at the stars. Sighing with relief, she relaxed as invisible currents massaged her lower back.

Thank you, she whispered.

Often, on those nights, the child inside her would rub a fist across her belly, as if waving to the air, the moon, and the stars. That was when Ariel was certain she was having a daughter and that her child would ride the wind like her ancestors. Ariel knew her child would be a strong wind rider.

I'll keep her safe, Ariel promised the wind. *I'll teach her.*

She already knows, replied the wind.

On some nights when pregnant Ariel sought relief in Up There, she fell asleep secure in the air's comforting arms. So tired from the needs of the growing baby, she didn't even wake when Ruddy came out of the house. She didn't see him shake his head with loving exasperation at the sight of his floating wife, didn't feel him tuck her drifting body into the safety of his embrace, didn't hear him whisper to the air, "I've got her now."

* * *

Ariel, still shaken from the discovery of the shoes in the barn, set the Harriet doll on her desk. She wondered: *Could she teach Meri all she needed to know to manage her gift?* It had taken Ariel years to figure out who she was and to find her place Up There. She had no teachers.

Ariel was ten years old when she first rode the air with confidence and began communicating with the wind. Her almost-five-year-old daughter was already talking with Up There, and Meri's accelerated pace worried her mother. Ariel knew that the call of the wind could overpower good sense and self-control. Meri had yet to learn to fear Up There and where it could drive her. She knew nothing of the sacrifices it could demand of her.

When Sahara married Echo Starling, the town physician

who had been courting her for years, she gave the Stevens farm to Ariel. The legacy had required Ariel to take a stand about herself and her life. Would she continue to hide her gift in a tiny Minneapolis apartment, or would she return home to the sweeping Cosette skies that allowed her to be who she truly was? The inheritance put Ariel into the cross hairs of tenacious real estate agent Melanie Harcourt, the representative of a group of investors who wanted to turn the farm's spacious fields and rolling hills into a golf resort. But Ariel denied Melanie and kept her home. Now, she realized it was the best decision she had ever made because she had a daughter who needed the sky over the Stevens farm.

✳ ✳ ✳

Ariel heard her daughter waking and prepared herself for the fight she knew would come. That child who had waved to the stars from the womb was strong-willed, like her mother.

When Meri crashed into her mother's second-floor office, Ariel calmly looked up from her laptop and into the huge eyes and long lashes of her daughter's cat sleep mask. Ariel glanced from Meri to the window. Outside, the swing in the oak tree had begun to move of its own accord.

"Can we go Up There now? Can we?" Meri bounced on her toes.

Ariel hardened her heart against Meri's plea and the adorable eyes staring at her from the mask. She said, "I'm working, Meri."

Meri pushed the mask to her forehead and leaned closer into Ariel's space. "Then can we go later? I really want to go."

Ariel saved the work on her laptop, swiveled her chair to face her daughter, and said firmly, "No."

Meri couldn't believe it. "But why?"

"You need to learn more about Up There before we go there again."

"I know everything already."

"No, you don't."

"Yes, I do."

When Ariel refused to give in to her daughter's request, Meri's bottom lip began to tremble. Then came the wailing. The sudden, instant, and loud weeping from the normally happy child always came as a shock. A Meri meltdown was like the blast of an erupting volcano—explosive, messy, and uncontrollable. Outside in the backyard, the swing twisted faster, and the chains tangled.

Ruddy, who had noticed the swing's wild gyrations from the windows in his office downstairs, rushed into the room. "What's going on?"

Immediately, Meri turned to her father and flung herself at his legs. Giving him her most pitiful look, she said, "Daddy, *she* won't let me go Up There."

A glance passed between Ruddy and Ariel. That glance said keep a united front. When it came to parenting decisions, they backed each other, even when they didn't entirely agree. But, on this occasion, Ruddy was in total agreement. He would prefer that Meri never returned to Up There, but he knew that was an impossible wish.

He patted Meri's shoulder. "Your mother said no."

Meri pushed away from him and swiped at the tears in her eyes. "But, but, it's so unfair. I know what I'm doing."

"You are only four," said her father.

"Almost five," Meri corrected.

"Still . . ." Ruddy tried to hug her, but she spun away and turned on her mother.

"Why did you show me Up There if you're not going to let

me go back? I want to go. Now." She ripped off the sleep mask and flung it to the floor.

Bending down to pick up the sleep mask, Ruddy said, "Meri, don't use that tone with your mother."

Meri looked him right in the eye and screamed.

Ruddy sighed. Sometimes he didn't know what to do with his daughter. He had little experience with tantrums. He was the son of a patient birdwatcher and a happy baker. Like them, he took life at an easy pace and believed life was good, no matter its ups and downs.

With hands on her hips, Meri faced her mother. "If you don't let me go back Up There, right now, I'm going to move to . . . a different state . . . on another planet. And I'm not giving *you* my address!"

The ultimatum made Ariel lift an eyebrow at Ruddy. "You had to show her the universe?" she said.

Ruddy, trying to hide his grin, said, "Science is sort of my thing."

Recently, Ruddy and Meri had been studying the world on computer maps. He had shown her where they lived, in a state called Minnesota. Then he explained that Minnesota was part of a country, the United States, and the country was part of a planet, Earth. He had provided books on stars and the universe, and Meri had started naming the paper stars dangling from her ceiling.

Ariel leaned forward in a face-off with her mulish daughter. In a tone of voice not to be ignored, she said, "Okay, here's the real deal. I took you Up There because shortly you'll turn five and then you will go to school. You have only a little time to figure out who you are Up There and what it means."

Meri didn't understand. "What does school have to do with it?"

Ariel pointed to the swing, which was now ensnarled in its chains. Meri looked at the swing in the backyard with shock. "What happened?"

"You happened," Ariel said.

Meri shot her mother a look, which quickly turned to denial. "I didn't do that."

Ariel pulled Meri into her lap. "Baby, you and I talk to the wind, and it talks to us. But it also picks up on our feelings. Sometimes, without meaning to, we can send signals and create problems."

Meri looked puzzled and a little scared.

"Not on purpose," Ariel assured her. "But that still doesn't stop these problems from happening. We must be careful. For some reason that I don't understand entirely, our feelings can have an impact. We are connected to Up There."

Ruddy knew Ariel was right. He thought this aspect of his wife's gift—managing one's emotions so carefully—sounded terrible and was too much responsibility for anyone, much less his young daughter. Not for the first time, he wished this gift from the Hamilton line had passed over his wife and child. But if that had happened, he wondered, would Ariel still be his Ariel? Would Meri be the wonder that she is?

Ariel continued, "We have people we need to protect. That is what having the gift is about. We must learn how to be a part of Up There and how to keep Up There safely inside of us."

Meri frowned. "I don't get it."

Ariel hugged her. "You will. This summer, you and I are going to train like crazy so when you go to school in the fall you won't be tangling any playground equipment by accident."

Meri looked doubtfully at the swing again.

Ariel tapped Meri on the shoulder and handed the Harriet doll to her daughter.

"Is this Harriet?" Like all the children in Cosette, Meri visited the Harriet statue in the city park and patted her size 80 shoes. Her grandmother Sahara had told her the story of Harriet Bunyan battling her big brother the lumberjack to save the natural world around Cosette.

"Harriet has been my friend for a long time," Ariel said. "And now she is yours. But don't take her to another planet. I would miss you both terribly."

Meri hugged the doll. "I can smell you on her."

"That's the smell of my love."

"Do I have a smell?"

"Yes," said Ariel. "I know your smell and will remember it all of my life. If we were ever lost in a dark-as-night cave, I would find you and hold you and know it was you just by your smell."

"Even if you couldn't see me?" Meri asked.

"Even then."

Meri caressed the doll. "Grandma Sahara says Harriet had superpowers. She was a giant like her brother, you know. She made our lakes and rivers and forests. And when her brother Paul wanted to chop down the trees, she said no, just like the Lorax in my book."

"That's how the story goes," said Ariel.

After several moments of thought, Meri turned to her father. "Daddy, what is your superpower?"

Ruddy laughed. "I don't think I have one," he said.

Ariel didn't agree. "He puts up with us," she told her daughter. "And that takes superpower."

"Yes," said Meri in an adult voice. "Because we're a *lot* of trouble."

CHAPTER 6

WE SAVE WHAT WE LOVE

MERI SCOOPED UP A box elder bug from the kitchen counter and, carrying it in her cupped palm, rushed to the back door, where she released it into the outdoors. Like her great-uncle Kal, Meri never met a creature she didn't try to befriend, even those that bit and snarled. She watched the box elder bug flit away then lifted her head and listened.

The wind called her today. Its voice was strong and made Meri feel as if ants were running around inside her. If she didn't go out soon and be with the wind, she would start rolling on the rug like Gus scratching his back. She needed to be outside. Now.

Entering Ruddy's office, Meri announced, "I'm going outside, Daddy."

Ruddy looked up from his computer with a frown. "Hold on." He was engrossed in a chapter he was writing for the new book, his second collaboration with Ariel. To their surprise, their first book, which wove his expertise on weather and at-mosphere with Ariel's passion for the environment and halting climate change, had been a best seller.

"Give me a few minutes, and I'll come with you," he said, typing the end of a sentence.

"I can go alone. I'm just going to be in the backyard," said Meri.

Ruddy didn't like the idea, but he was riding an irresistible train of thought in his research. He looked intently at her. "You'll wear the monkey backpack?"

She already had grabbed the monkey pack from its hook and eagerly held it up for him to see.

When Meri went outside, either alone or with others, she was required to use one of two child safety harnesses—a uni-corn one or a monkey one. The monkey pack was bigger than the unicorn pack and contained a two-pound dumbbell. At first Ariel and Ruddy had worried about weighing their daugh-ter down with a lump of iron, but as Ariel said, "It's better than the shoes." Still, Ruddy had conferred with his father-in-law, Doctor Echo Starling, to make sure the added weight wouldn't harm Meri's back or posture.

Since Ariel was in Minneapolis speaking at a symposium on the impact of environmental change on agriculture, the de-cision was Ruddy's. He said, "Okay. Go. But I'll be watching you from the window. No shenanigans with Up There."

Meri smiled, turned, and raced through the back door.

She stopped on the patio, pausing to check on her father through his office windows. Ruddy was already intently fo-cused on his computer.

Meri sat on a concrete bench, pulled off the backpack, and removed the bright pink dumbbell. She placed the weight on the ground beside the bench, then donned the backpack again. Gus, watching intently, didn't like this turn of events. He nosed the dumbbell and whined.

"It'll be okay, Gus," she said, patting his smooth head. "Don't be such a worrywart. I'm just practicing cartwheels."

Meri had studied gymnastics videos and was determined to turn a cartwheel. Her mother promised that once she mastered the cartwheel on the ground, she could try it in the air. But it was difficult, and Meri kept falling over instead of landing on her feet.

Wearing a red tutu with bike shorts underneath, a tie-dyed T-shirt, and the now light monkey backpack, Meri raised her arms, took a few running steps, and lunged. The result was the same as her previous efforts. She landed on her rear end. Her audience, Gus, nudged her in the grass to make sure she was all right.

Meri practiced until she grew tired and plopped under the oak tree to rest. She noticed that the birds in the tree were excessively noisy and wondered what had upset them. Looking for the source of the trouble, she spotted a fluttering in the nearby grass.

It was a baby bird.

"It must have fallen out of its nest," said Meri, studying the tiny creature. "I don't think it has its flying feathers yet, Gus."

Meri placed her hand on the dog's neck to make sure Gus didn't get too close as he sniffed the bird. Gus was big. He could step on the bird without realizing it.

"What do you think we should do?" asked Meri, in a worried voice.

The baby bird reminded Meri of a day by the lake with her great-uncle Kal, the family's wildlife expert. Sitting on the dock, they had watched a nest of baby wood ducks taking their first plunge into the water.

"I built that nesting box for them," said Kal. "Long ago."

The box was mounted on a pole planted in the water. "It's so high," said Meri.

"It must be high to keep the eggs away from predators. It's situated in the water so the babies can land in the water when they take their first step out of the nest."

Meri nodded in understanding. "So they don't crash into the ground. But it must be scary if they've never stepped into the air before. Look, there's one too afraid to jump."

It was the final fledgling. The bird stood at the door of the box, looked down, rustled its feathers, and chirped for its mother. Mother duck swam below in the water, offering encouragement, but the little bird just couldn't trust itself.

Meri turned to Kal. "Maybe we should help it."

Kal shook his head. "It has to do this itself. Mother Nature will see to it."

Finally, the baby duck let out a frightened squawk and flung itself from the nesting box to its new home in the waters of the lake. Landing with a plop, it swam to join its family without hesitation.

With the memory of that day still fresh in her mind, Meri looked from the oak tree to the baby bird. Should she return the bird to its nest? Or should she leave it for the mother to find?

"It's a dangerous world for baby birds," Meri told Gus.

She couldn't simply abandon the baby bird to struggle in the grass and be picked off by one of the cats. The cats really had no respect for birds. In fact, one was already approaching on stealthy paws hoping that Meri and Gus would leave soon so it could race in and grab its defenseless lunch. Meri turned and pointed a finger at the cat. "I see you," she said. The cat froze.

Gus nudged her as if to say, well, what are we going to do?

"We're returning it to its nest," she told Gus and scooped up the bundle of feathers. Tucking the bird close to her beating heart to calm it, Meri whispered words of comfort.

Listening to the squawking birds, she scanned the oak's foliage and decided that the baby bird's nest must be in there somewhere. *But how do I get up there?* she wondered.

We'll help, said the wind.

And before she knew it, Meri's feet had left the ground. She gasped as she rose. She clutched the bird against her chest. Gus woofed. She rose higher and higher. When she saw the nest, she whispered to the wind, *We're here.* She stopped and floated on a cushion of air as she carefully placed the bird back in the nest next to its sisters and brothers. The sight of an unknown creature—a rather large one, at that—hovering so nearby startled the nestlings and set off even more incessant tweeting. Before Meri knew what was happening, a mother bird dived in, answering the fearful calls of her children. Meri jerked back to avoid a collision with a sharp beak, scraping against the bark of the tree. She held her hands up in surrender.

"It's fine," Meri reassured her. "It just fell out of the nest. I brought it back to you."

The mother protectively fluttered above her children then landed on a branch overhead and angrily lectured Meri. The baby birds were still excited, and Meri thought she had better go.

But when she asked the air to help her down, she found herself stuck.

The strap of the backpack was caught on a broken branch. She tried wiggling off the protruding wood, but the tree held her tight.

Meri began to shout, "Daddy, help! Daddy!"

* * *

From the tunnels of his data-meandering mind, Ruddy heard a nagging sound. He brushed it aside and kept reading, focusing, calculating. He took notes. There was the sound again. He glanced out the window.

The backyard was empty.

Where was Meri?

Rushing into the yard, he followed Meri's voice to the oak tree. He stared at his daughter dangling high in the tree.

Hands on his hips, he shouted, "Meriweather Turnstone, what are you doing up there?"

Meri gave him a sweet smile and waved hello. "Hi, Daddy."

Ruddy pointed a finger at his daughter. "You've got some explaining to do. I'll get the ladder."

I'm in trouble now, whispered Meri to the wind.

With his stomach churning, Ruddy fetched the ladder from the barn. How he hated this piece of equipment. He leaned the ladder against the trunk of the tree and tested it to make sure it was secure. Then with a deep breath and a reminder to his acrophobic mind that he could do this, he started upward, careful not to look down. Nevertheless, his breathing soon became labored, forcing him to stop twice, close his eyes, and center himself. "Breathe," he told himself. "Look straight ahead."

From a distance, he heard Meri's voice. "You're doing great, Daddy."

When he reached her, he rested his head on a ladder rung to gather himself. Finally, he looked at her. "Are you all right?"

"Of course."

"At least one of us is," he mumbled.

Meri began, "I'm sorry . . ." Her voice trailed off as she watched her father struggling to breathe.

He nodded, happened to glance down, and hugged the ladder in panic. *How was he going to do this? How was he going to get both of them down?*

"Give me a moment. Let me figure this out," he said.

"Take your time, Daddy," Meri said. "I can wait."

Ruddy swallowed his fear and told her to loop her arms around his neck. Then with one hand still securely clutching the ladder, he reached up with the other and slipped the backpack strap from the tree. When Meri was free, Ruddy crushed his daughter to him.

He felt a small hand pat his back.

The ladder shifted slightly with the added weight, and Ruddy's heart lurched.

Slowly, he began to back down the ladder.

"I can fly down now, Daddy," Meri reassured him.

"No," Ruddy said. "Stay with me. I'll get us both down."

It seemed, to Ruddy, to take forever to reach the ground. When he finally felt solid land under foot, he sank onto the grass with Meri still in his arms.

"I'm good. I'm good," he said, more to comfort himself than his daughter.

"You are the bravest daddy in the world," said Meri, kissing his cheek.

"And you are in trouble," he said.

Meri looked him in the eye. "I can explain—"

"You were told not to go Up There." Flicking the suspiciously light backpack with his hand, he asked, "And where is your dumbbell?"

Meri tentatively pointed toward the patio. "I can't practice cartwheels with that. It weighs me down."

"That's its job. You promised to take the dumbbell."

Meri held up a finger, "Actually, I promised to take monkey. And I did."

"Meri," he said, drawing her name out in exasperation.

The child rushed to explain, "I found a baby bird, Daddy. It fell out of its nest. It couldn't fly yet. I simply had to save it."

"Of course, you did."

There was a saying around the Turnstone house: We save what we love.

The problem was: Meri loved too many things.

CHAPTER 7

THE DOG BITES

MERI HAD TWO GRANDMOTHERS: Sahara Lee Starling and Alice Turnstone. Sahara was the one who bought Meri new books, so many books that Ruddy had to build a new bookshelf in the child's room. Alice was the one who encouraged Meri to get her hands dirty in the Turnstone garden and to don a child-size apron in her kitchen.

As Sahara shared a playground bench with Alice, she thought of an article she recently read: "Grandmothers have a natural connection, woven of worry, generosity, and relief. At night, they take their concerns for their little ones to bed, where sleep is already illusive, hiding behind the boulders of aching and aging bodies. They have hearts that are never too full and never too busy for grandchildren begging for attention or homemade cookies. And they crumple into their chairs at the end of the day grateful that, even though they love them dearly, grandchildren do get to go home to someone else's care."

Nothing could be truer, thought Sahara.

"I love being a grandmother," said Alice, waving to Meri as the child climbed the steps to the slide. "But it sure is exhausting. We baked chocolate chip cookies yesterday. I had to take a nap after she left."

"Don't let her sneak the dough. Uncooked dough is an invitation for salmonella," said Sahara, a freelance writer-turned-novelist who had once written an article on the many types of bacteria eager and able to wipe out the human race. Now Sahara stuck strictly to the writing of her popular fantasy novels, and in her fiction, the bacteria never won.

Alice said, "I know I shouldn't let her sample, but it's tough to say no to her. She looks so cute in that apron I made her." Ruddy's mother, who owned nearly as many cookbooks as Sahara owned novels, was an award-winning baker, according to the judges at the Minnesota State Fair. She was the expert in all culinary matters in their family and a soft touch. Sahara, on the other hand, hated cooking and was not so easily manipulated. She had experience navigating the wiles of precious but conniving daughters.

The grandmothers observed the growing crowd at the playground. Summer was winding down; soon school would start and play days would be limited. "Maybe we should take her home soon," said Alice, her watchful eyes roaming the playground for potential problems.

"She's having fun," objected Sahara. "She can handle it." Sahara sounded more confident than she felt. Vestiges of fear and worry from raising her own wind-riding daughter lingered, but Sahara hid them well.

* * *

Alice hoped Sahara was right. She will never forget the day she discovered her granddaughter's true nature. She and husband

43

Arthur had made an unplanned visit to the farm and saw eighteen-month-old Meri toddling about the backyard. The child was wearing her safety harness, and Ruddy held the leash. Alice had rushed to them, saying "Take that silly leash off my grandchild so I can hug her."

"That's not a good idea, Mom—" Ruddy had started to object.

Before Ruddy knew what was happening, Alice had unstrapped the harness. Instantly, a giggling Meri began to levitate. Alice took a step back and screamed. Ruddy made a lunge for the floating baby, snagged her by a leg, and reeled her in. Arthur stared at the child in stunned silence.

After several moments in which Ruddy anxiously watched his parents gawk at Meri with disbelief, Arthur whispered in awe, "Our little bird." Arthur, who himself resembled a lanky, long-legged heron in a flannel shirt, found avian connections everywhere he looked. A lifelong birder, he worked with retired science teacher Dakota Blue to spread the word about the decline of bird populations around the world.

Hearing the commotion, Ariel ran from the house, took Meri into her arms, and produced a rattle from her pocket to distract the child. She held the baby, while Ruddy strapped Meri back into the harness. "She's not a bird," Ariel corrected. "She doesn't flap her arms. She is a wind rider. Like me."

Alice's eyes widened, now more perplexed than ever. "A what?"

Ariel and Ruddy exchanged nervous looks. When he nodded, Ariel explained, "I was born with the gift of flight, and so was Meri. She's too young to understand how to work with the wind and the sky, but she'll learn. I'll teach her."

"Extraordinary," said a grinning Arthur, reaching out his arms for Meri.

Alice looked at all of them as if they were crazy.

A child who could fly frightened her.

A glance at Ruddy's face—silently begging her to accept his family—stopped Alice. Shame overpowered her fear.

Meri had been too young to understand the sudden strained silence among her parents and grandparents. She shook the rattle to get her grandmother's attention, smiled at her, and offered the rattle to Alice—by slowly levitating it toward her. Alice gulped and, with tears in her eyes, cautiously accepted the rattle from the air. Ruddy and Ariel held their breath.

Arthur laughed in amazement. After a moment, a look of wonder bloomed on Alice's face too, and she handed the rattle back to Meri.

Seeing that the situation was under control, Ariel handed the baby to Arthur and said, "Don't let her fly over the barn." With a big grin, he nodded and began to walk with Meri, identifying birds in the yard and reciting their names to his granddaughter.

So much had happened since that day of revelation. Now, Alice worried when Meri didn't wear her harness and leash. At night, she had nightmares of Meri caught in power lines, while Arthur had begun researching avian language in the hopes that Meri could communicate with birds someday while she was Up There. "Imagine what we could learn," he told his wife.

* * *

Meri was wearing her monkey harness with the dumbbell today, no leash. She focused on keeping herself grounded by maintaining contact with the steps, the handles of the ladders, and the edges of the slides. Seeing the concern on Alice's face, Sahara said, "Meri's being careful."

45

Sahara had more than thirty years of experience protecting the secrets of a daughter who could fly—decades of worry and single parenting, a lifetime of trusting no one with her child. Being a grandparent with Alice, sharing the secrets of Ariel and Meri with her, had made Sahara realize that no one lives in a vacuum. *We all need others*, she thought, *even those of us with secrets.*

The grandmothers watched Meri settle on the platform at the top of the slide with a new friend. The girls were laughing when two boys, about the same ages as the girls, approached. It was a calm day but a little cool, and Meri was wearing a sweater, tights, and a frilly pink skirt with sequins.

"You look like a puff ball," said one boy.

"She does not," said the girl Meri had befriended and who was greatly enamored of Meri's sparkling ensemble. "She's a princess."

The boy laughed at them. His friend, however, did not. "C'mon, leave them alone," the friend said, beginning to edge away.

Watching the exchange, Alice rose to intervene, but Sahara motioned for her to sit back down. "Meri can handle it," Sahara said.

Alice wasn't so sure, and in truth, neither was Sahara.

As a nervous Alice perched on the bench, ready to leap to the rescue, Sahara studied the two boys. "One's Wren Wamsganz. His family just moved back to town. His father is Freddy Wamsganz. Freddy returned to Cosette to help run the family resort after his father died."

"A Wamsganz," Alice said with disgust.

The late Earl Wamsganz, Freddy's father, had never paid for the resort's website that Arthur had built for him, and Freddy's brother, Harley, had bullied everyone in grade school and high school including Ruddy.

The boy with Wren, a kid in a flashy jacket, flicked his hand at Meri's monkey backpack. "I've seen you. They have to put you on a leash. Like a dog."

Meri stared up at him and said defiantly, "I am *not* a dog."

Her tone, which sounded like an insult to the boy, made him draw closer. "Arf, arf. Here, puppy, want a dog biscuit."

The girls stood. "Leave us alone," said Meri's new friend and defender.

Wren grabbed his friend's arm and said, "Buster, let it go."

Buster shrugged him off. "First, I want to hear the dog bark. Can you beg, dog?"

When Sahara heard the name Buster, she immediately identified the boy.

"That's Buster Sweeney," she told Alice.

Alice looked the kid over and said, "The Sweeneys built that big house on the lake, right?"

During the year that everyone wore masks and kept their distance from each other, the Sweeneys had abandoned Minneapolis and converted their summer cabin into a permanent residence. The father was a former actor turned theatrical agent with a flair for the dramatic, and the mother was an interior designer with a fancy take on just about everything. Their Cosette home project had quickly gotten away from them—now the house was so large and top heavy it appeared ready to topple into the lake.

Buster's real name was Thomas, but he had earned the moniker Buster in day care. He was the kid who liked to knock down everything and everyone. No building block tower or castle, no child in his way was safe from Buster. He enjoyed being the monster, a game he had learned from his parents.

In the game, his parents would chase him around their massive Minneapolis mansion and laugh in an eerie singsong voice: "I'm a monster, you better run. I eat children, just for fun." Buster adored the game. It titillated his penchant for the dangerous, and it focused all his parents' attention on him. But his day care teacher began to worry when Buster started stalking children, whispering the song under his breath, "I'm a monster." The teacher had a discussion with the Sweeneys, who stopped playing the game (much to Buster's regret) and even considered therapy for Buster.

Up on the slide, Buster's taunts grew louder. "Here, puppy," he said, snapping his fingers.

Alice began to squirm. She eyed Sahara for guidance, but a watchful Sahara did not move to intervene. "Meri can deal with the boy," said Sahara, hoping she was right.

* * *

Humiliation and anger rose inside Meri, flooding the carefully constructed walls of defense that she had worked on all summer with her mother. Suddenly, Meri couldn't think of any of the techniques her mother had taught her to control her emotions. There was something about deep breathing and counting to ten but . . .

Meri was at a loss as to what to do. However, like her mother, there was something in her genes that would not allow her to back down—even when she was afraid.

She heard the words of her mother in her mind: *You will meet bullies, people who want to make you afraid, but you are not helpless. You are stronger than they are.*

Was this Buster a bully? Meri didn't know much about bullies. She'd never met one before. She didn't know what to say to him or how to act. He seemed to want her to feel small and helpless, but it wasn't working. Meri decided that Buster must be a bully and that she had to stand up to him.

"I'm not afraid of you," she said.

Meri's new friend stepped up to Buster and yelled, "Yeah, we're not afraid of you. Go away!"

Buster shoved the girl aside, and before Meri knew what was happening, she flung out her arm and drew a gust of wind to the platform. It caught Buster and sent him, with wheeling arms and stumbling legs, backward down the slide.

The Wamsganz boy yelled, "Buster!"

Giving Meri an incredulous look and clutching the new baseball cap the wind was trying to rip from his head, Wren plunked himself down on the slide and followed his friend. At the bottom of the slide, the boys got up and shook sand from themselves. "You all right?" asked Wren.

Buster rubbed the back of his neck and looked up at Meri with a puzzled expression. "Yeah," he said, "let's get out of here."

Sahara leaped to her feet and grabbed her backpack. "Time to go."

Alice, handbag already draped on her shoulder, was right behind her. "Yup."

The wind dissipated as Meri and her friend slid down the slide. When they reached the bottom, the grandmothers were already waiting.

Filled with guilt, Meri turned pleading eyes toward Sahara. "I-I-I didn't mean . . ."

"I know," Sahara reassured her. "It's okay."

But was it really? wondered Meri, as they drove home past the statue of Harriet Bunyan. A confused Meri glanced at the mighty heroine of Cosette and asked herself: *What would Harriet have done? Would she have been proud of Meri or disappointed in her?*

CHAPTER 8

DON'T BE ME

ARIEL AND RUDDY PONDERED how to discipline a daughter who had swept a boy off a slide with the flick of her hand. Buster might have deserved it, but that was beside the point. All children needed to learn control, but it was especially important in Meri's case. Despite her youth, Meri had to learn to manage her emotions, to be aware when they were rising inside her and be able to calm herself. If she couldn't learn this, the consequences could be dire.

Ruddy recalled his first experience with an out-of-control Ariel. She was in labor with Meri, and each time the pain ripped through her, the hospital windows shook. Although the nurses had been oblivious to the sudden change in the atmosphere, both he and Echo had noticed the disturbing synchronicity of Ariel's labor and the atmospheric events outside. Ariel's groans whipped the wind into a vortex, pushing and pulling at the medical center. At one point, a frowning Echo looked over the rims of his wire-framed glasses and said to Ruddy, "We've got to get the baby out before Ariel tears this place apart."

Cosette residents, recalling that day, said they had never experienced such wind as the one in which Meriweather Turnstone was born. They were right. Ruddy had consulted the weather data, and the day Meri made her entrance into the world, a record for wind velocity had been set in their area.

Now, Ruddy remembered that day and wondered if that long-ago climatic uproar had been entirely Ariel's doing. He suspected that his powerful daughter, struggling from the throes of birth, had contributed to the atmospheric mayhem as well.

No one had prepared Ruddy for having a child with elemental powers. Some days, life with Meri made him feel lost and ill-equipped for parenthood. Once he'd asked his mother-in-law how she had managed to raise someone as special as Ariel and Sahara had told him: "I treated her like any other child. When she broke the rules, I couldn't turn an eye or make excuses. Ariel's survival depended on me."

Remembering Sahara's advice, Ruddy gave his daughter a stern look and said, "Meri, you know you did something wrong at the playground."

Meri shifted in her seat across the kitchen table from her mother, glancing at Ariel then quickly away. She muttered, "Yes . . . but that boy was so mean."

Ruddy, leaning against the kitchen counter, said, "When it comes to you, Meri, there are no buts."

With wide eyes, Meri asked, "What do you mean?"

Ariel leaned forward, her eyes meeting Meri's. "He means that you and I are different; we must remember that. When we lose our tempers, people could get hurt."

Meri grumbled, "But it's so hard. He called me a dog."

Ruddy exchanged a look with Ariel. Both of them would like to have a few choice words with Buster Sweeney's parents.

Ariel said, "You must have felt the wind rising in you before you called it to deal with Buster."

Meri looked away from her mother. "Maybe, but I couldn't remember the stuff we practiced . . ."

"There are no buts, Meri, no excuses," said Ariel softly.

Meri persisted. "But I didn't *know* the wind was going to do that!"

Ruddy crossed his arms over his chest. With a sigh, he said, "Baby, you need to learn from this."

Meri didn't like the sound of that. "Are you going to punish me?"

"Yes," said Ariel and pronounced the verdict she and Ruddy had agreed upon. "No deer visits for a week."

Meri jumped out of her seat. "What? You can't do that!"

Ruddy hardened his voice and replied, "And you can't throw boys off slides."

Meri's mouth snapped shut. She knew that tone of voice; she hardly ever heard it from her father. He was the softer parent, the one who could be persuaded to see her point of view more readily. But not today.

∗ ∗ ∗

Ariel knew the punishment was justified but implementing it hurt.

Deer often came to rob the bird feeder in the backyard on quiet evenings, and it was a beloved family ritual to sit on the patio and watch them. House arrest—keeping the miscreant inside during the deer visits—had been the standard punishment for a misbehaving young Ariel, and now it would be the same for Meri.

This penance would be especially difficult on Ariel's daughter.

Instead of sitting quietly on the bench with her parents during the visitation of these wild creatures, fearless Meri had no qualms about crawling across the yard with bird seed in her pockets. She was determined to make contact. The deer would allow her to get close, but not too close. She knew enough to select a respectable distance in the dew-damp grass and wait for the deer to accept her.

Depending on their mood and skittishness, sometimes the deer took the gift Meri proffered, snuffling and vacuuming up the seeds from her palm. Other times, they ignored her and went straight for the bird feeder. Either way, Meri smiled at them, sent them calm vibes, and told them they were safe with her.

Ariel knew how it felt to have a deer trust her and eat out of her hand. She knew how addictive it was to be accepted by one of Mother Nature's constituents and how much denying this contact with the deer would hurt her daughter.

That night, after a subdued Meri was in bed, Ariel sank into Ruddy's arms and whispered, "Did we do the right thing?"

* * *

Sahara and Ariel tipped the front porch swing into action with their toes. Gus slept in his dog bed. Meri, Ruddy, and Echo were inside making dinner. It was spaghetti night.

The air was disturbed, running anxious fingers through the leaves in the trees. Sahara knew the unrest in the air reflected her daughter's state of mind. She reached over and took Ariel's hand. "Don't worry. Whatever it is, we'll figure it out. You are not alone."

Ariel gave her mother a desperate look. "School starts in a few weeks."

"I know." Sahara did not mention the heavy shoes that had

kept Ariel safe when she started school. Her daughter was the mother now of a special child and had chosen a different path with Meri. Sahara kept reminding herself not to interfere. She just hoped Ariel's course of action was the right one.

"I can teach her. I can keep her safe," said Ariel, but Sahara heard the doubt in Ariel's voice.

Neither mentioned the years that Ariel had not trusted herself and ran from her gift. Ariel had been only sixteen when she gathered too much wind, lost control of the situation, and accidentally injured her best friend, Blinka Trout. After the accident, Ariel refused to step one foot in Up There. She locked the doors to her heart and shuttered the windows, denying the wind access. She'd spent years cowering in an apartment in Minneapolis, until her mother lured her home to the farm where her reconnection with Up There had been irresistible.

"I'm stronger now," Ariel said, more to herself than her mother.

"You'll do just fine," Sahara assured her. "And so will Meri."

Ariel gave a laugh of disbelief. "Mama, I'm so afraid of messing up with Meri." She looked down at their clasped hands and whispered, "I don't want her to turn into me—"

Shocked, Sahara stopped the swing for a moment then started it again with a push from her toe. "Ariel, Meri would be lucky to turn out like her mother."

Ariel shook her head. "No. I don't want her to be frightened of who she truly is." She didn't utter the words: *As I was, and still am.*

Ariel said, "It's so hard to let her go, to send her out into the world . . ."

Sahara pulled her daughter into her arms and hugged her. "I know, I know."

Sahara thought, *Maybe I did it all wrong. The shoes. So many secrets. What did I let my fear do to Ariel?*

Ariel sniffed and wiped a tear from her eye. "I thought I had it figured out."

"What?"

"My place in the world. What I was supposed to be Up There and Down Here. Now I don't know. Who am I: a mother, a wife, a writer, a crazy woman who talks to the wind?"

Sahara laughed and squeezed her daughter. "I know one thing. We are all works in progress, Ariel. The world changes. We change. We are always baking. Don't shut off the oven and leave the kitchen. You are not done."

CHAPTER 9

WHEN DOLPHINS CAN FLY

THE TROUTS WERE MECHANICS in talent, inclination, and heart. Every one of them was on the tall side, as blond as could be, and had long fingers that pried open the mechanical secrets of all kinds of contraptions, from engines to toaster ovens to bicycles. Blinka Trout was the only girl in the family of seven children and the first to refuse a spot in the family business, Trout Auto. Instead, she rode out on her own—a streak on a ten-speed with strong legs and swinging braids. She pedaled into the future to build Bike the Babe, a bicycle repair and rental shop located in downtown Cosette across the street from the Paul Bunyan State Trail.

Grandmother Trout, the matriarch from whom all the Trouts had inherited their mechanical genius, always claimed she loved her grandchildren equally, but everyone knew she favored Blinka. After all, when Grandma Trout died, she'd left her house and all her money to her only granddaughter, who had promptly used it to finance her dream of owning a bike shop.

Blinka had been Ariel's best friend since kindergarten. She had stood by young Ariel when others teased the girl in the clunky shoes; when adult Ariel had shut herself off from her gift, paying the price in loneliness and unhappiness; and when Ariel ended her self-imposed isolation in Minneapolis and rediscovered who she was in Cosette. When Ariel, still bruised and bandaged from tangling with a tornado, had married Ruddy in the living room of Echo Starling's big house, Blinka had been Ariel's maid of honor *and* Ruddy's best man. They'd been a threesome since sixth grade. While Ariel often worried that she could do no right, especially as a mother, Blinka had always believed that Ariel as a human could do no wrong.

For the life of their friendship, Ariel had kept the secret of her gift from Blinka and felt guilty about it. Every time Blinka had defended her against the school bullies and insisted that it was okay to be different, Ariel had yearned to explain her gift and Up There to her friend, but she couldn't. Her fear of rejection had kept her silent. Ariel didn't know what she would do if Blinka ever turned away from a friend who was just too strange to love.

It was a hot, summer afternoon, and Blinka and Ariel were sitting on a tatty plaid blanket by the lake on Ariel's farm. Stevens Lake was their place. Secrets (but not ones regarding flying) had been revealed here and kept here. Whether they were swimming in summer or ice skating in winter, they had held each other here. It was here where Blinka had claimed, to Ariel's astonishment, that they were sisters of the heart, a confession that nearly unraveled Ariel's vow of silence.

Ariel and Blinka watched Meri splash and paddle in the lake. The child wore a bright turquoise swim vest. Even though Meri could swim well, the floatation device was non-negotiable. Meri didn't like the vest since it kept her from diving deep. Ariel and Ruddy liked it for that very reason. It kept their daughter on the surface and in view.

Keeping an eye on Meri had been Gus's self-appointed job from the moment the family dog had laid eyes on infant Meri. He sat on the dock now, never taking his gaze from the girl splashing and flipping over in the water a few feet away.

Meri shouted, "Look, I'm a dolphin." The child was obsessed with dolphins. She watched videos on dolphins and tried to "swim" like them, arching and looping.

Raising her head out of the water, she squeaked. "That's hello in dolphin, Gus." The dog barked hello in return.

Ariel and Blinka laughed.

"I wish I were a dolphin and could play in the water all day," said Blinka, flinging her long blond braids over her sweaty shoulders and pressing a cold pop can against her cheek to chase away the August heat. "It's been a miserable summer. We could use some relief."

"It's coming," said Ariel. Just this morning she and Ruddy had argued about the weather. She always sensed changes in the atmosphere long before his technology reported it. It frustrated him when she predicted a cooling front that he couldn't see coming with his maps and models.

"Didn't see anything on my weather app about a break in the weather, but I believe you," said Blinka. "You have a sense about these things."

Ariel closed her eyes and felt the wind rising. She smiled and whispered in her mind to the wind, *I told Ruddy. It's coming.*

But the wind did not answer.

Instead, it kept stirring and growing.

Ariel opened her eyes and observed the waving arms of

the trees. On the opposite shore of the lake the reeds were bending and the feathers of the heron fishing for a snack were riffling.

Ariel rose slowly, sensing trouble in the air. The wind rippled over the lake and raced through the trees. She searched the sky. The clouds had gathered, compacting in layers stretching as far as the eye could see.

"What is it?" asked Blinka, also rising. "Something wrong with Meri?"

Suddenly, Ariel felt a swish, and a current of air crossed the lake and scooped up Meri.

Hearing Meri yelp, Ariel's gaze snapped from the sky to the lake.

She ran for the water, with Blinka on her heels.

But Gus was already on the spot. With a bark, he leaped from the dock into the air, snatched the strap on Meri's swim vest, and pulled the child back into the water.

Ariel and Blinka dived off the dock and came up near Meri and Gus. Gus was desperately paddling toward the bank, towing Meri by the strap with his teeth. The women each grabbed one of Meri's arms. Ariel ordered Gus, "We got her. Get out of the water." Gus splashed to shore, shook his body fiercely, and anxiously waited.

Ariel, Blinka, and Meri dragged themselves from the water and collapsed on the blanket, their chests heaving. The wind whipped around them. Gus stood close by, dripping, panting. He brushed Meri with his wet nose. "I'm okay," Meri said. "Thanks, Gus." The dog sat down.

Ariel removed Meri's swim vest, wrapped her in a dry towel, and pulled the child onto her lap. She hugged Meri. "That was a close one," she said. "But you kept your cool, baby. You did good."

"I was scared at first," Meri admitted, "but I remembered you told me losing control just makes you lose control more."

Wringing water from her braid, Blinka nodded. "It's never good to lose your cool in water."

"Or the air," Meri said then gasped and slapped her hand over her mouth, as she noticed Blinka's confused expression. Meri's gaze flew to her mother's face. "Mama, I-I didn't mean . . ."

"It's okay, baby." Ariel gave her daughter a soft smile, as she dried Meri's long curls with the end of the towel. "She had to know sometime."

Blinka looked from Meri to Ariel. "Know what? What actually happened out in the lake?"

Ariel swallowed. The old icy fear roared back to life.

The wind whispered, *Tell her.*

Taking a deep breath, Ariel started, "Blink, there's something I have wanted to tell you. Like all my life."

Blinka gave her a strange but teasing smile. "Ariel? What deep, dark secret have you been keeping from me?"

After several moments, Ariel said, "I have a gift, an unusual gift."

Blinka didn't see why this should cause consternation. In her mind, gifts were always good.

Ariel continued, "The wind talks to me, and I talk to it. And it helps me go Up There." She pointed to the sky.

"Up There? What does that mean?"

Meri scrambled out of Ariel's lap, leaned toward Blinka's puzzled face, and whispered, "She can fly."

An expression of disbelief passed over Blinka's features, then she was grinning. "What game are we playing?" When neither Ariel nor Meri said anything, Blinka stopped smiling. "This *is* a game, right?"

Ariel looked down at her hands. The moment she had

always dreaded was here. The wind rose around Ariel, and her wet hair started to fly. When she raised her head, there were tears on her face. The edges of the blanket started flapping madly, and Gus grew restless.

"No game, Blink," she said.

Then, without a word, Ariel levitated into the air, her legs still crossed as if she were sitting on the blanket. She hovered before her best friend. When she spread her arms, the wind took her higher. The air pulled at her wet T-shirt, and the waves in her hair swirled around her head.

Blinka's mouth fell open. Unable to take her eyes off her best friend, Blinka said, "What the hell?"

Frightened by the power she felt in the air and the wretched expression on her mother's face, Meri screamed, "Mama!" and reached for Ariel.

"No, Meri!" shouted Ariel, unfolding her legs, but it was already too late. Meri had launched herself into the air. A playful breeze immediately snatched Meri and tried to spin her away, but Ariel grabbed her child and pulled her close. They floated together, in each other's arms, as the wind tore at them.

Enough, Ariel whispered to the air.

The sight of Ariel and Meri hanging for a moment in the air then gently drifting down to earth left Blinka speechless. When they landed, Ariel kept Meri's hand clasped in hers. The wind eased. But a storm was brewing. The air told her so as it raced across the lake.

Unable to look Blinka in the eye, Ariel said, "We should get back to the house," and began gathering their swim things.

Blinka reached out and stopped her. "Help me understand."

Hearing compassion in Blinka's voice, Ariel wilted into Blinka's arms, as the weight she had carried for so long lifted. It would be all right. They were still sisters of the heart.

On the walk back to the house, Ariel told Blinka everything: how the gift of flight was passed through the women in the Hamilton family, how it had caused trouble in her life, and how it had come to be a constant in her existence as a person and as a mother.

"I live a tricky life," Ariel said.

Blinka replied, "You live a scary life."

When they reached the house, Ariel sent Meri inside then turned to Blinka. "Don't tell anyone about this, Blink. Please keep our secret—for my sake and Meri's."

When Ariel became pregnant with Meri, she and Ruddy had discussions about sharing the secret of Up There with those involved in Meri's life. Ruddy, who had always enjoyed a transparent life, saw no harm in including their best friend Blinka. Sahara, however, advised keeping the circle of secret keepers to immediate family. She had been raised to protect secrets—first keeping her mother Anne's flying a secret from even her own brothers, then maintaining the silence she believed was necessary for Ariel's survival. It was difficult for Ariel's mother to trust others with the family's confidences.

Ariel said to Blinka, "I know this is a heavy secret and a big ask."

Despite being part of a boisterous and curious family of seven children, Blinka took after Grandma Trout, who was the world's best secret keeper. Grandma would motion zipping her lips over a secret and promise, "I'll take it to the grave, kiddo."

Now, Blinka did the same. "Consider it done," she said, zipping her lips. "To the grave."

When the rain came, suddenly opening the skies and drenching them, the women didn't move. They stared at each other, making a pact that would last the rest of their lives.

Finally, Blinka asked, "Why did it take you so long to tell me? Didn't you trust me?"

Ariel looked away, embarrassed. "I was afraid that you would think I was weird."

Blinka laughed. "You *are* weird. We both are. According to Grandma Trout, everyone is weird in their own way."

Ariel felt a flood of relief.

Then suddenly, Blinka grabbed her in a mighty hug that lifted her off the ground. "You are the coolest friend I could ever have," she shouted and swung Ariel around until they were both dizzy.

From the window of Ruddy's office, Meri and her father watched the two laughing women ignoring the rain and holding each other.

Ruddy thought, *At last. She has told Blinka.*

CHAPTER 10

SO YOU WON'T FORGET ME

ON THE DAY MERIWEATHER Turnstone was born, Helen Moongoose bought an infant car seat. She didn't know what she was doing. Why would she? Her abusive husband had ended both her babies while they were still in Helen's womb. That was why she became Cosette's only convicted murderer and never a mother. But she was determined to be a darn-good adopted auntie to Meri, the daughter of her longtime friend Ariel. And she had been.

She had relentlessly researched car seats, kept trading to another size as Meri grew. She'd pushed infant Meri in a stroller on the streets of Cosette and always maintained a selection of children's books in the reading room, the unofficial library Helen kept in a corner of Books & Bobs, her sister Sweetie Moongoose's hair salon. Helen's book collection came from yard sales and donations from enthusiastic book buyers such as Sahara. Helen encouraged salon clients to read as they sat under the bubble hair dryers or to take a book home with them.

When Meri graduated from the stroller to a safety harness, Helen didn't question why. She expanded their walks into the woods and told the child the stories her Native aunties had told her: fantastical tales of the coyote, the hummingbird, and the pine tree. If Helen noticed, on these walks, that Meri's tiny sneakers sometimes walked the air instead of the path—Helen said nothing.

Helen had always sensed there was something special about Ariel and that she carried a heavy secret, but it was not in Helen's nature to dig it out. Unlike talkative and gossip-loving Sweetie, Helen didn't want to know everything about everyone. She was reluctant to get too close to the secrets of others. In her experience, secrets could be dangerous.

August was nearing its end, and Meri had begged to visit Dakota Blue once more before school started. Dakota was in her eighties and, before her retirement, had spent years introducing Cosette schoolchildren to the mysteries and beauties of the natural world. She was a self-proclaimed environmental warrior, and although Ariel never had her as a teacher, Dakota was a much-loved mentor. She had played a significant role in Ariel's career direction.

Ariel was in the passenger seat of Helen's used Toyota. Meri sat in a car seat in the back with a tote of books for Dakota. Helen, in her mid-fifties, had been delivering books from the reading room to the beloved science teacher for years.

"Helen," Meri said, "hasn't Miss Dakota read some of these books already?"

Helen glanced in the rearview mirror at Meri. "So. You read your books more than once, don't you? Don't worry. Miss Dakota will enjoy these stories again."

Satisfied, Meri turned her attention to the window. They had left the paved county road and were now making their way along a tree-shrouded gravel drive. They crossed over the bumpy one-lane wooden bridge spanning the creek. Meri didn't remark, as she usually did, how she liked the way the trees formed a cozy cave here and how the creek glistened in the sun. She had something else on her mind.

Finally, as they pulled up in front of Dakota's house, she asked, "Helen, did you really kill a guy? That's what some kids say."

Helen froze, her grip tightening on the steering wheel. Ariel patted Helen's arm and gave her friend a smile. Helen turned sad eyes on the figure in the rearview mirror.

Ariel said, "Meri, don't listen to everything other kids say. That is a personal question. Everyone is entitled to their secrets."

"No," Helen said, "that's all right." With a sudden heaviness of spirit, she got out of the car and opened the back door. She leaned in and began unbuckling the car seat straps with careful hands.

Meri reached out and laid her hand on Helen's cheek, stopping her. "It was probably an accident."

Even now, with Meri's esteem for her on the line, Helen would not lie. Picking up that kitchen knife and stabbing her worthless husband nineteen times had been no accident. He had broken her arm, again, and lit her face on fire with his fists. She'd seen death in his eyes on that night.

When Helen moved back to Cosette after her time in prison, she returned a downtrodden woman wishing to disappear behind her baggy clothes and unkempt hair. But her work in the prison library and her love of books would not let her hide. She became a traveling librarian, building acceptance in the community one book at a time. She had evolved into a woman who took pride in her looks and in who she had become. She would never be as fashionably dressed as her trend-chasing sister, but she had emerged from her dark past.

Unable to meet Meri's gaze, Helen mumbled, "No accident."

On that long-ago day, when Helen had fought for her life, she'd felt no regrets—but then Meriweather Turnstone became her friend. When she was with this child, she wished more than anything that she had walked away that day from her scurrilous husband and that handy kitchen knife—that she had been then, the woman she was now.

Suddenly, a wisp of air comforted Helen and Meri said softly, "It's okay. You won't do it again."

Meri's trust in her made Helen swipe her eyes with the back of her hand and begin fumbling again with the straps of the car seat. "No. I won't."

When Helen lifted Meri from the car seat, the child clung to her, and Helen hesitated. Her heart reveled in this moment of forgiving closeness. Then Meri kissed her cheek and wiggled to get down.

Helen grabbed the tote bag of books and followed the running child into Dakota's house.

* * *

Ariel could never step into Dakota's old kitchen without remembering the first time Helen had brought her to visit the revered schoolteacher. She'd been thirteen. There had been shortbread on the butcher block table waiting for them and dishes in the sink, which Helen automatically began to wash. The living room hadn't changed since that first visit: dusty teaching awards and colorful quilt pieces hung on the walls, blankets drifted off the backs of the furniture, and Dakota's quilt, "Lost Loves," stretched in a frame in the corner. For as long as Ariel had known Dakota, she had been working on that quilt. Dakota maintained she would never finish her fabric homage to extinct species because nature's creatures continue to disappear.

Meri ran to Dakota, and Dakota opened her arms. As she hugged the child, the old woman closed her eyes and a blissful expression settled over her face.

When Meri stepped away, she reached into her pocket and pulled out a name tag. She carefully placed the tag on her dress. "I wrote it myself," she said. "I'll wear it every time I visit. So you'll remember me."

Meri had asked Ariel to buy name tags after she noticed that there were notes all over Dakota's house: "Turn off oven" in the kitchen. "Take blue pill BEFORE brushing teeth" in the bathroom. "Stand straight" on the walker. "Smile" attached to the mirror.

Dakota studied the name tag, slowly making out the wobbly letters. "Meriweather. Perfect penmanship."

Meri didn't know what penmanship was, but she felt good when Miss Dakota used her full name. Meri believed, due to all the awards on the walls, that Miss Dakota must be brilliant and surely said only brilliant things. Meri also believed that you could hear love in the way a person said a name. She had once told Ariel, "My name is safe in Miss Dakota's mouth."

While Meri could read many words, her motor skills were still rough when it came to writing. "Sometimes I mix up the 'M' and the 'W,'" she told Miss Dakota. "I forget which should be mountains and which should be valleys."

"Understandable," said Dakota.

Dakota struggled to get out of her comfy chair, and Meri

held the delicate woman's slender arm as she leaned into the walker. "Let's go see my quilt," Dakota said with a spark in her eyes and a mischievous grin. Meri stayed by Dakota's side as they slowly navigated the few steps to the quilt frame. At the quilt, Dakota pointed to one of the animals sewn in the quilt's design. "Today we will talk about the Japanese sea lion. This fellow has not been seen in a long time."

* * *

Ariel and Helen left Dakota and Meri to their animal stories and retired to the kitchen. Dakota had once told those same stories of long-gone creatures to Ariel. Seeing how fragile her beloved mentor had become pained Ariel. Dakota's passion for the Earth and all its creatures had inspired Ariel to pursue degrees in journalism and environmental science.

Ariel made a fresh pitcher of lemonade, while Helen fried bacon for Dakota's bacon, lettuce, and tomato sandwich. As Ariel stirred the lemonade, she said, "She's getting weaker, isn't she?"

Helen paused, glanced at Ariel, then turned her attention back to the splattering bacon. "Yeah. I'm terrified she's going to fall and break something."

"You're cooking a lot of bacon."

"I'll wrap the leftovers in little packs for her to munch on— when she remembers. Damn dementia."

They heard laughter from the living room.

When Ariel peeked in, she saw that Meri had helped Dakota safely back to her chair. Her friend looked tired. Helen placed the BLT sandwich on the table by Dakota's chair with a glass of lemonade. She plunked the tote of books at the side of the chair well within Dakota's reach.

"Now, you eat *all* of this sandwich before you tear into that bag of books," Helen ordered. "And there's more bacon in the fridge if you feel peckish."

Dakota rolled her eyes at Ariel, making her smile. "I don't get peckish," Dakota said. "I'm too puckish."

"All right, frisky schoolteacher," said Helen, holding Dakota's bony hand a moment longer than necessary. Then she brusquely turned away. "Let's hit the road, Meri."

Ariel and Meri said their good-byes with hugs, kisses, and whispers of "We'll be back soon."

The trio was quiet as they drove away.

It wasn't until about halfway home that Meri finally spoke: "Miss Dakota says people once made pipe cleaners from the whiskers of the Japanese sea lion. To clean their *smoking* pipes."

This fact obviously concerned the child who could spend hours at her craft table making "creations," as she called them. She worked with a variety of craft supplies including pipe cleaners.

"Is that a problem? I know you like your pipe cleaners," said Helen, who had been the recipient of many Meri creations.

After several moments of silence, Meri came to a decision. "Miss Dakota says even if we can't save the creatures already gone, we still should make a stand. I don't know about smoking pipes, but I'm never using pipe cleaners again in *my* artwork."

CHAPTER 11

THE ART
OF THE CANOE

HARLEY WAMSGANZ LOOMED OVER Nikki Diego with shaking fists. "You did this to spite me, Diego!" he shouted.

Harley's bombastic performance did not impress Nikki. She was no longer the shy girl who had hidden behind her drawing pad in high school and avoided Harley, the school bully. In the years after high school when she'd studied art in Europe, she had fended off sleazeballs with a growing self-assuredness, steel-toed boots she was not afraid to use, and arms made strong from hours of wrestling heavy metal and stone into stunning sculptures.

"What is that saying, Harley?" She pondered the clouds then snapped her fingers. "What goes around comes around."

Harley had been an exceptionally large child for his age and had earned his reputation for meanness. Through the years, he had relentlessly tormented and belittled fellow classmates including Nikki, Ariel, and Ruddy.

Nikki's flippant response to her old schoolyard nemesis elicited a guffaw from Freddy, Harley's brother.

Both of their attitudes infuriated Harley.

Harley's nephew, Wren, who had been watching with puzzlement the exchange between his agitated uncle and the cool-headed woman, said, "I think the canoe's awesome, Harley."

Smiling, Nikki bumped fists with the boy. She worked in metal, stone, and wood in the workshop she shared with her father Lars on the Diego farm. Lars was best known in Cosette for creating the statue of Harriet Bunyan in the city park. For years, he and Nikki had been collaborating on a project called Art for Earth, which included several gigantic sculptures with environmental themes erected on their property.

A proponent of recycling, reuse, and all actions intended to save the planet, Nikki had gladly accepted the commission to remove the dents out of Harley's old aluminum canoe. When she finished and set down her hammer, however, she studied the canoe and decided the job wasn't done. Filled with love for the long-abused canoe and a decades-old desire for revenge on Harley, she opened her cans of paints. She hummed as a garden of psychedelic flowers in screaming colors that she knew Harley would hate bloomed on the sides of the canoe. He was definitely a camo guy.

Harley pointed at the canoe sitting on the shore of the Wamsganz Resort. "I just asked you to hammer out a few dents. Not paint it. And I never asked for any *flowers*."

Wren drew his uncle's attention to the canoe. "Look, Harley. There are words too."

Harley bent down and examined the spot where Wren pointed. It said, *Nature First.*

He rose and glared at Nikki. "Damn it, Diego, you paint over that. I don't want your eco-propaganda on my canoe."

Freddy laughed harder. "Brother, you just don't get this environmental stuff."

"Oh, shut up," Harley said.

A voice came out of the woods with the swish of long gauzy skirts and the slap of sandals. "Boys, don't fight." Freddy went to meet his wife, took her hand, and led her to the canoe. She hunkered down, her skirt carelessly brushing the dusty ground, and studied the flowers. "It's magnificent," said Willow Wamsganz. "Soothing. Just what a canoe ride should be."

She rose and wrapped her arms around Nikki. The hug surprised Nikki and made her a little uncomfortable. She hadn't had much experience with Willow or her family; they had only been in town for a few months. Finally, Willow stepped back, folded her hands in namaste at her chest, and bowed to Nikki. "Thank you for brightening our life and bringing this calm, Nikki."

"Um, sure," Nikki said, casting a wary glance toward Harley, who hid his eyes and shook his head. "Well, I better get back to the farm."

"Wait, Diego!" Harley said. "You take this canoe back and repaint it!"

Nikki continued toward her truck. She tossed one last taunt at her old schoolmate, "Enjoy the canoe, Harley."

Harley fumed as Nikki drove away. He thought, *I'll show her. I'll repaint that sucker myself—good ole hunter green.*

* * *

The Wamsganz family had run the small resort on the lower end of Lake Cosette for as long as Harley could remember. He and Freddy had grown up chasing each other around the rustic log cabins, swimming in the lake, and exploring the woodlands that surrounded the resort. When they grew old enough, they were expected to help change over the cabins on summer Saturdays when other kids were fishing, and in winter, they had to pitch in to refurbish the cabins with their inept carpentry skills. No sleeping-in on Earl Wamsganz's watch, unless you wanted a slap or a pinch.

Their mother never stepped in when their father Earl was on a bender or in a mood. She hid. And even after a soused Earl fell off the dock and drowned, she continued to hide. She signed the resort over to Freddy and Harley with a swipe of the pen and went to live with her sister in Wisconsin. Although she loved and sometimes missed her sons, she hated the resort and never wanted to see it again.

Harley had barely tossed Earl's ashes into the trash bin before he was calling his old friend, Melanie Harcourt, the real estate agent. She looked over the paperwork and gave him the unwelcome news: he couldn't sell the resort without his brother's consent since they were co-owners.

"Too bad, Harley," Melanie had told him, "I could flip that property in a flash for you. Prime lakefront, old cabins begging to be ripped down, developers eager to divide that land for upscale homes. You could make a bundle."

The conversation with Melanie had led to the uncomfortable phone call with Freddy, whom Harley hadn't spoken to or seen in years. Freddy was living in California, of all places, at the time. Harley couldn't understand the appeal of a state with palm trees and little snow. He was a Minnesotan through and through—he wore shorts in every season, embraced the cold and snow as if they were life-giving, and had agreed with his mother that the fictitious Lake Wobegon town on the radio probably was a great place in which to live.

California was too far away for Harley. If he could ever unload the resort, he might move to Minneapolis and get a job as a bartender. He knew his way around liquor. Heck, it was practically a family pastime.

But then his brother refused to sell the resort, and he couldn't afford to buy out Harley's share. Instead, Freddy moved home to Cosette with his family, and Harley was stuck with them.

* * *

Freddy Wamsganz hadn't been able to leave Cosette, Minnesota, fast enough. With the ink still damp on his high school diploma, he'd escaped the fists of Earl Wamsganz and a dreary future at the resort—and never looked back. He'd left Harley and his mother behind. For a long time, Harley's anger at Freddy's desertion and his fury with his father were mixed up in Harley's head. But, during his saner and more sober moments, Harley understood. Freddy had always been the smart one, unlike Harley whose dismal grades had prevented him from getting the football scholarship he'd always talked about. Freddy went into the Navy, grew strong and worldly, got a college degree in electronics, then fell into the clutches of flower child Willow. Freddy had returned to Cosette a changed man—serene with a tender attitude and a sense of humor.

Some days Harley didn't even recognize the brother who'd left Cosette hell-bent on never returning. The brothers who had grown up together, hiding in the woods from their drunken father, had aged into quite different men. Freddy held himself military straight, where Harley slouched. Freddy was fit and hummed happily as he worked; out-of-shape Harley grumped and took breaks whenever he could. Freddy was the younger and Harley the older, but somehow Harley felt that he'd done nothing in life while Freddy had done everything.

When Freddy and his family arrived at the resort, they moved in with Harley in their parents' former house, a ranch-style abode positioned on a slight knoll with a clear view of the lake and the resort's seven cabins. Harley had planned to keep his old childhood room, but it soon became obvious to him that he needed to move out. The house felt cramped with Willow making decorating changes, Freddy helping her, and their son always underfoot.

Now, Harley's kingdom was the backyard trailer that used to be Earl's getaway. Earl had died more than a year ago, and Harley was still finding whiskey bottles stashed under the bed and in the closets.

Willow had taken one look at the trailer and instructed Harley, "Open all the windows. I'll get my sage." He had followed his sister-in-law around as she wafted the smoking sage in all the corners of the trailer and mumbled prayers. Harley thought the sage stunk and he doubted the efficacy of prayer, but Willow assured him it would release all of old Earl's vibes. Harley would put up with any nonsense to get rid of Earl.

Willow turned out to be a diligent worker, even though she traveled at her own pace and tended to make resort decisions without the input of anyone else. She'd created gardens everywhere, or so it seemed to Harley. He was constantly tripping over and smashing delicate, do-nothing flowers. Harley's mother had never been a gardener and certainly had never bothered setting welcoming vases of posies in the cabins. That was a waste of time and money, according to Earl. And yet, their guests seemed to like Willow's special touch with the tiny bouquets.

Guests also raved about the healthy options Willow had introduced in the snack bar. Harley had never heard of veggie crisps until Willow started making changes, and he personally hated yogurt. However, Harley was slowly growing accustomed to the Willow way of operating—how she delivered hugs as if they were free and how she found something positive no matter the situation or catastrophe.

Harley was thirty-six years old and had never been around children much, except the ones who showed up every summer to make his life hell. He avoided them as much as possible, had no interest in learning the ways kids think. He did not need to understand them; he just needed to take their money in the snack bar and ignore their complaints.

But his nephew was another matter. The kid followed him around and was always asking questions. One time Harley said to Wren, "You're five years old. Don't you know anything?"

Wren had pondered the question and replied, "I'm very smart, but not resort smart. Yet."

Harley thought that sounded like the boy was gunning for his job. "Be careful what you wish for, kid," he said.

In the rapid-fire changes in topic that were so typical with Wren, and that frustrated Harley, Wren said, "Mama taught me how to wish on stars."

"She would," Harley muttered.

"Do you wish on stars?" asked Wren. "Minnesota has a lot of them."

With a glance at the canoe that he probably would never get around to repainting, Harley said, "I gave up wishing a long time ago, kid."

CHAPTER 12

TROUBLE COMES TO TOWN

ARIEL AND MERI PRACTICED flying every day in the valley where Ariel's grandfather, Will Stevens, had found the bone of a giant bison. Below their feet were still buried the bones of those behemoths that crossed the Bering Land Bridge into North America from Asia during the last Ice Age. Above them was the meadow and the cliff where early hunters had driven the bison, forcing them over the edge and into the valley below. Archeologists called the valley a kill site, a planned place of death. But the Stevens family had always thought of it as sacred ground deserving respect. Here, where the now-extinct giant bison rested, Ariel's farmer grandfather had put away the plow and let the wildflowers grow.

Ariel was glad he had. The meadow and this valley were special places on the farm. She could feel a difference in the air here. When she was upset, she could breathe here. When she was happy, she could celebrate here.

During training, Meri did not have to wear either her unicorn or monkey safety harness. Ariel kept her daughter close by her side. They moved through the air together as Ariel imparted wisdom about navigating the air.

She taught Meri how to visualize her arms gathering the air and how to slow everything, especially her mind. "Let the air lift, support, and turn you," she said. "When you feel yourself dragging, that is gravity."

Meri said, "Gravity is in one of my planet books. Daddy says it keeps us from drifting off into space."

"He would know," said Ariel.

Meri tried flapping her arms. "No," Ariel said. "We are not birds. We are wind riders."

"But how do I steer?" asked Meri.

"Steer with your mind. In Up There, thought means as much as action. Use your thoughts to slow when you go too fast and to redirect you. Watch out for that tree, Meri . . ." The child covered her eyes with her hands. Ariel quickly snagged the back of her daughter's dress and piloted them both safely under the tree limb. "See. I changed our direction with thought."

When Ariel noticed her daughter tiring, she suggested that they take a break. They rested in the shadow of the meadow's cliff, sipped from bottles of water, and ate animal crackers. It was August, the start of school was only two weeks away, and Ariel prayed they were ready.

"Let's go over the rules again," she said.

Meri rolled her eyes. They'd been through this repeatedly. She put down her water bottle and said, "Rule number one: Never fly anywhere but on the farm."

"Good."

Meri continued, "Rule number two: Never tell anyone about Up There. Not even Helen or Miss Dakota or my new teacher or any kids at school or the police . . ."

"Okay, okay," Ariel said.

"But it would really be cool to tell people."

"No. This is a family secret."

Meri understood that family secrets were sacrosanct, but she did not know why.

Sighing, Meri popped another cracker in her mouth. She started to talk with her mouth full, but then after a look from her mother, swallowed and started again. "Rule number three: Do not use my gift . . ." She stumbled over the last word.

"Inappropriately," supplied Ariel.

"What does that mean again?"

"Don't use your gift when you're not supposed to."

"I don't get it."

Ariel's thoughtful gaze traveled over the purple asters and golden black-eyed Susans running wild and calm across the old field. She'd made so many mistakes with her gift when she was young. With all her heart, she wanted to save Meri from those burdens of guilt. Yes, she'd used her gift to bring a wisp of relief to tired brows and to blow snow from a dangerous road to avoid an accident, but she'd also sent her best friend into a ditch when she urged the wind to push their bikes faster and faster.

Ariel said, "Baby, sometimes we can hurt people even when we don't mean to."

Meri's eyes widened and she whispered, "Are we evil?"

"No, no. But sometimes when we use our gift, we think that we're helping and we're not. We must be careful."

A look of frustration furrowed her daughter's brow. "I don't like all these rules."

"Eventually, you will see why these rules are important. They are to keep you, and others, safe."

"Why wouldn't I be safe?" asked Meri.

Ariel wasn't ready to have this conversation with her young and impressionable daughter. She didn't want to tell Meri how people often were afraid of what they didn't understand, that they might fear those who were different and, sometimes, even try to harm them.

Hoping to distract the child from a topic that had grown heavy, Ariel pointed to a hawk, circling above them. They watched the hawk make a few loops then dive into the nearby woods with amazing speed and daring, skillfully skirting between trees.

"That's a sharp-shinned hawk," Meri told her mother. "Grandpa says they're small and fast so they can dodge trees and branches." Meri's grandfather Arthur never tired of talking about birds. Arthur had installed numerous bird feeders in his backyard and theirs. It was Meri's and Ruddy's job to keep them filled with seeds.

Meri continued with awe in her voice, "Grandpa Arthur has even *held* a sharp-shinned hawk."

"Really?"

"It was at a bird count. That's when they catch birds, count them, and tag them," Meri explained. "I thought that sounded mean, but Grandpa says it doesn't hurt them and it's important to know how many birds there are—so you know how many are missing."

"Sounds sensible."

"Grandpa said holding that hawk, for just a moment, made him so happy. I'd like to do that."

"I'm sure you will someday, if your grandfather has anything to say about it."

Meri stuffed the last cracker whole into her mouth and chewed. She handed the empty bag to Ariel for recycling.

After several moments, she asked thoughtfully, "Why do you think we are the way we are?"

How many times had Ariel asked herself that very question?

Before Ariel could formulate a reply, Meri continued, "Maybe we're supposed to be superheroes."

Ariel looked at her daughter with tenderness. She sensed Meri's yearning to do remarkable things like the heroes she watched on videos. Although Ariel and Ruddy tried to limit Meri's screen time, videos of kids saving the world awaited Meri at every click of the remote.

"Maybe we are supposed to be like Harriet Bunyan, a protector of nature?" Ariel suggested.

"And like Uncle Kal."

"Yes, Kal works every day to save nature in Minnesota's parks."

"Maybe I'll be a park ranger like Uncle Kal," Meri said, "when I'm not being a ballerina or a dolphin trainer."

"You've got time to decide," said Ariel, crossing her legs into a meditation position. "But now we have ten minutes of meditation practice, and then I'll show you a trick."

Meri immediately copied her mother's lotus position, arranged her purple tutu just so, then closed her eyes. She started taking measured breaths, in and out, in and out. She was supposed to be letting her mind settle. Instead, she thought of Harriet Bunyan and wondered how she would look in a tutu.

When meditation practice was over, Ariel stood and stretched her arms over her head. She stepped out into the field, rose into the air, and completed three slow-motion front walkovers in the air.

"I want to do that," shouted Meri, jumping up and down. "Teach me. Teach me."

Meri started toward her mother then suddenly stopped and turned toward the woods.

Someone was clapping.

Ariel immediately dropped to the ground and rushed to Meri. She positioned her body between Meri and the sound. After a few moments, a figure emerged from the dense woods that surrounded the valley. It was a small woman with straight black hair down to the waist of her worn jeans.

The woman said, "I think it would be cool to be a superhero."

The remark made Ariel wonder how long the intruder had been eavesdropping on their conversation. What had the stranger heard? What had she seen?

Ariel said, "This is private property."

The woman walked toward them. "I saw the signs."

"Leave," Ariel said. The woman shook her head.

Growing concerned, Ariel reached for the wind.

The wind rose, and air surrounded Ariel and Meri in a protective circle.

Hair blowing, the woman continued to approach.

Ariel thrust out her hand, and the wind grew stronger.

Meri peeked from behind Ariel and gasped. "Mama, look."

As the woman neared them, she rose into the air until her red Converse high-tops were kissing the heads of the autumn flowers in the field.

"Who are you?" Ariel whispered.

"I'm your cousin," the woman said with a smile. "My name is Trouble."

CHAPTER 13

SHAKING THE FAMILY TREE

SAHARA HAD COLLECTED HAMBURGERS from Marta's Diner, and now Trouble was reaching for a second burger. Trouble was built like Ariel and Meri, slight and deceptively fragile looking. Sahara wondered where this mysterious and previously unknown member of the family was putting all the food. As Trouble chewed with the grace and manners of a junkyard dog, she surveyed the tower room of the Starling house with its inviting view of Lake Cosette and pronounced, "This is a cool place."

The tower was normally Echo's domain, but he was not home. He was playing a game of Crazy Eights with Meri at Ariel's house. Echo had begun to cut back on his hours at the clinic. In his mid-sixties, he was not ready for full retirement, but his thoughts were taking a circuitous path to that end. He was still fascinated by medicine and still treasured the meetings with his patients, but there were days when his old leg injury complained too much. The pain and resulting limp were a reminder of the North Carolina hurricane that had devastated his life, ripping apart his home and killing his first wife and their five-year-old daughter.

Sahara believed her husband had earned the right to play hooky with his granddaughter; he'd overcome so much, from deadly hurricanes to harsh Minnesota winters to the distrust of narrow-minded patients. For more than thirty years, he'd been the lone Black physician doctoring the injured and ill of their predominantly white area of Minnesota. He'd stuck by this community that desperately needed his medical expertise and had earned their respect and support.

Sahara studied Trouble and looked for Hamilton traits in the young woman. Hamilton women like Sahara and Ariel tanned easily in summer and had messy auburn waves. As Trouble talked and ate, she tossed a curtain of solid black hair over her shoulder. Her face was unusually pale, and thick bangs nearly hid her dark eyes.

Sahara listened to the young women chat. They were of the same generation—Ariel was in her mid-thirties, and Trouble looked not much older than twenty-five. Already a friendship was blooming between the two.

Sahara knew that Ariel had long believed she was the only one of her kind. Trouble was someone Ariel had never thought she would meet: another adult wind walker. That formed a natural bond. While Ariel was eager to welcome Trouble, Sahara hesitated. There was a restlessness and recklessness about Teri "Trouble" Hamilton that bothered Sahara.

Sahara cleared her throat. "Trouble, I'm trying to understand what part of the family you are from, and why your last name is Hamilton."

Trouble said, "That's easy. All Hamilton women keep their

surnames. It's the custom. Grandma kept hers even though Grandpa didn't like it."

Sahara had never heard of this tradition. It made her wonder about her own mother's actions. Why had Anne Hamilton Stevens changed her name when she married Will Stevens?

"Let me get this straight," Sahara said. "My mother, Anne Hamilton, was raised with your grandmother Clarissa? They were cousins, grew up together, and flew the skies together?"

Trouble sucked her milkshake dry with a loud slurp. "Yup."

"But, according to Anne's journal, Clarissa drifted into the sky and never came back," Sahara said. "Everyone thought she was dead."

"Don't know about that," said Trouble. "Here I am. Living proof Clarissa survived."

Ariel asked, "What about your mother? Tell us about her."

Trouble, in the process of reaching for another fry, stopped. In a soft voice, she said, "Mom died when I was eight. Grandma and Grandpa raised me. First, Grandpa died, then Grandma. So I left."

"Left?" Sahara frowned. "Left where?"

Trouble looked at them and shrugged. "Home. Missouri."

Sahara and Ariel exchanged looks. Missouri was hundreds of miles away.

As the food disappeared, Sahara and Ariel pried more information from the reticent Trouble. She had no car, and her driver's license had expired. She traveled by bus, hitchhiked, or walked the sky. Her most recent mode of transportation was an old one-speed bike, which she'd found cheap in a yard sale. She'd been rootless for some time, working at "this and that" to get by. She had nothing but the clothes on her back (a black T-shirt and distressed jeans) and the items in a worn pack, which she insisted on keeping with her even during lunch.

"How did you find us?" asked Ariel.

"Grandma told me stories about this place."

Surprised and uneasy that strangers would know so much about their family, Ariel and Sahara tensed. "She told you about our farm?" Ariel asked.

Trouble shook her head and grabbed the last snickerdoodle. "Not your farm, but some place near Cosette. A house where the Hamilton women lived and flew. I'm going to find it."

"Why?" asked Ariel.

"To learn about our family, about our flying," said Trouble. "I thought you might know where it is—the old Hamilton House. Didn't your grandmother tell you about it?"

"I never met her," Ariel said. "All I know about Anne comes from her journal, which I found hidden in the barn."

Sahara said, "My mother was a secretive woman. She never discussed her past."

Trouble raised a black brow. "And you didn't ask?"

Ariel gave her mother a strange look. "Yeah, Mama, why didn't you ask?"

The questions startled Sahara. She had never felt the urge to explore her mother's side of the family. She wondered, *Why?* Spying her mother Anne, returning home wind-tousled and happy from a secret night flight, Sahara had never asked the important question: *Who are we really?*

Sahara felt uncomfortable now with her lack of interest, or was it fear? Was it because she didn't want to know too much? *Had I feared that I would miss what I could never have? Had the act of keeping Anne's secrets become so ingrained that I had lost my chance to truly know my mother?*

Anne Hamilton married Will Stevens, a farmer she met at a traveling carnival. They fell in love atop a Ferris wheel. They had three children: Sahara, the oldest; then Gobi; and finally,

Kalahari, the baby. Will had been handsome, sweet, and the owner of land that beckoned Anne with a most inviting wind.

As for Will, he had never met anyone like Anne. She spoke out when others remained silent, and she dressed in fluttery dresses and sassy cowboy boots when other Minnesota farm wives tugged on blue jeans and flannels. But most of all, she made Will believe that the impossible was possible. She was the magic in his life.

Without offering to fetch a drink for the others, Trouble rose, crossed the room to the mini-refrigerator, and snagged a can of pop. "What was Anne like?" she asked, slugging back half the drink in one gulp.

Ariel turned to her mother and said eagerly, "Yes, tell us about her."

Sahara thought for a moment. Memories flooded her. She said, "My mother was intuitive. She gave each of us what we needed. I wanted stories so she made up adventure stories for me. I knew that they were original because I was the star of every story."

"Was Grandma Anne a writer too?" asked Ariel.

Trouble turned to Sahara. "You're a writer? Have you written anything I'd know?"

Ariel answered for her mother. "She's S.H. Stevens."

Trouble stopped mid-sip and stared at Sahara. "*The* S.H. Stevens?"

"That's me," said Sahara, with a casual lift of her shoulders.

"But I *love* S.H. Stevens," said Trouble. "I've got one of your books in my bag."

Sahara smiled.

"But you don't put your picture on the cover and your bio is skimpy," noted Trouble. "What's the deal?"

Ariel answered for her mother, "Mama doesn't do publicity,

no interviews, no conventions. She likes her privacy. We all do."

"But doesn't everyone in town know who you are?" asked Trouble.

Sahara gave her a wink. "Yes, but they keep my secret. I've lived here all my life."

After a thoughtful pause, Trouble asked again about Anne Hamilton.

Sahara dredged up more memories. "My brother Gobi loved books and studying; I can't tell you how many times our soft-hearted mother did the dishes when it was his turn just so he could finish one more chapter. He's a lawyer now in Minneapolis and still surrounded by books." Sahara smiled at the reminiscence. "Then there's Kalahari, my youngest brother. He is the nature boy in the family. I remember one time Kal brought home a nest of motherless birds. He was distressed when he had to leave them and go to school. Mom sat in the barn all day, feeding those tiny birds with an eyedropper until Kal returned to take over the job."

Trouble took in this information and smiled. "Sounds like I have a whole family I never knew about, *and* I'm related to a famous author. Cool. I can't wait to fly with you," Trouble said to Sahara.

Silence.

Sahara and Ariel exchanged looks, and Trouble noticed.

"What's up?" she asked. "Don't you want to fly with me?"

Finally, Ariel said, "Mama can't go Up There."

"Up There?" Trouble frowned in puzzlement.

Ariel explained, "Up There is my name for the wind and sky that call me, that help me fly. Meri insists that there are two worlds: Up There and Down Here."

When Trouble still looked confused, Ariel continued,

"Down Here is everything that is *not* Up There: the ordinary grind, the arguments and the resolutions, the meanness, and the kindness."

Ariel did not mention, *And the secrets.*

"I am of Down Here, just like Ruddy, Echo, and everyone else," Sahara said, "The gift of flight skipped me."

"What?" Trouble, who was rummaging for food in the leftover sandwich wrappers on the table, stopped in astonishment. She gaped. "I've never heard of the Hamilton gift skipping a generation."

"So your mother was gifted like Clarissa?" asked Ariel.

"I always assumed so," Trouble said, "but now I wonder. I never saw her fly, and she died before I came into my gift."

"Surely, you saw Clarissa go into the air," said Sahara.

The young woman shook her head, her long hair spreading like a cape over her shoulders. "Grandma trained me, but she refused to fly herself. She gave all that up when she married Grandpa. All our lessons were in secret and at night."

Trouble gave Sahara a look of pity. Apparently, choosing not to use a gift, as her grandmother had done, was more acceptable than having no gift at all.

"A Hamilton woman who can't fly," Trouble said. "Bummer."

CHAPTER 14

A GOOD MERI DAY

MERI RAN DOWN THE stairs for breakfast, her new school backpack bouncing against her back. She slid into the kitchen banquette without removing the backpack. It was navy decorated with a universe of stars, planets, and rockets, and it was her first "real" backpack with no harness, no unicorn, and no monkey. She hadn't taken it off since it arrived in the mail two days ago.

Trouble, leaning against the kitchen counter sipping a glass of orange juice, laughed. "Never seen anybody so excited about school."

"Didn't you like school?" asked Meri, stuffing a forkful of pancakes into her mouth and dripping maple syrup down her chin.

"You've got to be kidding," said Trouble. Meri paused eating and stared at Trouble. Seeing the look of disapproval on Ariel's face, Trouble quickly amended her assessment. "Like it? I loved it."

Meri happily went back to her breakfast.

Trouble had moved into the guest room, formerly Ariel's office. No one knew how long this newly found cousin planned to stay, so Ariel had relocated her laptop and research materials to the dining room table. It was the same table that Sahara had used as an office for all of Ariel's childhood. To Ariel, the table had never felt like a place on which to dine but a place to work, explore, and create. It had family history. It was where her mother had written freelance articles to keep them fed for years until Sahara's fantasy novels found a loyal audience.

As Meri finished her breakfast, Ariel called, "Heads up," and tossed a moist washcloth toward her daughter. Meri caught it in one hand and swiped at her lips and sticky fingers. Then she scrambled from the table.

"I can't be late," she said.

Ruddy, Ariel, and Gus walked Meri to the bus stop at the end of their drive. On the way, the wind followed them, and Ariel sent a message to Up There: *Protect. No tricks.*

Ariel laid a hand on Meri's shoulder. It was their signal, a reminder: Keep in control. Stay grounded. Wear your backpack.

Ariel made sure the straps of Meri's backpack were fitted properly and the pack was evenly distributed on her shoulders. She double-checked that Meri's dumbbell was in the backpack. They had replaced Meri's usual two-pound dumbbell with an Echo-approved three-pounder, just as a precaution. Ariel worried that her daughter, who was extremely excited about attending school, would accidentally call the wind.

Ariel had already met with Meri's teacher, Astrid Lindqvist, and explained why Meri had to always wear the backpack. "It helps with her anxiety issues," Ariel had told the teacher. Astrid had examined the backpack and dumbbell with concern, but she consented to Ariel's request. Astrid thought the dumbbell was an odd solution, but she'd had other students who had required weighted clothing for their calming effect.

"Do you have your stone?" asked Ariel. In Meri's pocket was a smooth gray stone with pale white striations. It was small enough to fit in her fist. It was another reminder. If Meri felt the wind rising inside her, she could hold on to the stone and focus on filling herself with calming thoughts. It was an ordinary stone, one Ariel had found when she was a child and had kept on the windowsill of her room. Meri had gravitated to it, just as Ariel had, from the moment she saw it.

"Don't worry. I'll be okay, Mama," Meri reassured her.

Probably many children heading off to their first day of school said the same thing to their mothers. Ariel, however, was not like other mothers. She was the mother of a child who carried the family's greatest secrets and who could command the wind.

Ariel forced a smile to her face and said, "Of course, you will."

"And when I come home, we can go Up There, right?" Meri asked eagerly.

"Only if it has been a good Meri day," said Ariel, keeping her promise.

Meri nodded and repeated, "A good Meri day."

Clasping Meri's shoulders, Ruddy turned his daughter toward him. "And how do we make it a good Meri day?"

Meri touched her ear and said, "Listen."

Ruddy nodded.

Meri pointed to the corner of her eye. "Watch."

Ruddy smiled.

Finally, Meri placed her hand over her heart and grinned. "And be kind."

In approval, Ruddy hugged his daughter and swung her

around while Gus barked. "You're a genius. You already know so much." Turning to Ariel, he asked, "Why are we sending her to school again?"

Meri giggled at her father's teasing.

While Ariel focused on preparing Meri for life in a world where her gift could be looked upon with fear and suspicion, Ruddy considered his role was to keep his daughter in touch with the ordinary things in life. When he was a child, his mother had always sent him off to school with the mantra of listen-watch-be kind, and now he made sure his daughter started out the day with those same sentiments in her heart.

*** * *

The bus came on time.

Whistler Newton, an old friend of Sahara's and the entire Turnstone family, opened the doors. "Good morning, Meri."

Meri started up the steps, but Whistler held up a hand to stop her in her tracks. "Wait. Gotta get a picture." He pulled out his camera and snapped a shot. Whistler worked in construction, but his true love was photography. He'd been the "official photographer" at Sahara and Echo's wedding. He'd recorded every moment, including an inexplicable shot of Ariel rising in the sky with the tornado reaching for her. He didn't know how many times he'd sat and stared at that image. It filled him with something he couldn't name. He had never shown that photo to anyone and never would.

As the bus pulled away with a roar, Ariel remembered how it smelled, sounded, and felt on those long-ago school mornings. Whistler's father, Mr. Newton, used to drive the bus when Ariel rode it. She'd worn the clunky, heavy shoes then, and kind Mr. Newton had always offered a hand as she climbed onto the bus. But she'd resisted the offer every time.

Ariel had sensed from an early age that she was different, and she had to take care of herself. Now, she stood at the end of the drive, butterflies in her stomach, her arm threaded with Ruddy's, and watched until the bus disappeared. Gus sat beside them, bumped Ariel's leg with his head. "She'll be okay," she told the dog. Gus woofed in agreement. Ruddy nodded.

But none of them believed it.

* * *

As Wren Wamsganz waited for the bus, his mother noted that his chakras were open and balanced. "You are in excellent shape to have a great day," Willow told him, reaching to brush his shaggy blond hair from his eyes. He ducked from her questing fingers, making his father laugh.

Freddy wasn't a true believer of the seven energy centers that Willow professed would bring harmony to the spirit, mind, and body. But he didn't *not* believe either. His wife had a way of generating change. She meditated, talked to plants, and wore harmony like a delicate shawl. Willow opened her arms to the world, which for a long time Freddy had kept at a distance. His childhood had taught him it was safer to avoid friendship and trust—until he met Willow. He looked at the open and loving face of his son and once again was grateful for Willow. Wren had a good spirit—all because of her.

They could hear the bus approaching. Willow clutched Wren into a tight hug, and Wren's eyes sought help from his father. Freddy pried his wife's arms away and squeezed Wren's shoulder. "Hey, we'll toss some plastic when you get home," he said.

"Definitely," said Wren.

Wren and Freddy played disc golf, a sport Wren's uncle Harley found lacking in aggression. One of the first things

Freddy and Wren had done upon moving to the resort was to mount a portable disc golf practice basket behind the house.

On the steps of the bus, Wren paused and looked back, searching for his uncle. Harley stood in the shadow of the resort's office. "See ya, Harley," Wren waved.

Harley gave a half-hearted nod, almost lifted his hand, but then went back into the office.

* * *

Meri sat alone on the bus, just as her mother had done many years ago. She was worried about making friends. She didn't know any of these kids.

She closed her eyes and fingered the stone in her pocket. She breathed in the air of the bus and tasted the edgy excitement and first-day anxiety of the children. She heard the bus waking up, engine roaring and exhaust belching. It moved and she swayed in her seat. Then a breeze skipped down the aisle and patted her knee.

She opened her eyes and found a boy staring at her.

* * *

Wren looked at the empty seat next to the girl from the playground. Should he take it or not? There was something unusual about the girl. She made him nervous, but he also felt sorry for her. Wren didn't really understand what had happened on the slide, but his mother always said, "Open your heart, Wren. Who knows what wonderful things you will find?"

After a moment of indecision, Wren shrugged off his backpack and sat, perching the pack on his lap.

"Hey, we have the same backpacks," said the girl with a big grin.

He looked from his to hers. They were identical.

96

She said, "But mine doesn't have a cool zipper tab like yours."

Wren saw that his mother had attached a braid, made of yarn and some grass or vine, to his zipper. It also was probably blessed with one of her essential oils. It smelled like it. It embarrassed him, but then the girl touched it with reverence.

"I'm Meri," she said, not taking her gaze from the braid.

"Wren," he said.

"Nice name." She looked at him. "Like a bird. I'm trying to learn how to talk to birds, but it's a hard language."

She talks to birds, he thought, maybe it was not too late to change seats. But then he thought of his mother, who conversed with all living things: trees, flowers, rivers, birds. And he decided to stay.

He said, "I hear birds all the time, but I don't know what they're saying."

It was growing hot in the bus with all the bodies. Meri pushed her wild hair behind her ear, and, suddenly, a comforting breath of air circled them. "My grandfather has a book that tells what all the bird calls mean," she said. "I'll show it to you sometime."

"Does he have an app to identify the calls?"

"He has an app for everything." Meri laughed. "Birds, stars, plants, trees. He's kind of a geek."

"Neat."

Suddenly, Wren was glad that Buster Sweeney, the kid he'd met on the playground, was not on the bus. If Buster had been on the bus, Wren would have felt obligated to sit with him, and he wasn't sure he wanted to hang out with Buster. It was much more peaceful being around Meri. He bet Meri's chakras were in good shape.

CHAPTER 15

A BRUSH
WITH BUSTER

ASTRID LINDQVIST, KINDERGARTEN TEACHER, did not have grand aspirations to open young minds to the world's great opportunities. As she joked with her mother, "I'm just trying to keep them from killing each other." But in reality, Miss Lindqvist was a good teacher because she adored children, even the ones who set her teeth on edge. She understood that these initial experiences in the educational system—away from their families, their familiar toys, and the instant gratification they might be accustomed to—were challenging times. And often the human response to challenge was violence. She knew the squabbles, the crying, the hitting would get better as the school year progressed—or so she hoped.

She also knew there were some personalities that were destined to clash. After only a few weeks of school, she saw this was the case with Buster Sweeney and Meriweather Turnstone. Buster was the most aggressive child in the classroom, chasing children and muttering his monster threat in a growly, singsong voice. But he couldn't get Meri to run—which made him try even harder.

Miss Lindqvist had never encountered a student like Meri. There was something about the child, a carefulness, a control, the others didn't have. Again and again, Miss Lindqvist saw Meri express compassion for the downtrodden as well as the oppressor. Just take today, for example, Meri built a castle for a stuffed llama with a set of building blocks. Buster walked by and, of course, demolished the castle and tried to steal the llama. But Meri refused to let go of the stuffed toy.

"Give it to me," Buster shouted, pulling harder on the toy.

Meri kept her grip strong and her voice calm but defiant. "I had it first."

Miss Lindqvist had seen a red-faced and frustrated Buster kick and shove when he was denied, and she started toward the conflict before someone got hurt.

But Meri handled the situation herself. She regarded Buster and said, "You knocked down my castle."

"So? It was ugly."

Meri cocked her head and considered him as if he were a strange insect she had just discovered. "You're not very nice."

Buster didn't like the look in her eyes and didn't know what to do with her response. This was the first time someone had said that to him. Surprising both himself and her, he started to cry.

Immediately, Meri released her grip on the llama toy. "Here, take it."

Then she got up and walked away.

Miss Lindqvist, however, knew this was not the end of the conflict between Meri and Buster.

Buster was one of the few kids who did not ride the bus.

At day's end, the children always ran to the window to wave at Buster's mom, when she came to pick him up. Adrienne Sweeney insisted on driving Buster to school. She didn't trust buses, which she called "germ factories." Buster's mom was a favorite of the children. She remembered everyone's names and made them feel noticed, and she brought elaborately decorated cupcakes from bakeries in the Twin Cities for special treats.

On the day of the llama tug-of-war, Buster stopped Meri as she tried to join the others at the window to greet Mrs. Sweeney. "Not you. She's my mom, not yours," he snapped at Meri.

Wren, who avoided confrontation for the most part, stopped beside Buster and said, "C'mon, Buster. Don't be mean."

Buster crossed his arms over his chest. With a glance at the backpack Meri always wore, even in class, he said, "Dogs can't wave."

* * *

At home, Trouble found Meri sitting in the backyard, pondering the sky, and absently stroking Gus's head. Trouble recognized someone who had something on her mind and plopped down beside Meri. She gave the child the usual greeting, "Stay grounded today, kid?"

So far, after a month of school, Meri had not used her gift or answered the call of the wind once while at school or on the school bus. It had been more difficult to restrain herself than she thought it would be. She often found herself reaching for the small stone in her pocket, her "calming" stone as she had come to think of it. The stone reminded her of her promises to her mother, of the family secrets that must be kept.

"Buster crushed my castle today and wanted my llama," Meri told Trouble.

Studying the sky in silence with the child, Trouble asked, "What did you do?"

"I let him have the llama," Meri said, glancing toward Trouble and seeing a look of disappointment on her face. "I made him cry. I didn't mean to. Buster is mad a lot."

Trouble said, "You felt sorry for him. Don't let people like Buster push you around, kid."

"Mama says sometimes the best way to win is to let go," said Meri.

"That sounds like her," muttered Trouble. "But you really didn't care if you won, did you?"

Meri looked down at the hand scratching under Gus's chin and shook her head. "I was afraid," she muttered.

"Of Buster?"

Meri's hand stopped. "No," she whispered. "Of me. Of what *I* might do. Like on the slide."

Trouble had heard about the incident at the playground. She personally applauded Meri's actions. Trouble believed the many rules Ariel insisted upon when it came to Meri and her gift were silly, even dangerous. In her experience, a woman always had to look out for herself.

From the conversations she'd overheard in the Turnstone household and the things she'd seen, Trouble suspected that her gift was slightly different from Ariel's and Meri's. Trouble could ride the air, but that was about it. She had never heard the wind's voice. She had never been able to converse with the elements, like Ariel and Meri did. Her gift was weaker than Ariel's, and she certainly could never direct the air to toss a boy down a slide as Meri had done. She would give anything to have that power.

"Meri, the next time Buster is mean to you, you don't have to use your gift. Just give him a regular old punch in the nose."

Shocked at the idea, Meri sat up straighter and leaned away from Trouble. "What? No. That's not nice."

Trouble shrugged. "It's nicer than the alternative."

"The alternative?"

"Bottling up your frustrations and accidentally using your gift to bring the school down on Buster's head."

Meri jumped to her feet. "I can't do that, and I wouldn't do that!"

Trouble looked up at her and thought, *This kid doesn't have a clue what she could do.*

Slowly rising to her feet, Trouble reached out for Meri, but the child stepped away. "Hey, I was just kidding," Trouble said, quickly backtracking. "Your parents are right. Violence is never the answer."

When Meri continued to look at her with suspicion, Trouble said seriously, "But, Meri, I know one thing: bullies are little jerks." Meri's eyes grew wide at Trouble's language. "And they grow into big jerks."

CHAPTER 16

FALLING LIKE SNOWFLAKES

IT WAS A SATURDAY in December and the first snow of the season. Big flakes, shockingly beautiful and smelling of the promise of winter, sent a rush of happiness through Ariel. She loved the first snowfall. Meri had already built a snowman with her father and tried to teach Gus how to make snow angels. Now, she and Ariel were cuddled in the barn loft enjoying the view of the snow from the loft window.

The barn was frosty, and mother and daughter could see their breaths. They had not shed their down jackets and snow boots. Pulling their winter hats tighter over their ears, they watched the snowflakes swirl outside the open loft door and wiggled deeper into the bean bag chair they shared.

"We're in a snow globe," said Meri happily.

The loft had always been one of Ariel's favorite places. The rickety aluminum lawn chair Ariel had dragged up there so many years ago still waited for her, its frayed webbing fluttering in the chilly air. She'd read many wonderful books sitting in that chair. Now Meri found her own book adventures in the chair when she wasn't curled beside her mother in the bean bag.

It was so quiet today. There were no chattering baby birds in the rafters; they would come in spring. Below, the sleepy cats kept warm in the barn's dark corners and in the pockets of old blankets Meri had shaped into nests for them. The loft was where Ariel had found her grandmother's journal, read about her wind-walking heritage, and learned the legacy awaiting her in the sky. The same legacy that awaited her daughter. The day Ariel discovered the journal had changed her life.

"Should I close the loft door?" asked Ariel. "It'd be warmer."

"No," Meri said. "I like to look at the air."

"Me too," said Ariel with a smile. Sometimes, experiencing the beauty of Up There—the mysterious life in the air—filled the well of Ariel's soul, and even to think about ending that experience by closing a loft door seemed unbearable.

Ariel knew her daughter felt the same way. Like Ariel, Meri was all slender arms and legs, what her grandmother Alice called "a bit of nothing." Meri's chestnut brown locks, with a tint of bronze from her father, were forever tangled, as if the wind lived within them. The wind lived in Ariel's hair too.

The calm moment was interrupted by a question from Meri: "How do birds fly in snow?"

Ariel studied the white world beyond the loft door. "They have strong wings."

"Why don't we have wings?"

"Because we have strong legs to carry us, and besides, I think we'd look silly flapping our skinny arms, don't you?"

Meri thought for a moment. "Unicorns have strong wings *and* strong legs. They're lucky."

I am the lucky one, Ariel thought. There were days when Ariel still couldn't believe that she had a five-year-old child, that she lived with her best friend on the farm she loved, that she could have her family and the wind too.

This winter she and Ruddy were working on their second nonfiction book on climate change and the weather. They collaborated well. She put on the skids when he got too technical, and he reined her in when she climbed onto her soapbox. Their first book titled *Think of the Children: A Parental Look at Our Changing Climate and Weather* had been lauded for being "a combination of easy-to-understand science and environmental passion."

Meri asked, "Have you ever gone Up There in the snow?"

A memory startled Ariel with its fierceness. It had been a day like this one—the wind inviting, the snow laughing. She'd been eleven years old. It was the first time she had stepped off the cliff in the meadow, and it was the first time she had truly feared the wind. Ariel looked at her daughter and found Meri studying her with a quizzical expression.

"Yes, I have," said Ariel.

"Was it scary?" Meri asked.

Ariel didn't know how Meri did this—figured out what she was thinking and feeling at the times she most wanted to hide her emotions. Somehow, her daughter knew the unspoken, and her first impulse was to offer healing.

Ariel realized she wanted Meri to be smart and cautious Up There, but never to experience fear in that amazing place. Fear led to being out of control. Being out of control was a bad habit to get into for women like them. When Ariel had left the meadow's cliff that first time and stepped into the air, she'd lost control and panicked, severing her connection with Up There. She fell instead of floating and ended up unconscious at the bottom of the cliff. Although she'd lost confidence and control, Up There hadn't. She'd been lucky—nothing broken—because the wind had cushioned her fall.

On stiff legs, Ariel rose awkwardly from the bean bag chair and held out her hand to Meri. The child looked at her with puzzlement but took it. They walked to the loft door and looked out. The wind and snow churned in excitement. Gus the dog stared at them.

Ariel said, "Your great-grandmother Anne—"

"The one like us?"

"Yes. She would stand at this door, smile down at your great-grandfather, then step into the air."

Meri inhaled sharply. "Did he catch her?"

"Always. She floated right into his arms."

Meri, a romantic, smiled. "Did he hug her and kiss her?"

"Every time."

"I wished we could do that," Meri said, "but there is no Daddy below to catch us and kiss us."

Ariel glanced toward the house and saw Ruddy standing at his office window, staring at them.

She knew he was hoping they would turn around and leave the loft by the ladder, not the air. She didn't like scaring him. She wished he would be waiting below, his arms opened wide and welcoming.

She almost turned away from the window, but then she heard the wind: *Come. Play in the snow.*

* * *

Ruddy watched his wife and daughter standing at the loft window. "Don't do it," he whispered.

The thought had barely left his head when their right legs

shot out in a synchronized step and found the welcoming nothingness of the air. His fingers gripped the windowsill.

Their descent was gentle, their feet waving in slow motion, their grins growing bigger as cold snowflakes fluttered around them. Ariel turned them in a soft swirl, and Meri laughed. When their boots touched the ground, Gus was there, barking and dancing around them.

Meri, bubbling with happiness, kissed the dog's nose.

Ariel looked toward the house again and their gazes met. Ariel lifted her arms and shrugged, as if to say what else is one supposed to do on a wonderful snow day like this. Ruddy, unable to keep a stern look when faced with his wife's and daughter's obvious joy, just shook his head.

"You don't like it when they are in the air," said a voice behind him. "In fact, you hate it."

Ruddy turned to find Trouble in his office. She stared at Ariel and Meri then Ruddy.

Ruddy didn't respond.

In an annoying voice, Trouble continued, "Poor Ruddy, you're always Down Here waiting for them Up There. You must feel left out."

"Don't be ridiculous," said Ruddy.

"Are you ever jealous of them? A lot of people would be."

"Of course not. You wouldn't catch me Up There without a net, five extension ladders, and emergency personnel on call."

"Not a fan of heights, huh?"

Ruddy regretted showing this weakness to Trouble. He pushed past her and went to his desk. "I've got work to do so if you don't mind . . ." He tilted his head toward the door of his office.

Trouble gave him a cheeky grin and sashayed from the

room. She was wearing those red high-top sneakers again, even though he had repeatedly asked her to remove her shoes while in the house. Every Minnesotan, from the earliest age, was taught to follow this simple northland etiquette, but Trouble thought this courtesy was nonsense. "I'd spend all day taking off and putting on shoes," she'd scoffed.

Watching her leave, Ruddy realized he didn't like the way Trouble wandered the house. She moved too silently and explored too much. Once he'd even found her using his computer.

Ruddy never shut his office door, in case Ariel or Meri needed him, but he was rethinking his open-door policy—now that Trouble was living with them.

Outside, Ariel and Meri were lifting into the air, arms wide, and turning slowly. Their mouths were open, trying to catch snowflakes on their tongues. He heard them laughing and reached for his coat. He refused to let the wind have all the fun with his family.

CHAPTER 17

A MERRY HARLEY

THE FIRST DECEMBER SNOW melted and ceded territory to a stretch of cold nights and unusually warm days. Minnesotans did not like brown Christmases. Each morning they searched the sky for snow clouds, turned up the holiday tunes on the radio, and told themselves the weather forecasters had to be wrong.

The lakes hadn't frozen over yet. At the Wamsganz Resort, Willow was in her element, hanging greenery in the cabins and welcoming guests with fresh-baked holiday cookies. All this cheer made Harley want to jingle somebody's bell. He took off for town in his truck and didn't plan to be back until he was so drunk he couldn't hear the holiday carols drifting from his brother's house.

Hours later, Harley ended up on a bench at the park overlooking Lake Cosette, wearing the long red scarf Willow had knitted for him and which he wore only to keep peace in the family. Beside him at his feet were several empty beer cans and a bottle of his friend, Jim Beam. He had sat on this bench so many times with old Jim, trying to drown the desperate hope that his life would change—someday. This was his spot, whether he was avoiding his father's fists or Willow's relentless all-season gaiety. *They ought to name this sucker after me,* he thought patting the bench.

Down at the other end of the lake, he could see the Christmas tree on the dock of his resort. A freaking tree! With flashing lights! He told Freddy there must be a state law against shore decorations being this bright and cheerful. But Freddy just winked at Willow, who enclosed Harley in one of her patchouli-scented hugs and said, "Merry, merry, Harley."

A nearby sound drew his attention from the lake. He looked around and rubbed his eyes.

There was an enormous black spider scrambling up the statue of Harriet Bunyan. He blinked again.

The spider was placing a holly wreath around Harriet's neck.

This was too much for Harley's merriment meter. "Spider, get the hell down from there," he yelled. "Leave Harriet alone." Everyone raised in Cosette, even normally indifferent Harley, felt protective when it came to the town's icon.

The spider slid gracefully down, hung for a moment arm-in-arm with Harriet, then swung out into the air and landed on the sidewalk with a crash of sturdy black boots. Harley groaned. He recognized those boots.

"Hey, Harley," said Nikki Diego, who had tipped her spiky hair red for the season.

His old schoolmate and the defiler of his canoe sat down beside him, snatched the beer can from his fingers, and finished it. She spotted the pile of empties at Harley's feet. "You're going to recycle those, right?"

Harley snatched the can back, tossed it on the pile, and

crossed his arms over his chest thinking she'd go away if he ignored her. But she didn't go away.

Peering down the lake, Nikki said, "Nice tree on your dock, Harley."

Harley rubbed his face. He kept his beard at a stubble, like his brother. Neither Wamsganz son ever wanted to resemble their shaggy-maned father.

"That tree's an eyesore," he said.

Nikki laughed. "I like the way it flashes. Sort of resembles a mini lighthouse."

"That's it." Harley surged to his feet. "I'm going home where I can get some peace."

He leaned over to retrieve the half-full whiskey bottle. But when he straightened, he felt dizzy and stumbled. Nikki leaped up and grabbed him by the scarf.

With hands that were as strong as the jaws of the snapping turtle that lived under the Wamsganz dock, she forced him to sit down on the bench. "Hold on there, sailor," she said.

While she stomped flat the empty beer cans one by one with her steel-toed boots and tossed them into a nearby recycling bin, Harley glared at her.

When she lobbed the last crushed can, Harley saw an opportunity to escape and struggled to his feet. Taking two unsteady steps, he began searching his pockets for his car keys.

Nikki held up a set of keys. "Looking for these?"

He lunged for them, but she dodged and pocketed his keys. She was quicker than she looked in those heavy boots.

"Give 'em here," growled Harley.

"I'm driving."

"Like hell."

But somehow Harley found himself in the passenger seat of Nikki's truck. He closed his eyes and leaned his head against the car window. She couldn't drive worth shit, he thought, as they hit another pothole.

"Doesn't this thing have shocks?" he moaned, his head bumping the window again.

"Shocks are for wimps," she said.

When the interminable ride to the resort finally ended, Harley half-crawled, half-fell out of the truck. All was quiet in the cabins and the family house. He started toward his trailer, the leftover libations clutched to his chest. He expected Nikki to leave, but instead he heard her car door opening.

Before he knew what was happening, she was walking down the dock toward the Christmas tree.

"Hey, come back here." Harley quickly set down the whiskey on his doorstep and stumbled after her. His first step on the dock made his stomach career. He swallowed down the rising beer. He vowed he would not puke in front of Nikki Diego.

"Look, Harley, look at the colorful lights reflecting in the water. Isn't it beautiful?"

Harley could barely open his eyes, much less admire a bunch of lights. He could feel the vibrations of her big boots tap-dancing around the tree. The dock bobbed, and his stomach rebelled. Damn, if he wasn't replacing this floating dock with a permanent one before next summer.

He lost track of where he was, but he didn't forget who he was with. Suddenly, he asked, "If you like colors so much, why are you always dressed in black?"

Nikki ignored him. He felt her clumping toward him on the dock. As she passed him, she tapped him on the shoulder, "C'mon, Harley. I want to see the tree from the water."

"What?"

His head spun as he watched her gracefully spring off the

dock, walk over to the canoe he had yet to repaint, and flip it over.

"Wait, Diego. Nikki!"

But she was already hefting the paddles. "You coming?"

He shook his head. It was dark, the water was cold, and she was irritating. She didn't even have a life vest. She could fall in and disappear. Those boots of hers would drag her to the bottom. *That would teach her a lesson about messing with the Wamsganzes,* he thought.

But in the end, Harley couldn't let her go alone.

"Oh god, she's pushing it into the water," he muttered, stumbling off the dock, falling to his knees in the sand, and getting back up. He made one leap for the canoe and landed with one foot in the canoe and one foot in the icy water. "Shit!"

Nikki's calm voice called, "Sit down, Harley. You'll tip us over."

And then they were gliding out into the lake. She paddled with strong strokes. They hardly bobbled, but when they did, Harley's stomach rose up like a fish from the bottom. Finally, he couldn't keep it down and leaned over the side.

"Bet you feel better now," Nikki said.

"I'm gonna kill you, Diego."

She responded, "Probably," and began to hum *Feliz Navidad.* They paddled to the middle of the lake, then Nikki brought them to a stop. They drifted. The water surrounded them with quiet. The loons, herons, and shore birds were long gone, enjoying the sun and fish down south.

Harley felt terrible. From his seat in the front of the canoe, he twisted to look at her. "Can we go back now?"

Nikki smiled at him with sweetness, an expression he didn't trust.

"In a minute. First, look. Look at the tree, Harley."

The quiet canoe floated sideways, giving them a perfect view of the dock and the tree.

"Isn't it beautiful?" Nikki asked, her voice gently carrying to him.

Harley had to admit it was: the sparkling tree, the soft reflection of the lights in the water, the silent night broken only by the whisper of the water lapping against the canoe. The canoe rocked like a cradle, and he felt a calm that was strange to him. What was it? What was he feeling? Had Nikki sprinkled some kind of enchantment over this canoe with her crazy paint?

Nikki's voice came from what seemed like far away. "I wear black in mourning for the planet."

Harley shook his head and said, "You're nuts."

She didn't correct him.

Back on shore, they stored the canoe and paddles, and Harley walked Nikki to her truck. He couldn't get the beauty of the watery tree reflection out of his mind. As she opened the door, he stopped her.

Tugging the red scarf from his neck, he growled, "Would it kill you to wear a bit of color?" He wrapped the scarf inexpertly around her, from nose to shoulder. She watched him with big, silent eyes as he worked. Her intense stare made his fingers clumsy. She was tiny, barely reaching his shoulder, and the scarf swallowed her like a mummy.

That night Harley had drunken dreams of mummies with pixie hair and Christmas trees swimming away from him with laughter.

CHAPTER 18

FALSE ALARM

THE MONTHS AFTER CHRISTMAS break were calm in the Turnstone household. Meri was settled in school and enjoying kindergarten except for Valentine's Day, when Buster Sweeney refused to give her one of the fancy Valentine cupcakes his mother had brought for the class. After Miss Lindqvist admonished Buster for his behavior, she took a cupcake from the box and delivered it to Meri herself. But, by then, Wren was already sharing his cupcake with Meri, who simply looked at Buster and said, "No, thanks."

Spring had come in with its usual contrariness in Minnesota, mixing rain, snow, and heat. The only sure bet was the wind.

Meri tasted the cold April wind rushing across the schoolyard and clutched the calming stone in her pocket. The wind wanted her. It wanted all the children racing around the playground equipment, chasing each other; they just didn't know it. Meri felt the excitement in the air and knew it was energizing her classmates. The teachers, muffled from head to toe in miles of scarves, shouted for colliding students to slow down and be careful.

Meri heard the north wind laugh, *Let's play.*

Oh no, she thought. The stone warmed in her hand. Temptation rose inside her.

Then suddenly, in the chaos of the playground, someone rammed her from behind and knocked her down. She landed on her hands and knees and lost the stone. A voice inside her said: *Keep the stone. Don't let go.*

From above her, she heard another voice: the sneer of Buster Sweeney.

"Watch it, mutt." She looked up. Buster was the one who had run into her. He rubbed the forearm that he'd used as a battering ram, the one that had smacked into her backpack, which as usual she wore in school and out. Continuing to rub his arm, he demanded, "What do you have in that bag?"

Suddenly, he grabbed the backpack and tugged, trying to get it off her. His hand ripped off the braid on the zipper tab, the one Wren's mother had made especially for Meri. Buster tossed the tab to the ground and stepped on it.

"Hey," Meri said, pushing to her feet and trying to escape Buster's clutches. "Let go of my bag."

But Buster refused to release the backpack. "Why's this so heavy? What you got in there? A gun?"

The very idea horrified Meri. She searched her pockets for her calming stone, but it was not there. Before she realized what she was doing, Meri summoned the wind for help.

A blast of air crashed into Buster. He stumbled backwards and landed on the ground. He didn't see how she had done it, but he knew she'd done something to him. Just like the time on the slide at the park. It angered and frightened him. Scrambling to his feet, he began yelling, "Gun! Gun!"

Immediately, the schoolyard erupted into pandemonium. Screaming children rushed to hide under slides and swings. Teachers, whose first thoughts were lockdown and safety, shouted above the cacophony and tried to herd the children into the school.

Meri didn't move. She stood with the wind wrapped around her and her hair flying. She stared at Buster in shock. What was he talking about?

"Buster," she screamed over the wind, which was growing stronger by the second. She reached out for him.

He backed away from her in fear. "Get away from me! You've got a gun! You're gonna kill us all!"

"No!" she cried. "No!"

The powerful wind, fueled by Meri's anxiety, smashed into the play yard, tangling swings and toppling children as they dashed for safety.

Buster turned and ran.

Wren dodged Miss Lindqvist's arm as she directed him toward the school doors and headed for Meri. He fought through one gust after another to reach her. Frightened children ran past him, slamming into him. Buster pushed him aside. Wren kept struggling toward Meri, who seemed frozen all alone in the middle of the play yard. The wind was so strong. Her skirt and jacket were whipping back and forth. A dust devil whirled around her. Wren saw Meri begin to lift into the air and knew he was imagining things. He brushed dust from his eyes and grabbed for her, catching her arm. Meri gave him a lost look. It was as if she didn't know him.

Shaking her, he shouted, "Meri! We have to get inside!"

Awareness snapped into Meri's eyes. "Wren?"

He tugged her toward the school, but the wind wanted to keep her.

We'll keep you safe, it said.

Meri tightened her hold on Wren's hand. She took several deep breaths. *I know,* she told the wind, *but we need to stop now.*

We? Stop? puzzled the wind.

Meri wasn't ready to face what she'd done, how she'd lost control, how all this was her fault.

Please, she whispered.

By the time everyone, including Meri and Wren, were inside the school, the day had begun to calm.

But in the halls and classrooms, there was anything but serenity. Both children and adults were shaken. Anxious students cried and huddled together, while nervous teachers assured them that they were all safe. The police arrived, searched the premises, and determined there was no shooter. Eventually, parents were phoned to pick up their children early.

✳ ✳ ✳

One of the first parents to arrive was Adrienne Sweeney, who hovered over her babbling son as two tall officers questioned him. "If Buster saw a gun, he saw a gun," insisted Adrienne.

One of the officers, Jim Bubbleski, looked Buster in the eye and asked, "Did you *see* a gun?"

Bubbleski's stern tone and intense stare made Buster look away. "Well, not exactly," mumbled Buster. "I felt it. It was in her backpack." He turned to his mother. "She could have killed us all, Mom. I just know it."

Bubbleski sent the other officer to retrieve Meri's backpack. When it arrived, Bubbleski emptied the backpack and showed the Sweeneys what was inside: a pink dumbbell.

No gun.

"Are you sure there's no gun in there?" Buster peered inside the backpack.

"No gun," Bubbleski confirmed.

Adrienne pulled her son close but addressed the officers. "It was an easy mistake to make."

Bubbleski raised a skeptical eyebrow at Adrienne. He'd encountered overprotective parents before and their kids, who like Buster enjoyed being the center of attention. "You can take him home," he told Adrienne, "but make sure he understands how serious this was. False alarms are not funny. People could have been hurt."

✱ ✱ ✱

In the principal's office, Meri sat between Ariel and Ruddy on hard wooden chairs. She kept saying, "I'm sorry. I'm sorry."

Ariel and Ruddy exchanged worried looks. Was it time to reveal Ariel and Meri's secret? What if a child had been injured today? That was an outcome neither could accept. "Maybe it is time to think seriously about homeschooling," whispered Ruddy.

Meri turned pleading eyes on her father. "No, Daddy."

In the end, Ruddy left the decision up to Ariel—and Ariel lied.

"Meri must carry the dumbbell for medical reasons," Ariel told the police officers.

Jim Bubbleski gave Ruddy, his friend and old classmate, a look of disbelief. Ruddy said, "Bubble, it's true. Look at her. Do you really think she's capable of braining someone with a dumbbell? She's a little girl who is as scared as everyone else. Besides, she can hardly swing a flyswatter."

Bubble thought Ruddy was probably right, but there were rules, and surely a heavy object like a dumbbell in the hands of a kindergartner must fall within them. He was about to say so when Doctor Echo Starling and his wife, Sahara, swept into the room. Word had spread fast through the town about a possible shooting incident at the school, and Echo had rushed to the school to see if he was needed. Sahara insisted on coming along, especially when Ariel texted that Meri was involved.

"Hey, Jim." Echo, the picture of calm and efficiency, nodded at the officer. "What do we have here?"

"Don't think we need you, Doc," Bubble said. "Nobody hurt, except for a few skinned knees. The school nurse has already taken care of those."

Sahara and Ariel exchanged a silent look. Sahara winked at her daughter then patted her husband's arm.

Echo got the message. "Good, still while I'm here, I'll check Meriweather Turnstone. Besides being my granddaughter, she is my patient, and I heard she was pretty shaken up."

Bubble remembered that Echo had proudly discussed his granddaughter as he patched up Bubble's son after the boy broke a leg skiing.

"Well, Doc," Bubble said, "Ariel claims that her daughter needs to carry this three-pound dumbbell for medical reasons . . ."

Echo nodded. "True, true. While I understand such an object can be dangerous in young hands, it is essential in this case. I'm happy to write a note for the school's records explaining that, in my *professional opinion*, Meri needs this weight to help her with her . . . anxiety issues."

"Anxiety issues?" Bubble looked at Meri suspiciously. The kid looked calm to him.

Meri, who had refused to speak a word since the police officers had escorted her into the principal's office, kept her head down and stared at her feet, which didn't reach the floor. She had never heard her grandfather lie before. It made her feel even guiltier than she already did. She'd closed the school, and now everyone was afraid of her.

Meri didn't know that Echo had been lying for the Lee family for years, since the day he accidentally saw an amazing young Ariel somersaulting in the air. He'd given his heart to that enchanting child and, eventually, to her protective mother. He'd thrown his allegiance to Sahara and Ariel long ago and would continue to do so until his dying breath.

In the end, Bubble's report downplayed the incident. He thought that was best for all involved. After all, Doctor Echo Starling was the best physician in town and somebody had to doctor Bubble's daring, risk-loving son.

CHAPTER 19

WE DON'T RUN AWAY

TROUBLE FOUND MERI ON the porch swing looking as if her world had been sucked into a black hole. She sat down beside the child and pushed the swing into motion. The tops of the trees were bending as they had been all afternoon since the incident at school.

As air continued to sweep across the porch, Meri started talking. "Everybody hates me. They think I'm going to hurt them."

A silent Trouble kept the swing moving.

Meri said, "I would never do that. Never."

Gus, ensconced on his dog bed on the porch, lifted his head at Meri's appalled tone.

After a long pause, Meri whispered, "I don't want to go back to school."

In a considering voice, Trouble asked, "What do your mom and dad say about that?"

"Daddy thinks I should stay home for a few days, but Mama says, no, I have to go back."

"Did she say why?"

"She said because women like us don't run away. What does that mean?"

They sat in silence for a long time, rocking. Trouble didn't agree with Ariel. She thought there certainly were times that warranted avoiding people and situations, times when not being resilient was okay. That was just part of survival. But Trouble also knew that Ariel did not want Meri to get into the habit of running away from problems.

"Daddy's talking homeschooling," said Meri.

Trouble told the child that she had been homeschooled. "I missed having friends," Trouble said, "and I envied the kids who got to ride the school bus every morning."

"Really?" Meri asked. "Did you cause something bad to happen too?"

"No," said Trouble. "My mom just wanted me near her."

Trouble's grandmother, Clarissa, had kept the secret of the Hamilton women and their gift from everyone—especially her husband, Jack. She'd even kept the Hamilton legacy a secret from her daughter, Brooke, until Trouble was born and Clarissa sensed that her grandchild would be gifted. Brooke had been born like Sahara, giftless, and was clueless regarding the family heritage. Clarissa hadn't known when the gift of flight would manifest in her granddaughter, but she was sure it would. She tried to prepare Brooke but only succeeded in alarming her daughter, who worried about the day that Trouble's Hamilton talents would show themselves and get the better of her, just as Meri's had this day at school.

Brooke grew obsessed with keeping her child safe and always nearby. She insisted on homeschooling her daughter, although Brooke was awful at textbook teaching. She was drawn to Nature and escaped to it whenever she could. Nature touched something inside Brooke, something that she was never quite able to define. Often she abandoned the traditional school subjects of mathematics and reading and took Trouble romping through the fields on their Missouri farm.

When Brooke died unexpectedly from an unknown virus, Trouble and Clarissa were bereft. But the grandmother, in her early seventies at the time, had pulled herself together and taken over the raising and education of her eight-year-old grandchild. When late-blooming Trouble came into her gift at the age of thirteen, Clarissa secretly taught her granddaughter the lessons of being a Hamilton—how to ride the air, how to stay grounded when in the presence of the giftless, how to keep secrets.

There was resilience in the Hamilton gene, and Trouble recognized it in Meri. Remembering the words of supportive Clarissa, Trouble patted the child's arm and said, "So everything got away from you today, kid. It happens."

* * *

Wren sat on the resort's dock, staring into the water. He felt the dock shake as heavy footsteps approached. He was surprised when his uncle Harley sat down beside him.

"Tough day at school," Harley said.

"Yeah," said Wren. The boy couldn't stop thinking of what he'd seen on the playground.

Was it real? Why had Meri looked as if she was in a trance? Had the wind really started to lift Meri into the air? Maybe it was just the swirling dust that made it appear that way.

Rubbing his eyes, which still felt gritty, Wren said, "I hope Meri's okay."

Having little experience advising five-year-olds, Harley wondered what to say. He scrubbed his scratchy beard with his cracked and winter-roughened hands.

"I went to school with that girl's mom," he told Wren. "She used to wear these clunky shoes. That family has always been weird."

Wren frowned at his uncle. "Meri's nice!"

Recognizing the boy's defensive tone, Harley let out a sigh and got to his feet. He placed a hand on Wren's shoulder and gave it a slight squeeze. "Maybe so. But her mom never closed the school. You be careful around that Meri girl."

CHAPTER 20

A NIGHT UP THERE

THAT NIGHT THE PEOPLE in Cosette tossed and turned in their beds as the wind howled around them. It had been a terrifying day for the town.

In the Turnstone living room, Ruddy recognized this meteorological turmoil. It was more than the typical gustiness of April. He'd felt this same agitation in the air the day Meri was born. He only knew one thing to do: be the rock when Ariel and Meri were adrift. He pushed calm into the atmosphere, into his wife, held her tight, and talked to her.

"Breathe. It's over. All is well."

Ariel turned desperate eyes toward him. "Is it?"

"No one was hurt," Ruddy reminded her. "It was just a big misunderstanding. A kid got scared and freaked. Kids do that."

"What are we going to do—about Meri?" wondered Ariel. "She's so young, Ruddy. I was ten when I came into my gift and learned how to handle the wind inside me. Ten doesn't sound terribly experienced, but it is a heck of a lot more mature than five."

The wind rattled the bones of the house, as if to agree. Ruddy placed a calming hand over the fists clutched in Ariel's lap. "I still think we should consider letting her sit out the rest of the year. Homeschool."

The idea shocked Ariel. "What? You want to take her out of school? No. She has to learn how to handle these situations."

"She will but . . ."

Ariel shook her head. "She doesn't give up, and neither do we."

"I'm not giving up, Ariel," Ruddy protested. "But she turned that playground upside down today. And look outside. Do you even realize what *you* are doing out there?"

Ariel glanced at the shuddering windows. Every day she preached control to Meri and hadn't realized how much she had lost the handle on her own emotions.

She closed her eyes and took deep breaths. She whispered to the wind, *We're okay.*

It took a while, but eventually, the tension around Cosette eased. The edginess slipped from the air, the wind settled, and so did the sleeping denizens of Cosette.

* * *

Meri knelt at the top of the stairs, eavesdropping on her parents. They were talking about homeschooling—again. The word, "homeschool," sliced through her, and a fistful of dead leaves outside flung themselves against the window of her room across the hall. When she felt a tap on her shoulder, she jumped.

It was Trouble.

She motioned for Meri to follow her into the guest room and closed the door behind them. Trouble, in her signature black leather jacket, invited Meri to join her on the bed.

Sitting beside Trouble, Meri twisted the folds of her flannel nightgown and kicked at the rug on the floor with her fuzzy bunny slippers. She began to cry. "I want to go back to school," she mumbled.

"What? You said before you didn't want to go."

"I want to see my friends."

"Are you sure you still have any?" Meri turned hurt eyes on Trouble, who threw up her hands in apology. "Sorry, sorry. I didn't mean that. Just kidding."

Meri started kicking the rug again. "Maybe I should be homeschooled," she whispered. "Maybe I'm dangerous. Maybe I'll never get it right."

As the wind shook the window of Trouble's room, Trouble made a decision. Tossing her long hair over her shoulder, she rose and said, "Come on."

She walked to the window and raised the sash. The wind whipped into the room.

Meri looked at her with shock. "What are you doing?"

"We're going out."

Meri stuttered, "You-you mean Up There? Now? But it's night and dark."

"So?"

"I'm not allowed to go Up There without Mama—and we *never* go at night."

Trouble propped her hands on her hips. "I do it all the time. It's like nothing you've ever experienced."

Meri's gaze slid toward the closed bedroom door. Her parents were still talking, still discussing her, their disappointing daughter.

Slowly, Meri rose from the bed with a squeak of the springs and tentatively approached Trouble.

"We won't go far?" Meri asked. "You won't let go of me?"

"I got you, kid, and you got this."

Trouble held out a hand, and Meri, still in her nightgown, took it.

* * *

They climbed through the second-floor window and up onto the roof. When Meri looked down, she experienced the same excitement she had felt standing at the loft door with her mother. Only there was no cushiony snow below, and there was no reassuring mother at her side. There was only the black night, the wind, and Trouble. A thought flashed in Meri's mind: *Should she trust Trouble?*

But before the thought could crystallize, Meri heard the wind whisper her name: *Meri.*

She turned to Trouble and said, "Let's do this."

* * *

They rose into the night—a woman in black leather and a child in fuzzy slippers—and with a friendly gust, they were off.

Meri couldn't see much in the dark, but she felt the occasional brush of trees. Trouble guided them around obstacles as if she were a night bird. They drifted, and the stars laughed with them. They floated on the songs of owls and coyotes. They swam through the aromas of sleeping earth. The moon lit Trouble's happy smile, and the air tousled her dark bangs. Meri thought her cousin, with her long hair streaming behind her, had never looked prettier.

Glancing below, Meri saw the golden lights in the living room of her house. She could see her parents, huddled together, still thinking, still talking. She watched her mother drop her head on her father's shoulder, and Meri begged the wind: *Don't tell her.*

In Minnesota, April nights can recall the crispness of winter. After a while, Meri grew cold, but she didn't want to turn back. The night air's touch was strange yet comforting. Encased in her jacket, Trouble seemed impervious to the cold, but Meri's flannel nightgown was flimsy protection in a night ride. Meri shivered. Trouble looked at her and lifted a brow, as if to ask if they should return home. "Not yet," shouted Meri.

So, they walked the night air a bit longer.

When they did land, it was in the meadow. The cold, wet grass tickled Meri's ankles as she stepped from the air, and she shivered again. Trouble pulled off her leather jacket and dropped it around the child's shoulders. They stood in the middle of the meadow's expanse, two tiny figures in a massive universe. The starry sky went on forever, as far as they could see. Staring up, Meri whispered, "The stars are so bright. So pretty. And there are so many of them. They make me feel funny."

Trouble understood. "There's something about night flying. It gets inside you. It makes you feel closer to . . . everything."

Trouble's grandmother had told her stories of night flights like this one, when the sky opened its arms to earthly visitors and filled them with wonder. She'd also told tales of a house of women who frightened away their men with their gift, who lived for each other, and who took to the sky together at night when no one could see them.

They were Hamilton women. Women like Ariel, Meri, and Trouble.

Night flying was in their blood, but it could be a lonely business, as Trouble well knew.

Trouble usually flew solo at night. Intent on keeping the secret of the Hamilton women from her husband, Clarissa had never accompanied Trouble on her night travels. Trouble had never felt the love and camaraderie of flying with family before. This, she thought, was what Clarissa had missed.

"The sky is magical at night," whispered Meri.

Trouble, still thinking of her grandmother, said, "Yes, it is."

Meri continued to chatter, "I feel magical when I am Up There. I am never giving up the sky."

Giving up the sky? The very thought was like biting into bitter fruit for Trouble. She had run from home and the man who had given her the black leather jacket—instead of giving up the sky. Now, she was sure she had made the right decision to explore her heritage and find out who she truly is.

Trouble knew she would complete her journey with Ariel and Meri at her side. She would find the Hamilton homestead. She would take her grandmother's ashes home. She would be the Hamilton woman she was always meant to be.

"You got this," she said to herself and Meri.

CHAPTER 21

EARTH DAY IN COSETTE

EARTH DAY WAS AN official holiday in the Turnstone household. Everyone took the day off from writing and researching. They donned gloves and their worst clothes. As Ariel explained to Meri, it was their turn to clean their tiny part of the planet's messy room. Ruddy consulted his weather instruments and resources and predicted this April 22 would be a perfect one. Ariel agreed with him. There wasn't a cloud in the sky. The rainstorms she felt stirring were hundreds of miles away. The wind was content.

Ariel had been pregnant with Meri when she organized her first Earth Day project in Cosette. Ruddy had worried as she bent over to pick up a scrap of paper or a discarded beer can. When he saw her lugging useless and abandoned auto parts from ditches along the highway, he nearly blew a gasket. The next year found him planting trees and building compost bins with infant Meri strapped to his chest in a baby carrier.

The family tradition grew to encompass grandparents Sahara, Echo, Alice, and Arthur. Then, to Ariel's surprise, the event exploded into a platoon of community volunteers. Somehow, the chore of organization always fell to Ariel. She was the one who enlisted volunteers and ordered supplies of work gloves and trash bags. Volunteers looked to Ariel for assignments to junk-filled yards, wind-littered fields, and debris-strewn byways.

Leaving from her shop, Bike the Babe, Blinka led a crew to pick up trash along the Paul Bunyan State Trail and the parking lots that served it. Sahara, Echo, and some of Echo's co-workers scoured the city park and lakeside for debris as well as planted new trees to replace those that had fallen or died. The Moongoose sisters, Helen and Sweetie, prodded their fellow downtown merchants to join them in cleaning up Cosette's Main Street from one end to the other.

When Helen caught Main Street tenant Melanie Harcourt locking up her real estate office on Earth Day, she stopped Melanie and asked, "Coming to join us?"

Melanie, wearing a crisp spring dress and high heels, stared at Helen. "Do I look like it? Some of us have *real* work to do, Helen."

Helen eyed the campaign posters tucked under Melanie's arm. She was running for town council in November. "Melanie, today is a day to clean up the roadways and yards, not add more trash," said Helen.

Melanie harrumphed, skirted around Helen, and headed to her car with heels clacking.

Helen had spent many hours discussing science and the environment with Dakota Blue. She had heard Dakota's personal stories of the first Earth Day in 1970, which had been a "teach-in" aimed at showing humans that they had a role in repairing the planet they were destroying. In 1970, people saw the destruction—polluted land and rivers on fire—on their televisions. Today the failing planet was not just something that happened on television. It was personal now in the crop-killing droughts, unpredictable snows, torrential rains, and unbearable heat they all experienced.

Still, Helen knew there would always be people like Melanie who maintained it was not their problem, people who refused to realize that they were on the same sinking ship as the rest of the world.

Sweetie Moongoose had never been as fierce as her younger sister. She was the one who preferred pretty things and cheerful thoughts. Seeing Helen's frustrated face as she watched Melanie drive away, peacemaker Sweetie nudged her sister. "Let it go. There's a trashy alley up ahead calling our name."

* * *

This year, the school was the hub of Earth Day activities. It was a Saturday so the building was supposed to be closed, but Ariel had persuaded the principal to allow them to open a few classrooms. Children could join Nikki in one classroom to create their own Earth Day art. In another classroom, Dakota shared stories of extinction, of creatures that were long gone. As usual, Dakota mesmerized the young minds who were drawn to her sense of humor and her love of nature.

Most of the action, however, was outside on the playground where The Incident, as it was known in the Turnstone house, had occurred. Standing at the top of the steps with Wren, Meri beheld with shame the many people working on the playground to correct what she had wrecked a few days ago. Remorse this intense was a new feeling for Meri, and she didn't like it.

"What a mess," said Wren. Trash and recycling bins had been knocked over by frightened stampeding children. Wind-driven leaves, papers, and debris were lodged against the school building and the fence. Swings remained tangled. The hungry wind had eaten up the sand, leaving large bare spots on the playground. The science class's bird feeder had disappeared. The spring drawings and paintings created by the art classes and taped along the fence were either ripped or gone.

"I'm so sorry," whispered Meri.

Wren looked at her. "It's not your fault. My dad says it was just a freak weather thing."

"Yeah," said Meri, "a freak thing." She did not add, but thought, *My freak thing.*

Ariel, who was raking leaves into piles, called to them, "You two, grab a trash bag and get to work."

Wren nudged Meri and smiled at her. "Coming," he said.

Ruddy held a ladder while Wren's father, Freddy, climbed to the top of the swings and untangled them. "Check the bolts," Ruddy told him. "Might as well tighten them while you're up there." In fact, the volunteers checked the security of all the playground equipment that had weathered the fierce winds.

"Roger that," said Freddy with a smile.

The entire Wamsganz family had shown up for the clean-up. As Freddy climbed down the ladder, Ruddy said, "I'm surprised to see Harley here. He's never participated in Earth Day before."

On the ground, Freddy dusted his hands on his worn jeans. "Willow made him come."

"Your wife is a powerful woman," said Ruddy.

"You have no idea."

They turned and watched Harley approach Lars Diego's pickup truck, which was loaded with sand and wheelbarrows.

Harley, being a big fellow, easily lifted one of the wheelbarrows from the top of the pile of sand and growled to a couple of nearby parents with shovels, "Well, don't stand there. Load 'er up."

Harley wheeled and dumped load after load of sand. He looked up once and saw Nikki standing on the school steps, grinning at him. That made him huff and yell, "Get your ass down here and rake this sand in place."

She shook her head. "I'm the art teacher today. Not the sand raker."

"You're filling those kids' heads with climate nonsense."

Dressed in ripped black jeans, a black sweatshirt, and the red scarf Harley had given her, she marched down the steps and stopped in front of Harley. Even with her short hair at its spikiest, she barely reached his shoulder. Harley leaned against his upended wheelbarrow and looked down his nose at her. She kicked the wheelbarrow with her heavy boots, almost toppling him.

Nikki rose on her tiptoes and got in his face. "The glaciers in the Arctic are melting, dummy, and the sea levels are rising."

Harley looked bored. "As far as I know, we don't have any ocean-front property in Minnesota."

Nikki poked his chest with a finger. "We have lakes, and they're getting warmer. The fish will die, and the fisher people, your customers, will stop coming."

"I'll be long gone by then. It will be someone else's problem."

He grabbed her hand before she could poke him again. She snatched her hand away. "Harley Wamsganz, you are a-a-a . . . turd."

He laughed. "What? Are we in third grade?"

"Sometimes it feels like it," Nikki retorted. "You are being your usual negative, do-nothing self. You'd rather cause trouble than help."

Their raised voices had begun to draw attention.

Willow stuck her head out the door and interrupted them, "Nikki, we've run out of drawing paper. Where can I find more?"

Nikki gave Harley a cross look.

"I'll be right there, Willow."

Without another word for Harley, she turned and strode toward the school and up the steps. Just as she reached for the door handle, Harley yelled, "Like the red scarf, Diego."

Nikki stopped, turned, and stuck her tongue out at Harley.

Wren and Meri, who'd been taking in the entire scene, gasped then began to giggle.

* * *

Willow had purchased spring flowers to plant in front of the school. Being from California, she didn't know what would grow in Minnesota's wintry zone so she consulted an expert: the young clerk at the hardware store. He suggested the hardy yellow and purple pansies on display in the front of the store. "Not much else is safe until May fifteenth or so," the clerk told Willow. "Gotta watch for those late frosts. But after that, let 'er rip."

Ariel heard Willow and Freddy laughing and talking as they planted. Harley's brother was two years younger than Ariel. She didn't remember him from their school days, but she imagined growing up in the shadow of his ornery father and angry brother had not been easy. She was glad he'd found Willow with her luminous spirit and accepting style.

Ariel turned and saw Ruddy raking sand as Harley dumped it. She found Wren and Meri crawling under slides to retrieve errant litter. Ruddy's father, Arthur, had arrived with a new birdhouse, which he was erecting on the post of the former one. Alice Turnstone had baked dozens of cupcakes for the volunteers, and Marta Diego was distributing sandwiches she'd brought from the diner.

As volunteers gathered on playground equipment and on school steps, eating and sharing stories of Earth Day, a light breeze touched them. Ariel closed her eyes, inhaled the taste of the contented air mixing with the voices of people happily working together, and smiled. It was moments like this that made her feel ordinary and a part of the collective Cosette family. She was sorry that Trouble had chosen to miss it.

CHAPTER 22

A PLACE THAT SHIMMERS

WHILE THE FAMILY CLEANED, Trouble snooped.

First, she fired up Ariel's laptop and performed her usual searches, tunneling through the internet and social media. There were certain people she kept her eye on, people who also were keeping an eye out for her.

No sign of him. He was still where he was supposed to be, where she'd left him—at home. Leaving him had been a difficult decision, but it had been the right thing to do.

Next, she turned to news reports, community blogs, and official channels.

No arrest warrants for her. Yet.

She had told herself that she hadn't done any real damage when she lifted that woman's expensive leather wallet in Chicago. She only took the cash because she was hungry. She deposited the wallet, with credit cards and driver's license, in a collection basket at a church, even though churches gave her the creeps.

Trouble shut down the laptop and rifled through Ariel's materials on the dining room table. She found boring books and papers on the environment. She searched the bookshelves. There were books everywhere in this house: dining room, living room, hall, even bathroom. *Who needed so many books?*

Once again, she did not find the object of her hunt.

Finally, she entered Ariel and Ruddy's bedroom. She scanned the room, eyeing the queen bed, the closet, the nightstand. Where would Ariel hide something precious? Under the mattress? Trouble stuffed searching fingers between the layers of bedding. Nothing. She was overthinking this. Ariel didn't know about hiding things; she only knew about hiding herself.

Trouble approached the nightstand, forced open a squeaky drawer, and smiled. There it was. The journal of Ariel's grandmother.

"You like to keep it close," she muttered.

Trouble flopped onto Ariel's bed, not bothering to remove her red high-top shoes, and opened the journal. "While everyone else honors ridiculous Earth Day, I'm going to find your secrets, Anne Hamilton Stevens."

Unknown to Ariel and Ruddy, Trouble had continued to ride the air at night. She had passed over the countryside searching for the "lone house on the hill" her grandmother had described to her. Grandmother Clarissa had made it sound like a magical and welcoming place where the air and life itself shimmered.

Clarissa had spoken of the Hamilton homestead as a house of women. There were no strict fathers or know-it-all uncles. Clarissa accounted for this with a simple statement: "Men never lasted long around us." So, the females became set in their ways and strong in their beliefs. They made decisions for themselves and became adept at chasing off possible gold-digging suitors coveting their land. At night, they walked the sky together in a constellation glimmering with sisterhood and felt a depthless love for each other and their gift. Anne, Ariel's grandmother, had lived a wondrous life in that house with Clarissa, Trouble's grandmother—until the day Clarissa left.

From Clarissa's reminiscences, Trouble had pieced together her grandmother's sad story: how Clarissa had fallen in love with a man of weak character, a man who discovered her gift and rejected her, a man who did not picture himself married to a "freak." Clarissa had been crushed and nothing the women in the family could say or do would bring her out of her despair. She stopped going on family walks in the night sky. She stopped eating and grew frail. Then, one day she drifted away on the wind, like a lost leaf, never to see her family again.

Trouble turned the pages of Anne's journal, looking for references to her grandmother Clarissa. She was shocked to learn that the family had thought that Clarissa had died when she disappeared. No one had gone looking for her. No one had searched the sky for her, night after night.

They didn't know that days after the wind had swept Clarissa away, it had gently deposited her, exhausted and weak, in a field on a small farm in Missouri. There bachelor farmer Jack Harper found her, nursed her back to health, and married her. Once her strength had returned, a grateful Clarissa gave up the sky. She never told Jack about the Hamilton gift or curse, as she often thought of it. She dared not risk Jack's affections.

Clarissa would suffer Up There withdrawal all her life. Her refusal to reach for the arms of the air pitched her into days of dark spirits and silent moods, but she never told her husband why. Jack, a simple man raised to balance the unpredictability of his farming livelihood with the dependability of his faith, never questioned the source of these downturns in his wife's spirits. He prayed for her. Clarissa, from a family of women who followed their own dogma, prayed that the child she was carrying would not inherit the Hamilton gift.

Clarissa's prayers were answered. Her daughter, Brooke, did not inherit the gift of flight.

But Brooke's daughter did.

Trouble closed the journal. Anne had written little of her early life with Clarissa and the other women of Hamilton House. There was nothing here to tell Trouble where to find the house. Anne had been a secret keeper, just like Sahara and Ariel. Her journal talked mostly about her life with her husband Will Stevens and their children—and her experience with storms. Anne claimed she'd ridden storms to keep her family and Cosette safe. Trouble wasn't sure she believed it.

Clarissa had never mentioned riding storms to Trouble, but she had often spoken of her desire to return to that house on the hill, the one place where she had been truly happy. When her loving grandmother died and Trouble felt so alone she could hardly bear it, when the bank claimed the farm and took her home, Trouble ran away. She gave in to the call of the sky and the driving need to visit the house her grandmother had so wistfully described and so endlessly loved.

Trouble tossed the journal aside. It had been no help. Where should she look now?

Trouble was determined to find Clarissa's shimmery place.

"It's time to hit the sky again," she told herself.

CHAPTER 23

A FIELD TRIP WITH TROUBLE

SCHOOL WAS OUT. MERI had survived kindergarten. They all had made it through without further wind-related and Meri-driven problems. Now summer was here in Minnesota, a time to forget the frigid winter days that took one's breath away and the mountainous snowbanks one had to climb. Outerwear suitable for a visit to Everest could be pushed to the back of the closet. Echo could stop worrying about treating snowmobile accidents and focus on sunstrokes and water injuries. Ariel and Blinka could take Meri and Gus swimming. Ruddy could mow the lawn, a repetitive chore he found creatively inspirational and especially helpful in his writing, which never seemed to come as easily as it did for Ariel.

It also was the time of year to retrieve the bikes from the barn, pump up the tires, and ride. When Trouble first came to Cosette, Blinka had taken one look at Trouble's one-speed garage-sale mess with the bent basket and bald tires and declared, "What a piece of junk. You can't ride that." A few days later, she gave Trouble a working ten-speed that rode as if on ice. When Trouble tried to pay for the bike, Blinka refused. "It's used," Blinka had told her. "Been planning to take it out of the rental inventory long ago. My brother Jake checked it out, replaced parts and tires. It'll get you where you want to go."

Trouble and Meri, who continued their occasional and secret nighttime excursions, also had begun riding bikes together on the back roads around the farm. Meri had never required the use of training wheels. She had taken to riding a two-wheeler with an unusual sense of balance for someone her age.

Although she wasn't always comfortable with Trouble's actions or ideas, Meri enjoyed being with Trouble because she didn't insist that Meri always be in control of herself. "Let's cut loose, kid," she would say as they raced down the road on their bikes.

This was a day to cut loose.

Meri had no clue where Trouble was leading her. They started on the paved county road, keeping carefully to the shoulder, and headed away from Cosette. They pedaled into the country, past woodlands, cornfields, and dirt drives marked by mailboxes and barking dogs. Trouble's ten speed was faster than Meri's smaller bike. Blinka had ordered the bike especially for Meri's size. It had seven speeds, kid-friendly gear shifter and hand brake, and an adjustable seat for a growing child. Blinka had taught Meri how to ride the bike on the Paul Bunyan Trail, which ran near Blinka's bike shop.

As they pressed on, Meri noted that Trouble appeared to be looking for something. They both wore bike helmets, a stipulation of Ariel's, and Meri had on her monkey backpack with dumbbell, a condition of Ruddy's. Meri grew tired after a while and was glad that Trouble carried snacks and water bottles in the panniers on her bike.

"What are you looking for?" yelled Meri.

Trouble waved her on. "It's not far. I just need to find the road."

"Slow down. Where are we going?" asked Meri, pushing her helmet more securely on her sweaty head. Her legs had begun to ache.

With a glance at Meri, Trouble adjusted her speed. "Hang in there. It's a surprise. I spotted it on one of my night flights."

"What kind of surprise?"

With a grin, Trouble said, "You'll see."

Moments later, Trouble stopped. "Ah. I think this is it."

Meri eyed the strange, barely there path. It was deeply rutted and taken over by woods and brambles. It looked narrow, uninviting, and scary. Towering trees loomed over the long-forgotten road in a hovering canopy. The birds were ominously silent here.

Meri tentatively asked, "Are you sure?"

"Come on." Walking her bike, Trouble entered the path. "Let's check it out."

Meri had noticed that Trouble often erred on the side of adventure rather than safety. She was sure that her parents would not want her to go into those woods, but she didn't want to be left alone by the side of the road either. So, Meri bumped and wobbled over the ruts and tufts of grass, desperate to keep Trouble in sight. Bushes clawed at Meri's legs and arms. It seemed to take forever to push through the dark, sunless tunnel to an opening in the foliage.

Then, finally, they were out.

Meri looked around her. They were at the bottom of a hill—the tallest hill Meri had ever seen. Overgrown with waist-high weeds and grasses, the hill rose like a thumb from the earth—and at the tip of the thumb was a house.

Meri and Trouble continued, pushing their bikes up the hill, through the dense prairie toward the house. It was tough going. The hill was steep, the grass was thick, and the wind blew harder as they climbed. Meri felt as if this place did not want them to visit.

Breathing heavily and with screaming calves, Meri asked, "Are you sure we should do this?"

Unworried, Trouble said, "Of course, this is our place."

Meri gave her a questioning look. "Our place?"

When they reached the summit and stopped, Meri collapsed onto the grass, exhausted. Trouble, too excited to sit, stood and eyed the house.

To Meri, it looked inhospitable and scary. And yet, there was something about the house that intrigued her. Half the windows were gone. The paint rolled up the sides of the house like the peeling bark of a birch tree. Wind-ravaged and listing shutters creaked. Everything about the rickety house shouted *Don't come near.* It was a wonder it hadn't tumbled down this hill long ago.

Meri knew her parents would not like her going in there. *It probably has ghosts, monsters, and hidden dangers,* Meri thought. *Probably poisonous gases and trapdoors too.*

"What is this place?" Meri whispered.

Trouble couldn't take her eyes off the house. "It's the Hamilton homestead. This is where my grandmother Clarissa and your great-grandmother Anne lived."

Meri's eyes rounded, and she looked at the house again. "Really?"

They left their bikes lying on the ground, doffed their helmets, and cautiously stepped toward the house. "I'm sure of it," said Trouble. "My grandmother told me stories about this place. It matches her description perfectly."

Enchanted by the mystery of the house, they hadn't noticed that the day had turned threatening. Dark clouds now blotted the sun. Shadows crept closer. The wind roared.

When Trouble placed a foot on the bottom step, Meri grabbed her arm.

"Are you sure we should go in?"

"Kid, I've come all the way from Missouri to see this house."

Meri eyed the house and heard the air whisper: *Don't go.*

"I think we should come back with Mama," said Meri.

Trouble turned and looked at her. "If you're scared, you can stay here and wait for me. I won't be long. I just need to see inside."

"But . . ."

As if caught in the house's siren song, Trouble shook off Meri's grasp and slowly mounted the crooked steps.

"Trouble . . . Trouble, wait." Meri followed her cousin. The steps groaned, and it felt as if the whole world was wobbling. The wind tried to steer Meri from the house, but she pushed on.

Trouble crossed the porch, dodging broken boards. As she reached for the doorknob, the door suddenly flew open and a cloud of bats blasted out. Meri shrieked and jumped, and her foot broke through a rotten step.

At Meri's shout, Trouble turned and saw the girl lying on the porch steps, her foot caught in a hole. She rushed to the crying child. "Meri, it's okay. Let me see."

Sobbing, Meri said, "It hurts! The house has me! I can't get out!"

Trouble yanked on the broken boards, ripping them away with her hands and tossing them aside. She carefully released

Meri's foot from the house's grasp. When Trouble ran her hand over the injured area, Meri pulled away. Her ankle had already begun to swell.

Giving Meri a reassuring smile, Trouble said, "Doesn't look too bad. Can you walk?"

She helped Meri stand, but the child cried out when she tried to put weight on the ankle.

"You can't ride your bike like this," Trouble said. She thought for a moment. "I'll ride back to the house and get your parents."

Meri clutched Trouble's arm. "No! Don't leave me here!"

"But you can't push down on the bike pedals with that ankle."

"Please. I'm scared."

Trouble helped Meri sit on the ground. She found a small First Aid kit in the pannier and wrapped Meri's ankle tightly with an elasticized band. Then she retrieved crackers, a banana, and water bottles from the bike pannier. They ate and considered the situation.

"Better?" Trouble asked.

Meri nodded. "Let's call Mama to pick us up."

Suddenly, Trouble looked uncomfortable. "I-I don't have my cell phone. I lost it, again."

In a desperate voice, Meri cried, "Trouble, what are we going to do? We should never have come here. How are we going to get home?"

Trouble patted Meri's knee. "Kid, we Hamilton women are resourceful. We are not afraid of rampaging beasts, bothersome inconveniences, or injured ankles. We prevail."

"Prevail?"

"We triumph against all odds."

"How do we prevail in this situation?" asked Meri.

Making a decision, Trouble rose to her feet and held out a hand for Meri. "We fly home."

Taking Trouble's hand, a shocked Meri began to babble, "What? It's daylight. We're far from the farm. I'm not allowed to . . ."

"You go night flying with me," said Trouble as she began unbuckling the weighted backpack and slipping it from Meri's shoulders.

"That was at night, and we stayed on the farm where no one could see us."

"Did we?"

Meri gaped at her cousin. "But you said . . ."

Trouble saw the look of distrust on Meri's face and cut off the complaints with a stern voice, "Look, we're wasting time. We need to get you to your grandfather. We're going to fly home, and you are going to have one of your nice conversations with the wind to help us get there safely and unseen. Now, hand, please."

CHAPTER 24

YOU DID WHAT?

ARIEL WALKED DOWN THE drive and checked the road again. "Where are they?" she wondered. "They've been gone for hours."

Ruddy, too, was disquieted. He sensed *something was wrong*. He had visions of his daughter's bike crumpled on the roadside and Meri thrown in a ditch. "I'll take the car and start looking for them."

"Call Echo to go with you," said Ariel. "Tell him to bring his medical bag. Just in case."

Ruddy and Ariel exchanged worried looks. Ruddy nodded and pulled out his phone. "Just in case."

As Ariel's anxiety grew, the rustling in the spruce trees in the backyard increased. Gus, who had been keeping pace with her, barked. Then Ariel heard the wind: *They're coming.*

She peered at the road, saw nothing, and turned to the sky. *Oh surely, they had not,* she told the wind.

Echo and Sahara had just pulled into the drive and Ruddy was about to trade places with Sahara in the passenger seat to begin the search for Meri when Ariel shouted for the others to wait.

She pointed to two specks amid the clouds, floating nearer.

They all gathered in the backyard and watched the specks grow larger.

It was Meri and Trouble. But why were they Up There?

When Ariel realized that the two were having difficulty in the agitated wind, she lifted into the air to help them. She met them aloft, wrapped her arm around Meri's waist, and said to Trouble, "I've got her."

"Soft landing," Trouble instructed in an exhausted voice. "Watch the ankle."

A tired Trouble stumbled as she landed, but Ariel, with her precious cargo clasped tightly, glided to earth.

* * *

Ariel had barely touched ground with Meri in her arms before Echo was kneeling over his granddaughter and examining her ankle. He pronounced it a sprain but still insisted that it be X-rayed at the clinic. After it was confirmed that the ankle was not broken, Echo wrapped it tightly and ordered elevation, ice, and bed rest.

Back at the house, Ruddy handed Meri her Harriet doll and tucked her into bed. The child was so exhausted she didn't even count all the stuffed animals sharing the bed with her. Instead, Ruddy verified that all were present.

Watching her father fuss with the covers, Meri mumbled sleepily, "What does bed rest mean?"

"You have to stay off the ankle for a few days," Ruddy explained, propping a pillow under her foot. "Keep it up and the ice pack on."

Meri wrinkled her nose. "It's too cold."

"You'll be back to running around in a few days."

"A few days!" Meri's eyes shot open, and she rose on her elbows. "But Wren and I are playing disc golf tomorrow."

"We'll reschedule," said her father.

Meri flopped back onto her pillow. "This is terrible."

Ruddy sat on the edge of the bed. "Meri, what were you doing with Trouble today?"

Meri yawned. "We went to see an old house. It was creepy."

"A house? Why were you there?" asked Ruddy.

Meri's words began to slur. The painkiller that Echo had given Meri was starting to take effect. She would be asleep in moments, and Ruddy didn't have all the answers he wanted.

"What else do you do with Trouble?" he pressed.

Meri gave him a puzzled look. "We ride bikes together, and she takes me flying at night . . ."

Concern froze Ruddy. Meri was not allowed to go Up There without her mother.

"Where do you go—at night?" he asked, as casually as he could.

In a drowsy voice, Meri said, "Up There is so pretty at night, Daddy. You should see it. And it feels different. We're so high, I can almost touch the stars."

Ruddy's concern grew. He said, "Meri, you're not supposed to go Up There without . . ." but the child was asleep.

✳ ✳ ✳

When Ruddy entered the living room, Ariel could tell that something had happened.

Instead of pulling up a chair beside the rocker where Ariel sat, Ruddy took a stance near the fireplace. His silence, and the fact that he had not given her shoulder a comforting squeeze as he passed, a signal between them that all was well with their

152

child, unnerved her. Sahara and Echo, seated on the sofa, and Trouble, ensconced on the floor by the coffee table, did not notice that something was amiss.

Ariel glanced nervously from Ruddy to Trouble. She knew that Ruddy wasn't Trouble's biggest fan. He found her presence in his home disruptive, and maybe after today's events, he was right. But Ariel wasn't ready to think the worst of her cousin. They were family; they shared a gift. As she had explained to Ruddy, "There's no one like us, and I have to hold on to as much of us as I can."

Before Ariel could ask Ruddy what was wrong, he fired a question at Trouble, "Why did you take Meri to an abandoned house? Meri knows she is not allowed to enter strange houses."

"An abandoned house?" a confused Ariel asked Trouble. "Is that how she got hurt?"

Trouble shrugged away Ariel's concern. "She was with me. Everything was cool."

"How do you figure that?" persisted Ruddy.

Trouble glared at him. "Because it's *our* house. The Hamilton homestead."

Ariel and Sahara both sat up straighter. "What?" they said in unison.

With a roll of her eyes, Trouble enunciated, "You know, the place where my grandma Clarissa and your Anne grew up."

Puzzled, Echo asked, "How do you know this?"

"I know because Grandma Clarissa told me about it. She described it to me a million times. She missed that place." Trouble lifted her chin. "And I wanted to see it."

Ariel asked, "But how did you find it?"

Trouble was not looking as confident now. When Ruddy moved, Trouble flashed him a wary look. "I go out at night sometimes and search for it."

"You *fly* at night," said Ruddy, accusation heavy in his voice.

"Well, I'm not supposed to let anyone see me in the daylight," Trouble grumped. "Those are *your* rules."

Ruddy had never wanted to shake someone so badly. "Tell Ariel who you take with you, Trouble. On these night flights."

With a puzzled look, Ariel turned to her cousin. "Trouble?"

Trouble averted her gaze. "Sometimes Meri comes with me," she said softly.

Ariel launched herself, sending the rocker rocking. "You what? You take my daughter Up There at night?"

Sahara rose and gestured for calm. "Let her explain, Ariel."

Ariel ignored her mother. Her voice rose, "You take my five-year-old daughter, who doesn't know nearly enough about her gift, flying at night! My daughter, who could fall out of the sky and die!"

Suddenly, wind blasted through the open window, knocking over a lamp. Trouble scrambled to her feet, casting a nervous glance toward Ariel. With hands up, as if to fend off Ariel, Trouble shouted, "I hold her hand the whole time! I swear! I never let her go. Not for a second. I would never do that."

With hair flying and hands fisted at her side, Ariel stepped toward Trouble. Ruddy quickly grabbed her arm. She wanted to throw Trouble out of the house, keep her far away from Meri.

"Why would you do such a foolish thing?" Ariel stared at Trouble. "Why would you endanger Meri like that?"

A tear slid down Trouble's cheek. "Because Meri needed it."

Ariel remained incensed. "I will take Meri walking the air at night when she's ready. She knows that." Brushing her wind-electrified hair aside in exasperation, Ariel added, "I don't know what you were thinking, Trouble."

Sensing there was more behind Trouble's actions, Echo

leaned forward and asked, "Trouble, why did you think Meri needed to fly at night?"

The young woman shifted her feet. Finally, she addressed Ariel and Ruddy. "Do you remember the time at school when that kid accused her of carrying a gun? She heard you talking about homeschooling and was afraid you'd make her leave school."

Ruddy sighed impatiently. "What does this have to do with the night flying?"

"Meri felt like a failure." Trouble looked at them with pleading eyes. "She didn't trust herself. I thought-I thought doing something she'd never done before would . . ."

"Build her confidence," said Echo.

Trouble glanced at him. "Yeah. Sort of. I thought it might help her. I mean, I got such a buzz my first time at night."

Echo nodded in understanding, but Ariel couldn't speak.

She was remembering her first time walking the night air. She'd been afraid and exhilarated at the same time. In the darkness, with only the stars for company and guidance, she felt herself expanding. She'd returned from that walk feeling strong and empowered as well as humbled.

Ariel glanced at Sahara. From the expression on Sahara's face, Ariel knew her mother was remembering that night as well, how Ariel had stepped from the total darkness and into her mother's waiting arms. They'd sat on the grass in the back-yard, looking up at the sky, and young Ariel couldn't stop chattering about all she'd seen and all she'd felt.

For a few beats, Ariel hated Trouble for stealing that moment—Meri's first night flight—from her. It was supposed to be *their* thing, *their* mother-daughter moment. It was supposed to be wonderful, not a guilty secret that Meri felt she had to hide from Ariel and Ruddy.

Recognizing Ariel's disappointment, Sahara tried to calm her daughter. "Ariel, what is done is done."

Ariel knew her mother was right. She had to forget this sadness, but it would be some time before she forgave Trouble or trusted her with Meri.

Suddenly tired, Ariel held out her hand for Ruddy, and they started for the stairs. In a grave voice, she said, "Tomorrow we investigate that house."

CHAPTER 25

THERE WAS A HOUSE ON A HILL

A DENSE CURTAIN OF foliage successfully hid the Hamilton House and its forbidding hill from the road. "How did you find it?" Ariel asked Trouble.

Trouble, eagerly hovering between the front and back seats of Ariel's Subaru, said, "Grandma told me it was always windy on the Hamilton homestead. So, I flew over the countryside looking for old houses on hills in places that offered good updrafts."

Ariel had to admit that was a smart approach.

Sahara assessed their location. "This can't be more than five miles from our farm. I never knew we lived so close to Mom's family home. She never talked about it."

The woods had reclaimed whatever drive there had once been. Ariel put the car in gear and pressed through the wall of foliage, which snapped shut behind them, leaving them in a dark tunnel of trees, bushes, and bone-jarring ruts.

When the car bottomed on the rough terrain, Ariel muttered, "We should have used Echo's car." Doctor Echo Starling, a former fair-weather North Carolinian still not trusting of Minnesota winters despite surviving more than thirty of them, maintained an all-wheel-drive SUV. It was capable of delivering him to any patient, in an emergency, in any weather—and it had a high carriage.

They continued muscling their way through the dark jungle of strangling woods, until suddenly they burst into a sunshine-bright clearing and stopped. All three women got out of the car and stood, blinking with disbelief at the steep hill before them and the ramshackle house sitting at the apex like a topper on a wedding cake.

"Isn't it incredible?" whispered Trouble with awe in her voice.

Ariel examined the area around them. "There's no drive to the house."

Sahara said, "Perhaps they parked at the bottom of the hill and walked."

"Or flew," suggested Trouble.

In winter, the hill would have challenged the most daring skier. In summer, it cascaded from the house in an untamed, multicolored veil of grasses and wildflowers. Amid the tall bluestem, switchgrass, and Indiangrass was a canvas of white campion, orange butterfly weed, golden black-eyed Susans, purple prairie phlox, and pink fireweed.

Trouble started up the hill on foot. "What are you waiting for? Let's see what's inside."

"Don't step on the flowers," called Ariel, hoping to save some of Mother Nature's work from Trouble's careless steps.

"They're just weeds," Trouble scoffed and proceeded.

As Sahara and Ariel followed, Ariel felt a change in the air's mood. The wind swirled around her like an exuberant child: *Welcome, Hamilton blood.*

Sahara, who was in decent shape for a woman in her sixties, began to huff halfway up the steep hill. Ariel instructed the wind: *Help her.* And suddenly, a tailwind so strong it made them stumble gave them a push.

Flinging her arms over her head, Trouble laughed. "Isn't this the greatest place?"

When they reached the top, the women stopped in their tracks. The wind buffeted them in an unending assault. In the yard, a lone apple tree huddled, gnarled and bent, sculpted by the wind. It had learned to stay low and live.

The tree wasn't the only thing that had figured out how to survive in this place. The wind-ravaged house stood two stories tall, too proud to hunker down, but that pride came at a cost. Dangling shutters banged against the house, the porch railing had been ripped halfway off, and shingles were missing from the roof.

Trouble kicked aside a withered apple and started up the steps to the porch.

"Careful," said Ariel, eyeing the hole where her daughter's ankle had been lodged. She suspected nothing in this house would pass inspection.

Trouble reached the door. Glancing back at them, she warned, "Keep your head down. There might be bats."

"Bats," muttered Sahara with a shiver, as she and Ariel skirted the hole in the steps and joined Trouble.

Trouble opened the door cautiously, but this time, the house did not expel a cloud of creatures.

With caution, they stepped inside.

The house creaked and moaned around the women. A strong breeze entered via the broken windows, swirling dust motes.

They stared at the ragged rugs, the broken chairs, and a cracked kitchen table made of walnut. Stuffing exploded through the worn and eaten damask upholstery of a sad-looking Victorian sofa. "What do you think lives in there?" asked Ariel, eyeing the vintage mess.

The first floor was a single area serving as living room, dining room, and kitchen. Stairs led to the second floor. Looking out the kitchen window at an outhouse with tall lilac bushes on each side, Sahara said, "No indoor facilities."

Trouble headed for the rickety staircase. Ariel instinctively began a warning but stopped, knowing it would do no good. She followed her curious cousin. While eager Trouble took the steps by two, Ariel tested each one before trusting it.

Upstairs, they found three bedrooms, each with faded and water-stained floral wallpaper similar in pattern and condition to the wallcovering downstairs. Rain and snow had entered the shattered windows, leaving a moldy smell on the disintegrating mattresses and linen.

When Sahara joined them, Ariel asked her mother, "How long do you think it's been vacant?"

"No idea. It's hard to imagine my mother living here. It's a depressing place."

Trouble, kneeling on the floor, brushed away a layer of dust. "It must have been happy at one time. Look."

Sahara and Ariel crouched beside Trouble. In a corner of the floor were carved initials: A H and C H etched in a circle of stars. Anne Hamilton and Clarissa Hamilton.

"They must have shared this room," said Ariel.

Trouble's fingers traced over her grandmother's initials, and she heaved a sigh. "She loved this place. More than anything."

Sahara asked, "She never come back, not even for a visit?"

Trouble said, "Grandma claimed it was too hard here with

the wind always reaching for her. She gave up walking the wind, you know, when she got to Missouri. Never told my grandfather about her gift. She thought it was the only way to keep him. Grandpa was a decent guy, but he didn't believe in 'hogwash,' as he called anything that disagreed with his views."

Ariel felt sympathy for Clarissa. She knew how difficult the decision to leave the sky forever would have been for her. Ariel had given up riding the air after she had unintentionally injured her best friend Blinka in a wind-related biking accident. They had been only sixteen at the time. The wind, summoned by Ariel to make them go faster, had gotten out of control, and Blinka had ended up in the hospital. Ariel had never forgiven herself. For years, afraid she might hurt someone else, Ariel had denied the wind and her place Up There.

Trouble poked through the closets and wrestled open dresser drawers, swollen with age and damp. "According to Grandma, she and Anne were born the same year, first Clarissa then Anne," said Trouble. "But Grandma Clarissa's mother died in childbirth, so Anne's mother, Annabelle Hamilton, raised them both as sisters. There were never any men around. I don't think either Anne or Clarissa knew their fathers."

"Annabelle must have been an amazing woman. How did they live here, feed themselves? How did she raise two children alone?" wondered Sahara aloud, staring out the bedroom window. She could see no neighbors, no fields once planted with crops. There was no barn, but there was an overgrown garden and what appeared to have once been a chicken coop.

Ariel turned to Trouble, who continued to rummage. "What are you looking for?" she asked.

"Anything," said Trouble, lifting her hands in disappointment that they weren't helping her snoop. "Anything that says something about us, our family, who we were and are. Why do we have this stupid gift, and what are we supposed to do with it? I mean, it has to be of more use than knocking a snot-nosed kid off a slide."

Sahara and Ariel exchanged glances. Neither mentioned how Anne and Ariel each had used their gift to ride storms, attempting to quell their destructive force.

Sahara asked, "Well, what have you done with your gift?"

"Jack shit," said Trouble, a note of futility in her voice. "All I can do is go Up There and float around. I can't talk to the wind or hear it, like Ariel and Meri. I can't ask what I should be doing. I just feel this urge to be Up There and find myself in the sky. I'm basically drifting through a meaningless life."

Sahara approached Trouble and enfolded her in a hug. "Honey, I don't know if we will find any answers here."

Trouble pushed away. "There have to be." She brushed the bangs from her teary eyes. "I need to know more!"

CHAPTER 26

COVERED IN SNOW-IN-SUMMER

SILENTLY, ARIEL AND SAHARA joined Trouble in her search. They looked under dusty beds and smelly mattresses. They swept their hands over filthy shelves and pushed the cracked dishes and cups aside. They even shined a light from Ariel's cell phone into the innards of the decaying sofa but found . . . nothing.

There were no notes or messages tucked into the many books on the shelves, books that disintegrated in their hands as they thumbed through them. Again, no letters were hidden inside the rotting sleeves of the records for the Victrola, which had been turned into a nest by some unknown creature. It felt as if the past had slipped away from them.

Finally, an exhausted Ariel and Trouble leaned against the warped kitchen counter, while Sahara wandered the first floor again, reexamining every nook and cranny they had already searched. She turned to them, hands on hips, and said,

"Where did Annabelle go? Something tells me she stayed here until the very end."

"You think she died in this house?" asked Ariel.

"We didn't find her remains nestled with the mice in one of the beds," noted Trouble.

Sahara stepped to the kitchen window. Could she smell the lilacs by the outhouse, or was that her imagination? It was late for lilacs to be blooming, and the bushes were old and past their prime. She walked to the back door and stepped onto the stoop. Lilac air whistled around her.

Ariel followed her mother, and Trouble joined them.

"Do you smell that?" Sahara asked.

They inhaled the scents not only of the lilacs but also the honeysuckle bush on the opposite side of the yard. Sahara stepped off the stoop and walked toward the large honeysuckle, which beckoned with a powerful aroma. Like the lilac, it was old and yet still full of life. Sahara was not gifted with flight, but she was a Hamilton and something here demanded her attention. She noticed a mound under the honeysuckle covered in small white flowers that brought a smile to her face.

"Snow-in-summer," she whispered, kneeling to run her hands through the ground cover. "I haven't seen it, or even thought about it, for years."

"It's a lovely plant," said Ariel, admiring the delicate silver leaves and the tiny flowers. "It looks like a fresh snowfall."

"Your grandmother Anne loved this flower," Sahara said.

Trouble gauged the mound and suddenly stretched out beside it in a corpse pose. "I think we found Annabelle."

Ariel and Sahara looked from Trouble's cadaver position to the blanket of white flowers. Ariel frowned. "But who buried her?"

"Somebody had to. She couldn't have buried herself," said

Trouble, sitting up. "Does this mean there are more of us somewhere in the world?"

"Why do you think it is a relative?" asked Ariel.

"Because who else could get through that wind," said Trouble, motioning toward the hill. "This place is thoroughly Hamilton."

Sahara, who had continued to absently stroke the snow-in-summer, suddenly stopped. "There's something here." She pushed her fingers deeper through the covering of flowers.

Trouble lifted a suspicious eyebrow. "I hope it's not Annabelle's elbow you're digging up."

It was a cookie tin, square, with the design of a holiday scene—a family riding a horse-drawn sleigh—on the lid.

The women gathered in a tight circle on the grass and stared at the tin.

"Well, open it," said an excited Trouble.

Sahara struggled with the lid, which was welded in place by rust, dirt, and age. Finally, she popped open the tin. Inside was a single page written in cramped and wobbly penmanship.

It was the last will and testament of Annabelle Hamilton.

Once upon a time there was an old house sitting on a hill in the middle of Minnesota. The house craved new paint, and the wind, which was wicked strong on that hill, played lovingly with us but mercilessly with the broken shutters. From the outside, the house appeared lonely, perhaps even haunted, which kept the curious away. Inside, it was anything but. It breathed with marvelous books, dancing music, and strong hugs. In the house lived three women. And each of those women could fly. I was one of them.

I raised Anne Hamilton and Clarissa Hamilton in that house as if they were sisters. What one got the other got. While Anne was my birth child, Clarissa was my adopted daughter. Her mother, my dear sister, died in childbirth. Both Anne and Clarissa were loving children, extremely talented in the sky, and came into their gift of flight at about the same time, when they were seven. I took them into the air then to help them understand what it meant to be a Hamilton.

Their favorite times were the family flights at night, streaking into the stars, high over the trees and country-side. We listened to the wind inside us and went where it took us. When we flew home on those cold nights, we always warmed ourselves with mugs of hot chocolate. These family flights were a celebration—of who we were and what we had been given.

I taught Anne and Clarissa ordinary school subjects as well as how to ride the air. Homeschooling seemed the best option when they were young and unable to control their gift. I scavenged books in yard sales and in the trash bins behind the school in Cosette. I taught them at home until the grade of nine, when they started at the local high school. By then, they had learned a measure of control and ability to hide their gift, and they were eager to stretch their social skills. I trusted they would be smart and keep our secret, but I hadn't counted on the vulnerability of the human teenage heart.

When Clarissa fell in love, my happiness for her was tinged with sadness. In my experience, and in the experience of many Hamilton women, the male of the species did not take kindly to women who were more gifted than they. We dented their egos, threatened their masculinity, and did not always listen to them. We were not ordinary, and, when it comes right down to it, few men value the extraordinary. Extraordinary requires work.

Therefore, I was not surprised when the young man Clarissa had given her heart to eventually spurned her. I had warned her not to tell him about her gift, nor to show him. But she was so young, so eager to share everything of herself with him.

His departure from Clarissa's life, just days after their high school graduation, sent her into a tailspin. She refused to accompany us on night flights because he said only freaks could ride the air. She ate little, slept little, and spent days mooning around the house. She only went outside to feed the chickens, which had always been her favorites. As she flung chicken feed, tears dropped to the ground with the pellets. Anne and I tried everything to make her realize she was better off without that arrogant nitwit. She didn't believe us. To this day, I hope he lands in the hottest spot in hell.

On the night of her twentieth birthday, Clarissa left her bed and floated into the sky, never to be seen or heard from again. She did not say good-bye or leave a note.

✳ ✳ ✳

Trouble interrupted Sahara, who was reading the will aloud. "Grandma regretted that. That night haunted her. Said she stood in the doorway of their bedrooms, trying to figure how to tell Anne and Annabelle of her decision: to end her life."

Ariel was shocked. "She was going to kill herself?"

"Grandma had planned to just let the wind take her wherever it wanted," Trouble said. "She had packed no food, water, or money. She thought she would eventually grow so weak that she would just drop out of the sky, plummeting to a quick death on hard earth. Grandma didn't want to fall into a lake or a river. She couldn't swim."

"She was choosing between death by falling or drowning?" said Ariel, aghast.

Trouble noted, "Grandma considered drowning a horrible way to go."

"That poor girl. She must have been in unbearable pain," said Sahara softly.

Trouble gave them a grin. "But the wind wouldn't let her fall. It whisked her through the nights and days until it could gently deposit her in a field in Missouri, where my grandfather discovered her."

Ariel said, "So she found her love, after all."

Trouble thought for a moment, a frown forming on her face. "I don't know. She never seemed overly affectionate toward Grandpa Jack. She maintained the farm for him—kept everything running, meals on the table on time, bills paid, house clean. They went to church together, but that was about it. They didn't socialize or celebrate much, except when my mother Brooke was born."

Trouble continued, "To celebrate their child's birth, Grandpa baked a cake for Grandma—the worst one and the only one he ever baked, according to Grandma. But I think the gesture made her happy."

Ariel imagined a man and a woman eating cake in bed together, a baby tucked between them. It sounded romantic, but Ariel doubted that moment of closeness between Clarissa and Jack had changed their lives. She suspected it had not because, no matter what, Clarissa would always miss Up There.

Ariel nudged Sahara to read more.

* * *

Eventually, Anne and I realized that Clarissa was not returning, no matter how much we scanned the sky for her. She was gone, and our world changed. Anne, who had planned to attend college, decided to stay home with me—a decision I detested and argued against. I knew this house and this hill were my place, but they were not Anne's.

When she met Will Stevens at a carnival in Cosette, I had never seen Anne so happy. At last, the house came to life again. We danced and laughed, and after Anne and Will were married, my circumstances improved considerably. I didn't have to depend on the garden and the chickens for my nourishment. Anne visited me at night, floating through the sky like an angel delivering stories of her life and baskets of food. When she brought Will to meet me the first time, they parked the truck at the bottom of the hill and climbed to the house. He shook my hand and said, "That's quite a hill, Miss Hamilton."

I said, "We like it."

He laughed as the wind stole his hat from his head.

We watched as the eager air greeted Anne, wrapping around her, lifting her into the air. I slanted my eye toward Will to assess his reaction to this reunion and saw the most beautiful expression on his face. "Isn't she marvelous?" he whispered, not taking his eyes from his laughing, flying wife.

That's when I knew Will Stevens was not like other men. He was a good match for my Anne, and he became a good friend to me.

If you are reading this, I am long gone. And if Anne has followed my instructions, she has buried me under the honeysuckle so I can always smell its sweetness. My guess is that Will helped her; he always did. They knew I never wanted to leave my hill or the wind I'd found here. We Hamilton women are partial to our winds.

I really have nothing to leave anyone, except for this house, this hill, and this wind.

Anne brought her daughter, baby Sahara, to visit. I do love babies, but I could tell as I held that precious child in my arms that she did not inherit our gift. My sympathies, Sahara, but I have a feeling you will have a gifted daughter.

Since Anne is quite happy with her wind on the Stevens farm and my dear Clarissa is long gone, I pass my house and my hill to the daughter of Sahara Stevens. If my great-granddaughter has not found her wind elsewhere, maybe it is waiting for her here.

Love to all those who come after me.
Annabelle Hamilton
Witnessed by: William Stevens

✱ ✱ ✱

Ariel and Trouble stared at each other, one in shock and the other in disbelief.

Before Ariel realized what was happening, Trouble scrambled to her feet and raced down the hill.

"Trouble, come back," yelled Ariel.

CHAPTER 27

WHERE THERE'S A WILL . . .

TROUBLE STORMED INTO THE house, pushing past Ruddy, taking the stairs two at a time, and finishing by slamming her bedroom door.

"What's going on?" he asked as Ariel ran past him, rushing after Trouble.

Sahara entered more slowly, more calmly, but said not a word. Instead, she handed a piece of paper to Ruddy and continued to the card table in the corner of the living room. There Echo was playing Crazy Eights with Meri, whose injured ankle was cradled by an ice pack and propped on a pile of pillows. Sahara leaned against Echo, her hand on his shoulder. Long attuned to her feelings, he placed his hand over hers. "Whatever it is, we'll fix it," reassured her husband, so skilled at maintaining composure in the worst circumstances.

She sighed and kissed the top of his bald head.

Meri's eyes went from one adult in the room to another.

Finally, she pushed the ice pack off her ankle, limped to Ruddy, and sat beside him on the sofa. He absently patted Meri's arm as he continued to read the paper Sahara had given him.

"Daddy? What's wrong with Trouble and Mama? Did they have a fight?"

"I don't know, sweetheart."

Pointing to the paper in Ruddy's hand, she asked, "What is that?"

"A problem," he said.

* * *

Ariel tapped on Trouble's bedroom door. "Trouble, open up."

"Go away!" yelled Trouble.

"We need to talk," said Ariel.

Silence.

"I'm not leaving until you let me in," Ariel warned. "You found the homestead. Isn't that what you wanted? I don't understand why you're so upset."

Suddenly, the door flew open with such force that Ariel fell back a step. Trouble glared at her. "You wouldn't. You have everything! And I have nothing!"

"You have us," Ariel argued. "We're family."

"Family, ha! You didn't even know I existed. No one knows who I am."

"Trouble, calm down. Let's sit down and figure this out . . ."

Trouble shoved Ariel, forcing her to take another step back. With fire in her eyes, she advanced. "How do you really know I am who I say I am?" Trouble asked. "I don't have any ID to prove it. Are you just so gullible that you take in every tramp who comes along? What kind of mother are you?"

Ariel told herself to remain calm. Her cousin was in pain and striking out, but she was landing punches in Ariel's most vulnerable spot: her ability to be a fitting mother, especially to a child as special as Meri.

"I know you walk the air like me," said Ariel, trying to sound reasonable. "Who else could you be, but a Hamilton?"

But Trouble wasn't finished. "You don't appreciate what you have. You live in a house mired in secrets and fears. Ruddy's afraid of who you really are . . ."

"Stop it!" Ariel snapped.

"And your daughter's confused by all your stupid rules."

"They're for her protection!"

Trouble shook her head and with a sly look asked, "Or are they for your protection, Ariel?"

Pain and anger mixed in Ariel, and flurry of air whipped through the hallway.

Trouble noticed and said, "What are you going to do now, Ariel? Summon the wind to throw me down the stairs? That's a good example for the kid."

Ariel peered down from the landing at the top of the stairs and saw everyone in the living room staring at them, listening, waiting. She saw a look of horror on her daughter's face.

Seeing his wife in distress, Ruddy yelled, "Enough, Trouble!"

Trouble gave him that cocky grin he detested and taunted, "Sending me to my room, Ruddy? Playing the strong husband and father?"

Her tone and her words had Ruddy bristling. He barged up the stairs toward the women on the landing. Ariel had never seen that expression on her husband and best friend. As he reached them, she placed a hand on his arm. Still believing she could defuse the situation, she said, "Ruddy. She didn't mean . . ."

"Oh, yes, she did." Through gritted teeth, he said to Trouble, "Get out of our house!"

For a moment, Trouble was too shocked to respond. Then she shouted, "Fine!" Whirling, she raced into the bedroom and slammed the door.

Fifteen minutes later, Trouble marched down the stairs, backpack flung over her shoulder, long hair swinging defiantly. Ariel followed her.

Meri leaped to her feet, winced, and hobbled toward Trouble as she stormed toward the front door. "Trouble, don't go! Mama, don't let her go."

But Ariel stood silently watching her cousin, the only other woman of her kind, walk out the door.

* * *

Sahara and Echo followed Trouble. They found her cursing and struggling with the bike rack on the back of Ariel's car. Before leaving the Hamilton House, they had collected Meri's monkey backpack and strapped Trouble's and Meri's bicycles to the bike rack on the Subaru.

Echo approached the young woman. "Let me," he said, in a gentle voice.

Trouble turned away and wiped her eyes as he fiddled with the contrary straps of the bike rack.

Finally, he freed the bike and handed it to her.

Sahara asked, "Where will you go?"

Refusing to meet their eyes, Trouble said, "I don't know."

Sahara and Echo exchanged looks.

"I do," said Sahara.

CHAPTER 28

COSETTE'S NEWEST LAND TYCOON

THE TALL, WAVING SUMMER grasses of the meadow hid Ariel from sight, as they once did when she was young and miserable in her heavy shoes. In times of distress, her mother always knew where to find her. So did Ruddy. Today she sat, in Ruddy's opinion, dangerously close to the edge of the cliff—her preferred spot. He approached her, spooned in behind her, his legs stretched on either side of her. He was her buttress, and she leaned back against his chest with an exhausted and frustrated sigh.

With arms wrapped around her, he said, "Tell me about this house that has everyone in an uproar."

When she spoke, he heard both puzzlement and awe in her voice. "It is an incredible place. The wind is tremendous."

"Really?" He didn't like the sound of that.

"It is desolate and inhospitable—a shabby old house on top of a hill with a ferocious wind guarding it. It's falling apart, and the path up to it would challenge a Humvee or a mountain goat."

Hearing hesitation in her voice, he asked, "And yet?"

She twisted to look up at him. "And yet, I felt welcomed there." Her eyes widened. "Ruddy, that place recognized me."

Ruddy froze for a moment with fear. He heard temptation in her voice and tightened his arms around her.

She leaned her head back against his shoulder and continued in a soft voice, "I felt my ancestors there, Ruddy. My grandmother Anne grew up there. It was where she learned about her gift and first felt the wind inside her. She was happy there with her mother, Annabelle, and Clarissa, who was the nearest thing to a sister."

"Clarissa was Trouble's grandmother, the one who disappeared, right?" asked Ruddy.

"Yes. It must have hit Annabelle and Anne hard when Clarissa vanished without a word. Trouble said Clarissa always wanted to return home but never had the courage. Instead, she filled Trouble's head with stories of the magical house where the Hamilton women were happy and reigned oblivious to conventions."

"Being unconventional *is* a Hamilton trait, it seems," said Ruddy.

"And our curse," Ariel said.

Ruddy knew that while they were growing up and for years after, Ariel had run from the idea of being different. They might never have married if she hadn't finally come to accept who she truly was and had trusted him to see the extraordinary in her.

Ariel smiled for the first time since he joined her in the meadow. "You married a freak," she teased.

He returned her smile. "I love freaks."

Ariel and Ruddy relaxed as evening light submersed the meadow. They had earned this quiet time. It had taken several stories and songs to settle Meri for the night, after an argumentative dinner. Meri had insisted that her mother go after Trouble, but her parents had maintained, "Trouble needs time to herself."

"I don't get it," grumbled Meri. "What was in that house that made everybody so grouchy?"

Soon the fireflies would be out flashing their love songs, and the owls would be hunting. The air in the meadow gently sang with the song of crickets. The serenity was the kind that got inside Ruddy and made him thankful for his life with Ariel. He wouldn't give this up for anything.

Ariel shifted in Ruddy's lap and pressed her cheek against his shoulder. He felt her warm breath on his neck as she whispered, "What am I going to do about that house?"

A moment of déjà vu descended on Ruddy. Years ago, they'd sat in this same spot, discussing the fate of the farm where they now lived. Ariel had just learned that she had inherited the farm from her mother. Back then, still unsure of where she belonged—of her place Up There or Down Here—Ariel hadn't wanted the farm. Now he knew she—and he—couldn't live anywhere else.

"You seem to be constantly saddled with property that you don't want," he teased. "I never dreamed that I would marry a land tycoon."

She laughed. "Seriously, I don't even know if Annabelle's will is legal."

"Your grandfather witnessed it, but it has never been notarized," said Ruddy. "There are probably back taxes owed on the property."

"No doubt. I bet Grandma and Grandpa paid the taxes

until they died. They took care of Annabelle, as much as she would permit. She was independent and certainly sounded stubborn about leaving her house and her wind. But no one has paid the taxes in the last thirty years because we weren't aware the property even existed."

Ruddy said, "I don't like the idea of that tumbledown house tempting Trouble and Meri again. We should burn it down."

He felt Ariel stiffen in his arms. "Trouble would kill me!" she cried.

With exasperation in his voice, Ruddy said, "Then give it to Trouble!"

"I can't. The place is rotting away. She'll get hurt if she tries to live there."

"So don't do anything with it," suggested Ruddy. "Let the house fall down and the wind take it away."

The loss of that bit of Hamilton heritage bothered Ariel. "That's a sad ending to the Hamiltons."

"It isn't an ending. You, Meri, and Trouble will carry on the family gift."

"I don't know," said Ariel, in a considering voice. "Both Grandmother Anne and Great-Grandmother Annabelle believed that we are pulled to places where 'our' wind whispers for us."

Ruddy's breath caught. *Would that damn house lure his Ariel away from him?* Waiting for her to make her decision had his stomach churning.

Slowly, as the first firefly blinked into view, she snuggled closer to him and said, "My wind lives here with you and Meri."

Contentment settled on him like an evening dusk. He held her and looked at the sky stretching far before them, far into the future.

CHAPTER 29

NO COUCH
IN THE TURRET

TROUBLE WANTED THE TURRET room, but Sahara said, "Absolutely not. That's Echo's."

"But I've always wanted to live in a tower," Trouble pleaded. The turret was a circular room attached to one corner of the large Starling house, and through its many windows, Echo could see all of Lake Cosette. It was his favorite place to read, drink morning coffee, and watch the loons. Kind-hearted Echo would relinquish the spot to Trouble, but Sahara would not think of it.

"There is no bed in the turret. Not even a couch."

"I'll sleep on the floor."

Sahara led her troublesome guest down the hall from the turret room and opened another door. "You'll have the lilac room. It's a soothing place and still has a lake view."

Tossing her backpack on the double bed and eyeing the walls painted a soft lavender, Trouble pouted, "I hate purple."

* * *

Sahara and Echo's house, which had belonged to Doc Weatherly and his wife before the doctor retired and sold it to Echo, was what Trouble and her grandmother would call "a fancy house." The elegant Queen Anne-style house was large and sat amid a manicured landscape, thanks to Mrs. Weatherly. Tulips crawled from the cold ground in spring and perennials waved in summer. Hard-to-contain shrubbery gave Sahara and Echo privacy, and a number of trees in the big yard kept the two-story house comfortable on hot days and maddened Echo in leaf-dropping season. The Weatherly landscape was planned, orderly, and quite different from the wildflower gardens Sahara had planted—then let take over—on the Stevens farm.

While the yard still carried the regimentation of Mrs. Weatherly's spirit, the inside of the house was thoroughly Sahara. She had painted and neatened it after her wedding to Echo seven years ago, and then promptly let it all dissolve into homey disorder with books stacked everywhere, sweaters draped over chairs, shoes left wherever one stepped out of them, and Meri's games and toys escaping the shelves. She had warned Echo that her housekeeping was subpar, but he hadn't cared. He understood his wife's priorities—writing came before cleaning and gardening.

That night, after the dinner dishes were cleared, Trouble, Sahara, and Echo sat in uncomfortable silence at the kitchen table. While Trouble fiddled with the salt and pepper shakers, Sahara nudged Echo. He had experience with people who refused to talk and could crack the most stubborn cases.

She lifted a questioning brow at him, and he sighed. With a mug of coffee clasped in his hands, he casually leaned toward Trouble. "Why were you so angry with Ariel?"

Trouble looked at him with distrust. "I don't know why I should tell you, you'll just take her side."

"I was trained not to take sides," said Echo.

When Echo didn't press, just kept staring at her with those understanding eyes, Trouble shifted in her seat. She did not like when people tried to get their way with a facade of kindness. She wanted to tell Echo that she saw through him, but instead found herself admitting in a forlorn voice, "I have nowhere to go."

"Is that really true?" asked Echo.

"Ariel wants me to believe all this family stuff," said Trouble, "but when it comes down to it, when I really need her, where is she? She has a home and Ruddy and Meri. She doesn't need that house.

"And you do?" asked Sahara.

She gave Sahara and Echo a defiant look. "Yes! There's nothing left for me back home. Grandma and Grandpa are gone. Grandpa's farm is gone. There is nothing and no one holding me there."

Trouble was insistent, but Sahara wondered if that was true. She heard a hesitancy in the woman's voice; Trouble was hiding something.

Secrets, Sahara thought. Hamilton women always came with secrets.

∗ ∗ ∗

That night lying in bed surrounded by all that disgusting purple, Trouble thought of Hamilton House. When she had started to climb the hill to her ancestors' house, she'd felt part of something greater than her.

She'd felt belonging.

Trouble believed Sahara and Echo could never understand

her or her feelings. He was a well-liked doctor, and she was a successful writer. They had no idea what it felt like to be so alone and so . . . purposeless. Trouble had been wandering for a long time.

Now, when a home was within her grasp, it was Ariel's.

Trouble kicked off the covers and began to plan. She lifted the small sewing box from her backpack and ran her hand over the fabric lid. The box had belonged to her grandmother. Once it had contained spools of thread, needles, and pins. Now it held the ashy remains of Clarissa Hamilton.

Ariel didn't need that house on the hill. She already had a farm, a husband, a child. She had a gift that was stronger than Trouble could even dream of possessing. She had a life.

Well, Trouble was going to get what should have come to her—a life as beautiful as Ariel's.

As Grandpa Jack used to say, "You can whine or you can do, Trouble."

Trouble secured the lid on the box. With a loving pat, she said, "We're going home, Grandma."

CHAPTER 30

FRIES WITH A SIDE OF REGRET

TIMOTHY LEE HAD NEVER really been a father, so he had no idea how one went about being a grandfather. But he was determined to try. He savored the juicy cheeseburger, flat-grilled just the way he liked it, in Marta's Diner and considered ideas for introducing himself to his granddaughter, Meriweather Turnstone.

He swirled a French fry in ketchup and took in the diner with its narrow booths, vinyl-covered stools, and speckled counter. Little had changed since the last time he was in Cosette years ago. But then things seldom changed in this small Minnesota town. He and Sahara had lived here when they were first married. They'd made a love nest on the farm like two swallows in the barn and, for a while, it was enough for this city boy. But then, Cosette and the responsibilities of family and fatherhood closed in on Timothy.

He sucked on the straw of his milkshake and listened to the

locals complaining about the weather (as usual) and the price of everything (again as usual). He waited for the familiar feelings of claustrophobia to rise inside him.

But there was nothing. Why? he wondered.

Maybe it was age, he thought. He was a musician still rocking in his sixties, still playing in bars to increasingly smaller crowds, and still writing songs that never quite hit it big. He had friends who would lend him a couch when he needed one but no family—except those who were barely on speaking terms with him here in Cosette.

Maybe he was tired. His nomadic life began the day he walked out on his wife Sahara Lee and infant daughter. Ariel had been only ten months old. Sahara's fiction writing career hadn't taken off yet; she'd still been writing freelance articles at the dining room table with baby Ariel crawling at her feet. He'd left them, sailing off for the promised land of Rock 'n Roll Hall of Fame. But he never reached that distant shore.

Timothy had always told himself that his abandonment of his family had been for the best—he would have screwed up their lives anyway. Then he became the abandoned one. Sahara divorced him and became a best-selling author. Ariel grew into a smart and independent woman who didn't need him. He had tried, shortly before Sahara's wedding to Echo, to establish and repair his relationship with his daughter, but Ariel had wanted nothing to do with him. For years, his emails to her went unanswered.

Then came an unexpected text: *I have a daughter. She is five. Her name is Meriweather, and she is just like me.*

Timothy had read between the lines. It was an announcement, a defiance, and a warning. She would not risk, or tolerate, his rejection of his granddaughter—as he had rejected her.

The message was clear: "Stay away," but that hadn't stopped him. All Timothy could think of was: *I have a granddaughter.*

He remembered the day he left Cosette for good and why. He recalled the fear he'd felt of his own child. She had been so different from everything he had expected. Baby Ariel loved being tossed into the air. Her toys flew through the air as if levitated. He saw now that the rattle she had hurled at him with unforeseen force had been a game to the child; she'd just been trying to get his attention. But at the time, it had angered him.

Then, there was the wind. Whenever Ariel was outside, the wind whipped around them in such a spooky way, as if trying to pull the baby out of his arms.

Taking his phone out of his pocket, he read the text from Ariel again: *Her name is Meriweather.*

It was an odd name, he thought, *but that was par for the course in Sahara's family, which had three kids named after deserts.*

He took a deep breath, pushed a twenty-dollar bill under his plate, and rose. He picked up his guitar case from the floor.

Timothy had driven from Texas to Minnesota chanting: "Meriweather. Meriweather." It was a drumbeat, a song, a prayer.

Although Timothy wasn't a religious man, that didn't stop him from sending the occasional heavenly plea. As he left the diner, he prayed: *Let me get it right this time.*

CHAPTER 31

THE UNFORTUNATE TEXT

TIMOTHY STEPPED OUT THE door of the diner and walked straight into his ex-wife.

"Timothy?" Sahara gave him a surprised look. "What are you doing here?"

Her sudden appearance flustered him. He wasn't prepared for this reunion. He hadn't figured out what to say or how to approach Sahara or Ariel. This felt like one of his nightmares in which he stood on a stage and forgot the words to his song, and not just any song—but the words to the song he wrote for his daughter, his one big hit, "The Girl Who Played with the Wind."

Timothy boyishly swept his graying hair out of his eyes and considered his ex-wife, who had rendered him speechless by their unexpected meeting and by her incredible appearance. Man, he thought, she was still as pretty as ever. She could still rock a T-shirt, he realized, sucking in his stomach. Her long hair carried off the silver streaks better than his dark mop did. Some days, when he looked in the mirror, he didn't recognize the old man he saw there.

Sahara snapped her fingers in front of his eyes, pulling him from reminiscence. "Timothy."

He immediately flashed a smile. "Good to see you, Sahara."

The bell over the diner door jingled as customers entered and exited. It was a busy summer day in downtown Cosette. Without warning, Timothy crowded closer to Sahara, his guitar case bumping her knee, and planted a kiss on her cheek. Her eyes widened.

Why had he done that? he wondered, suddenly embarrassed. He stepped back, smacking her leg again with the guitar case. She looked at the case and asked, "Are you playing somewhere around here?"

Timothy shook his head. Then before he could stop himself, he blurted, "I'm here to see Ariel . . . and my granddaughter."

Shocked, Sahara glanced at the busy sidewalk filled with summer tourists then said, "Let's take a walk."

* * *

Sahara led her former husband down the street to the city park. When she sat down on a bench, he joined her.

Scanning the empty playground, Sahara was glad she had not brought Meri to the park today. The child's ankle was much better, well enough to go bird-watching with her grandfather Arthur.

Sahara studied Timothy. His lifestyle of late nights, noisy bars, and uncertain gigs showed. He looked rough around the edges: tired eyes, sagging face, and nervous hands. But he was still a crisp dresser. She'd never known another man who ironed his T-shirts.

"Are you still living in Texas?" she asked.

"Yeah."

"Still writing songs?"

"As much good as it does me."

There was the old Timothy she remembered—the one who sank into negativity when life was difficult. He must be between gigs and bands, she thought, nowhere to go and nothing to do except try to mend the past.

Pondering the quiet lake before them, she thought of the estrangement between Ariel and Trouble, how the family was still grappling with the presence of this mysterious cousin and the revelations of Annabelle Hamilton's will.

She said, "Timothy, this really isn't a good time to see Ariel and Meri."

Timothy looked away from her. He mumbled, "Sahara, I'm not going to upset them."

"I know you'll try but . . ."

Timothy turned to her with desperation. "Please, Sahara, give me a chance. I know I disappointed you and Ariel, but I'm . . ."

"Different? Changed? Lonely?" Sahara sighed. "Timothy, when are you going to think of someone other than yourself?"

Timothy's busy fingers tapped his knee. In a low voice, he said, "I want to be a grandfather. I want to be better than I was."

Sahara struggled to keep herself from softening toward her ex-husband. She knew that Ariel had never revealed her gift of flight to Timothy, and Sahara had kept her daughter's secrets, as always. "You don't know what you're asking, Timothy, or what you are getting into."

They sat in silence for a long time. As much as her instincts wanted to protect her daughter and Meri, Sahara felt sorry for

Timothy. He had missed so much by leaving Ariel's life. And in reality, Sahara felt she had no right to keep Timothy from Meri. She *was* his granddaughter.

With a sigh, Sahara rose from the bench. Before she could walk away, Timothy touched her hand. She knew the feeling of those calloused fingers, recognized their plea for understanding.

She pulled away, searched his sad but yearning eyes, and said, "Don't you dare hurt them, Timothy."

* * *

Sahara left Timothy and rushed to Ariel's house. Huffing as if she had run to the farm on two legs instead of driving there like a Formula One racer, she pounded on the door. When Ariel answered, Sahara pulled her out onto the porch and shoved her toward the swing, their customary place for heavy discussions.

"Your father's in town," Sahara announced.

Placing a calming hand on her mother's arm, Ariel said, "Mama, take a breath."

But Sahara couldn't stop babbling. "I tried to talk him out of it. I did."

"Out of what?"

"Aren't you listening to me? Timothy is here. He wants to meet Meri."

As the situation became clearer to Ariel, she froze in con-sternation. "Meri? Timothy?"

Ariel had never called her father "Dad" or even thought of him as one. For most of her life, he had been nothing but a song in her head—"St. Judy's Comet," the Paul Simon lullaby that Timothy had sung to his baby girl as she drifted to sleep. Ariel was twenty-nine when she first actually met her father, and it was not a songfest. That meeting, which had taken place here on the farm a few days before Sahara's wedding, had filled Ariel with anger and confusion. He had wanted to be friends, and she had wanted nothing to do with the father who had abandoned her until it suited him. She had sent him away without a good-bye.

The wind swirled around the porch mixing with Ariel's memories and bringing Gus in a flash from the side of the house. After so many years living with Ariel, Gus could sense when there was distress in the air. He leaped up the steps and went directly to Ariel. When he reached her, he tilted his head in a quizzical expression and leaned against her knee.

The wind pushed the back of the swing, and the chains groaned.

Sahara reached for her daughter, just as Ariel sprang from the swing and shoved past Gus. She began to pace across the porch and back. The curls of her hair rose in wild tangles, and a flurry of air rippled her T-shirt. Her thoughts raced: *What was she to do? She had to protect Meri.*

Always on the alert for changes in the weather, both professionally and personally, Ruddy came out of the house and immediately stepped in front of Ariel. Halting her mid-step, he wrapped her in his arms. When he felt a disturbance moments ago, he spun from the computer and peered out the window. He saw nothing impending. Then something inside him whispered, *Ariel,* and he went to find her.

Ariel searched his eyes with desperation. "Meri! I have to get to her."

Ruddy tensed. "She's with my mom. Is she in danger?"

"Yes! My father is coming."

Ruddy cast a puzzled glance toward Sahara on the porch swing. His mother-in-law shook her head refusing to explain.

Ruddy had been raised by two parents who doted on him. He could not fathom being distant from his father Arthur, much less dislike him or fear him. Arthur had taught him about computers and birds and patience (which Ruddy had needed in his long quest for Ariel's heart). And if other fathers didn't keep binoculars at the dinner table in case an interesting bird dropped by the feeders outside the window, that was just their loss. Arthur had shown his son that passion—for any-thing—was good and important.

Ruddy had never met Timothy Lee.

"Tell me why this is bad," he said to Ariel in his soothing zephyr voice.

She clutched the front of his shirt. "Because I've never re-ally told him about Up There. He doesn't know who I truly am and what I can do. He doesn't understand and will never understand. Meri and I don't fit into his world view. We can't let him near Meri!"

"Maybe he has changed," Ruddy suggested.

She shook him. "Don't you get it! We can't take that chance! He's going to reject Meri just like he rejected me."

Ariel collapsed against Ruddy's chest.

Ruddy couldn't imagine anyone rejecting his beautiful daughter. He felt the storm of sadness eddying around his wife, and he began to rock her. After a while, they were slow dancing on the porch as Ariel sniffled and Ruddy whispered words of comfort.

As the tension eased, Sahara sneaked away with a nod to Ruddy, who continued to sway with Ariel. He held Ariel's hand close to his heart and tried to think of a solution to this dilemma.

Finally, he threw out the most impossible suggestion he could think of—it was an unusual tactic for Ruddy. He was not a go-wild-or-go-home guy. "I know what we'll do. We'll lock you and Meri in the house until your father leaves town," he said. "I'll stand guard at the door, night and day, ready to fend off your father—armed with the heaviest book I can find."

Ariel's sniffs turned into giggles. "A book. Like Shakespeare?" They both still had their five-pound tomes of the complete works of William Shakespeare from their college days.

Ruddy said, "I believe in fighting with words rather than weapons."

That dissolved them both into laughter.

When Ruddy sobered, he said softly, "You know I would die for you and Meri."

The romantic wind sighed and so did Ariel.

After more turns of slow dancing around the porch, Ariel said in a dispirited voice, "This is all my fault."

"What is?"

"Timothy. I'm the one who told him that we had a daughter."

Ruddy stopped dancing and stared at her. "Why would you do that if you don't want anything to do with him?"

"Because I'm an idiot." Ariel shook her head. "I answered a few of his emails . . . but I said *nothing* that could be construed as I forgive you or you can come back into my life. Then about two weeks ago I heard your father patiently answering Meri's endless questions about the birds flitting around them."

"He always answered my questions, too, when I was a kid," said Ruddy. "No matter what he was doing, he would stop and tell me about the birds."

"On that day, a sentimental wind must have slipped inside me," confessed Ariel, "because I started thinking about what

Timothy could teach Meri. Music, maybe. She does love to sing."

They continued to sway.

Ariel said softly, "And I thought about never meeting my grandmother Anne or my great-grandmother Annabelle. I wished I had known them, Ruddy."

Ruddy understood his wife's eternal search for belonging and said, "Before you realized what you were doing, you fired off a text to him."

"Yeah," said Ariel. "I regretted it as soon as I sent it, but it was too late."

Ruddy held her close. "We all make mistakes," he said. "That's why we keep our Shakespeare."

CHAPTER 32

WEATHER FASCINATION

RUDDY HATED WHEN HIS wife rode the storms.

She had not been called to calm a tornado since Sahara and Echo's wedding day, but she had worked with smaller storms. Thunderstorms full of bravado, hail, and sneaky lightning were the worst. Ruddy had experienced being struck by lightning—twice. He remembered the feeling of a lightning jolt traveling through his arms and legs and his body flying in the air. Afterward, he woke, feeling foggy and disconnected, not part of this world.

Every time Ariel went Up There in stormy conditions, Ruddy begged, "Don't go," then held his breath and waited for the worst news he could imagine.

This time, she kissed him, smiled, and lifted into the air. "See you soon," she called.

He watched her until he could no longer see her then dashed inside to his office. He consulted the radar and prayed that the blobs on the screen would decrease in severity and disappear. He cast frequent glances at the rain-lashed window looking for Ariel.

He called his mother. Meri was baking with Alice that afternoon.

When Alice answered, he immediately said, "Keep Meri in the house."

"Of course," Alice said with a grin in her voice. "I know the routine when it comes to children fascinated by weather. I did raise you."

Ruddy felt a new tension. "Is Meri interested in the storm?"

Hearing the strain in Ruddy's voice, Alice answered thoughtfully, "She's certainly distracted this afternoon. She broke eggshells into the first cookie batter, and we had to throw it away. She can't keep her attention off the kitchen window. The bird feeders in the backyard are swinging in the wind and rain like Gene Kelly." Ruddy's mother loved old movies, especially musicals. *The Wizard of Oz*, with its mesmerizing scenes of weather, for Ruddy, and singing Munchkins, for Alice, had been regular family viewing in the Turnstone household.

Ruddy didn't care for the idea of his daughter being hyperaware of the storm.

Alice lowered her voice and issued the words he feared, "I think she wants to go out there, Ruddy. She says it's calling her."

Oh god, Ruddy thought. "Don't let her go outside, Mom. Keep her in the house. No matter what."

"I will."

* * *

When Ruddy saw a dripping Ariel trudging across the backyard, he ran from the house. Her hair was a cloud of tangles, her shirt was ripped, and she had lost a shoe. Without a word, he pulled her into his arms. They stood in the rain, she too exhausted to speak and he too grateful to scold her.

That night, Ruddy listened to the house settle. Ariel's warm hand drifted down on his chest. With a pat, she said, "You're not sleeping."

"How can you tell?"

"I know your breathing."

"Remind me to hold my breath while I'm pondering the crazy stuff my wife does, so I don't wake you."

Ariel lifted his arm and fitted herself next to him, her head on his chest. Pat.

"It was just a little storm," said Ariel with a yawn. "A baby, really."

Ruddy sighed heavily, and his arm tightened around her as he told her about the conversation with his mother.

Suddenly alert, Ariel jerked up and stared at her husband. Moonlight illuminated the fear and sadness in his face.

"Meri felt the storm calling her?"

"Yes."

"But she's so young—"

"I know." He paused then said the words he knew were terrible for her to hear and that he dreaded to speak, "I want you to stop riding storms, Ariel."

Shocked, Ariel felt the words automatically tunneling up from her heart—"Of course, of course, whatever you want"— but she didn't utter them. Memories held her back, memories of the years she'd lost when she refused to answer the call of the wind. She had holed up in her apartment in the Twin Cities, afraid to come home to the farm and face the wind.

She was not that woman anymore.

"I've been careful," she said, a note of pleading in her voice.

"I know, but each time you go . . ." Ruddy gathered his courage and rushed on. "I'm afraid of the day that Meri follows you."

"Ruddy, it may be years before—"

His expression was a mix of love and terror. "You don't understand how hard it is to watch you . . . to think about . . . I found your broken body after the tornado, Ariel. I couldn't take it if I had to do that for our daughter."

He waited for her promise. Silence.

"You and I both know the weather is growing more unpredictable," Ruddy said. "There will be more storms, more droughts, more strange weather. You feel the change in the climate better than anyone. Please, Ariel, promise me."

* * *

The next afternoon, Sahara sat on the porch swing with Ariel and felt a restlessness around them. Something was bothering her daughter. "What's wrong?"

Ariel told her mother about Meri's reaction to the storm. Sahara was not surprised. For a long time now, Sahara had wondered and worried about the strength of her granddaughter's gift. She remained silent.

After a long pause, Ariel said, "Ruddy wants me to stop riding storms."

Sahara inhaled sharply. "What did you say?"

Suddenly, a current of air rushed across the porch, waking the sleeping Gus who lifted his head and automatically searched for Ariel. With downcast eyes, she whispered, "I promised him that I would."

Sahara remembered her mother Anne had often been called by the wind to settle storms and been unable to resist. Ariel had done the same when she tried to calm the tornado ripping toward Cosette on Sahara and Echo's wedding day. Days later, when Ariel was still in the hospital recovering from the effort, Sahara had asked her daughter why she had done such a dangerous thing, and Ariel had replied, "The wind was out of control, and it needed my help."

Now, Sahara wondered, "Will you be able to keep that promise?"

"I don't know, Mama. I don't know."

Sahara put on her best assured mother smile and said, "You'll deal with that when the time comes. As for now, don't worry about Meri. Even when she was inside you, you felt she was a different kind of Hamilton woman."

That was true—Ariel knew Meri would never let herself be separated from Up There, as Ariel had done when she denied the wind so long ago. Meri would always answer when the wind called. Ariel just hoped Meri discovered, before it was too late, that the wind could not always be helped—or trusted.

CHAPTER 33

THE WIND GOLFS

STRETCHED ON HIS STOMACH on the dock, Wren Wamsganz studied the fish swimming in the lake. When the floating dock began to rock, he knew his uncle was approaching. Harley's footsteps were different from his father's, heavier. When Harley's shadow fell over him, Wren asked without looking up, "What's the name of that fish?"

Harley peered where Wren was pointing and said, "Blue gill."

"And that one?"

"Blue gill."

"And that one?"

Harley sighed. "They're all blue gill. They see you hanging over the dock and think you're gonna feed them. Dang kids keep tossing them cracker crumbs. They've turned all the fish into beggars."

"What's wrong with that?"

Harley nodded to the dark approaching head with the pointy snout sneaking up to the surface. "Because all the attention attracts him. That's a snapper, kid. He's old, big, and smart. If he got a hold of your finger, that turtle would never let go."

Wren didn't know if that was true, but he decided not to test his uncle's claim. He quickly retracted the fingers he'd been lazily dipping in the water.

"Will you teach me to fish, Harley?"

Wren fully expected his uncle to refuse. Harley had the snack bar shift this morning, and Wren sensed that his uncle really didn't like spending time with kids. Their eyes met, Wren's pleading and Harley's unconvinced. Wren added an inducement he knew his uncle wouldn't resist, "I'll help you sweep the cabins on Saturday."

Harley looked as if he didn't know whether to trust his nephew. Then, abruptly, he turned, headed back up the dock, and said over his shoulder, "I'll get the night crawlers. You get the life jackets."

They fished for an hour, tossing their lines over the side of the small boat. It was hot. His uncle wore his raggedy Minnesota Twins hat pulled low. Wren wished he had a hat like that, a hat that looked as if it had been places.

Harley didn't talk much, except to issue orders about hooks ("that's a weapon in the wrong hands") and bait ("don't be afraid of a little worm"). They caught a few sunfish or "sunnies," as his uncle called them, and plenty of seaweed. When Wren lost Harley's fishing net overboard, Harley called it a day.

Freddy was waiting for them at the dock, a puzzled expression on his face. He helped secure the boat. As Wren stepped ashore, the boy excitedly told his father, "Dad, we caught sunnies. They're kinda pretty, but they have sharp fins. They were too little to keep, Harley said. We tossed them back."

Freddy watched his brother gather the fishing gear and step

out of the boat. When Harley was on the dock, his arms full of fishing poles and tackle box, Wren suddenly flung himself at his uncle's legs, giving an awkward hug. "Thanks, Harley, for taking me fishing." Then the boy ran toward the house.

Startled, Harley watched the boy clatter up the dock. Harley threw a glance toward Freddy and noticed him struggling to keep from smiling.

"That kid of yours doesn't know one end of the hook from the other," Harley growled, shoving past Freddy. "I could have lost an eye out there, the way he casts."

A silent Freddy followed his brother.

While Harley stored the fishing gear in a small shed attached to the office, Freddy said, "I guess you took Wren fishing to get out of working in the snack bar this morning."

Unsure if Freddy was needling him or glad that he'd spent time with Wren, Harley stopped and faced his brother. "If he's gonna live on a lake, he should know how to fish. It's a more useful sport than disc golf, if you can even call that a sport. Besides, I left a note saying the snack bar would be open later. Nobody's gonna starve because they didn't get their bag of veggie crisps."

* * *

Meri knew it was going to be a good day because the wind told her so. It filled her with happiness as if tiny bubbles were floating inside her. She was excited to be with Wren and to learn how to disc golf.

She watched her father talk with Wren's uncle Harley. She knew they had gone to school together, been in the same class with her mama, but it was difficult to believe. Her father looked so *young*, compared to Harley. Maybe it was her father's friendly shoulder-length coppery curls or his relaxed stance.

He looked like the kind of guy who would laugh with you and hold you when the monsters came for you. Harley, on the other hand, with his bristly buzz cut and frequent frowns, was not a man she would instinctively run to for help. Harley was probably a friend of monsters.

But Wren insisted his uncle was an okay guy. According to Wren's mother, Willow, Harley needed to adopt a happier attitude. "Mom's trying to get him to do yoga with her and Dad," Wren told Meri. "She says Harley is too tight."

Meri waved as Ruddy drove away. She followed Wren around the side of the house. "Harley probably needs to meditate too," said Meri. "Mama and I meditate." She did not tell Wren it was a crucial part of her training for walking Up There. "It kind of makes you feel all calm."

"Sounds cool," Wren said.

As they reached the backyard of Wren's house, Willow came out the door. She welcomed Meri with a hug, the "mushy" kind Wren had warned her about.

"I'm off to deliver a bassinet to cabin five," she said. "Don't you love babies?" Willow did not wait for a reply. "There are drinks and cookies in the kitchen, and don't chop anyone's head off with those discs."

Meri caught Willow's teasing expression and laughed. "Yes, Mrs. Wamsganz."

"It's just Willow, honey," said Wren's mother, climbing into the all-terrain vehicle used to haul supplies to the cabins.

After Willow left, the disc golf lesson began. According to Wren, the object was to throw the plastic discs into a basket set up in the backyard behind Wren's house. It did not look like any kind of basket that Meri had ever seen. It was a metal cage attached to a pole. Above the cage streamed looped chains, which chimed when Meri ran her hand along them.

The chains were supposed to catch the disc as it flew by and guide it into the basket.

Wren handed Meri one of the discs. "They're frisbees," she said.

Wren shook his head. "Not exactly. They're made from a harder plastic to go far."

The discs were decorated with images of birds, bears, snakes, squirrels. "So many animals," she said. "Pretty."

"It's a nature sport," said Wren.

Wren showed her how to grip the disc, how to stand, how to throw. But tossing the disc into the basket proved to be more difficult than Meri had imagined.

Discs flew in all directions—into the nearby woods, on the road, on the roof of Harley's trailer—and Meri and Wren soon were laughing so hard that they fell onto the ground.

When Wren's father, Freddy, came up the dock to check on them, Wren invited his father to toss a few. "Dad is super good," he told Meri.

Watching Freddy throw was like watching a ballet. His body moved in ways Meri had never seen before. He twisted his body as he did a run up, then uncoiled quickly, whipping his arm out and releasing the disc. The disc shot from his hand and exploded into its own dance. It whistled through the air, then began to dip and weave to a music only it could hear, until finally, it drifted to the ground.

"Wow," Meri said. She stared at the disc in her hand, a bright orange one with a fairy on it. When Wren's father threw, his disc slipped between the currents of air as if it was a natural element of the cosmos. The disc didn't fight the air; it became a part of Up There—just as she did. She wanted to throw like that. She wanted to be like that.

Wren nudged her. "Hey, you okay?"

Meri's head snapped up from her thoughts. "Sure. Freddy, that was wonderful."

He bowed to them then announced it was time to have a snack. Wren, however, begged him to try just one more.

"My dad can ace it from far away. I've seen him do it," Wren told Meri.

And before Freddy could say anything, Wren grabbed his father's hand and pulled him down to the end of the dock. The dock was between Wren's house and the snack bar. With wide eyes, Meri followed them. The basket was now a long distance away, past the house and snack bar. She doubted *anyone* could throw that far.

Wren said, "Please, Dad, show Meri how you can put it in the basket from here."

The snack bar door opened, and Harley stepped out. Leaning against the side of the building, arms crossed over his chest, Harley called, "Yes, brother, show us."

Meri stepped closer to Wren and asked, "Does Harley play?"

"No," he said.

Freddy gave his brother a hard stare then took the disc Wren handed him.

With an encouraging nod from Wren, Freddy took a step, spun, and launched—the disc leaped from his hand eager to fly.

It cruised high over the house and Harley's trailer.

It rode the air. It bobbed.

Then it began to veer wide.

It was going to miss the basket.

Meri glanced at Wren. He was mumbling under his breath, "Turn, turn."

Meri knew she was not supposed to call the wind; that was

one of the rules. But watching the disc head off course, Meri could feel Wren's disappointment.

Come on, she whispered to the wind. *Turn.*

Suddenly, air swept past them. When Meri felt the change in the air, a sense of happiness bloomed inside her.

She watched the disc sketch an unexpected arc in the windy sky.

Then she heard the disc hit the chains with a clang and slide into the basket.

Freddy had made an ace. From what seemed, to Meri, like miles away.

Wren, all smiles, pumped a fist in the air and shouted, "Yes, Dad! You did it!"

Wren and Freddy laughed with excitement. "I didn't think it was going to make it," confessed Freddy. "It turned like a magnet toward the chains."

"I know," said Wren. "I thought it was going into the woods . . . but it didn't."

Listening to Wren and Freddy, Meri glanced toward Harley.

He watched the celebration, then with a nod of respect for his brother, Harley went into the snack bar and slammed the screen door.

CHAPTER 34

RUNNING FOR YOUR LIFE

IT WAS PAST MIDDAY, and Marta's Diner was nearly empty, except for a trio of women huddled in the back booth.

"No," Ariel said for probably the fifth time. "Why can't one of you do it?" In the booth across from her sat Blinka Trout and Nikki Diego. They exchanged conspiratorial glances. This was supposed to be a friendly lunch, Ariel thought, not an ambush.

Blinka answered first. "I have a business to run. Bikes don't rent themselves. Summer's my busiest time, Ariel. Jake and I are up to our ears in repair work." Jake, Blinka's youngest brother, worked for her in Bike the Babe. Tourists biking the popular Paul Bunyan State Trail, which ran through Cosette, patronized Blinka's shop as well as many of the businesses in Cosette.

"I run a business too. Articles and books don't write themselves," Ariel retorted, before turning to Nikki. "And what's your excuse?"

Nikki shrunk back into the booth, reminding Ariel of the timid girl Nikki had once been, a child who would rather hide behind her art sketchbook than face the bullies of the world. "I don't do public speaking," she mumbled.

Ariel's hands flew up in disgust. Nikki was the picture of revolution—from her spiky ruffled hair to her tattooed arms to her steel-toed work boots. She wore her life motto inked on her forearm: "Never Be Ordinary." If anyone can compete against Melanie Harcourt for a spot on the town council, it should be someone who epitomizes change, someone who doesn't care about shaking up the status quo. Nikki lived for that stuff.

Blinka tapped the table for Ariel's attention. "You are the perfect choice, Ariel. You are a natural leader. Look at how your Earth Day project has grown."

Nikki nodded. "And you have a child in school, which Melanie doesn't have. You are invested in the education of Cosette's children and the *positive* growth of our town."

"By positive, you mean . . ."

Nikki looked her in the eye. "This race is a choice between raging economic development and saving our town's natural and unique appeal. We need someone to help Cosette navigate the coming years of climate change and preserve Cosette's way of life in concert with nature."

When Ariel looked doubtful, Blinka chimed in, "You are accomplished in your field. Your writing and your book about climate change make you a celebrity. And you *do* do public speaking. You speak at environmental conferences around the world."

Ariel did not like that aspect of her work: the attention and especially the criticism. Social media had been both brutal and supportive of her perspective. When Ruddy saw the online trolls getting her down, he ordered, "Stop reading the internet." Then he would take her hand, pull her from the computer, and cajole her into a quiet, screen-free walk in the woods.

Ariel's gaze ping-ponged between Nikki and Blinka. Although Blinka was aware of Ariel's gift, Nikki was not. And even Blinka didn't fully understand Ariel's bond with her gift and the world of Up There. Not only did Ariel believe in saving the planet, but she was compelled to do so. Her closeness to Up There was a chain she could not break. She had tried to sever the tie when she denied the wind for all those years after Blinka's accident, and it nearly tore her apart.

"I hate politics," grumbled Ariel.

"Who doesn't?" Nikki gave her an encouraging look. "But you can beat Melanie in this election."

Seeing Ariel waver, an excited Blinka said, "You know she just wants to turn Cosette into a tourist destination for the rich and open it up for out-of-control development."

"Development dollars that will line her pockets," said Nikki.

Marta Diego, Nikki's mother and the owner of Marta's Diner, approached the booth with three slices of luscious French silk pie. Marta had barely slid the plates on the table before all three women were digging in and sighing with pleasure. "Mmm," Blinka said, "Marta, you should enter this pie in the state fair contest. You'd win for sure."

Marta straightened the apron encasing her round belly and grinned. "It wouldn't be fair. I *am* a professional."

Before Marta returned to work behind the counter, she caught Ariel's eye and said, "They're right. You should run. We need fresh blood around here, and you are just the one to bring it." She turned away, adding over her shoulder, "Here's your first campaign contribution. Free pie for all your planning sessions."

Nikki and Blinka bumped fists. "How can you turn down an offer like that?" asked Blinka with a smile.

Ariel finished her pie and pushed the empty plate aside. "So how long have you two been cooking up this scheme?"

Blinka and Nikki exchanged guilty looks.

Nikki admitted, "Since Melanie's signs went up. But it's a good idea. C'mon, Ariel, you have always been able to hold your own with Melanie."

"Yeah," Blinka said, "Remember how she tried to get your farm so she could turn it into a golf course. Boy, oh boy, did you shut her down."

Ariel rubbed the spot between her eyes where a headache was materializing. "She scares the crap out of me."

Blinka placed a hand on Ariel's arm. "She scares everyone. But you are different. You have resilience."

Ariel and Melanie had a long history—from childhood when Melanie led others in the ridicule of Ariel's heavy shoes to adulthood when real estate agent Melanie set her sights on Ariel's farm. Sometimes it felt as if Ariel had spent a lifetime standing up to Melanie Harcourt. Although she may dream of sweeping Melanie off a high slide with a blast of well-placed wind, Ariel always held back. She could never retaliate as she wished. She had a responsibility to her gift and secrets to protect, secrets that were now even more essential since she had Meri.

"I don't know," Ariel said. "This is not a good time. I'm fighting with Trouble, and now Timothy is in town."

Blinka eyes grew big. "Your father?"

"Yup. He wants to meet his granddaughter."

Blinka, who knew exactly what that meant for Ariel and

her daughter, leaned back in the booth in thought and said, "Yikes." She had helped a confused and angry Ariel pick up the pieces after her first meeting with Timothy. At that time, neither Blinka nor Timothy was aware of Ariel's secret life Up There, and as far as Blinka knew, Timothy still didn't.

Frowning, Nikki eyed her friends. "I don't get it. What's the problem?"

Blinka said, "Ariel's dad left when she was baby . . ."

"And didn't come back for nearly thirty years," finished Ariel.

"Wow," Nikki said. "If my dad did that, my mom would track him down, slice him up, and bake him in one of her pies. She can be hotheaded when it comes to family."

Both Ariel and Blinka eyed their empty pie plates.

"I don't really know my father," said Ariel, "and I don't trust him. Especially with Meri."

Being the daughter of Lars and Marta Diego, Nikki understood the passion and inseparability of tangled family relationships. Lars was the product of a Norwegian artist mother and a romantic Mexican migrant, and Marta was one hundred percent Mexican and one hundred and fifty percent Catholic.

"We will pray for you," Nikki said.

Ariel had no experience with organized religion. Her church was Up There; her hymns, the songs of the birds; her sacraments, the walks in the wind that sustained her soul. Still, she appreciated Nikki's offering and nodded her thanks.

After a moment of reflection, Nikki said, "Forget about your dad. We have a campaign to plan. I've already started designing your campaign materials." She quickly flipped open a notebook on the table and searched through the pages of drawings. When she came to the sketch she'd been searching for, she showed it to Ariel and Blinka. It said, "Ariel for Town Council. The Nature First Candidate."

Blinka, who often forgot how strong she was, wrapped her long arms around petite Nikki and squeezed. "Nature First Candidate. It's perfect."

"Okay, don't mangle me for life," Nikki said, unraveling herself from Blinka.

"I'll be your campaign manager," Blinka told Ariel. "I'll put my family to work for you. We know everybody—or at least, their vehicles."

The Nature First Candidate.

Ariel felt a tingle inside her. This decision could change her life as well as Ruddy's and Meri's. On the one hand, how could she protect the family's secrets as a public figure? On the other hand, how could she face Meri if she passed up her chance to make this a better world?

Do it, the wind said. *For us.*

Ariel studied the sketch for her campaign poster. "I'm not promising anything. But I'll talk to Ruddy."

CHAPTER 35

DUELING POSTERS

HARLEY DIDN'T KNOW IF he was happy or irritated to see Nikki stride through the door of the Wamsganz Resort's office. Lately, Harley had been unsettled, searching. There were moments when he found himself standing on the end of the dock thinking about the vastness of life. And he wasn't even drunk when these bouts of reflection occurred.

He blamed this navel-gazing on anything and anyone but himself. It had to be the fault of Nikki and her ridiculous painted canoe. Maybe it was Willow and the damn ringing of her Tibetan prayer bowl or Freddy's general good-naturedness. The Freddy of Harley's youth had never been so affable and impossible to rile. And then there was the kid, Wren, always asking questions and making Harley feel stupid when he couldn't identify a specific tree or insect. Who cared about bugs?

Nikki slapped a rolled paper into his palm. "Here you go, Harley. A little decoration for your window."

He unfurled the paper. It was a campaign poster for Ariel Lee Turnstone.

"You're kidding," he said. "The Nature First Candidate?"

Nikki placed her hand on her narrow hips and tapped her black combat boot. "Harley, don't be an idiot. You are in the environment business, whether you want to admit it or not. Who will want to come here if the fish disappear and the trees die?"

They'd had this conversation before, and maybe, just maybe, Nikki's ideas were starting to take root in Harley. Harley had to concede that the rising level of Lake Cosette was nibbling away at his beach, and that last winter's early thaw had melted the resort's much-needed ice-fishing business. Still, Harley wasn't totally sold on this climate change business. He wanted to be hopeful, but the logical and pessimistic side of him believed that when it came to life on this planet, it was too late for all of them. Humans were screwed, according to Harley.

But he didn't voice that sentiment to headstrong, crusading Nikki. Instead, he accepted the poster, to Nikki's glee. As she went out the door, his mind was more on her rare and quirky smile than on town politics. He stored the poster on the shelf behind the check-in desk and forgot it.

✻ ✻ ✻

Two hours after Nikki left, Melanie barged into the office.

"Busy day for the Wamsganz Resort," Harley muttered to himself.

Melanie marched up to Harley, slapped her hand on the desk, and demanded, "Where the hell is my poster, Harley? You were supposed to display it in your window. I gave it to you a week ago. Don't you support me?"

"Of course, I do," he said, searching desperately behind the desk for Melanie's poster. His hand brushed Ariel's poster, then snagged Melanie's poster and a roll of tape. Under the watchful eye of his old friend and to the impatient tune of her tapping high heels, he quickly taped Melanie's campaign poster to the office window.

"There, Mel. Happy now?"

"Don't call me Mel," she said.

She scanned the desk with its stew of pens and papers. The rest of the room was just as cluttered with T-shirts, sweatshirts, soft toys, child-size fishing poles, candy bars, chips. In one corner was a mountain of used games and puzzles to occupy antsy bodies and bored minds on rainy days.

As Melanie wandered the snack bar part of the office, she said, "Have you talked to your brother about selling, Harley? I could have this place listed in a week. In fact, I have a blank contract in my car."

Actually, Harley had not raised the topic of selling the resort since his brother and family moved in. In fact, he had not thought about it in months. Selling the resort and moving into a new life was not such a priority with Harley anymore.

At Melanie's penetrating look, Harley quickly contrived an excuse: blame his brother. "Freddy's stubborn," said Harley. "He doesn't make snap decisions. Between you and me, I think he's enjoying being the lord of the manor."

"Well, light a fire under him," snapped Melanie, irritation in her voice.

Melanie had been testy for months, ever since her mother died in a senior facility. Rumor was that Melanie came to clean out her mother's apartment and the nurses found her sitting on the floor surrounded by mounds of clipped coupons and sobbing. Melanie's bargain-hunting mother, Stacy Harcourt, had saved coupons all her life, even when she had no need to redeem them. As Melanie left the facility, she handed three garbage bags of coupons to the staff with instructions to burn them. She walked out of the facility carrying a single item: her parents' wedding photo in the silver frame she'd given Stacy many Mother's Days ago.

As she passed Harley and headed for the door, Melanie said, "Stay on that brother of yours."

Later, when Wren came in for a candy bar (the kind his mother did not approve of but Harley always let him have), he found Harley taping Ariel's poster on the window of the office beside Melanie's poster.

"What are you doing, Harley?" Wren asked. "Hey, isn't that Meri's mom?"

"Yup." Harley stepped back and assessed his work. "I'm declaring Wamsganz Resort an election-neutral zone."

"Why?"

"It'll be safer for everyone," Harley said.

CHAPTER 36

A STRANGER FROM HOME

ARIEL PAUSED BEFORE ANSWERING the door. She swept a hand through her tumbled locks and found a pen tangled in the mess. Tossing it on a nearby table, she opened the door. "Yes?" she said absently. She did not know the man interrupting her writing time.

The stranger took a step back at her tone, then gave her a hard look from behind black-rimmed glasses. When she raised her eyebrow in question, he abruptly stuck out his hand and introduced himself, "Mick Dunn."

Ariel did not shake hands with strange men at her door. Instead, she shook her head and said, "I'm sorry, I'm sure whatever you're selling is fabulous, but I'm not buying."

When she started to close the door, he quickly said, "I'm not selling. Really." He held up his empty hands. "I'm looking for Trouble. Is she here?"

Ariel stopped.

"What do you want with Trouble?" she asked, eyeing the stranger.

"She's my fiancée," he said.

Ariel stepped back, surprised, then motioned. "You better come in."

* * *

They sat in the living room, Ariel and Ruddy together on the sofa, and Mick Dunn in the rocker facing them. Mick had the presence of a well-dressed bouncer crossed with an Amish farmer who had lost his way. He was a sturdy man in black motorcycle boots, black jeans, black vest, thick black beard, and a pristine white shirt rolled up on his well-muscled arms. She imagined he was bald under his jazzy black fedora.

Suddenly nervous under their scrutiny, Mick swept off his hat and spun it between his long fingers. She'd been right about the cue ball.

Ruddy asked, "How do you know Trouble?"

Mick answered with a story about a thirty-year-old construction worker and part-time piano player (him) who looked up from the keys one night in a bar and felt drawn to a mysterious woman with secretive eyes and incredibly long, silky hair (Trouble). He knew, from that first glance, that she would harmonize with him and together they would play the perfect tune. But then her grandmother died, the bank served foreclosure papers, and Trouble disappeared.

"Trouble was scared," Mick said.

"Why didn't she run to you—her *fiancé*?" asked Ariel, suspicion filling her voice.

Mick's face reddened. "Okay, maybe that is a slight exaggeration." Ruddy stirred, and Mick held up his hand. "Wait, don't throw me out yet. I was ready to propose, honest, but then she vanished." He looked down at his hat. "I don't know why."

So, Ariel thought, Mick doesn't know about Trouble's search for her Hamilton heritage.

Ariel and Ruddy exchanged glances. Ariel knew Ruddy was thinking that Trouble had brought another mess to their door, but Ariel felt sympathy for her cousin. Obviously, instead of revealing her gift to Mick and facing the possibility of rejection, she had run, like her grandmother Clarissa.

Mick continued, almost to himself, "There was always something she kept from me, some secret. It used to drive me nuts, like the notes of a song on the edge of my memory."

"And now?" Ariel asked.

"Now, I don't care what she's hiding. I just want her back."

Ariel gave a heartfelt sigh. Like the other Hamilton women, Trouble was quite adept at running and hiding.

With a pleading look, Mick begged, "Please help me find her. I know she thinks she can take care of herself, but she really is lousy at it. She loses her cell phone all the time. She takes crazy risks, like running away with an expired driver's license and no money."

Ruddy asked, "Why do you think she's here?"

"I'm a handyman, and I used to do odd jobs around her grandfather's farm," explained Mick. "Trouble's grandmother talked about a place in Minnesota where she once lived. Trouble was obsessed with the place. Her grandmother was named Clarissa Hamilton, and she mentioned a cousin named Anne. So I began tracking Hamiltons in Minnesota. I discovered an Anne Hamilton Stevens lived and died in this town."

Ariel cocked a head. "But how did you find us?"

"I went to the local real estate agent, a Ms. Harcourt," Mick said. "She was glad to help me. Told me all about Sahara and you and this farm. She even gave me directions."

Ariel tensed and gripped Ruddy's hand. "I bet she did," snarled Ariel. Suddenly, she rose. "I have to make a phone call."

She left Ruddy in the living room with Mick and went to the kitchen. When her mother answered the phone, Ariel said in a soft voice, "Where is Trouble?"

Her mother sounded puzzled. "Trouble? I don't know. She's gone."

"Gone! Where?"

"I found a note on her bed. It said she was going home. Do you think she means Missouri?"

Ariel studied the quiet scene outside the kitchen window and felt the wind rising inside her.

"No, not Missouri," Ariel told her mother. "But you can bet that when I find her, she will wish she were back there. We *will* have words. First Trouble, then Melanie Harcourt."

"What does Melanie have to do with this?"

"She sicced Trouble's fiancé on me."

"Her what?" Sahara gasped.

CHAPTER 37

THE SQUATTER

ARIEL LED THE WAY through the tunnel of foliage protecting the Hamilton homestead. In her rearview mirror was Mick Dunn on his motorcycle. He'd traded the fedora for a helmet and donned a leather jacket, which shielded him from the aggressive, overgrown, and possessive bushes and branches that guarded the path. When they broke through the green gauntlet, Ariel stopped and got out of the car.

Mick stared at the hill before him, the steep climb, and the rickety house at the top. He was at a loss for words. Finally, he removed his helmet and handed it to Ariel. "Put it on," he instructed then patted his bike. "This baby can take us up there."

Ariel looked from the hill to Mick and, after a moment, shoved the helmet on her head and climbed behind him. She had never been on a motorcycle in her life.

With a heavy roar, they spun up the hill, and Ariel wished she had been able to take the wind to the house. The gravity pulled at them with strong hands, and the hill bucked them. Worried that she might fly off the back of the bike, she wrapped her arms tight around Mick, leaned into him, and closed her eyes.

And then they were at the top of the hill.

Mick parked the motorcycle beside a bicycle lying on the ground. Trouble's bike.

Ariel had been right. This was Trouble's new home—the house that technically belonged to Ariel, the house that was falling apart from roof to cellar, the house the wind guarded with ferocity.

As she thought of the wind, she realized that it now had them surrounded and was blasting them from all sides. She recognized it, and it recognized her Hamilton blood. But it was not her wind; it would never be *her* wind. Her strength came from the wind she'd found on the Stevens farm.

It's all right, she told the wind on the hill. *I understand.*

The squall eased a little around her but kept fighting Mick.

Mick in the fedora he had retrieved from the saddlebags on his motorcycle, leaned toward the house but was unable to take a step against the powerful headwind. Clutching the hat to his head, he shouted, "Where did this wind come from?"

Ariel didn't answer. She was watching the house.

Finally, the door flew open.

A defiant Trouble stood framed in a portrait of peeling paint, raggedy shutters, and broken windows.

The women glared at each other. The world narrowed around them, and all else—the wind, the house, the man struggling to stay upright—fell out of focus.

"Go away, Ariel!" screamed Trouble, and the wind screamed with her.

"No," Ariel raised her voice over the wind.

The house moaned.

"Leave me alone! Leave us alone!" shouted Trouble.

"Not a chance," said Ariel, stepping toward the house. Trouble had claimed she could do no more than walk the wind, but the air at the Hamilton homestead certainly seemed to be responding to her. "We *will* talk, Trouble." Then in a stern voice, one that Meri always knew meant business, she growled, "So ground your thoughts. Before you sweep Mick Dunn off this hill."

Trouble's eyes flashed to the man fighting to get to her. "Mick?"

In a snap, the air changed. Tension fell like snowdrops, and Trouble leaped off the rotten porch. She slammed into Mick, wrapping her legs around his waist, and he clutched her to him.

"Trouble, Trouble," he whispered, a name turned into a prayer.

Ariel watched the couple's reunion and suddenly felt old. They were young, obviously in love, but had no clue of the bumpy road ahead of them. And before they could start down that path, Trouble had some explaining to do—to Ariel and Mick.

Ariel cleared her throat, and Trouble looked at her. She slid down Mick's body and out of his arms. But he wouldn't let her go. He grabbed her hand before she could step away.

In a far-from-welcoming voice, Ariel asked, "What are you doing here?"

Trouble lifted her chin and stared Ariel in the eye. "I'm living here."

Ariel started up the porch steps, dodging the holes and heading for the door. "Oh, no, you're not."

"Ariel!" Trouble hurried after her, followed by Mick.

When Ariel entered the ramshackle house, she found that Trouble had already made herself at home: her backpack and clothes were strewn on the living room floor along with a sleeping bag that Ariel recognized as belonging to Sahara.

"You're squatting," accused Ariel.

"Nobody lives here," said Trouble in a rebellious voice. "Nobody wants this place. Except me."

While the women scowled at each other, an amazed Mick toured the living room, dining room, and kitchen. The carpenter in him tested floorboards, rapped on walls, and examined rotten windowsills. He stopped at the staircase to the second floor, peered up into its decaying depths, almost started up, then thought better of it.

One glance at Trouble's stubborn expression sent Ariel's heart plummeting. She knew she had to be cold-blooded, even if it broke the budding relationship she had with the only person in the world who utterly understood what it was like to be a gifted Hamilton woman. This house, hill, and land were Ariel's responsibility now, and she could not bear the thought of anyone being injured here. For Trouble's own sake, Ariel had to save her from this run-down and dangerous inheritance.

Ariel hardened her heart against Trouble's pleas. "No, this house is not yours," she said gruffly. "Great-Grandmother left it to me. I have the paperwork. This is my house, every rotten inch, and I refuse to let you stay here."

"You're just being greedy," charged Trouble.

Ariel shook her head. She had known from the moment she stepped on this hill that although she was welcomed here as a Hamilton, it would never be hers. Ariel's grandmother Anne had noted in her journal that Hamilton women searched for the places where they belonged, where the air embraced them and yearned for them. Ariel had found that place of acceptance and belonging on the farm where she grew up. Ariel didn't know if Meri would find her "wind," as Great-grandma

Annabelle called it, on their farm, or if she would need to seek the winds in other places.

Suddenly, wind shrieked through the broken windows, bringing the powerful and persistent scent of lilac and honeysuckle. The house shivered. Ariel knew she was not causing this. Her cousin was feeling too much; she was out of control.

"It's mine! Mine!" Trouble shouted at Ariel. "You have *your* farm."

"I'm trying to protect you!" yelled Ariel.

Mick stepped closer to Trouble, touched her arm. "Honey, this place is—"

Trouble shrugged his hand away. "It's mine," she turned to Mick with pleading eyes. "I can fix it up. You can help me."

"Trouble, this house is a mess—"

Trouble suddenly threw her head back and screamed. Wind tore through the open door, grabbed a corner of the water-stained wallpaper above the rotten and animal-infested sofa, and ripped off a chunk. The paper flew straight for Ariel.

Ariel batted it away and advanced on her cousin. "Stop it! Get a grip! You'll have this whole place falling down upon us."

Mick frowned, obviously bewildered by what was happening. "Trouble, what's going on?"

Trouble ignored Mick. She trembled, struggling for control. Dust swirled around them, and the chandelier overhead started to swing. Finally, she took a deep breath and focused on Ariel, reaching for Ariel. Their hands connected, and Trouble clutched Ariel as if she were a lifeline.

She said softly, "Ariel, I can *hear* the wind here."

Those words hit Ariel in the heart. She gasped. The hope she saw in Trouble's eyes gripped Ariel. Could this place help Trouble find who she truly was—just as the wind on the farm had shown Ariel?

Ariel didn't know what to say. Unlike Ariel and Meri, Trouble claimed she had never been able to hear the wind or talk to it. From everything Trouble had told her, Ariel thought her cousin couldn't communicate with Up There at all. She simply walked the air when emotion rose inside her and the air took her into its arms.

Ariel whispered, "You can *hear* it calling?"

Trouble burst into a smile as tears of joy streaked her cheeks. "Yes, a bit. I never understood why you and Meri made such a big deal of it. But this feeling . . . this feeling of belonging . . . it's amazing, isn't it?"

"Yes," Ariel said softly.

"This feeling is bigger than me. And I know it will get stronger the longer I stay here. Please, Ariel, help me."

Ariel cast a sideways glance at Mick, who was warily watching them. *The poor man doesn't know what he's in for,* Ariel thought. She tilted her head toward Mick. "And him?"

Trouble sent a quick glance and soft smile toward Mick. "I'll talk to him," she promised Ariel.

Ariel nodded, then silently wandered to the kitchen window and gazed thoughtfully at the backyard, where Great-Grandmother Annabelle lay under the blanket of blooming snow-in-summer. The hedge of honeysuckle was still happily guarding the old woman.

What am I to do? she asked the wind. Could she really take this chance from her cousin? Her heart was screaming at her: remember when you ran away from the wind and Up There, remember those twelve long years of searching for who you truly were, remember what it did to you?

During those lost years, Ariel had turned away from the people who loved her. She had given into the darkness of her fears—and almost disappeared. If she had never found her way back to the farm and Up There, she would not have Ruddy or Meri.

The scent of honeysuckle softly wove through the broken window where she stood. The wind lifted her hair and said, *Remember.*

Finally, she turned and saw Trouble leaning into Mick, his arms enclosing her. "Okay," she said, "here's the deal. We need to talk more about this. But for now, you can stay here."

"Yes!" Trouble ran to her and hugged her.

Ariel held up a hand. "But you can't sleep in this house. It's a death trap."

"I'll be careful—"

"No, this part is nonnegotiable," said Ariel. "You'll come back to the farm with Mick and get our tent. Set it up in the backyard by Annabelle. You'll pack a supply of food and water, and you'll reassure Meri that we are no longer fighting. You hurt her feelings when you stormed off without a good-bye, Trouble. That's my best offer."

"I'll take it," said Trouble eagerly.

CHAPTER 38

CATCHING LOST TIME

A MAN WITH A guitar case stood at the corner of a house where he once lived. Timothy Lee remembered this backyard, where he sang songs to his baby girl under the arms of the spreading oak. He remembered it was never hot here, always a breeze rustling the guardian spruce trees and tickling the wind chime. And now, from his place of hiding, he watched a child trying to teach her dog how to play disc golf.

"Gus, you have to twirl around like this then throw," said the child. The girl spun in a circle, and the dog imitated her, chasing its tail. The dog stayed on his feet; the girl did not. She fell, got up, and threw the disc again. When the disc flew a few feet farther, the dog watched it drop to the ground then ran to retrieve it and brought it back to her.

"Don't let it touch the ground, Gus. You're supposed to leap into the air and catch it between your teeth. Just like in the videos."

Gus tilted his head. He was trying to understand her. He always wanted to please the girl.

"Look. Catch it in the air. Like this." And with those words, the girl floated into the air, pretended she was grabbing the disc using her fingers, not her teeth, and hung there for a moment. "See?" Then she drifted back to the ground with a grace impossible for the average gravity-bound human.

Timothy sucked in his breath, not believing what he'd just seen. But then the girl did it again. His heart fluttered, and he placed a hand against the house to steady himself.

This was his granddaughter, Meriweather Turnstone.

This was the most beautiful, most amazing thing he had ever seen.

He didn't understand how Meri could do what she was doing. How could she break the shackles of gravity and become a part of the air? How could she return to the ground in the slowest of motion with a control that appeared natural to her?

After many years of hard lessons, Timothy finally had learned there were some things in life too lovely for words. They cannot be written on a sheet of notebook paper or played on a guitar. They must only be felt. And if you blinked, you would miss them.

Timothy was determined not to blink this time.

His granddaughter was a remarkable song wrapping around him until he could barely breathe. When it reached its crescendo, he felt his knees weaken and an explosion shuddered inside him. For the first time in years, there were tears in his eyes.

He knew, then, that he would fight for Meri, as he had not done for her mother. He would fight his own fears. He would be better this time. He would be a part of her life.

So, when the disc landed at his feet, he picked it up and stepped out of hiding to meet his granddaughter.

* * *

"Can I play?" he asked.

Meri stopped and stared at him. With a growl, Gus took up a guard position between Timothy and the girl.

Timothy held up his hands in surrender. The girl continued to eye him with suspicion.

"My name is Timothy, and I used to toss discs with my friends. I'd like to play a game of catch with you, Meri."

With distrust in her voice, the girl said, "How do you know my name? I'm not supposed to talk to strangers."

Gus growled and took a step toward the stranger.

Keeping an eye on the dog, the man said, "That's right, and I don't want to make you uncomfortable, so I won't come any closer. But I have been looking forward to meeting you." The man took a fortifying breath. "I'm your grandfather."

Meri was not falling for that one. "No, you're not."

"Your mother is my daughter, and you are hers." He pointed to his chest. "That makes me your grandfather."

"How come I've never heard of you?" asked the doubting child.

"I live in Texas. Far away. I don't get to Minnesota often."

"Don't they have phones in Texas?" she asked, crossing her arms over her chest.

"Yes, and I do email and text with your mother." He did not mention that such communication was rare, and that the door to a relationship with Ariel had only opened recently and briefly. Navigating their estrangement had been a slow process, one he had vowed to take at Ariel's pace.

He could feel the child softening toward him. He pointed

to the guitar case lying on the grass near the house. "If you play catch with me, I'll sing you a song."

"You play the guitar?"

"For years."

"Are you any good?"

Timothy smiled at her. "I played for your mother when she was a baby."

Without turning her back on the man and motioning Gus to follow, Meri went to the center of the yard. "Okay, but don't lose that disc," she said. "My friend Wren gave it to me."

They started at short distances—light, erratic tosses that both inexperienced Meri and rusty Timothy could easily catch. Gradually, they stepped farther apart, and the throws grew longer.

Since Meri had yet to master precision, she was better at catching than throwing. As Timothy shook off the rust, his throws grew more accurate and the discs intentionally flew higher and just out of Meri's reach. Without realizing it, Meri automatically lifted into the air in her attempts to catch them.

* * *

Ariel entered Ruddy's office and saw him at the window staring at something intently. His office, converted from the old sun-room at the back of the house, was lined with windows and had a panoramic view of the backyard. The windows were open, and they could hear voices.

"What are you watching?" she asked, coming to his side.

"Your father . . . playing with Meri."

"What?" Ariel shrieked, starting for the door.

Ruddy snagged her wrist and stopped her. He tugged her to him.

"Wait. My first impulse was to keep this guy away from

Meri too. But I've been watching them and listening to their conversation. They're having fun."

Ariel didn't believe it.

She saw Meri, so focused on the game that she was inadvertently walking the air as she tried to catch the disc.

Ariel's eyes whipped to her father to see if he noticed. He was laughing and applauding Meri's performance.

This was the man who had flown into a rage when infant Ariel had socked him in the eye with a rattle. She had been ten months old at the time and was just learning to levitate objects with the wind's help. He'd been tired from touring with his band, frustrated because he wasn't writing the great and powerful songs he wanted to write, and beginning to sense that there was something different about his family, and especially his child. He didn't know what it was, but his family had changed and it scared him.

Sahara had told Ariel that Timothy's life was constructed on ritual and orderliness, on the familiarity of gigs and bars, on explainable events. Flying rattles were not neat, organized, or explainable. They were unpredictable. Was that why he had run away and abandoned his family? Had he felt like a stranger in his own home?

* * *

When Ruddy called Meri and Gus in for a snack, Ariel stepped out of the house to face her father. She eyed the guitar case by the side of the house and the man who had planted a song—and not much else—in her heart. Sahara had raised Ariel alone. Timothy had never been in the picture. Their one meeting as adults, which occurred shortly before the wedding of Sahara and Echo, had been awkward. But over the years, abandoned Ariel had thawed toward the father she did not trust, and Timothy had kept trying to reach the daughter he wanted to know.

When Ariel stepped into the backyard, she heard in her head "St. Judy's Comet," the song that would never leave her alone and the song she would never sing.

Ariel and Timothy stared at each other. Although communication had eased between them, they were still essentially strangers. Ariel didn't know if she believed everything he wrote in his emails. Timothy claimed he followed her writing, had even bought copies of her book to proudly give to his friends.

Now neither knew what to say or do.

When Ariel said nothing, Timothy shoved his hands into the front pockets of his jeans and looked down at his shoes.

The wind gave Ariel a gentle push. Finally, Ariel spoke, "Please, Timothy, if you have ever loved me, don't hurt Meri."

Timothy's head snapped up.

"Hurt? I would never . . ."

Ariel held out a palm to forestall his excuses. She said, "Don't reject her because she's different or she makes you feel uncomfortable. Please."

Timothy's expression was puzzled. "Reject? Ariel, she's the most beautiful thing I've ever seen. She blows me away with just her smile." After a moment, he added, "She has your smile."

When Ariel said nothing, Timothy asked in a tentative voice, "Can you do what she does? Is that what you meant when you said she was like you?"

Ariel's emotions slammed into her, and the wind wailed through the pines. Timothy noticed the change in the air, the stirring of the spruce boughs, but instead of running away from her as he'd done in the past, he stepped toward his daughter.

"You don't have to tell me, if you don't want to," he said.

Ariel felt her face crumbling. The years of fear, the waiting for rejection, were lodged so deeply inside her. She forced herself to breathe.

Then, keeping her eyes locked on Timothy's, she lifted into the air. The wind welcomed her, and she gathered courage from it. She spread her arms and began to turn in a slow and elegant circle. The air filled all the lonely and fearful parts of her, and suddenly a thought rocketed through her: *If he doesn't like who I am, that is his problem.*

But then, she saw an expression she never thought she would see on her father's face: wonder . . . and pride.

Slowly, she drifted back to the ground.

Timothy walked to her and pulled her into a tentative but warm embrace. "My beautiful girl," he whispered in her ear.

* * *

Meri and Ruddy sat at the breakfast table watching Timothy and Ariel embrace.

Meri slipped a cookie to Gus under the table then stuffed another into her mouth. When she had stopped chewing and took a sip of milk, she said to Ruddy, "He says he's my grandfather."

"That's true."

"Then that means I have three grandfathers." This revelation amazed Meri.

"You do," said Ruddy.

After a moment of pondering, Meri said, "That doesn't seem fair. Maybe I can give one to Wren. He doesn't have any."

With another glance out the window, Ruddy smiled and said, "That is very thoughtful of you. But I don't think any of your grandfathers would be willing to leave you."

Meri studied her mother and grandfather now sitting in

the grass, heads bent together, talking. She said, "Maybe I'll just lend one to Wren for a day."

CHAPTER 39

UNEASY CONNECTIONS

FOR THE REST OF the afternoon, Ariel and Timothy sat in the shade of the oak tree and connected. He brought out his guitar and, in breaks in the conversation, occasionally strummed a tune. A companionable waft of air wove around them, and a contented Ariel found herself telling him about Trouble and the house on the hill.

"She's like you and Meri?" he asked.

"Yes, she can walk the air, but she doesn't seem to be able to converse with it very well."

Timothy's fingers paused on the guitar strings and one of his eyebrows lifted. "And you and Meri can?"

Ariel hesitated, plucking a blade of grass and floating it in the air. "Meri and I hear the wind calling and try to answer it the best we can."

"Answer it? What does that mean?"

Ariel wondered how to explain her gift to Timothy, or if

she should even try. Could she trust him with their secrets? Seeing him with Meri, feeling the beginning of a relationship, was battering her long-held defenses.

"Sometimes the air just wants to play, and sometimes it calls for help," she said. "On the day Mama married Echo, a tornado called to me. It was so confused and scared . . . and it was headed for Cosette. I knew I had to help it."

In a soft voice, Timothy asked, "What did you do?"

"I stepped into the tornado and let it become part of me."

The light tune Timothy had been strumming suddenly crashed to silence. He stared at her. "You what?"

Shifting her gaze, she said, "I think my job in these cases is to offer support, to soothe, to calm. And hope the elements will settle. I don't exactly know how it works, but it helps when I'm Up There."

"You must have been hurt—"

"Yes. But I survived." She did not tell Timothy that her grandmother Anne had died riding a storm.

Timothy took a long time thinking about this unexpected aspect of his daughter's life. "Will Meri grow up to do this too? Risk her life in some storm?"

Ariel wished she could tell him that Meri would always be safe. "I'm not sure. Meri's gift is so strong, and she is so empathetic. She understands things way beyond her years. I can't deny that I'm afraid for her."

Timothy watched his daughter levitate the cap of an acorn lying on the ground and weave it through her fingers like a magician's coin. He felt a powerful urge to place his hand on her bent head as he had done when she was a baby, to feel the softness of her hair, the preciousness of her again. Inside he wept for what he had so foolishly thrown away.

Without giving it a thought, he began to play the lullaby

he always thought of when he thought of Ariel—"St. Judy's Comet." Ariel's head immediately came up. The acorn cap paused in mid-air. He grinned at her with the dimpled and devilish look that had beguiled many women including her mother Sahara. After a moment, the same impish expression crossed Ariel's face. It slammed into his heart, this part of him reflected in her. And right then, he who had always chased fame and legacy realized he had given this world something far more extraordinary than one hit song.

He cleared his throat and sang to his baby girl once again.

* * *

As it grew close to dinnertime, Ruddy fired up the barbecue grill. Ariel heard him muttering to the charcoal. He was not a guy who liked to play with fire. He teased that he got enough excitement living with her and Meri.

Ariel and her father had talked for hours, so long she had to help him rise from the grass. "Growing old is a bitch. Everything gets stiffer than it used to," he said, brushing off the grass from his jeans. "Don't know how Jagger does it."

With a smile, Ariel helped him dust off his clothes. "Mama says you always liked everything . . . tidy."

"I need structure," he admitted, continuing to neaten his appearance. "Always have. I need clothes a certain way, songs played perfectly, rehearsals beginning on time."

Ariel shook her head. "Mama is as messy as can be, so am I. I don't know how you ever lived with her."

Timothy stopped and turned an astonished look on her. "I loved her."

At Ariel's expression of surprise, Timothy suddenly became preoccupied with zipping his guitar into its soft case. "Your mother always made adjustments for me, even though it went against her grain," he mumbled. "I realize that now, but I didn't appreciate it at the time. I have always loved Sahara and you."

When he had the guitar situated exactly as he liked it, he straightened, eager to change the subject. "So, what are you going to do about the house on the hill and your cousin?"

Ariel swept her hands through her hair in frustration. "I don't know."

Timothy eyed her. "Why don't you just give her the house? You don't want it. You love it here. This is your home."

They'd begun walking toward the house, and Ariel stopped and stared at him. "It's not that simple."

"Why not?"

"The place is falling down!" exclaimed Ariel.

Timothy shrugged. "Then let's fix it."

Ariel let out a laugh. "Says the musician who worries about the crease of his trousers."

"Hey," he said, "I've worked a lot of jobs between gigs: bartender, cab driver, construction worker. Trust me, I can use a hammer."

She looked at him with disbelief, and suddenly, Timothy wanted more than anything to make this one problem go away for his daughter. This need to take care of her was an unfamiliar feeling.

He pressed, "You said her boyfriend is in construction. We'll put him to work—"

"What is this *we* stuff?" Ariel interrupted him. "And you have no idea how much this will cost. That place is a money pit."

"I've got some money put aside—"

"We couldn't take your savings!"

He waived her concern aside. "We'll tap your mother and her rich doctor husband."

They continued walking. "Echo's not rich," she corrected

him. "And you just dropped by to meet your granddaughter. Now you want to rebuild a house?"

She had revealed Meri's friendship with Trouble, and Timothy wasn't above using it to help his daughter. "Doesn't sound like Trouble is going away," he said. "You know Meri will visit her, and the house has to be safe for my granddaughter."

They reached Ruddy who was still fussing with the barbecue grill. Ariel introduced Timothy to Ruddy. When Timothy stuck out his hand to shake, Ruddy hesitated then took it. From the look Ruddy gave him, Timothy knew his son-in-law didn't like him or trust him.

Ariel told her husband, "Timothy wants us to rebuild Trouble's house for her."

"Trouble's house?" Ruddy looked puzzled.

"The Hamilton House," she said.

As they talked, Timothy's mind automatically shifted into organizing mode and began making lists: help his daughter, win over his son-in-law, spend more time with his granddaughter. He had a few weeks before he had to go on tour again. Summertime was prime time for outdoor festivals in the upper Midwest.

Meri and Gus came out of the house and joined the conversation. Talk of rehabbing the Hamilton House excited Meri. She asked, "Grandpa, are you really going to help Trouble?"

Hearing himself called "Grandpa" for the first time sent a thrill running through Timothy. He almost didn't know what to do with this much happiness. Mentally, he started another list. Things to do with Meri: play the guitar, toss golf discs, meet her friend Wren, buy her a burger at Marta's Diner.

That night, he stood at the window of the guest bedroom in Ariel's house. His daughter's invitation to stay with them had surprised him. Then when Meri had asked him to read her a bedtime story—a ritual that was Ruddy's domain apparently—Timothy's spirits had risen to the stars.

From the window, Timothy watched Ariel and Ruddy swaying in the moonlight in the backyard. *Had he ever danced with Sahara like that, so slow and so immersed in each other?* He tried to remember.

But then he noticed that Ariel's feet were in the air, just inches from the ground. She was tethered to this world by the arms of Ruddy Turnstone. Ruddy seemed to pay this amazing phenomenon no mind, which made Timothy experience a strange and paternal thought: *She is safe with him.*

As Ruddy continued to swirl Ariel in slow circles and the night softened, a whiff of magic drifted into the room with a laugh. Before he realized what he was doing, Timothy pulled out a notebook he always carried with him but had not opened in a long time.

He heard a melody in his head and began to write.

CHAPTER 40

A SPY IN THE SKY

WILLOW ROUTINELY CRASHED COMPUTER programs, locked up laptops, and annihilated apps on her cell phone. She had come to accept that her vibe was toxic to technology.

It was not the case with her husband or son. Freddy could just step into a room and any technology present would stand straighter, salute, and obey. Her son Wren had a similar compatibility, having worked a cell phone expertly since the age of three. The common refrain in their household was: "Did you try turning it off and on again?"

Willow really didn't want to go online and order the beeswax candles that she desperately needed. She was certain the order would go awry. Saying a prayer to the gods of all things electronic, Willow entered the resort office and found Harley at the computer. She came up behind him and peeked over his shoulder. "What are you ordering?" she asked, startling Harley.

"Willow. What the heck? Wear a bell or something."

"Sorry," she said, continuing to eye the online sales page

that Harley had been perusing so intently. "Are you buying a drone? Whatever for?"

Harley ducked into his shoulders and mumbled, "Thought the kid and I could have some fun with it."

Willow had difficulty thinking anything electronic could be enjoyable or that her brother-in-law would choose to spend time with her son. "Wren? You want to play with Wren?"

"Might as well. He's always underfoot," replied Wren's gruff uncle.

Willow thought about it for a moment. "Wren does like techie things. This is sweet of you, Harley."

Harley reared back in his chair. "I am *not* sweet," said Harley. "Don't be getting that idea into your head."

Willow slid a piece of paper with writing on it beside the laptop keyboard. "Since you're ordering, Harley, will you please order some beeswax candles for me? Two dozen will do."

"Candles?" Harley frowned. "I'm ordering manly stuff, Willow."

"Just have them delivered with your drone. Use that delivery option Nikki told you about."

Nikki was on a crusade to educate Harley on the elimination of excessive packaging. The delivery of a big box with only a single item rattling around in it was a sin in Nikki's world. She insisted he set up a delivery date where all items could be grouped in one package. "Do us all a favor, Harley. Save some gas," she told him. "What the heck do you need all those cardboard boxes for anyway?"

"Okay! Okay!" Harley gave in to Willow. "But if that wax melts all over my new drone . . ."

A smiling Willow wrapped her arms around her brother-in-law and squeezed. As Harley was shaking off the irritating Willow hug, she skipped outside where one didn't have to turn the trees or flowers or turtles off and on again to enjoy them.

* * *

A week later, Willow lit one of her new beeswax candles and waved her hand in the air. She sent the candle's scent and a prayer out the window toward the boy and the man sitting shoulder-to-shoulder at the picnic table in the backyard. She whispered, "May you have love. May your heart be open."

The prayer traveled as most prayers do—silently, gently, on the wings of faith, and with no surety of its success. But Willow wasn't too worried about the prayer. She had plenty of prayers inside her, and it gave her a tickle of delight knowing how much Harley, if he only knew, would detest being the target of her invocation.

In the backyard, Harley felt a shiver run down his back. He ignored it and focused on the drone in his hand. Wren hovered close, as intrigued by the device as Harley. They had read the instruction manual three times and charged the drone. Finally, they looked at each other and shared excited grins.

"Let's do it," they said together.

Wren placed the drone on the grass and ran back to his uncle's side. Harley, standing with the controls, pressed a button and the black drone lifted into the air. It hovered in front of them. It wasn't as noisy as they thought it would be, and it was fast.

Harley moved a control, and suddenly the drone rose above their heads and zipped around the yard barely missing his trailer. It skirted the trees and climbed, its camera offering a view of all the cabins of the resort.

"The lake," Wren whispered. Harley sent the drone buzzing up the lake toward Cosette.

It circled the head of Harriet Bunyan in the park, and Harley and Wren marveled at how different the statue appeared from the sky. In fact, everything in Cosette looked different from the air.

"There's my school," said Wren, pointing at the image on the screen of the controller.

Working the joystick, Harley concentrated on learning how to steer the drone.

Wren continued to chatter, "And there's Blinka's bike shop. Dad says I can get a new bike when I stop wrecking the one I have. Meri is really good at bike riding. Do you think it's okay that she is better at that than I am, Harley?"

"What?" He steered the drone in a circle and headed for home. He wasn't sure how much battery power the drone had left. He didn't want to take the chance of dropping it into the lake on the first day. "Your mom says girls can do anything."

"But what do *you* think?" asked Wren.

Harley shrugged. "Maybe Meri can ride a bike better than you, but you can throw a disc better than she can."

Wren thought about that for a moment then smiled. "Yeah, but I'd never tell her that."

They landed the drone and looked at the video they'd just recorded of the lake and downtown Cosette.

Growing hungry, Wren said, "This was neat, Harley. Maybe next time I can steer."

Still focused on the controls with head bent, Harley said absently, "Sure, kid."

Unexpectedly, Wren flung his arms around Harley and gave him a hug.

"Great! Thanks, Harley," he said, then headed toward his house.

* * *

That evening, after the drone had been charged, Harley drove toward Nikki's house. He pulled to the side of the road well out of sight of the Diego farm, parked the truck, and took out the drone.

The light was soft yellow, and the streaky sky was edging toward blue and violet. Harley imagined the rays of the setting sun glancing off Nikki's steel art pieces and setting them aglow. It would be quite a sight and make a spectacular video. Nikki had shown him her sculpture garden named Art for Earth, but Harley worried that he had not reacted as well to the tour as he might have. They'd walked below the towering statements on climate change, and he hadn't known what to say. Nikki gave him the details on each one: her inspiration, the issues she'd had to overcome in the construction process, how they made her feel.

Harley was uncomfortable with Nikki's artistic shouts of defiance. He didn't understand her kind of passion. Sometimes, Nikki's drive and strength confused him and left him with that old high school feeling when he'd been ambushed on the thirty-yard line by a bruiser from the competing team. After the sculpture garden tour, he'd driven away knowing he'd disappointed Nikki with his reaction to her work. She had expected something from him, something more than an inane "This is nice." He hoped a sunset video of her strange garden would make up for his earlier blunder.

Distracted by thoughts of how he'd screwed up the first time he'd seen Art for Earth, Harley sent the drone into the air—in the wrong direction. He watched the screen looking for the tall sculptures, but there were no grand pieces of art.

Wait a minute. He was flying over Ariel's farm instead of Nikki's. The two farms were neighbors. He recognized Ariel's farmhouse and barn. He sent the drone swooping in a wide circle to return to his intended course when something strange caught his eye.

What was that?

He edged the drone closer, flipped on the video recorder, then let it hover above a grove of thick trees edging a meadow.

When he realized what he was seeing, he nearly dropped the controls.

It was Ariel Lee Turnstone.

And she was in the air.

Flying.

His mouth fell open.

She drifted and floated, walking the air with ease. She didn't fall to earth as humans trying such impossible things were supposed to do.

He scrubbed his eyes. *This can't be.*

Suddenly frightened, Harley recalled the drone, packed it up, and roared off in a spray of gravel.

Back in his trailer, he slugged down two beers, one after another. Then he sat at the tiny built-in dinette and exported the drone video footage to his laptop. The video was surprisingly clear with the glow of the setting sun highlighting the arch of Ariel's back, the curve of her graceful arms, the wildness of her tousled hair.

Harley cracked open another beer and slowly drank it as he replayed the video again.

This was an Ariel he had never seen before. She was relaxed and happy. She was dandelion fluff riding the wind. She was a feather drifting from a hawk's wing. She was a balloon escaping into the clouds.

Now, where had those thoughts come from? wondered Harley. He'd never owned a balloon in his life, and he never thought about dandelion fluff.

"Damn Nikki," he muttered. She was turning him soft with her painted canoe and big sculptures.

Harley clicked off the video.

He should erase it.

It felt so . . . private. Like he had been spying on Ariel.

He reached for the delete key.

Stopped.

Tapped "play" again.

He couldn't look away.

Seeing Ariel like this reminded him of that Christmas tree reflection in the water and how Nikki had whispered with awe in her voice, "Isn't it beautiful, Harley?"

CHAPTER 41

GOOD BONES

THE GROUP STARED AT the house on the hill, their stances almost identical—feet apart for balance against the wind, hands akimbo in thought. The wind roared around them, waiting for a decision. It picked apart the braid of Ariel's hair. It snatched Ruddy's baseball cap and tossed it down the hill. It fought Timothy's tidy appearance, freeing the T-shirt tucked into his jeans. But no matter what the wind did, it could not budge Whistler Newton.

Whistler was a human mountain himself—big, solid, confident. A longtime friend of the Stevens family, he had known Ariel since she was a child. He had two loves in life: taking photos and building things. He'd had a hand in constructing or remodeling most of the structures in Cosette. His photo skills ranged from loon images on display in Marta's Diner to Sahara and Echo's wedding photos. But the photographs dearest to Whistler's heart were of massive items—such as the biggest skillet in Iowa and the world's largest walleye sculpture in Minnesota. From the numerous giant Paul Bunyans lumbering along Minnesota's roadsides to the fifty-five-foot-tall Jolly Green Giant in Blue Earth and the colossal L.L. Bean boot at the Mall of America, Whistler could never get enough of giganticness.

He also couldn't stand by when something needed to be done. He saw an issue and tackled it—no questions asked. When his father, Mr. Newton, could no longer drive the school bus, Whistler stepped into the job. Now he was answering Ariel's call to give his assessment of rehabbing the old Hamilton House.

"Can it be done?" Ariel asked.

It was a big job and definitely in need of doing, Whistler thought. He rubbed his bushy beard with thick, scarred fingers and ran his gaze over the pitiful excuse for a house. He glanced behind him at the hill guarding the house. "That's a heck of a hill. Getting supplies up here is going to be a challenge," he said. "But the house . . . it has good bones."

Trouble and Mick, who had been waiting anxiously for the verdict, whooped and hugged each other.

Ariel gave her cousin a stern look. "It's going to cost."

"Yup," said Whistler.

Mick stepped forward. "I've been saving for building us a house in Missouri. Don't know why we can't use that money here."

Trouble looked at him in shock. "You have? But . . ."

"I can find work in construction here. I'm a good carpenter. Maybe Whistler will put in a word for me."

"I'm looking forward to seeing what you can do," said Whistler.

Trouble shook her head. "But your family . . . they're all in Missouri . . ."

Mick gently lifted a strand of her long hair and slid it

behind her shoulder. "Haven't you heard? People have these things called cell phones and emails."

Trouble's eyes met Ariel's, and Ariel knew that Trouble had not yet told Mick her Hamilton secret. She saw the worry and guilt in Trouble's eyes. She wanted to grab Trouble, shake her, and shout: *Tell him. Tell him who you truly are. Tell him before he upends his entire life for you. He deserves to know.*

But Trouble looked away and Ariel sighed in disappointment.

* * *

As secrets go, the Hamilton property was a good one. A driveway that had disappeared through the years, a tunnel of dense woods as protective as any moat, a rapacious hill that challenged engines, and a wind that denied visitors—no one had seen or stepped foot on the old Hamilton property for years. It had vanished from nearly everyone's mind.

In fact, it had slept on the county assessor's records unnoticed. Then Ariel marched into the county office with a will, a claim of ownership, and a check for the back taxes.

Before Ariel had driven away, the assessor was on the phone to her good friend, Melanie Harcourt. "Melanie, the strangest thing just happened," she said.

* * *

In the following days, Hamilton House awoke and groaned as a troop of Hamilton family and friends wielded hammers and paintbrushes. Those with strong arms lifted and carried. Those with trucks and large vehicles hauled supplies in and took garbage away. The wind was confused by all this activity but hadn't rolled anyone off the hill—yet.

Whistler and Mick, the project's generals, led the troops.

They sketched plans and puzzled over complicated situations—such as rejuvenating the ancient plumbing and bringing the electrical system up to code. Timothy dismantled the rotten front steps that had "nearly taken his granddaughter's leg off," as he described the incident. He rebuilt the steps and secured the porch. Ruddy and his father worked together on the interior staircase. "It's bigger than a birdhouse," Arthur told his son, "but we can handle it." Some days, Ruddy wasn't so sure.

Alice and Sahara fed the crew. Gus occupied Meri in the backyard and kept her away from the work zone. Echo bandaged cuts and scrapes and assessed minor calamities caused by errant hammers.

Ariel and Trouble stripped the smelly and moldy wallpaper from the walls. Removing the broken and disintegrating upstairs furniture, they tossed cushions, pillows, and parts of beds through second-floor windows into the wind that shaped neat piles in the yard.

"Are you sure you want to live here?" Ariel asked, startling a mouse fleeing the tufts of an old chair. "Even with all the work we've done, it is still inhabitable."

"Windows with glass and a roof that doesn't leak will make a difference," Trouble said. "We'll be out of that tent soon."

Trouble and Mick had spent every night during the rehab project in their tent in the backyard beside the grave of Great-Grandmother Annabelle. They made occasional trips to town for food and to Ariel's to use the shower.

"The place is still a mess," said Ariel, sneezing as she stirred up dust. "Glad it's you and not me living here."

As the work on the house progressed, and the family gathered for lunches on the lawn, the wind quieted. It took breaks when they did.

* * *

When it came time for Timothy to leave for the summer concerts, he hugged Meri and Ariel. "The house is not nearly done," he said, "but the porch is ready for Meri."

"Yes, it is. Thanks to you." Ariel smiled, and Timothy saw a softness in her eyes. "Next time," she said, "don't wait so long to visit."

His breath caught at the invitation, then he broke into a grin. "I won't," he said.

Meri clung to Timothy's leg.

He patted her on the head and promised, "I'll be back to do some more on the house—and to see you both."

As he opened the car door, Meri thrust a disc into his hands. "Wren's giving me another one," she said. "You take this one. Practice with your band friends. You need it."

He laughed.

Driving away, he watched them in the rearview mirror. He didn't want to lose sight of his daughter and granddaughter— ever again. As the miles took him farther and farther from them, he imagined playing his guitar, sitting on the porch steps of Hamilton House with his granddaughter.

CHAPTER 42

CAMPAIGN WITH PIE

MARTA'S DINER WAS THE unofficial headquarters for the Ariel Lee Turnstone campaign for town council. It was here where campaign manager Blinka and public relations director Nikki brainstormed plans for victory. It was the perfect place, plus how many campaign headquarters had an endless supply of free pie?

As Ariel entered the diner, she glanced at the sparse mid-afternoon crowd and was surprised to see Harley perched on a stool at the counter, a cup of coffee—not a beer—in his hands. Even more shocking was the boyish smile that flitted across his face when Nikki approached him with a carafe of fresh coffee. Ariel noticed Nikki's body language as she leaned invitingly over the counter toward Harley. *What was going on*?

As she passed Harley's seat, his head came up then quickly ducked. He'd given Ariel the strangest look, before he had adopted an intense interest in his coffee.

She stopped and tapped Harley's shoulder. "Is Wren still coming over to swim with Meri and Ruddy?" she asked.

"What?" Harley glanced her way but didn't meet her eyes.

"Play date? Today?" Ariel reminded him.

After a long pause, Harley said, "Oh, yeah, I guess." Then, sounding more like the Harley she knew, he added, "Freddy's in charge of the kid's social calendar."

With a nod, Ariel continued to the booth at the back, where Blinka waited. Sliding into the booth opposite her friend, Ariel said, "Harley's acting even weirder than usual."

Blinka looked up from the papers she'd been studying. "Nikki says he's had something on his mind for a couple of days, but he won't tell her what."

"Nikki?"

Blinka leaned closer, her blond braid dusting the papers on the table, and lowered her voice. "I think they are seeing each other."

Ariel sat back, flabbergasted. "Nikki and Harley? On what planet is that even possible?"

Grinning Blinka tapped Ariel's knuckles lightly with a pencil. "Behave."

"But I don't think Harley can even spell 'art.'"

Blinka shrugged. "They don't have much in common, but, as Grandma Trout used to say, 'Love is blind . . . or stupid.'"

"Your grandmother got that right," said Ariel, glancing again at Harley and Nikki.

✳ ✳ ✳

After Harley left, Nikki joined them with three iced teas and three slices of coconut cream pie.

"Sorry, Blinka, I gave Harley the last slice of French silk," said Nikki.

Blinka and Ariel frowned at the pie in front of them. French silk pie was a campaign meeting tradition.

Unaware of the sudden silence at the table, Nikki forked into her coconut cream pie. "What are you two talking about?"

Ariel and Blinka exchanged glances. "Nothing," said Ariel quickly.

Blinka agreed. "Just talking strategy. Campaign stuff."

Nikki's fork stopped in mid-air. "Is there a problem?"

Before either Ariel or Blinka could reply, they were interrupted by a woman hurrying toward their booth. It was Astrid Lindqvist, Meri's kindergarten teacher from last year. She smiled at Ariel and said, "Don't have much time now. Just wanted to thank you and tell you that I'm voting for you."

As Astrid left, Ariel frowned. "That's odd. She's the third person this week who has sought me out and claimed they were supporting me. The election is months away."

Nikki wiggled like an excited puppy. "That's my social media campaign. It's working!"

"What social media?" asked Ariel with suspicion in her voice.

Blinka suddenly developed an intense interest in her coconut cream pie.

Tapping sugar packets to sweeten her tea, Ariel said, "Blinka?"

Blinka threw down her fork. "I confess. Nikki and I made an executive decision. To broaden your reach. We're communicating your platform through email and weekly position papers."

Sugar granules flew out of the opened packets. They swirled like a snowflake dervish in the air for an impossible moment before landing on the table. "Platform? Position papers?" Ariel said, a cautious tone in her voice. "I thought I was the 'Nature First' candidate. That's it. I have one position: stop harmful and unnecessary development in Cosette to preserve our environment."

Refusing to meet Ariel's glare, Nikki squeaked, "Now you have a few more."

The sugar crystals on the table shifted, and a few rose into the air. When Ariel realized what she was doing, she took a deep breath and the crystals settled. "What have you two done?"

"Well," Nikki said in a bright voice, "you support new equipment for the fire department."

"I do?"

Blinka jumped in. "And you believe that Cosette needs a program for providing free school supplies for needy families."

Ariel asked, "And where am I supposed to get the money for fire equipment and school supplies?"

"We'll apply for grants for the fire equipment," said Blinka. "Get the civic clubs involved."

Nikki continued with excitement. "And for the free school supplies, we'll have a warehouse of sorts where teachers can shop for their classrooms and students. We'll use one of the empty storefronts. We'll call for volunteers. Just like the way people help with Earth Day. We can ask families to buy a little extra when they shop for school and donate to the program."

"Wait. Wait." Overwhelmed, Ariel ran her hands through her hair, dislodging a few sugar crystals. "Stop promising stuff I can't deliver."

Blinka and Nikki exchanged guilty glances.

"I know you mean well," said Ariel. "But I'm not a politician. This is not me, making impossible promises for votes."

Ariel considered her friends. "One of you should be challenging Melanie for the town council seat, not me," she said. "You both want this more than I do. I just want to get through to November and then hide . . . again.

Blinka touched her hand. "You're the one people trust. You always stood up to Melanie."

"That was ages ago. We're grown up now," Ariel said, recalling the years of resisting the torment of Melanie, who had taken an instant dislike to Ariel from the moment they met. Melanie, Harley, and their gang had made life miserable for many schoolchildren, including Ariel, Blinka, and Nikki.

"I hid behind my sketchbook every time I saw her," admitted Nikki.

"I got so mad I could hardly talk," confessed Blinka, "and you know how I like to talk. But you always kept it together."

Recalling all the years she'd stayed away from Cosette, years searching for the courage to be who she truly was, Ariel shook her head. "I was terrified inside."

"It never showed," said Nikki.

Ariel muttered, "I ran away."

"You were composed," said Blinka. "Sure, you left Cosette for a while, but you came back."

Unlike Nikki, Blinka knew about Ariel's gift, why she'd stayed away from Cosette for so long, and how carefully her friend guarded her actions. Rather than engage, Ariel had always used restraint. Blinka could not imagine how difficult that must be. If she had her way and Ariel's power, fiery Blinka would hang Melanie by her toes in the air.

Nikki said, "Plus no one can forget that you fought for your farm and won. You kept Melanie from digging up the trees, evicting the wildlife, and poisoning the land with her golf course plans. If you hadn't stopped her, she would have turned your old home into an ecological disaster, just to make a few bucks."

According to whom you talked, Ariel's refusal to sell the family farm to Melanie's developer clients was either a blessing or a curse. It all depended on whether you thought keeping Cosette's way of life—the pristine environment Harriet Bunyan had envisioned—was better than more jobs and more tourism dollars. Even those who supported increased development knew that the supposed benefits came with drawbacks—more stress on infrastructure (overcrowded roads wear more quickly), a toll on the community's resources (especially water supplies), and rising property values (which impact locals' taxes).

Blinka said, "Melanie has manipulated and bullied people for years, but she has never been able to pull her tricks on you."

Ariel didn't mind being in the spotlight at conferences and forums; she knew her stuff when it came to talking about the environment and climate. She had studied environmental issues for years, kept up-to-date on various views, written enough about the climate crisis to paper a trail to the moon. Even more importantly, she felt this crisis inside her every time she stepped into the worried arms of Up There.

She was not so confident, however, about stepping into the new spotlight of civic leadership. It could cast a revealing glare on the secrets she had lived with and protected all her life. She and her family had more to lose than an election. Ruddy, who supported her decision to run, claimed, "People would be fools not to vote for my smart and beautiful wife." He didn't believe Melanie could hurt him or Meri.

But Ariel knew better.

Blinka, who'd always thought Ariel could do anything but also knew Ariel often doubted her many strengths, quickly backtracked. "Okay, maybe we got carried away. No more email blasts without your approval."

Nikki nodded. "Right. But, Ariel, there is so much we can do for Cosette."

Ariel knew they were right. Cosette had many needs, and

economic development ala Melanie Harcourt wasn't the only way to answer them.

With a glance at her hopeful friends, Ariel said, "Okay, but cut back on the social media stuff and no more executive decisions."

Blinka clapped with relief. "Now, let's talk about the debate . . . I mean, town hall meeting."

Sugar crystals fountained into the air. "What meeting?" asked Ariel.

CHAPTER 43

MELANIE ASKS FOR HELP

HARLEY WAS HOLED UP in his trailer with his laptop watching—again—the drone video of Ariel in the air. The interior of the trailer was dark, lit only by the screen. He didn't understand what he was seeing. And he didn't understand why the footage captivated him so. *Why did he click on this video again and again?* It had been two days since he accidentally flew the drone into the sky over the wrong farm and recorded a moment that his brain maintained was impossible. No one can lift into the air as Ariel had done. No one can walk the wind and cartwheel through the sky. No one can defy gravity in this unimaginable manner without falling to the ground.

And yet, Ariel did it.

If he were honest, Harley had never liked Ariel. When they were in school together, she hadn't been as much fun to tease as the other kids. There was an air about her that gave him the creeps. At times, when he had pushed and pushed to elicit a reaction from her on the playground or at a school dance, she had stonewalled him. His partner in crime back in those days, Melanie Harcourt, used to laugh at his frustration. Melanie was a wait-and-get-even type. She tended to ignore what did not fit into her world view—until she wanted something from them.

When they all graduated from high school, Ariel left for college and didn't return. For years, Cosette and Harley were free of the specter of Ariel Lee, that strange girl he could never break, unravel, or forget. Then she moved back home and married Ruddy Turnstone, another weirdo, in Harley's book. Harley still didn't understand how anyone could make a living staring at the clouds.

He started the video again.

Harley had never really thought about the concept of beauty, where it came from, how it made a person feel. And yet he was looking at beauty in the video and he was feeling something—he didn't know what, but it scared him.

He pushed up the reading glasses he never wore outside the trailer and leaned closer.

How had a Clodhopper transformed into a butterfly? he wondered.

* * *

The loud banging on the door of Harley's trailer sent Harley into a panic. He ripped off the glasses, hid them under a pile of papers on the table, and slammed the lid of the laptop closed.

"Harley?" a voice called.

It was Melanie.

He got up and flung open the door. "What?"

Melanie shouldered her way inside. "I've got to talk to you. Geez, why is it so dark in here? Turn on a light, for Pete's sake."

Harley snapped on the overhead light and winced at how bright it was. Casting a glance to make sure the laptop was closed, he motioned Melanie toward the trailer's ancient recliner. With a put-upon sigh, Melanie plopped into the recliner, a leftover of Earl Wamsganz's. It reeked of beer, and she wrinkled her nose.

As Harley shuffled onto the bench of the dinette, the only other seat in the trailer, he suddenly felt tired.

"What's the problem?" he asked, because Melanie only came to him when she needed help.

Melanie crossed her legs, hiking up the skirt of her daffodil yellow suit, but Harley paid little attention to the display. They had tried sex in high school and found they were incompatible. They made better friends than lovers, even when they drove each other crazy.

Melanie's lips pursed in a pout, and she twisted the tress of blond hair that had fallen out of her usually restrained bun. "It's this election, Harley."

"What about it?"

"I never thought it would be this *hard*," she whined.

"If it were easy, everybody would do it," Harley said.

"Thanks for the insight, Einstein," said Melanie, the recliner moaning as she rocked. "Shut up and give me a beer."

Without leaving his seat, Harley opened the mini refrigerator and stared inside. "Don't have any."

"What? You always have beer. What's wrong with you? Are you sick?"

Harley shrugged. "Guess I forgot to shop."

Melanie eyed him suspiciously. "You're never out of beer."

Harley rested his hand on the top of the laptop. Melanie noticed the gesture and asked, "What where you doing in here in the dark? Porn?"

Harley growled at her. "You came to me, Mel. What do you want?"

Sensing she was losing Harley's attention and patience, Melanie stopped rocking, uncrossed her legs, and leaned forward. "I'm worried, Harley."

Harley recognized this Melanie voice. It rose from some childhood place inside her, where she wanted to cry but didn't dare, where she hoarded the memories of her precious father. While she had always dismissed her mother as a silly woman, Melanie had idolized her successful real estate agent father. From an early age, she had shadowed him, learning all the tricks of his trade. She was thirteen when her congenial, always upbeat father died, but she had never forgotten his words: "Mellie, look for your assets. Those are your opportunities." She had built a business on maximizing assets and downplaying liabilities in the style of Felix Harcourt.

"What are you worried about?" asked Harley.

In a muffled voice that drew Harley nearer, she said, "I can't find my assets, Harley."

"Your assets?"

"My opportunities."

"I don't understand what you're talking about," Harley said.

Melanie frowned. "Keep up, Harley. Assets equal opportunities. I have to tell people about my assets. What I can do for people, what I bring to the game that Ariel doesn't. But I'm not getting through to voters. I can just feel something's wrong. When did I turn into the Wicked Witch of the Midwest?"

Harley's eyes unwittingly went to the laptop. If Melanie knew what assets Ariel had . . .

He cleared his throat. "I don't know what you want me to do, Mel. She's running on quality-of-life issues. And those are hot right now."

Melanie snorted. "Quality of life? I'll tell you what quality of life is: it's having a roof over your head and a job to pay for it. The deer and rabbits and squirrels can find their own housing."

"You might want to tone down that kind of talk, Mel. People around here like their deer, especially in hunting season."

Frustrated, Melanie abruptly leaned back, making the recliner squeak. "Why can't people see that we need progress to survive? Progress is logical and makes us happy."

In Harley's opinion, Melanie just wanted things her way, but don't most people? He studied the distressed woman sitting in his trailer and repeated something Nikki had told him, "People don't vote with logic; they vote with emotion."

"I hate emotion," muttered Melanie. "What if I lose this election, Harley? What if Ariel beats me?"

Knowing it was always wiser to appear to sympathize with Melanie, Harley said, "That is unlikely. You are a winner."

"I need an edge, Harley," said Melanie. "Has Nikki said anything about their strategy?"

"Nikki?"

"Don't play dumb with me, Harley. I know you're dating her. The whole town knows. If you drink any more coffee at Marta's Diner, you'll float away."

"I don't know what you're talking about . . ."

"Come on, Harley. Help me," begged Melanie.

Harley's impulse to come to Melanie's aid was difficult to ignore. All the strings of their old friendship pulled at him. They had known each other since kindergarten and had enjoyed being the "mean" kids in school. They had been leaders, once upon a time. He had been the football star, she had been the president of the class, and everything had been theirs for the taking—until they grew up.

His hand traveled to the laptop.

Maybe showing Melanie the video wouldn't be a big deal.

Maybe she would see the beauty that he did.

And maybe Nikki would kill him.

His hand moved away from the laptop.

"Harley, can you help me?" Melanie asked again.

Before he could answer, there was a banging on the door and Wren burst into the trailer. "Harley, you gotta come! A kid has a fishing hook stuck in his thumb. He's screaming bloody murder."

"Well, tell Freddy," said Harley.

"Dad's with Mom holding the yoga class on the beach. You gotta take the hook out. The kid's dad took one look at it and almost fainted."

"Damn kids," Harley muttered, hauling himself out of his seat. "Damn yoga."

* * *

Harley ushered Wren out the door, leaving Melanie to roam his living quarters. *What a slob,* she thought. She didn't know why she put up with Harley, except some days he seemed to be her only friend in Cosette.

When Melanie, a divorcée determined to restart her father's old business, moved back to town after years away, Harley was the one who helped her establish an office. She discovered that he was a decent painter and a surprisingly careful furniture mover, which came in handy when she had tricky restaging projects. After her mother Stacy died, he'd offered to help Melanie sort through Stacy's belongings at the assisted living facility—an unexpectedly kind and sensitive gesture that Melanie had declined, of course. No one, not even Harley, was allowed to see Melanie cry.

Melanie's gaze traveled over the wrinkled clothes left on the floor, the dirty dishes in the tiny sink, the blinds missing slats. She eyed the laptop, which was the only thing in the trailer that appeared to be clean and cared for. Curious, she slid onto the dinette bench, grimaced when her skirt snagged on the cracked vinyl cushions, and lifted the laptop lid.

CHAPTER 44

KEEP OUT

RUDDY WALKED OUT OF the house on a muggy August day and automatically peered into the sky. There was a bank of dark, marshmallow-puffy clouds to the west. He'd seen them on the radar, knew they were coming, and had grown excited. If anyone enjoyed a good storm, it was Ruddy Turnstone— unless his wife was riding it.

When Ruddy was struck by lightning, he was doing exactly what he was doing now: being too enchanted, and too engrossed, by the storm to find shelter inside. Today, he would really be asking for it. His work for the day was to check the condition of all the "No Hunting" and "No Trespassing" signs around the farm. He also had new signs to post around the land that surrounded the Hamilton House.

Yup, Ruddy told himself, *it was a grand day to be carrying metal poles and digging holes. So he had better get to it and beat the storm.*

The sky rumbled in agreement.

Today, Ariel and Meri had hair appointments with Sweetie

Moongoose at Books & Bobs. Afterwards, Blinka, as campaign manager, had scheduled an afternoon of campaigning and door knocking. Ariel hated door knocking. Talking about herself—with neighbors or strangers—was torture.

Ruddy, however, thought it would be good for his secretive wife to open up a little to the people of Cosette. Before moving back to Cosette and marrying Ariel, he had been a meteorologist at a television station in Burlington, Vermont. His youthful appeal, easy-going manner, and preference for casual flannel clothing, even on television, had appealed to his New England viewers. He had been a relatable media star who always smiled and stopped to chat whenever he encountered his devoted viewers. Whether he was at the grocery store or attending a special event, he was always willing to listen to their weather complaints.

He knew Ariel's long-instilled instinct was to pull into her shell and protect herself, but Ruddy honestly believed there was more good in people than bad—and he wanted her to experience that.

The door knocking had another purpose. Ruddy trusted Blinka to keep his wife and daughter occupied with campaigning and their minds distracted from what was happening in the sky. He prayed that the winds did not call to Ariel today. Could she keep her promise of no more storm riding?

"Come on, Gus, let's get these signs up so we can enjoy the storm," Ruddy said, patting his leg for the dog to follow him.

They headed for the barn, where the signs and poles were stored.

Suddenly, Gus stopped, looked at the sky, and gave a woof.

Ruddy turned to the dog. "I know a storm's coming."

But Gus wouldn't budge. He lifted his head again, sniffed the air, and stared over the tops of the spruce trees at the cloud wall in the west. Ruddy examined the clouds and after a few moments saw movement. It was too small to be an airplane. It grew closer.

Ruddy squinted. He couldn't believe what he was seeing.

"It's a drone," he told Gus.

The purpose of the "No Hunting" and "No Trespassing" signs was to keep the farm's air space safe for Ruddy's wind-riding wife and daughter. He wasn't taking any chances that a duck hunter could mistake airborne Ariel or Meri for one of Minnesota's waterfowl. Discouraging strangers from wandering the woods around the farm helped keep his family and their secrets safe.

This drone presented a problem.

It could be a joyriding child with a joystick, or it could be someone with a more meddlesome nature. Either way, Ariel would not like it, and neither did he.

Ruddy raised his fists at the drone and waved for it to go away. Gus leaped into the air with several barks, adding his own threats.

The drone ignored their actions. It continued to hover and watch them.

Suddenly, Ruddy rushed into the barn and grabbed a large piece of cardboard from the recycling bin. He pulled a black marker from his pocket and began to write.

Then he hurried outside and raised the cardboard sign into the air: "No Drones! Keep Out! This Means You!"

The sky growled, and the wind gathered.

The drone was tossed from side to side in the bucking wind.

For a moment, Ruddy thought it was going to crash, but instead, it recovered and buzzed away.

After the drone left, Ruddy stood in the yard with Gus. With shoulders slumped, Ruddy said to the dog, "Now we have to worry about hunters *and* drones. I'm going to need more signs."

Slowly, the pair turned toward the barn. The drone's threat had swept away their enjoyment of the storm. It also had ruined their time line. Now, they had to sit out the storm in the barn and then post the signs.

CHAPTER 45

SECRET THREAT

HARLEY OFTEN MISUNDERSTOOD NIKKI. She had a way of confusing him and making him feel slow-witted. He never knew if his actions would please her or set her off—even more puzzling, he didn't know why he cared.

Nikki was at the resort to see the drone footage he'd shot of her sculptures. After the first disastrous flyover of Ariel's farm, Harley had tried again and succeeded to capture the sun setting on the metal giants gathered in Art for Earth, Nikki's sculpture garden.

Now, Harley and Nikki hovered together at the wooden picnic table beside his trailer, viewing the drone footage on his laptop. Intent and silent, Nikki leaned closer to the screen and examined the video. She replayed it, not saying a word.

Growing nervous at her lack of response, Harley said, "I thought you might like to see your sculptures from the air. Like a different angle. Don't you think the sunset colors reflecting in some of the metal pieces are cool?"

Nikki straightened. "You did this for me?"

He felt his face warm. "I was just practicing. Trying to learn how to navigate the darn thing."

"You parked on my road, shot this footage, but never stopped by to see me?"

"I wanted to surprise you. Wasn't sure how it would turn out. It took a couple of trials to get the drone going in the right direction and not crash into your sculptures."

Nikki laughed. "I'm glad you didn't crash."

Suddenly, she leaned closer to Harley and planted a kiss on his lips. Harley froze.

"This was sweet, Harley. Thank you."

Stunned, he looked at her with big eyes.

Nikki leaned back from their first kiss and Harley's astonished face. *How did they find themselves here?* she wondered.

It began with a canoe, a Christmas tree, and a red scarf.

Nikki'd had fun painting the crazy and colorful designs on the canoe, picturing with each swipe of the brush Harley's horror when he saw it. It had been a righteous revenge for all those school years Harley had made her life miserable, but that momentary act of spite was supposed to be it. She had gotten even and had planned to delete Harley from her life and memory. But then she'd found him drunk under Harriet Bunyan one holiday night and he had somehow touched her heart.

Milo, her art teacher in Italy, had often spoken to her of breaking the limits of imagination, of self, of compassion. He believed that true art came from an unbounded and unfathomable place inside us. As she had bedecked Harriet in holiday garland, she had realized that Harley was the most limited person she knew. He never considered dreaming beyond his horizons.

That star-whispering night started a chain of events that neither Nikki nor Harley had predicted. They were an unlikely couple. They had nothing in common. He was lethargy, and she was energy. He was hopelessness, and she was optimism in kick-ass boots. He seemed blind to beauty, and she saw it everywhere.

She gave him a coquettish smile and turned back to the laptop. "Let's see what other videos you have," she said, and before he could stop her, her fingers were flying over the keyboard.

"Wait!" he said.

But it was too late. Nikki had clicked on the videos of Ariel's farm.

The most recent one—Ruddy motioning angrily at the drone and holding up an obviously homemade sign—made her laugh. The next video she clicked on, however, choked her into stunned silence.

Harley tried to place his hands over the screen to block her view. "Don't look at that one! It was a mistake. I should have deleted it."

Nikki pushed his hands aside and watched.

It was Ariel in the air.

Nikki gave Harley a furious look. "You've been spying on Ariel and her family," accused Nikki.

"No, no." He rushed on, "It was an accident. These drones are harder to fly than you think. Please, Nikki, I didn't mean any harm."

"I find that hard to believe," Nikki said, poking Harley in the chest. "I don't know how you manipulated this video, but this is just the kind of crap you would pull when we were in school. Anything to embarrass someone. I don't know why I wasted my time on you, Harley Wamsganz."

She believed he had doctored the video.

Abruptly, she stood but before she could stalk off, he grabbed her wrist. "I'm not that guy anymore, Nikki. At least

I'm trying not to be. And even if I wanted to, I wouldn't know how to edit a video. This is real."

That stopped Nikki, and she slowly sat down.

She pressed a key and stared at the video.

Together, they watched Ariel float in the air above the meadow on her farm, drifting high and turning in slow motion toward the ground only to rise again with grace. Her hair wildly lifted from her shoulders as she swayed and pirouetted. Her arms curved as if to embrace the air. She did a cartwheel in slow motion in the sky—and right off the cliff.

Nikki gasped. "When was this shot?"

"A week ago."

"But-but I talked to her yesterday. She was complaining because Blinka made her campaign, knock on doors. She's fine. How could she go over that cliff a week ago and be okay yesterday?"

Harley lifted his shoulders as puzzled as she was. They looked at each other then back at the video.

Nikki replayed the video again, freezing it at one point. "Look at her. She looks so happy," whispered Nikki, with tears in her voice.

"Yeah, I know," said Harley.

Suddenly, Nikki turned to him and gripped his shirt in a fist. "You can never let Melanie see this. Promise me, Harley."

He felt the strength in the fingers that easily wielded heavy hammers and bent steel. He studied her intense dark eyes and those disorderly tufts of pixie hair that on anyone else would look weird but on her screamed "don't mess with me." Instead of her usual black T-shirt, she was wearing a dark purple tee depicting a raised fist and the letters "RBG." He didn't know who or what RBG was, but guessed it was someone strong. Nikki wouldn't admire anyone less.

He had known how to handle the shy, easily spooked schoolgirl of his past. This spirited woman—this Nikki he couldn't stop thinking of—was another proposition.

"I promise," he said.

✳ ✳ ✳

Melanie Harcourt leaned back in her office chair, propped her feet on the edge of her desk, and tented her fingers in thought. She watched, once again, the video that she'd copied from Harley's laptop.

She smiled. "Harley, my old friend, you've been a bad boy. And I love it. The good old days are back."

CHAPTER 46

A GOOD PLACE TO DIE

DAKOTA BLUE DIED, NOT like an explosion in her old chemistry lab, but like the last nightly chirp of a bird heading to its roost.

When Dakota entered hospice care, her circle of friends gathered and created a schedule for her care. Dakota wanted to stay in her house until the end, until she closed her eyes for the last time—so her friends made it happen. They took shifts, administered medicine, read to her, made food she barely ate. She slept nearly all the time. Her breathing was labored and halting, which wrenched the hearts of those who sat in vigil beside her.

During her few lucid moments, she recalled former students. She rambled as memories surfaced: "Sahara Stevens burned off my eyebrows once; she could not mix chemicals correctly to save her life." "Earl Wamsganz could never pass up a fight." "Arthur Turnstone used to hide bird eggs in his desk."

These moments of clarity never lasted long. As Dakota tired, she would sink below the waters of memory like one of her lost creatures.

Ariel was with Dakota on that final night shift, talking to her in those dark hours, whispering of nonsensical things and inescapable thoughts. Even though Dakota never responded, Ariel kept up her litany as the wind, feeling her sorrow, rustled the autumn leaves outside the house.

Ariel had turned the lights down low, and now she sat by the bed, stroking the sleeping woman's head. Dakota's silver hair was even thinner than Ariel remembered, and her cheeks were sunken. "I never got the chance to show you my greatest secret, Dakota, my gift," said Ariel. "I think you would have loved it. I wish I had told you about Up There. I wish I had drifted past your window, waved, and seen you laugh with joyful surprise. I'm sure you would have clutched your hands to your chest, as you did whenever you saw something amazing and wanted to see more. I would have given you more. I would have flown around your house and above your trees. You would have come out to your porch, clapping and laughing like an excited child."

Ariel wiped moisture from her cheeks, tossed the used tissue into the growing pile in a wastebasket beside Dakota's hospital bed. The bed was positioned so Dakota could see, in the moments she was awake, the quilt she had spent her life sewing.

Glancing at the "Lost Loves" quilt, Ariel said, "I wish we could talk again. I want more stories of the birds and animals that have disappeared, the ones you sewed into your quilt. Stories I could tell Meri, and she could pass on to her children."

Dakota had attended marches and demonstrations for the environment and, as a teacher, had pressed her students to truly see and think about this great ball on which they lived.

"This planet is your home," she had told them with serious eyes and in a not-to-be-ignored voice. "Respect it. Take your environmental shoes off when you enter. Keep it clean. Fight for it."

"You were smart and brave," Ariel told the sleeping woman. "Always sure of your place in this world."

Tucking the cotton blanket more securely over the bird bones of Dakota's shoulders, Ariel recalled one of her last discussions with a clear-headed Dakota. They had sat in this room, festooned with teacher awards and quilt pieces. Ariel had confessed to the older woman that she was afraid, that she doubted she could win the election for town council—and that, in fact, she didn't even know if she wanted to win. Although she didn't voice this to Dakota, Ariel had feared that she had put everything in danger—all the family's secrets, her daughter's future, her husband's peace of mind. She had wondered, *How had Up There become her easy place and Down Here so hard?*

Dakota had listened, nodding in understanding. Then she said, "Stepping out of our comfort zone, pushing past our limits, is always hard. Especially for one like you, who guards her privacy. But remember: we save what we love. Passion creates action. If we do not love, nothing gets done. I love everything about this world. I think you do too. Ariel, my dear, you have always had more love inside you than you realized."

The clock on the mantel ticked closer to four. Ariel grew weary, her voice raspy from talking, her mind unfocused. The hospice worker had told her that one of the kindest things one could do for a loved one on the threshold of the beyond was to relieve them of *our* worries and fears of losing them.

Could Ariel do that?

Could she say good-bye to her mentor and friend?

Was that what Dakota was waiting for? Permission to move on? Assurance that her friends and this world she loved could carry on without her?

Could Ariel be the one to give it to her?

Taking a deep breath, Ariel pushed aside her own fatigue and took Dakota's frail hand. Softly stroking it, she began talking again. The night air quieted and gathered outside the window to listen. An owl hooted encouragement in the forest as if to reassure Ariel that her next words were the right ones.

Ariel leaned forward and whispered, "Hear the owl, Dakota. It is saying good-bye. All your friends are here: the rabbit in the garden, the mice under the porch, the moon in the sky, the wind in the trees. You can let go, dear friend. We will hold you in our hearts. You will always be loved—by them and by me."

After several moments, Dakota Blue released a rattling breath and left her earthly life behind.

For a long time, Ariel sat in the silence of the small house with its awards, quilts, and books. Dakota had built a nest festooned with her accomplishments, her dedication, and her love. It had been a good place to live and to die.

Finally, Ariel rested her head on the bed beside Dakota and cried. And the wind wailed with her.

CHAPTER 47

GOOD-BYE, DAKOTA

THE CELEBRATION OF LIFE for Dakota Blue, retired science teacher and lifelong environmentalist, was held in a wildflower field on the Diego farm. Dakota had never married, had no family, neither distant nor near. All of Dakota's belongings, her house, and her final instructions had been left to Nikki Diego, her heir. One of those instructions was to scatter Dakota's ashes in the Art for Earth sculpture garden.

The garden, situated beside the Diego family's barn/workshop, was populated with tremendous sculptures crafted in metal and wood by Nikki and her father, Lars. Some people in Cosette deemed them a tourist trap, but Nikki insisted they were a statement. "People can walk the garden, study the pieces, and see that humans aren't the most important entities in this world," Nikki said. All the sculptures featured one of nature's creatures and had an environmental theme.

Originally, Lars had wanted to locate the sculptures along the gravel road leading to the Diego workshop, so visitors lured by such bizarre creations would be curious enough to purchase other art by Lars and Nikki. But Marta, Lars's wife, insisted the sculptures would be more powerful presented en masse. "Let them rise from a pollinator-friendly park," Marta had advised. "A forest of art."

Every time Nikki fired up the tractor to move a massive sculpture into place, she knew her mother had been right. The spirit of the place felt good, this tribute to the planet, this "scream for help," as Dakota had called it the first time she strolled among the enormous sculptures, patting their metal legs.

Dozens of people, many of them former students of Dakota's, showed up at the memorial. The day was pleasant with the feel and scent of autumn. The gray, puffy clouds were somber. There was a silence in the air as if the world had paused in respect for Dakota Blue.

Although Ariel didn't know everyone gathered there, she was happy to see a few familiar faces: Ruddy holding Meri's hand, Sahara and Echo, the Turnstones, Blinka's family, Trouble and Mick Dunn, Helen Moongoose who had kept Dakota in reading material, and her sister Sweetie who had styled Dakota's silver hair in the same fashion for decades. All the Wamsganzes, including Harley, had made an appearance as well as Whistler Newton, who was taking photos. Even Melanie Harcourt had come, probably to campaign, Ariel thought unkindly.

Since Nikki found public speaking as odious as mass-produced hotel art, Ariel had been tapped to give the eulogy. Ariel didn't know what she could say that these people didn't already know about Dakota. She cleared her throat, fighting against the grief lodged inside her. She did not want to cry. A reassuring breeze caressed her shoulder. *For Dakota,* the wind whispered.

Ariel stood by a steel sculpture titled "The Last Passenger." The work was a collaboration of Nikki and Dakota, with Dakota providing the research and Nikki the construction. The sculpture depicted an enormous passenger pigeon flying into extinction via a fifteen-foot-high oscillating electric fan. The fan's blades actually revolved. Some of the pigeon's lost feathers were attached to the blades, while others were artfully strewn at the base of the sculpture.

Looking up at the metal bird towering above her, Ariel began, "The last known passenger pigeon disappeared from Earth on September 1, 1914. It died, not in the sky where it longed to be, but in the Cincinnati Zoo. Its name was Martha. Dakota taught me about Martha. Unlike some of you, I never had Dakota as a teacher in school, but she was my mentor. She helped me become who I am, as she did for many of you.

"What I loved about Dakota was that she remembered Martha the passenger pigeon. She remembered her name. Dakota personalized nature. She knew that we would fight to save what we know and what we love. That was why she wanted all of us to know this place where we live, our planet home, and to realize it wasn't a thing. It was alive."

Ariel didn't realize that her cheeks were damp with tears until Nikki stepped up and slipped a tissue into her hand. She did not use it. Suddenly, it was not important to hide her grief or love for Dakota. The air stirred around her, and people began looking at the sky.

Sensing the atmospheric change, Sahara took a step toward her daughter. "Ariel . . ."

Ariel gave her mother a reassuring nod. She was okay.

Taking a steadying breath, Ariel continued, "Dakota was a much-loved and many times-awarded teacher. The first time I met her she told me the story of a chemistry student who shall be unnamed . . ." Ariel grinned at said student, her mother. "A student who caused a fire in the lab that burnt off Dakota's eyebrows."

Glancing at Helen, Dakota's personal librarian, Ariel continued, "Dakota loved reading, carried a book everywhere she went and even had her own book delivery service. She paid for that service in shortbread." A ripple of laughter ran through the crowd.

"But most of all, Dakota loved environmentalism and was considered an expert on the topic. Environmentalists across the nation consulted with her. She encouraged many to become involved in saving the planet." Ariel smiled at Arthur, who had worked with Dakota to save vanishing bird species.

"Dakota attended the first Earth Day event in 1970 in Minneapolis. I bet not all of you knew that. There she was, an unknown schoolteacher from Cosette, marching on a stockholders meeting of a major industrial polluter carrying a coffin of electric appliances."

Several people shook their heads. They'd had no idea of Dakota's part in that day of activism.

Ariel continued, "Dakota was a gifted quilter and sewed her environmentalism into a quilt she called 'Lost Loves.' It was a tribute to the planet's animals, fish, birds, and plants that have vanished. She had hoped to finish it but knew she never would—because species are still disappearing."

Ariel paused and took a deep breath. "Today, we gather not for a funeral, but for a celebration. There will never be another Dakota Blue. But, I believe we all have a little of Dakota inside us. The next time you smile at the birds at your feeder or stop in awe at the sight of a deer in the woods or listen to the call of a loon—remember this: Dakota would be proud of you. You saw and heard the world around you, and that is the first step to love."

With a bow of her head, Ariel moved to the side and Nikki approached with a wooden box she had carved herself. Nikki had barely opened the box of ashes, when the wind rushed in and whisked Dakota Blue into the sky, as if eager to touch an old friend. Ashes swirled around the sculpture, caressing the bird's wings, tangling with the blades of the fan. Ariel remembered the day she visited Dakota and found Nikki and Dakota drawing sketches of the passenger-pigeon sculpture. She had been jealous of Nikki that day because she realized then that Nikki—not Ariel—had been the one destined to continue Dakota's environmental legacy.

Now, she glanced at Ruddy and Meri and realized her destiny was elsewhere. She didn't need Dakota's legacy; she was making her own.

Feeling more at peace about Dakota than she had since her death, Ariel turned to Nikki and smiled. The women took a step toward each other, hugged, then looked up at the pigeon art and the drifting remains of their friend.

"Safe travels, Dakota," said Ariel.

"We love you," said Nikki.

The somber mood of the crowd melted into a true celebration as people began to talk, laugh, and trade memories of Dakota. Some meandered toward the refreshment table Marta had decked out with some of Dakota's favorite pies and cakes. Others strolled in the garden to see the sculptures.

Everyone stopped, however, when Nikki's father, Lars, sounded an alarm. "Get in the barn! Everyone!" he shouted. "A storm's coming!"

CHAPTER 48

THE WINDS OF CHANGE

EYES TURNED FROM THE refreshment table and the sculptures to the dark, advancing clouds. Stunned silence turned into shouts. The crowd rushed from the garden and ran for the open barn door.

Ruddy took one look at the clouds and grabbed Meri's hand. Ariel began to follow Ruddy and Meri but then a shift in the air stopped her. She scanned the surrounding fields, the garden of sculptures, the people hurrying for cover—and listened.

The wind was calling her: *Help.*

When Ruddy realized that Ariel wasn't beside him, he turned. "Ariel, let's go!"

She walked toward him with sorrowful eyes. "I can't."

Ruddy shook his head. "No, no, no. Don't do this. Come to the barn with us."

The sculptures, the wind whispered.

Meri cried, "Mama!"

Ariel kissed her daughter and her husband. "Take Meri. Keep her safe." When Ruddy started to argue again, she said, "There's no time. Take her to the barn and make sure the barn doors are closed."

Ruddy's shoulders slumped in defeat. He'd seen this look on Ariel's face before as she stood at the cliff edge of the meadow and about to face a tornado. "I love you," he mouthed. Then he lifted Meri into his arms and ran with her as she screamed and reached for Ariel.

"What are you doing?" Meri cried. "Put me down. I can help her."

In Ruddy's mind, it took days to reach the barn. Stepping inside, he shoved Meri into Sahara's arms and began to pull the heavy barn doors closed. But they refused to budge. The old, cumbersome doors were stuck. Lars and Whistler stepped forward to help Ruddy. The men grunted and succeeded in nearly closing the door. It left a gap, however, just wide enough so Ruddy could watch helplessly as his wife calmly walked toward the storm.

Meri wiggled out of her grandmother's arms and ran for the opening in the door. She threw herself toward the opening, but Ruddy caught her. He wrapped Meri in his arms and turned her away so she wouldn't see what was about to happen to her mother.

When Meri realized she couldn't get to Ariel, she beseeched Ruddy, "Go get her, Daddy!" He just shook his head. She desperately looked around the barn, seeking Trouble. Their cousin cowered in a back corner of the barn behind a pile of steel and iron pieces. Meri wiggled out of her father's arms and ran to Trouble.

"Help her," she demanded, tears streaming down her face.

Trouble refused. "No. I can't."

"Can't you hear the wind crying? This is too big. It needs help. Mama needs help."

Trouble scooted further into the dark safety of the barn.

"You have the same gift," Meri pleaded. "Mama can't do this alone."

Trouble shook her head. "I don't know how."

Except on the hill where the Hamilton House stood, the wind didn't talk to Trouble as it did to Ariel and Meri. Even when Trouble spoke to the wind on the hill, she wasn't sure it ever made a difference.

Trouble said, "Ariel will be okay. She's done this before."

"You're afraid," Meri said, disappointment in her voice. "You act brave, but you're not."

Trouble couldn't meet her eyes.

Meri ran back to her father, leaned against his leg, and sobbed. Others in the barn thought the child was simply upset about the storm; few realized Ariel was not among them. Two people did notice, however. Nikki edged closer to the opening and stared. She looked up as Harley joined her, placing a hand on her shoulder.

* * *

While Ruddy and Meri sprinted toward the barn, Ariel turned toward the sky. This was not like anything she had ever seen. This was not a small storm, not an angry tornado either. The clouds didn't spiral in a slender cone. This storm felt different. It was a wind catastrophe of immense size, a forest of shelf clouds marching across the horizon toward her, and she felt tiny and helpless against it. When they were composing their book on weather and climate, Ruddy had told her about these storms.

She was facing a derecho in all its fury.

This inexplicable phenomenon was not one storm but a cluster of fast-moving thunderstorms that materialized out of nowhere and formed a band of danger. The ominous, low clouds barreled in one direction spawning straight-line winds and powering a swathe of destruction.

Today, this derecho was heading for her family, friends, and—the sculptures in Art for Earth.

The dark clouds appeared so low that Ariel felt she could touch them without leaving her tiptoes. Suddenly, the wind ripped at her dress and grabbed at her hair. *Pay attention,* it said. She tried, but the voices of so many storms screamed at her, pleaded with her. Gusts beat against the sculptures like drums, and the metal creatures shivered, groaned, and started to bend. The fan blades of "The Last Passenger" began to whir, and the steel feathers of the pigeon trembled, tore from the sculpture, and flew into the air. Ariel didn't know how Nikki had anchored the sculptures, but she doubted their foundations were strong enough to withstand these tremendous winds.

With one last look at the barn and a deep breath, Ariel flung herself into her first derecho.

Rain needles pricked her skin and immediately soaked her. A furious and unexpected wallop of air ambushed her from the side, slamming her into the pigeon sculpture. Metal wings scraped her arms and slashed her back. Shoving the wind-whipped hair from her eyes, she rose higher.

Don't do this, she told the storm. *Leave this place.*

The storm didn't listen. It was beyond reason.

When the wind shook her like a dog with a toy, Ariel cried out to the long-gone wind walker who had passed this gift to her, "Grandmother, help me."

The wind howled with rage.

"You are fine," said a calming voice in her mind. "Keep talking to it, just as you did for Dakota."

And so, Ariel told the wind what she thought Dakota would say: how she loved this world and how it desperately needed nature's peace.

Be calm, she begged. *For Dakota.*

But the wind had gone insane. It was beyond listening and calming. Ariel cried. *Was this the end? Would she ever see Ruddy and Meri again?*

* * *

Inside the barn, the crowd huddled in groups. Some cried; some stared in shock. A worried Lars, holding Marta in his arms, observed the swinging ceiling lights and wondered how much longer the roof would hold out against this punishing assault. Blinka, knowing what Ariel was attempting, stood amid her brothers, head bent, and prayed. Sahara curled into Echo's arms, her face in his chest.

Harley watched as the wind tossed Ariel and ravaged her hair. Suddenly, he flashed on a memory from childhood of an angry Ariel with hair flying and hands clenched at her sides. He remembered how sometimes the air around that young Ariel had frightened him. He stepped closer to Nikki. When Ariel crashed into one of the sculptures, Nikki cried out.

The barn shook and the wind howled. Ruddy watched his wife's battle and felt helpless. There was nothing he could do.

A few people crowded behind Ruddy, attempting to see the storm through the gap in the barn door. Whistler moved to block their view. When Melanie raised her camera phone to record the storm, Harley snatched the phone from her hand

and tossed it into a pile of metal scraps. "What the hell, Harley?" she complained. That's when strong Whistler tried again to close the door. With a mighty push and a roar, he slammed the door completely shut with a bang.

Meri, who had been standing beside her father watching her mother's struggles with disbelief, dropped his hand and ran to Trouble. She tried, again, to get Trouble to help.

"You have to do something!" Meri shouted at Trouble.

Trouble shook her head. "I can't!"

"If you don't help her, I will," Meri threatened.

"No!" Trouble jumped to her feet. "You're not strong enough yet."

Mick looked from Trouble to the child. He didn't understand why they were arguing. He glanced toward the barn door and said, "What's going on?"

Rain pounded the barn's metal roof. Meri shrieked over the racket, "She's trying to save us, Trouble!"

Unable to look away from the child's desperate eyes, Trouble's heart sank. The barn rocked. The sound of dishes, chairs, tables, and pies hitting the barn, the sound of the wind and rain, was so loud Trouble couldn't think. It scared her to death. She turned to Mick. Her glance roamed his gentle but puzzled face, that unruly beard she loved, those nerdy glasses that she teased him about but adored.

Trouble thought, *He deserves a normal love. He doesn't belong on a crazy hill with a crazy woman. He should have peace and happiness.*

She kissed Mick on the lips then turned away. When Mick realized her intention—to slip out the back door without anyone seeing—he grabbed for her but was not quick enough. Instead, he followed her, and Meri followed him. Mick came to a halt at the side of the barn, watching in shock, as Trouble marched into the field of sculptures. Meri stood beside him, slipping her small hand into his.

✻ ✻ ✻

Suddenly Ariel felt a shift in the air. *Was it weakening? Was she getting through to it?* She looked around her; something had altered the conditions. Then she saw a wind-whipped Trouble angrily striding toward her.

In moments, Trouble ascended and floated beside Ariel, absorbing the buffeting of the wind. Rain plastered her long hair to her body.

"I don't know how to do this!" Trouble shouted over the roaring air.

Ariel reached for her hand. "Just talk to it. Mind to mind."

"You're crazy!" Trouble moaned, as a blast took them sideways and slammed them into a sculpture.

"Hold on!" Ariel called.

Again, the storm threw them, and Trouble banged an elbow on the sculpture. "Ow! Fricking wind. Stop that!"

Ariel laughed.

Trouble glared at her, then found herself laughing too.

"Okay," Trouble said. "You do it your way. I'll do it mine."

And that's what they did.

Ariel was the voice of calm, hope, and Dakota love. Trouble shrieked and demanded. She treated the wind like a child.

One moment they were beseeching, commanding, shouting, cursing, and the next they were drifting in a serene silence.

As quickly as they had appeared, the powerful winds of the derecho vanished.

"This is going to hurt," Ariel warned as they began to drop.

"Of course, it is." Trouble shook her head as if she would expect no less from her cousin.

The two women plummeted to the ground in exhaustion and pain. They lay there, looking up at the rain still coming down. It ran down their faces and calmed their worried souls. They listened and heard the wind quieting. They couldn't tell if the derecho had moved on or dissipated. Finally, they crawled to their knees and helped each other to stand. They pushed their rain-streaked hair out of their eyes and assessed the sculptures, some bent but all still standing.

Ariel pulled her battered cousin into her arms. "You did it," she whispered.

Before Ariel knew what was happening, Meri dashed through the rain and catapulted herself into her mother's arms, staggering Ariel. She glanced back at the barn and saw people emerging cautiously. She couldn't interpret what they were feeling, couldn't hear what they were saying, didn't know what they'd seen. They looked terrified, grateful to be alive, and, most of all, curious about her. *What was she doing out here, soaked and bedraggled amid the storm-ravaged sculptures? Why hadn't she gone to the barn with everyone else?*

An old fear crushed her like a toppled tree. In that moment, Ariel felt again: she was Clodhopper, the Other, the Different One.

Her shoulders sank.

She watched warily as Ruddy approached. She was drenched, shivering, and so exhausted she could barely stand. He shrugged off his jacket and wrapped it around Ariel. Later, at home, he would be angry when he saw the cuts and bruises on her body and find the slash down her back where the sculpture had scored her. But for now, he just needed to hold her.

CHAPTER 49

BROKEN PROMISES

MERI HAD NEVER HEARD her parents argue like this. Neither had Gus. He leaped onto the bed beside her and buried his head under her covers. She tightened her grip on the Harriet doll. The concerned wind outside jolted her window. Gus snuggled closer. Meri stroked Gus's head and sniffed. In a teary voice, she reassured him and the wind, "It'll be okay. Right, Harriet?"

The doll did not answer.

* * *

Ariel had changed into dry clothes after a silent Ruddy bandaged the cuts on her back, arms, and legs. Neither said anything as Ruddy made hot chocolate and quietly placed a cup on the coffee table in front of her. Ariel, bundled in a blanket and already battling the aches and pains from fighting the storm, leaned her head against the sofa's cushions.

Ruddy did not sit.

There were too many emotions roiling inside him. This

overload of fear and anger, this feeling of powerlessness, drove him to an edge where he had never been. He was supposed to be Ariel's zephyr, the one who brought calm to her and their relationship. *How could he do that when what he really wanted to do was shake her?*

"If you're going to yell, do it quietly. Meri is asleep," Ariel said in a weary voice.

Ruddy glared at her. After several long, uncomfortable minutes, he said softly, "I thought you were going to die."

"Me too," she said. "I'm sorry I frightened you."

Ruddy gave her an incredulous look. "That's all you can say?"

Ariel tried to explain. "I couldn't turn away, Ruddy. I couldn't run into that barn with you. I had to help. Even when I was plastered to the wing of that damn pigeon sculpture, and the wind felt so strong and I felt so weak, I couldn't . . ."

She held out her hand pleadingly, but he ignored it. "I couldn't let the storm have you, Meri, all the people, the sculptures."

Ruddy said, "I know weather, Ariel, and I know the danger you were in, the chance you took."

"What would you have had me do?"

"How about thinking about us—Meri and me—for once? Do you know I had to restrain Meri from going out there with you?"

"Oh, no." Ariel jerked her head back in shock.

"She wanted to help you, Ariel. She thought *she* could help." Ruddy's shoulders fell. Anger and sadness warred in his voice. "She is only six years old. She wants to be just like you. She wants to save the world, just like her mother."

"I never thought—"

Ruddy shook his head.

"That's the problem. You think more of your winds and your Up There than of us," he said.

Ariel scrambled from the sofa, shedding the warm blanket. "That's not true."

"So you saved the world but at what cost?" Ruddy's voice rose. "Half the town was in that barn. Half the town might have seen you walking the air."

"Surely not."

"Your secret is out. *Our* secret is out. What's our next move, Ariel? Sell the house and join a circus in need of a flying woman?"

"That's harsh," said Ariel.

"What about Meri? How is she going to face the kids at school? People will talk. Kids will hear their parents discussing the strange events at the sculpture garden."

Ariel stood speechless.

Ruddy shook his head, brushed his bronze curls from his watery eyes. "I thought I had lost you. Don't you get it?"

She took a step toward him, reaching for him. "I'm sorry. I don't know what else I could have done."

He stared at the hand extended toward him then into her eyes. His voice was ominous and hard. "You could have stayed on the ground. You could have acted like the rest of us *ordinary* humans and run for safety."

Ariel looked as if he had slapped her. She dropped her hand.

Ruddy couldn't believe he'd said those words to her.

He didn't recognize himself. He had to get out of there before he said something unforgivable, something that he didn't mean and couldn't take back, something that would lie between them forever.

With disappointment in his voice, he said, "What could you have done? You could have kept your promise!"

* * *

Long after Ruddy stormed out the front door, slamming it behind him, long after Ariel heard the engine of his car fire then the gravel on the driveway spitting, she sat on the floor in a puddle of disbelief and pain.

He had left her.

Was this how her mother had felt the day Timothy walked out?

Ariel rubbed her chest. She hadn't known a broken heart could really hurt. She sobbed, and the house shook with her grief.

CHAPTER 50

TRUTH AND DOUGHNUTS

WHEN TROUBLE LOOKED FOR Mick after the storm, he was nowhere to be found.

Sahara and Echo gave her a ride to Hamilton House.

"Are you sure you're okay?" asked a worried Sahara.

Trouble climbed out of the car and into the rain. "Yeah," she said.

As she began the weary, wet trek up the hill, Trouble made a promise: she would tell Mick everything about her gift. But when she reached the house, his motorcycle was not there and his clothes were gone.

Standing in the rain beside Annabelle's grave, Trouble said, "Grandma Clarissa was right, Annabelle. Love is not stronger than the wind."

As night descended and the rain softened to a drizzle, an extremely tired and aching Trouble lay down by Annabelle's snow-in-summer grave. She wished more than anything that the Hamilton curse had passed her by as it had Sahara. She didn't want to follow in the footsteps of her lonely and heartbroken grandmother Clarissa. She didn't want to calm storms like Ariel.

She curled up and cried herself to sleep.

When Trouble woke, the day was calm, not a storm in sight. The winds felt like the usual winds on the hill, her winds. The sun was weak but shining. The birds crowded the air with their conversations. The house groaned its usual grumpy expression of "good morning."

Rubbing the dried tears and crusty sleep from her eyes, a stiff Trouble struggled to sit. Everything hurt, and then she felt a helping hand at her back.

With surprise, she looked up into the shining eyes of Mick Dunn.

* * *

Mick had almost reached the Iowa border when he realized he was going in the wrong direction—away from Trouble and Hamilton House. The sight of the woman he loved drifting in the air with no visible means of support had scared him, so he ran. He was hundreds of miles away before his heart slammed the brakes on his logical mind, and he realized he didn't want to leave that crazy woman in the red high-tops. The thought of never looking into her dark eyes again, of never threading his fingers through her long silky hair, of never holding her as they drifted to sleep in their tent—it stopped him in his tracks.

With that revelation, he made a U-turn and roared back north, the way he had come. He stopped only once—to buy a dozen doughnuts. Trouble adored doughnuts. She liked them raised, glazed, frosted, sprinkled, filled with cream. It didn't matter as long as they were sweet and full of doughy goodness.

As the engine of the motorcycle throbbed beneath him, he tried not to dwell on what he had seen in the storm. He was sure there was a logical explanation, and if there wasn't . . . what had he expected from a woman like Trouble? She hadn't earned that name by being traditional or ordinary.

Now, Trouble and Mick sat on the front steps of Hamilton House drinking coffee and eating doughnuts. The sun turned the autumn leaves bright, and the air was happy. Mick leaned over and gently swept away the sprinkles caught in the corner of Trouble's lips. She smiled at him. He stroked her soft waist-length hair and waited for her to take the lead in the conversation that neither of them wanted, but both knew they needed to have.

"I wish we could just stay here, like this, forever," said Trouble with a sigh. She wanted things to go back to the way they were, to hide from the world, just the two of them.

Mick surveyed the hill, the broken-down house, and the woman who could fly. These weeks with her, days of working and loving, had been the best times of his life. Each day his purpose had become clearer—build a life with Trouble.

What he had seen in the sculpture garden had badly frayed that goal, but Mick loved Trouble and was willing to see if their relationship could be rewoven.

"Can you help me understand what happened?" he asked.

She gave him a sad look. "What happened was I screwed up."

"What do you mean?"

"No one was ever supposed to know—not you, not the town." When she saw his puzzled but still calm expression, she explained, "The women in our family are born with a gift. We can walk the air."

"Walk the air?"

"You would call it flying, but it is so much more." Trouble's voice grew excited. "It is like this special connection with the world: the wind, the sky, the trees, all things in nature. I didn't realize this until I came here and met Ariel. I just thought my ability to fly was a neat trick and a big secret. I didn't know anything about Up There."

"What is Up There?"

Trouble rose from the step, turned, and drifted into the air. She floated in front of him, and his eyes widened. She wasn't being swept up by a storm or lifted by invisible ropes. She gave him a quirky smile. "This is Up There. The connection."

When she landed lightly in the grass and slowly walked toward him, he rubbed his eyes. He was caught between disbelief and astonishment. As he had ridden back to her, the miles disappearing under his tires, his mind had rationalized what Trouble had done. He'd worked out excuses and possibilities, none of them correct.

He had questions but couldn't find the words. Trouble helped him.

"Let me tell you everything," she said, perching again on the porch steps but careful to leave a space between them. She told him about coming into her gift at the age of thirteen, long after her mother Brooke had died, and how her grandmother Clarissa took on the responsibility of her training. They trained in secret, often at night. Trouble had been a slow learner, probably because her grandmother refused to join her in the air and show her how it was done. Thus, Trouble wrecked things, flying into a chicken coop, knocking down fences, and scattering hay bales. The morning her angry grandfather found her lying near the broken chicken coop, he started calling her Trouble, and the nickname stuck.

Mick listened and looked concerned. "If he didn't know about your gift, why did he blame you?"

"Grandpa always assumed I'd been playing and got out of control. I *was* out of control but for a different reason."

Mick remembered Jack Harper, Trouble's grandfather. He'd been a hard man to get to know, not exactly friendly, but he was honest and always paid his bills. Mick, a carpenter who took on odd jobs, had been called to the Harper farm several times—to repair a broken window, fix a fallen fence, rebuild a shattered chicken coop. Now, he wondered how many of those odd jobs had been the work of Trouble.

Jack's wife, Clarissa, had liked Mick. She always had a glass of lemonade waiting for Mick when he finished his work and often sent him home with some sweet she had made. He had difficulty imagining farmwife Clarissa drifting into the clouds.

"Why did Clarissa refuse to walk the air?" he asked.

"My grandmother Clarissa grew up in this house with her cousin Anne. Anne was Ariel's grandmother. Both had the gift, and both were warned by Annabelle Hamilton to keep it a secret, always. You see, Hamilton women had a history. They seldom found men who could accept them, men who would stay. But Clarissa didn't listen."

Trouble looked into Mick's eyes. "Clarissa fell in love. She revealed her secret to her suitor and was rejected. It destroyed her, and she ran away. She always feared the same rejection from Grandpa Jack. I think she hid her gift so deep inside her that she lost contact with Up There forever. In the end, I believe she was *unable* to walk the air, even if she had wanted."

Mick couldn't meet Trouble's eyes. "And I ran away from you," he whispered, rubbing his work-roughened hands. "Just like Clarissa's boyfriend."

Trouble scooted closer to him and rubbed his shoulder. "I don't blame you. I understand. What I do, what I want from life and feel for this house, isn't normal. I'm crazy obsessed with this place, and you shouldn't feel chained to it. You deserve to love someone who isn't as messed up as I am."

When he started to object, she placed a finger over his lips. "I know I shouldn't have kept this from you, let it get this far. But secrets are part of who Hamilton women are. We can't seem to escape them."

He took her hand and kissed the storm-ravaged knuckles. He ran his finger along the scratches on her arm. What she did was not easy work. "I have never felt chained, and I still don't," he said softly, lightly caressing the bruise on her cheek. "But I don't like seeing you like this."

Trouble exhaled deeply. "Taming storms is not as easy as Ariel makes it look. Even though we are the same, we are different."

He tilted his head. "What do you mean?"

"I can't do some of the things Ariel or even Meri can do—" Trouble slapped a hand over her mouth and looked anxiously at Mick.

Slowly, he asked, "Can Meri ride the air too?"

Trouble clutched his arm. "You can never tell anyone about Meri. She is a child. This could ruin her life. Please, please, promise you will never reveal Meri's secret. I don't care what you tell people about me . . . but keep Meri safe."

He gently cupped her face in his hands. Staring into her dark, fearful eyes, he said, "I would never endanger you or Meri or Ariel. They're your family."

Trouble closed her eyes in relief and realized how good it felt to admit, "Yes, they are."

"And you are my family," he said.

Her eyes popped open in surprise.

A bubble of happy shock rose inside her, but she forced it down. "Don't make this decision lightly, Mick. Things could get messy if our secret gets out. You know, mobs-with-pitch-forks messy, and I don't want to drag you into it."

"What are you saying?"

"You can go, Mick. I'll be sad and crushed, but I will survive. I am stronger than Clarissa. I know that now. It's something Ariel has taught me."

Mick shook his head. "I'm not going anywhere."

"You deserve a normal life . . ."

He silenced her with a kiss.

When they took a breath, he said, "I deserve to be happy, and the only place where I'm happy is with you. Your fight is my fight. Your people are my people. I don't care if we have to live like hermits on this hill in this god-forsaken wind."

The air enveloped them in happiness and ripped Mick's black hat from his head.

"Bring that back," he shouted with a smile in his voice.

The wind only laughed as the hat rolled down the hill.

CHAPTER 51

WHAT DO WE DO NOW?

ARIEL SWEPT HER HAND over Ruddy's empty side of the bed and woke in sadness. They had seldom slept apart since their wedding. She moved her stiff and aching arms and legs and groaned. The cut on her back still burned. She pushed her impossibly tangled hair out of her face and opened her eyes.

Meri was standing beside the bed with a serious expression. "Where's Daddy?"

Ariel glanced at the chandelier, which was swinging over the bed. It was not her doing. She reached out for Meri, who was clutching the Harriet doll.

"Climb in," Ariel said lifting the covers. "He'll be back."

Meri scrambled into the bed, and Ariel wrapped her arms around the small figure of her daughter. She inhaled the unforgettable scent of her child then breathed out the calming air from Up There and sent it funneling through the chambers of Meri's distress. Eventually, the chandelier slowed and stilled.

Ariel looked around the room and realized they were not alone.

Standing at the foot of the bed, in silence, were Blinka and Nikki.

"What are you doing here?" asked Ariel.

Blinka handed her a glass of water and two ibuprofen.

Nikki just stared at her.

* * *

The video on Harley's computer took on new meaning in light of what Nikki had seen yesterday. The vision of Ariel being tossed about in the air above the sculptures in Art for Earth was nothing like Ariel in the video. It was scary, not beautiful.

"Explain," demanded Nikki.

Ariel sighed. "I'm sorry. I should have told you about myself."

Not yet ready to forgive being excluded, Nikki crossed her arms over her chest. "Tell me what, Ariel? I want to hear the words."

Meri watched the exchange between the friends with tense eyes. Ariel looked at Blinka, who gave her a nod.

"I can fly," said Ariel. "I have a gift that I use to calm storms. I can talk to the wind, and it talks to me. It is like a calling."

Nikki understood callings. She felt them every time she picked up a chisel or a hammer. Slowly, her stance softened, and her shoulders relaxed.

"How long have you been like this?" she asked.

"Forever," said Ariel sadly.

The silence in the room grew unbearable.

Nikki exhaled in exasperation. "Ariel, you didn't think you should have mentioned this calling of yours to your PR manager—not to mention your friend?"

"I'm sorry I kept you in the dark," said Ariel. "It's just the more people who know about me, the more dangerous it is for my family."

Nikki decided now was not the time to mention the video on Harley's computer. Adding Harley to the list of people who shouldn't know about Ariel's gift—but did—was not helpful at the moment.

"Okay. Let's talk damage control," said Nikki with a nod. "People are talking, but mostly no one really knows what happened at Dakota's celebration. They are still freaked about the storm. So far, no photos or videos have been posted online."

Blinka agreed. "Ruddy, Harley, and Whistler acted quickly to contain the gawkers in the barn. They got the door shut, and Harley even snatched Melanie's phone when she tried to record the storm."

"Really?" asked Ariel, surprised Harley had helped.

Blinka continued, "We can't worry about who saw what and who recorded what. We need to prepare for the meet-the-candidates town hall. It's tonight."

Oh no. Ariel had forgotten about the town hall.

Nikki said, "With gossip running wild, it's going to be standing room only in the school auditorium."

Meri interrupted their discussion. "What about Daddy? We have to find him."

With a wave of her hand, Nikki said, "Don't worry about it. I've got Harley on that."

Ariel stirred. Harley had been assigned to corral Ruddy? People were asking questions? She had to face the voters—and Melanie—tonight? Ariel didn't know what to do. This was grade school all over again—she was the center of unwanted attention and wanted to hide. Only this time it was worse. She wasn't alone in the spotlight. Ruddy and Meri were there with her, innocent bystanders. It was a disaster.

Ariel started to pull the covers over her head, Blinka stopped her. "What you need is food," she said. "Nikki's brought pastries from Marta's Diner."

Meri scrambled out of bed. "Yes!"

Nikki nodded. "Chocolate frosted ones. Your favorite."

Ariel and Blinka heard Meri chattering with Nikki on the way downstairs. "We have to save one for Daddy," Meri instructed.

"Of course," said Nikki.

Blinka caught Ariel's eye. "See? Food makes everything better."

* * *

While everyone ate breakfast, Sahara arrived. She declined a pastry and motioned for Ariel to join her on the porch.

For generations, the Stevens farmhouse had been painted white, and it still was. The porch swing and matching front door, however, had changed colors through the years. The current shade of whimsicality was Cherry Bomb Red, which was a fitting hue for Sahara's mood.

She was ready to fight someone, anyone, because her baby was hurting. Sahara tipped the porch swing into explosive motion with her toe. She had always sought balance in this place. Here her mind could drift into a metronomic state, and harmony and calm could be hers. When she was a child and ignored by her brothers—Kal being too busy with his rescue animals and Gobi too attached to his books—her mother Anne would find her on the swing, sulking. When Timothy left Sahara, she had spent the entire night on the swing, holding infant Ariel, crying, cursing, and seeking the strength to carry on without her husband. When she was bereft of words for her stories, she had found the words here, lodged like floating leaves caught on a crag in a stream waiting for her to free them.

And now, she hoped the swing would help her face the day she had worked so hard to prevent, the day her child's world collapsed. She realized she had been waiting in fear of this day since she saw infant Ariel conducting the animals in the mobile over her crib, making them bob and weave with the wave of her tiny fists.

Now the waiting was over.

When Ariel came out of the house, Sahara plastered a welcoming smile on her face. Ariel plopped onto the swing without it missing a rocking beat.

"What do we do now?" she asked.

Sahara studied her daughter. "What do *you* want to do?"

Ariel's breath exploded from her. "Run away. Turn back time. Become a hermit and live with Trouble at Hamilton House."

"The winds there wouldn't suit you."

"Neither would that ridiculous camel-hump hill."

The women rocked.

Sahara broke the silence. "Whether you like it or not, your running-away days are over. You are a wife, a mother, and the head of the family now."

"No, you are . . ."

Sahara shook her head. "I can't go where you go, can't lead the Hamilton women into the future. That is your responsibility."

Despite the blustery fall day, a soothing wind slipped through the porch balusters.

Now, you're all sweetness, Ariel told the wind. *I'm still mad at you. A derecho. Really?*

Sahara recognized the preoccupied expression on her daughter's face. Sahara had seen it many times, and she had begun to spot a similar look on Meri's face. Ariel was conversing with the air.

Sahara recalled the first time young Ariel clattered into the house in her heavy shoes, too excited to contain herself, and exclaimed, "I talked with the wind, and it talked to me."

Sahara pulled her worried daughter close. Ariel leaned her head on her mother's shoulders. Sahara said, "Ariel, the sky has never been your limit."

"What do you mean? I have spent years battling who I am and what I am supposed to be Up There."

"And now, the battle is Down Here." She tapped the temple of Ariel's head. "The limits are inside you, Ariel; they always have been."

"I'm not ready for this. Our secret is out," said Ariel with sadness. "Everyone knows about us."

"Probably."

"How am I ever going to protect Meri now?" Tears crept into Ariel's voice. "I can't bear to see her hurt, Mama."

"I know exactly how you feel." Sahara stopped the porch swing and turned Ariel to face her. She wiped the tears from her daughter's cheeks with her thumbs. "Being the mother of a Hamilton daughter is the hardest thing you will ever do."

CHAPTER 52

CRAZY TO TURN YOUR BACK ON THAT

RUDDY HAD NEVER PASSED out on a wooden park bench before. Waking up, he found it hard, uncomfortable, and noisy. He covered his ears and curled into a tighter ball to escape the pounding in his head and the screams of a hungry gull.

A commiserating voice said from over his shoulder, "Hang-overs are a bitch."

Ruddy groaned. *Not Harley,* he thought, *not today.*

Harley shoved Ruddy's feet off the bench to make a seat for himself. As Harley sat, his boot connected with several empty beer cans tossed on the ground. The clatter resounded in Ruddy's aching head. He propped his elbows on his knees and cradled his head in his hands.

"Go away, Harley."

"Can't. Nikki told me to find you, and if I don't bring you home, she's going to kick my butt with those heavy boots of hers." Harley lowered his voice. "She has a mean side."

A gull swooped over their heads and landed on the shoulder of the Harriet statue. Harley pointed his half-eaten doughnut at the bird. "Don't you shit on Harriet. Show some respect." He tossed the remains of the doughnut toward the beach, away from the statue, and the gull pounced on it.

"From your current location and demeanor, I would guess there is trouble in paradise," Harley said. "And I'm not referring to that cute but strange cousin of Ariel's."

"Harley, I'm not in the mood for assholes this morning."

Ruddy picked up one of the cans near his feet, squinted into the opening for any remaining drops. He was so thirsty he could drink all of Lake Cosette. Harley shoved a bottle of water into Ruddy's hands, and Ruddy guzzled half of it in one drink.

Harley leaned back and spread his arms casually along the back of the bench. He peered at the lake, sparkling in the morning sun, and said, "That was some show we saw yesterday in Nikki's sculpture garden."

"Yeah."

"Is that what you argued about?"

Ruddy remained silent, not willing to discuss his marriage with Harley.

Harley continued, "But you already knew about her tricks, didn't you?"

Ruddy thought of all he and Ariel had done to protect their secrets, all the years of being careful, all the sleepless nights worrying about how to protect Ariel and Meri. In one rash moment, she'd blown everything apart, and he'd stood helpless, unable to stop her or protect his family. The fire of anger roared back to life.

Ruddy squeezed the empty water bottle in his hands. "She promised she wouldn't ride any more storms. She promised!"

Harley looked at Ruddy in surprise. Normally, the weather geek was unflappable. Harley said, "Riding storms. Is that what you call it?"

Ruddy pushed to his feet, kicking over clattering cans. With arms akimbo, he glared at the large man on the bench. "Yes, my wife can fly. You want to make a big deal out of it, Harley? You live for this. I'm sure you can make it worse, find some way to humiliate her and hurt her. You were always good at that."

At first, Harley didn't react. Ruddy was ready with his fists. One crack from his old enemy and he would punch Harley in the nose. Ruddy would probably break his hand, but Ruddy thought it would be worth it. Everything else in his life was breaking.

"Actually," Harley said, reaching into his pocket, "I want to show you something."

He took out his phone and clicked on the drone video recording of Ariel in the air.

Ruddy stopped. Slowly, he sank onto the bench and took the phone. He couldn't take his eyes off the screen.

"How did you get this?" Ruddy whispered. "Are you the one flying drones over our farm?"

"It was an accident," said Harley. "I didn't mean to spy on her. I planned to erase it, but . . ."

Ruddy looked at him sharply. "What?"

"It was so damn cool watching her," Harley said. "I'd never seen anything like that. How she moved in the air. And the look on her face. Isn't that one of the most beautiful things you've ever seen, man?"

Ruddy stilled and watched his wife. She thought she was alone in the meadow; he recognized the location. She was letting go, filling herself with peace and wind and happiness. She was one with Up There. No matter how many times Ariel had tried to explain this feeling to him, he had never understood—until now.

Head bowed, Ruddy asked, "How long have you had this?"

Harley shrugged. "Days."

"Have you shown it to anyone else?"

Harley looked uncomfortable.

Ruddy watched his old schoolmate closely and realized that there was something different about him. Lately, Harley had not been his usual grumpier-than-Grinch self. Ariel said Harley and Nikki were seeing each other. Ruddy had thought at the time, that it was an improbable match, but now he wasn't so sure. *Was he seeing the humanizing of Harley Wamsganz?*

Ruddy eyed Harley with speculation. "What do you want to keep quiet about this?"

Harley looked insulted. "Aw, man, I'm trying to do you a favor. Only Nikki has seen this, and no one else will. I don't understand this thing Ariel does, but Nikki believes Ariel saved her sculpture garden. Maybe she did; maybe she didn't. Nikki believes a lot of weird stuff."

When a breeze lifted off the lake and gentled the air around the two men, Harley continued in a gruff voice, "Nikki says there are some things you don't mess with, Turnstone. Some things are too extraordinary, too special, and we just need to leave them alone and be grateful for the experience."

Ruddy stared at the video.

Frustrated, Harley flung his hands into the air and said, "How can you walk away from that, man? I'm not your enemy. Go home and love that weird flying woman."

Ruddy found this philosophical side of Harley disturbing. He didn't know what to do with it, so he rose from the bench, handed the phone back to Harley, and patted his pockets for his keys. "Thanks."

Harley stood and towered over Ruddy, just like the old days. "You're going to recycle those beer cans before you go, right?"

Ruddy laughed. Nikki had created a monster.

* * *

When Ruddy walked into the house, he entered a room awash in mid-morning sunlight and in arguing women armed with a whiteboard, laptops, and too much coffee. Ariel, Blinka, Nikki, and Sahara were discussing, rather loudly, campaign strategy.

He'd forgotten: tonight was the night of the town hall, a chance for the candidates to present their positions to the voters. The timing couldn't have been worse.

Slowly, the room grew silent.

Everyone was staring at him, but he had eyes only for Ariel.

She looked happy to see him but also sad and hesitant.

They walked toward each other, meeting halfway.

Ruddy stared at Ariel, waiting for her condemnation. He deserved it. He had done exactly what her father had done— abandoned his family when they most needed him.

"I'm sorry," he said.

She pulled his head down and kissed him. He wrapped her tighter and deepened the kiss. When they came up for breath, she gave him the confident smile of Anne Hamilton Stevens, and he knew no matter what she planned to do—tonight or in the future—he would follow her.

He whispered in her ear, "I have faith in you."

CHAPTER 53

DOESN'T EVERYBODY WANT TO FLY?

MERI MISSED THE SCHOOL bus during the emotional morning of Ruddy's return, doughnut eating, and campaign planning. Ariel and Ruddy decided it was just as well to keep Meri home until they assessed the fallout of the events of the previous day.

Meri, however, was distraught about missing a day of first grade. While her mother and her friends planned for the town hall, Meri moped in the backyard, wondering what would happen to her family now that their most precious secret was no longer secret.

By midafternoon, the strategy session had broken up, and Meri was pacing like a caged animal. It was then that Sahara suggested that she and Echo take Meri to the park.

Ariel did not like the idea. "What about the other kids?" she asked Sahara.

"She will handle them. She's your daughter." Sahara pressed

Ariel's shoulder in reassurance. "Echo and I will be right there. We'll keep her safe."

As Sahara and Echo talked quietly on a bench within sight, Meri sat alone on the sandy beach in Cosette's park. None of the other children on the nearby playground approached her, and she dared not climb up to the slide to join them. She glanced at the swings, which were all occupied, and looked away. Suddenly, she wanted to sit on a swing and pump her legs, rising higher and higher. She wanted to take the swing to an elevation that no one had ever seen before and then she would jump off. Everyone would be shocked and waiting for her to crash, but she would continue rising into the sky. Just like her mother.

But unlike her mother, she would never come back.

Meri scooped up handfuls of sand and let the grains sift through her spread fingers. She didn't understand everything that had happened yesterday at Dakota's party or why everyone was so upset. Her mother had broken the family rules regarding Up There. Meri thought that should be okay because she did it to save people, but somehow it had created a big problem. Meri had an uneasy feeling. It felt as if everyone were holding their breath to see what would happen next.

Meri wore the monkey backpack with the pink dumbbell inside. Her father had insisted. Everyone's feelings were on edge, and he worried that Meri's emotions might overpower her today.

Sand slipped through the cage of Meri's fingers. The wind whisked the grains away and piled them neatly on the toe of a sneaker standing nearby. The sneaker belonged to Wren.

Wren lifted his foot to dislodge the sand and sat down beside Meri. She looked back at Sahara and Echo and found Wren's mom, Willow, sitting beside them.

"Why aren't you playing?" Wren asked.

Meri glanced at the raucous children shouting and pushing each other on the platform at the top of the slide. "Don't feel like it," she said.

He nodded in understanding.

Meri started drawing in the sand with her finger. She sketched a car, a stick person, and a dog.

After a few moments of silence, Wren said, "I know what happened. With your mom."

Meri ducked her head, adding more detail to her drawing—a suitcase for the stick person.

"Harley says I'm not supposed to talk about it," Wren said. "But I think it's cool."

Meri stopped and looked at him. "You do?"

"Doesn't everybody want to fly? I wish I could."

Meri never thought about it that way—that some people would envy her gift. She wished she could tell Wren about Up There and show him that she could fly like her mother. But she didn't dare. Instead, she swept the sand with the palm of her hand, erasing the drawings and any idea of sharing her secret.

Suddenly, hoping to cheer her, Wren said, "Hey, look, I got a new disc." He handed her a golf disc with a swirling pattern of shades of purple and sparkles. "It makes me think of you. I don't know why."

Meri examined it carefully then returned it. "Nice."

With head bent, she silently began scooping sand and pouring again.

Wren looked down the lake toward his family's resort. It was quiet. Fall mainly attracted fisher people, such as the one trying his luck from a boat in the middle of the lake. He said, "My mom says that people will forget what happened yesterday. It will blow over."

"I don't understand what's going on." Meri stopped sifting the sand. "Everybody's upset. I hope Mama and Daddy don't start talking about homeschooling again."

Wren turned to her, eyes wide. "They can't. I don't want you to leave school."

Meri shrugged as if the matter was out of her hands. "What if they sell the farm and make us move away?"

"No!"

"I don't want to," Meri said. "I love the farm, and I'm not sure what my mom would do if she couldn't live there. But . . ."

They were interrupted by a kick of sand.

"Bird boy, what are you doing talking to her?" said Buster Sweeney. Buster reminded Meri of a video game where all the characters were made of blocks. His new haircut for this school year, fresh from an expensive salon in Minneapolis, made him look like he was wearing a box on his head. He had gained weight over the summer and already had started throwing it around. Meri thought Buster's mother fed him too many sweets. If Mrs. Sweeney thought that would sweeten her son's personality, it wasn't working.

"Go away, Buster," said Wren in a weary voice.

"No," Buster leaned into their faces. "She's a freak, like her mother, and you shouldn't be sitting with her."

Both Wren and Meri rose to their feet, forcing Buster to step back.

Meri said nothing. She didn't want any trouble, especially not today.

Wren growled, "Don't say that about her. She's not a freak."

"She is too. My mom says the whole family is," Buster said.

Before this could escalate, Meri tried to intervene, "Wren, it's okay. Go play with Buster."

Wren frowned at her. "I don't want to play with this jerk."

Buster knocked Wren on the shoulder. "Who you calling a jerk?"

"You!" said Wren, his tone growing loud. "Why would I want to hang with you? I hate you!"

From the bench came Willow's mellifluous voice, "Wren, remember, we don't hate people."

Wren rolled his eyes. "Then I strongly dislike you, Buster."

"Who cares. You're a freak too. You and your woo-woo mom."

"Take that back," Wren said, launching himself at Buster. Buster was bigger, but Wren was faster. Willow, Sahara, and Echo immediately rose to separate the boys who were rolling in the sand.

In that moment, everything slowed in Meri's mind. She didn't want Wren to be hurt. Without realizing what she was doing, Meri called a column of air to part the boys.

"Stop!" she shouted. "Stop, Wren. Stop, Buster. Please."

Wren untangled himself and scrambled to his feet. Buster rose more slowly. Breathing heavily, the two boys glared at each other.

From behind them, Echo's authoritative voice ordered, "Buster, go join your friends on the playground."

Buster cast a glance at the parents staring at him, then turned away. Spotting Wren's new disc in the sand, he grabbed it and flung it as far as he could into the lake.

"My disc!" shouted Wren, starting after it but stopping at the water's edge. The disc plopped in the water, too far away to reach.

Buster laughed and ran away, kicking sand at them in his wake.

Willow joined Wren and placed her arm around her son's shoulder. He turned and hid his face in her sweater. "My new disc," he muttered.

Meri was shocked to see the disc begin to sink. She didn't know that discs couldn't float.

This was all her fault.

Meri recalled a time on this very playground when the wind responded to her anger and pushed Buster off the slide. Now she felt a desperate need to help Wren, to set things right instead of hurting people.

She exchanged glances with Willow, who simply gave her a kind shrug as if to say "Not to worry. It is what it is." But that didn't seem right to Meri. She felt a helping wind rise inside her, and she knew it wanted to come out. Moments later, Meri and Willow watched as the quite-sinkable disc began to spin on top of the water. Slowly, it started to skim toward the shore. Saying nothing, Willow smiled as the disc approached.

The fishing boat had moved to a new spot, creating small waves on the lake.

The disc rode the waves.

Meri said, "Look, Wren, it's not gone."

The boy turned, just as the disc washed up on the shore, and Wren gave a happy shout. He ran to get it.

As Wren and Willow turned toward their car, Willow looked back at Meri and winked.

CHAPTER 54

A NERVE
OF NEIGHBORS

ALTHOUGH FEW PEOPLE KNEW it, public speaking was one of Ariel's phobias. When she spoke on environmental topics, she appeared calm and professional and not at all like a trapped bird beating its wings to get free—because she had a system. Her system to distract herself from anxiety and to quiet the frightened wind inside her was based on a childhood game she had played with her mother. She recited collective nouns.

On the night of the town hall meeting, Ariel stood on the stage of the Cosette Middle School gymnasium and mentally recited a litany of collective nouns: a parliament of owls, a swarm of gnats, a romp of otters, an exaltation of larks. She always ended with larks. Up There adored the larks.

The gymnasium was a hot box. The only fresh air entered the room from a row of small open windows placed near the ceiling, offering little relief to the increasingly large crowd.

When the folding chair supply ran out, people set up their own canvas chairs pulled from their trunks and the backs of their pickups. They blocked the aisles, probably violating fire codes. People without chairs lined the back of the room, where the doughnuts and apple cider were going fast.

The two contenders for town council, Ariel Lee Turnstone and Melanie Harcourt, stood behind podiums with stationary microphones. They were positioned several feet apart with the moderator, schoolteacher Astrid Lindqvist, standing between them. There was a large empty screen on the wall behind the podiums.

In the front row, in easy view of Ariel, sat Ruddy, Sahara, Echo, Blinka, Nikki, and Harley. She spotted Helen and Sweetie Moongoose in the row behind them sitting with Whistler Newton. Trouble and Mick had offered to stay home with Meri. "The fewer Hamilton flyers they have to contend with, the better," said Trouble. "But we have your back. Call if you need us."

Ruddy winked at Ariel and gave an encouraging nod. He had wanted her to skip the meeting—"Let things settle down, let people forget"—but she knew she had to face the town, and Melanie. The wind inside her said, *Time to speak the truth.* But Ariel wasn't sure. Maybe she could get through this meeting—and the election—with her secret intact.

Astrid tapped her microphone, and the audience quieted. She introduced Ariel and Melanie and emphasized that this meeting was a friendly one. "This is an informal chat with neighbors," insisted Astrid, in a voice that brooked no disagreement. "I expect you all to be civil, orderly, and Minnesota nice. Is that understood?"

She cast a stern look, one familiar to her students, over the crowd. Several adult heads nodded obediently.

Melanie won the coin toss and was the first to speak. As Ariel expected, Melanie led off with the shortage of housing in Cosette, the empty storefronts, and the need for fewer zoning regulations and more tax breaks for developers.

"I know real estate, folks, and I know the resources of our region," said Melanie. "We are sitting on a gold mine of tourism. While our family resorts are fading, and that's a shame, we have plenty of room for high tax-paying properties, large resorts, and beautiful homes. We can't wait for the next plague from China or wherever to drive people into our town."

Melanie continued, "We need to build now and create an infrastructure that will take us into the coming decades. We need *grounded* leadership, people who know what it is like in the trenches. You all know me. You know my strengths. I am the candidate to take Cosette into the future."

The emphasis on "grounded" sent a shiver through Ariel. She looked at Ruddy, who was frowning.

Astrid cleared her throat. "Thank you, Melanie. Ariel?"

Ariel swallowed. She recalled those dreaded days of dodge ball in grade school when her clunky shoes made dodging difficult. During those games, she faced the fear by telling herself, "Keep standing. Just keep standing." She had expected Melanie to hurl her own form of dodge ball. Now it was time to stand.

As Ariel thought about how to begin, several collective nouns for neighbors, some real and some fanciful, came to mind: a quarrel of neighbors, a nuisance of neighbors, a chatter of neighbors. But the one that Ariel was recalling now was: a nerve of neighbors from James Lipton's book, *An Exaltation of Larks.*

Larks, whispered the wind happily as it pressed against the gym windows.

Quiet, Ariel told the wind.

A nerve of neighbors.

It was fitting given the tension in the room.

With another glance toward Ruddy, Ariel started, "My campaign signs say I am the 'Nature First Candidate.' That is not entirely true. Harriet Bunyan was the first one to campaign for nature in Cosette—"

Melanie interrupted with a snark that had a few people tittering, "Harriet is fictional, Ariel." Melanie paused. "Folks, we need leaders who don't have their heads in the *clouds.*"

Ariel's eyes went to Ruddy again. She saw the pain in them. The high windows in the gym convulsed, and she took a deep calming breath.

"Harriet was fictional, but the ideas that brought her to life were real," said Ariel. "The concept behind Harriet was to emphasize Cosette's environmental paradise. It reminds us why we want to live here and visit here. It is important for our children to have clean water to drink, clear lakes to swim in, and unpolluted lands to play in. Yes, we need progress, but we can have progress *and* quality of life. We owe it to our children and to ourselves to find a way."

A tingle of concurrence touched the nerve of the audience.

Melanie saw some people nodding in agreement and immediately tapped her podium to get attention. "There is no progress without building. There is no growth without expansion. Do you want Cosette to die?" Melanie stared at Ariel. "Pigs will *fly* before I let that happen."

While the "grounded" and "heads in the clouds" remarks were subtle and flew past many people, the flying statement landed like a roaring jet. Silence was loud in the gymnasium.

Astrid, the moderator, looked nervously at Ariel.

Although a rush of air through the open gymnasium doors

in the back of the room scattered napkins from the doughnut table and knocked over paper cups near the cider jugs, Ariel appeared composed.

"Are you calling me a pig, Melanie?" Ariel asked softly.

Astrid quickly jumped in. "There will be no name calling. Let's keep this polite and neighborly."

Melanie stepped from behind her podium and walked past the schoolteacher. "Oh, shut up, Astrid."

"Now, see here—" Astrid sputtered.

Melanie pointed a finger at Ariel. "You are not one of us. You never have been. And you cannot have a say in this town."

"I was born here, just like you, Melanie," Ariel said.

Melanie turned to the crowd. "I don't know what she is, but she doesn't belong here. And I have proof."

Melanie clicked a remote hidden in the palm of her hand and the screen behind the podium came to life.

Astrid objected, "No one gave you permission to play a—"

It was a video of Ariel in the air—not one recorded at the celebration of life but one taken on Ariel's farm.

* * *

Ruddy spun toward Harley with disbelief. "You liar! You said you wouldn't give that video to anyone."

Looking baffled, Harley held up his hands in defense. "I didn't. I swear, Ruddy."

"What have you done, Harley?" asked Nikki in a sad and disappointed voice.

Blinka muttered, "Harley, you jerk."

But Harley only had eyes for Nikki. He pleaded, "I didn't do it, Nikki, honest. She must have stolen it from my computer."

Ruddy said, "I'm putting a stop to this." He started to get up to go to Ariel, but Sahara halted him with a hand on his arm. Ruddy turned pleading eyes on his mother-in-law. "We have to help her."

Sahara shook her head. "My daughter has never needed rescuing from anyone—but herself."

Ruddy suspected his mother-in-law was right, but it went against his protective nature. Earlier, before leaving for the meeting, he had held Ariel's hand as they stood in the back-yard. The wind had been confused, even he could feel that, and he had been so afraid for her. She'd told him, "If I have to reveal my secrets, I'll do it on my terms."

Now Ruddy stared at Ariel, both the one on the screen and the one frozen in shock on the stage. He regretted not telling her about the video, not preparing her. His heart cried to her: *I'm sorry. I'm here for you.*

Ariel couldn't take her eyes from the video. She had often wondered what she looked like when she walked the air. There were no mirrors Up There. If she flew over a lake or a stream and looked down, she might see a blurry reflection of herself, depending on how the light hit the water or the condition of the day's cloud cover.

Sahara had never photographed her daughter in flight; she hadn't wanted to risk leaving evidence for others to find. Ruddy and Ariel had a similar prohibition on photos of a wind-walking Meri. Phones could be easily accessed, a lesson they learned when their mischievous daughter had swiped Ruddy's phone and used it to text Ariel: "Don't be mad at Meri for eating all the Oreos."

This was the first time Ariel had truly seen herself as she appeared Up There. She saw a woman swooping and skimming the air, swirling and floating, sketching a dance on the clouds as Up There became her music.

I look happy, she said to the wind.

Yes, said the wind, pressing against the building. *You look like a lark.*

Suddenly, Ariel found herself smiling.

The crowd, which had been stunned into silence, stirred, and people began speaking at once:

"Never seen such a thing."

"It's beautiful."

"I wish I could fly."

"It's wrong, on so many levels."

"She's a devil."

"She's always been different."

"We called her Clodhopper in school. Can you imagine?"

"She's a superhero!"

Some people began clapping, but the applause died out after Melanie shot a glare into the crowd.

"I demand that Ariel Lee Turnstone step down from the race for town council," Melanie shouted.

"On what grounds?" asked Astrid.

"Obvious ones," Melanie said, sweeping her hand toward the video. "She doesn't understand us because she is different from us. She is like some-some alien. Who knows what kind of crazy regulations she'll try to implement here? Do you want a freak making important decisions about your lives and the lives of your children? Do you want an alien telling you what you can and cannot do with your property?"

Someone from the audience shouted out, "How do we know that video is even real? Maybe it's some artificial intelligence stuff."

"It is real," Melanie maintained. She turned to Harley. "Tell them."

Harley looked at the video and felt, as he did each time he saw it, humbled. He realized it was like the Christmas tree on the dock, something out of place but enchanting. A gift. There had not been many such gifts in Harley's life, and he couldn't destroy this one.

He shook his head.

Melanie couldn't believe Harley had abandoned her. They had been compadres, seeing eye to eye, since first grade.

"Harley, you spineless piece of . . ."

Standing, Harley pointed at Melanie. "You stole that video from my computer!" The crowd buzzed and turned to Melanie.

"Somebody has to protect this town from people like Ariel Turnstone," retorted Melanie.

Harley turned to his neighbors around him. He pleaded, "So she can fly. Why is that so bad?"

"It's not normal!" shouted Melanie. The room filled with murmurs and whispers, doubts and accusations.

Ariel tapped her microphone, and the crowd fell silent. She studied the faces in the crowd, people she'd seen at the grocery store, greeted at PTA meetings, and worked beside on Earth Day. "I'm not normal," she said softly at first but gained strength. "I've never been ordinary. I can't do anything about it. I am a woman who can fly."

"See. She admits it!" said Melanie with satisfaction.

"I was born this way. It is not something I asked for," said Ariel. She looked at Blinka and Nikki and saw support in their eyes. "But you know what? Being different has taught me one thing: I don't stand down, and I don't give up. I'm an oddball with a strange gift. I won't explain it to you or answer your questions about it. I will, however, make this simple promise: I will use my gift and everything I am to protect you and your children."

And with that, Ariel stepped away from the podium.

Everyone began talking at once.

Melanie turned to the crowd. "She admits she's strange and weird. She wears it like a badge." She motioned toward the image of Ariel on the screen. "Do you want her flying around town, drawing the attention of snoopy reporters and crazies wanting to fly too?"

The mutters and questions in the crowd increased.

Ariel held up her hand for quiet. "I'm not interested in turning Cosette into a media circus," she reassured them. "I value my privacy just as much as you value yours. I want to protect this town." She paused. "And all of you can help me."

"How?" someone shouted from the crowd.

Helen nodded encouragement, and Whistler gave her a thumbs up. With trust in his eyes, Ruddy smiled at her.

She took a deep breath and said, "I've kept this secret for more than thirty years. Now, I'm asking *you* to help me keep it."

Ariel felt the air in the room change. She didn't know if she had gotten through to them, but slowly, people began to rise from their chairs and head toward the door. Some grinned at Ariel with approval. Some looked at her with suspicion as they talked among themselves.

Melanie wasn't ready to end the meeting. "Are you all crazy?" Melanie shouted, stamping her stilettos. "She's a freak!"

The crowd continued to disperse, even as Melanie begged them to come back.

✳ ✳ ✳

Infuriated and frustrated, Melanie sat on the lip of the stage, her wrinkled business skirt hiked up and her heels dangling over the edge. She couldn't stand this feeling of ineptitude. She always knew how to win; her father had taught her.

How did this event go so wrong? she wondered.

While the gymnasium emptied, Ariel lingered. Finally, when they were alone, she approached Melanie and sat down beside her. Melanie looked away.

"I was right all along," said Melanie.

"Yes, you were," Ariel said. "I have always been different, and I always will be."

Melanie didn't take consolation from Ariel's confession.

"I've spent most of my life writing about nature because I need it—to live the way I do. You need it too, Melanie."

Melanie made a sound of disbelief.

"Nature is the glue that holds together our world, Melanie," said Ariel. "Without it, our planet will unravel and so will we."

"Save it for the campaign poster," said Melanie.

A soothing whisper of air flitted around them, and Melanie closed her eyes.

"Melanie, we want the same thing. To save all of this." Ariel lifted a hand. "Don't you think your father would understand that?"

Felix Harcourt was remembered as a top real estate agent but also as an unfailing cheerleader of all things Cosette. From high school sports teams to civic organizations, Felix always had time to support a cause or promote an action he believed was good for the town.

Suddenly, as if Felix had tapped her on the shoulder, Melanie felt her father and knew how she'd lost. Her eyes popped open. Ariel had beaten her at her own game, the one Felix had lived by: "Maximize assets and turn liabilities into opportunities, Mellie."

"You turned your liability—this flying business—into an opportunity," Melanie said with disgust, banging her heels against the side of the stage.

Ariel said, "I'm not sure I know what you're talking about, Melanie, but I'm tired of fighting with you. I'm tired of fighting a lot of things."

The banging stopped. Melanie glanced at her. "Does this mean you're dropping out of the race?"

Ariel grinned at the hope in Melanie's voice. "Not a chance," Ariel said.

Melanie swept an escaped lock of blond hair back from her face. Her ranting and raving had ruined her trademark updo. "I had to ask."

"I know," Ariel said. "You don't give up either."

Melanie's eyes narrowed. "Don't you dare think we are anything alike."

Ariel hid a smile. "Of course not."

Melanie studied the empty room and the jumbled rows of chairs. "Did you know they would support you and your secret?"

The women stared at each other. "No," said Ariel. "I took a chance. But we've been looking after each other in Cosette for generations. It was time to start trusting."

And stop hiding, whispered the wind.

They rose. Melanie, in a tight skirt, struggled until Ariel held out a hand to help. After a moment, Melanie took it.

As they crossed the empty gym floor, someone began to click off the lights. In the dark vestibule, Melanie paused and said, "You know, I've always wanted to fly. Can you teach me?"

"No," said Ariel.

Pushing through the gym doors, Melanie laughed. "I thought not. See ya at the ballot box, Clodhopper."

CHAPTER 55

ONE STEP AT A TIME

THERE WERE TIMES WHEN Ruddy could not believe his great fortune. Times like this: when he could sit on the new bench in the meadow and observe his wife and daughter floating on tufts of air, legs crossed, and pretending to have a tea party in the sky. *How many men get to see this?* he wondered.

Ruddy remembered a day when he confessed his feelings of helplessness to his father: "The women in my family are destined for dangerous places, and I can't stop them."

Instead of commiserating with his son, Arthur had simply said, "Why would you ever want to?"

On this golden October day, Ruddy smelled the lure of autumn in the air. Soon he would be raking leaves and Meri would be leaping into the piles. With a laugh, he would join her and bury her with leaves, until the Meri-called wind would whisk the leaves away, uncovering the giggling child. She never played fair in the leaf game.

As Ruddy and Gus the dog watched, Ariel poured from an imaginary teapot into imaginary teacups. Then she held out an empty hand, offering an imaginary scone to her floating daughter. Meri took the scone from Ariel's palm and made nibbling motions. She rolled her eyes in a pretense of swooning at the savory morsel. "Airy," Meri pronounced, "but a little salty."

Ariel pretended to take umbrage at this aspersion on her culinary skills. "What!" she shouted, sweeping her arm across the imaginary table and scattering the invisible tea party. Then to emphasize her disgust she suddenly did a back flip in the air and stood, afloat, fists on her hips, a mock glare on her face.

Meri fell backward in giggles.

Clapping his hands, Ruddy shouted, "What an exit."

Ariel grinned at him then curtsied.

"I want to learn that," said Meri. "Teach me."

The lesson in how to perform a back flip led to other aerial tricks and demonstrations.

A voice from the woods behind Ruddy said, "There is no Gibson, no Stradivarius, that can create music as beautiful as that." Ruddy looked around and spotted Timothy Lee, stepping into the meadow, guitar case in hand.

Without an invitation and without taking his eyes off the pair in the air, Ariel's father sat down beside Ruddy and patted Gus.

Watching his family, Ruddy thought, *Timothy is right. They are meant to be where they are, like fish in the sea or deer in the forest. Was there anything more stunning than a being living its true nature?*

Suddenly, Ruddy realized it had been a long time since he had felt the sad feeling of waiting and being trapped Down Here. He was no longer unsure of himself, of what his family needed, of how he could love them as thoroughly as they needed to be loved. He had known how to do it all along. It was his nature to protect and believe in—the magic of Ariel Lee Turnstone.

That realization filled him with a peacefulness and happiness that he could not explain.

"You look good," said Timothy.

Ruddy glanced at the man beside him.

Timothy appeared tired and oddly disheveled. The cuffs of his jeans were muddy, and his shirt was wrinkled. But there was something else different about the aging musician. What was it?

"You look terrible," Ruddy said. "Tough tour?"

"Yeah." Timothy slouched on the bench with a sigh. "Lotta rain. Mud and water in everything. What a mess. Outdoor festivals used to be fun. Now everybody looks and acts like they're twelve. Some of them even *are* twelve. I'm getting old, man."

Ruddy hid a smile.

"My hearing is shot," Timothy continued, "the lights are too bright . . . and the fireworks. Fricking fireworks. Can't hear the songs."

"It's all about the spectacle, not the music," said Ruddy.

"Yeah," said Timothy. "I need to get out of this business."

Timothy sounded grumpy, but Ruddy noted the look of rapture on his father-in-law's face as his gaze followed the aerial antics of his daughter and grandchild. "You missed them," Ruddy surmised.

Timothy turned to him with a boyish grin, the one that first captured the heart of his ex-wife, Sahara Stevens, on that long-ago night in a Minneapolis club. "You got me. I haven't stopped thinking of them since I left. I don't know if I'll ever tire of seeing them like this," Timothy said in a tone of bewildered awe. "I feel better when I'm watching them, you know? I was a chickenshit for leaving so many years."

Ruddy understood because he too had walked a tightrope of wonderment and phobia when it came to his wife. Except, unlike Timothy, Ruddy had never feared who and what Ariel was. He was convinced that he had seen her specialness, even when they were kids. His unease had come from worry that he would not be enough for Ariel or Meri.

Timothy asked, "Have you ever wished you could fly?"

"Never," Ruddy said. "Heights and I don't mix."

"Huh," Timothy said, "and yet you married my daughter."

"She *is* irresistible."

"Yeah, she is." Timothy plucked a blade of grass, tucked it between his thumbs, and blew. No sound. He tossed the grass aside. "I was always better at the guitar."

Ruddy smiled. He had started out hating Timothy for his abandonment of Ariel and Sahara. But now, he realized that Timothy was just like the rest of them: searching for his place in this world. Maybe that was the change Ruddy sensed in Ariel's father. Timothy had finally accepted who he was.

Timothy said, "Seeing them like this reminds me that I used to dream of flying."

"Where did you fly?"

Timothy unzipped the guitar case, took out his guitar, and softly played a few bars of "Let It Be."

He said, "I crossed the ocean in my Yellow Submarine pajamas and flew to England. There the Beatles spotted me in the sky and invited me to jam with them."

"Good dream," said Ruddy, sharing a grin with his father-in-law.

"Yeah, it was," said Timothy. He ran his fingers over the strings, checking the tuning.

"Hey, Grandpa," waved Meri.

"Hey, Pumpkin," he waved back.

"Look, Timothy," Ariel shouted. "I'm walking the Stairway to Heaven."

Ariel took one step after another, walking air stairs, like a mime, rising higher in the air with each one.

Ruddy said, "Ariel told me that the day she came into her gift, the day she learned that she could take the wind inside her, she performed that trick for Sahara. Sahara nearly fainted when she saw her ten-year-old daughter climbing the invisible staircase."

"Don't blame her," said Ariel's father.

Timothy began plucking out the tune to Led Zeppelin's "Stairway to Heaven," and both Ariel and Meri turned to him with surprise. Then mother and daughter began swaying and pirouetting in the air to the moody opening of the song. Timothy began to sing. As the music shifted into a thumping tempo, the movements of the air dancers changed from balletic to break-dancing with twisting and spinning.

In a pause from singing but continuing to play, Timothy said, "Heard you had some trouble here in Cosette."

"We weathered the storm," said Ruddy.

Timothy dipped his head and continued to play.

With his head bent over the guitar as if the answer didn't matter, Timothy asked, "You care if I hang around Cosette for a while?"

There was a long pause, and Ruddy felt a soft breeze.

"Not at all," he said, rising and walking into the middle of the field.

When Ariel and Meri saw him, they touched down beside him like moths drawn to a flame. Ruddy drew Ariel into his arms, and Meri and Gus began to prance in the grass around them. Timothy played one song after another as the family danced.

Ariel's arms circled her husband's neck. Their hips swayed together. She whispered in his ear, "There's something I must tell you."

Suddenly, Ruddy was back in that hospital room when Ariel first uttered those words to him. He'd had no idea then if they were a prelude to heartbreak or the greatest adventure of his life. But this time he was not afraid.

"What is it?" he asked, kissing her.

"Meri thinks she needs a pony . . . and a little sister."

Ruddy missed a step. *Another Hamilton daughter?*

He shook back his long, burnished hair and stared at her. That smile, the one that is said to glow like her grandmother's after a night riding the air, slowly spread across her face. She lifted a questioning eyebrow.

"Don't know where we'll put her," Ruddy warned, swinging Ariel back into the slow dance. "Your father's in the guest room."

"We'll figure it out," she said, pressing closer. "We always do."

Looking down, he saw his wife's feet brushing the tops of the late summer grasses. He was her anchor, and he always would be.

He met her sheepish grin, and both Up There and Down Here echoed with their laughter.

ACKNOWLEDGMENTS

GRATITUDE IS THE THING that reminds us how lucky we are. In the past year, I have survived three surgeries, finished this book, and spent many precious moments with the people I love. I have sat and listened to the wind in the trees, talked with the crows in the backyard, and played card games with my grandchildren.

I have been fortunate to find intelligent and amazing writer friends. I thank all of you for your support and faith over the years: Christine DeSmet, Marlys Dooley, Lois West Duffy, Miriam Karmel, Janet Hanafin, Jean Housh, Laura Matthiesen, David Kostik, Marla Okner, Ann Woodbeck, and especially, my mentor and editor, the generous Faith Sullivan.

I highly appreciate the support of the Indie Author Project, the Minnesota Author Project, the Minnesota Library Association, the Metropolitan Library Service Agency (MELSA), the Anoka County Library, Lyrasis, and Biblioboard. Thank you for helping my work reach readers not only in Minnesota but throughout the nation.

Thank you as well to others who have inspired me with their kind words and endless patience: Gini Ewers, Debbie Gawrych, David and Elizabeth Gibbar, Patricia Morris, Diana Philliber, Gari Plehal, Geanette Poole, Beverly and George

Roberts, Glenn Roberts, and Gloria and John Ruff. They have believed in my journey from the beginning.

Special gratitude goes to Bill Newton, a delightful and savvy friend who gives me straight talk and wise advice.

My love and gratitude go to Sarah Roberts Delacueva, my brilliant editor, and Suzanne Roberts Claseman, my eternal supporter and avid reader. Everyone thinks they have the best children, but I really do.

Finally, and most importantly, thank you to Tony Roberts. He has had the unenviable job of pushing me up the mountain of rehab and reaching down with a helping hand when I am deep in the valley of writing despair. He's the one who tells me to write more and make the words sing. He believes in me more than I believe in me. He is the best friend to have in tired times and happy ones.

To my readers, I say thank you for joining me on this book journey and wish you a long gratitude list of your own. I firmly believe that when we fill our hearts with gratitude, we leave no room for hate. Every one of your thank yous—to your children, to your neighbor, to a stranger on the street, to your server at lunch, to the exhausted delivery driver at your door—makes this world a better place.

ABOUT THE AUTHOR

SHERRY ROBERTS is the author of award-winning mysteries and contemporary fiction. Her novel, *Up There*, won the Minnesota Indie Author Project presented by the Minnesota Library Association and the Minnesota Library Foundation. It was also a Midwest Book Award finalist.

Sherry's other contemporary novels include *Book of Mercy*, also a Midwest Book Award finalist and an Indie Author Project Select title, and *Maud's House*.

Her cozy and magical Minnesota mystery series includes *Down Dog Diary, Warrior's Revenge,* and *Crow Calling*. All are Indie Author Project Select titles, and *Down Dog Diary* is a Midwest Book Award finalist.

Sherry has contributed essays to national publications such as *USA Today* as well as short stories to anthologies and magazines including *Saint Paul Almanac; Dark Side of the Loon; Minnesota Not So Nice; It Was a Dark and Stormy Night, Dontcha Know;* and *Mystery Magazine*.

She lives in Apple Valley, Minnesota. Visit Sherry's author website at sherry-roberts.com. Her essays can be found at The Hearth: hearth.sherry-roberts.com.

WHAT'S NEXT?

SIGN UP FOR SHERRY'S EMAIL LIST (sherry-roberts.com) for updates on future writing news and offers available only to fans! Your email will never be shared, you can unsubscribe at any time, and Sherry promises not to paper your inbox with emails.

§

LEAVE A REVIEW. If you enjoyed this book, please consider leaving a brief review online at your favorite retailer site. Readers spreading the word to other readers is incredibly important to authors and their work. If you're shy, just drop me a line on the contact page of sherry-roberts.com. I value your support and ideas and promise I'll write back.

§

CHECK OUT SHERRY'S OTHER BOOKS. *Up There*, the first book about Ariel Lee's flying adventures, won the Minnesota Indie Author Project presented by the Minnesota Library Association. Other contemporary fiction includes *Book of Mercy*, a dyslexic woman takes on a town banning books, and *Maud's House*, an artist loses her creativity but finds love.

Sherry's cozy mystery series features crime-fighting yoga teacher Maya Skye and journalist Peter Jorn. You'll find their exploits in *Down Dog Diary*, *Warrior's Revenge*, and *Crow Calling*.

All of Sherry's books are available in paperback and eBook. Look for them at sherry-roberts.com, osmyrrahpublishing.com, Amazon, and other retail outlets. If you can't find her books in your local bookstore or local library, please ask for them. Thank you.